INSIDE THREAT

ALSO BY MATTHEW QUIRK

Red Warning

Hour of the Assassin

The Night Agent

Dead Man Switch

Cold Barrel Zero

The Directive

The 500

INSIDE
THREAT

A Novel

MATTHEW QUIRK

𝒲𝓂

WILLIAM MORROW

An Imprint of HarperCollins*Publishers*

INSIDE THREAT. Copyright © 2023 by Rough Draft, Inc. All rights reserved. Printed in the United States of America. No part of this book may be used or reproduced in any manner whatsoever without written permission except in the case of brief quotations embodied in critical articles and reviews. For information, address HarperCollins Publishers, 195 Broadway, New York, NY 10007.

HarperCollins books may be purchased for educational, business, or sales promotional use. For information, please email the Special Markets Department at SPsales@harpercollins.com.

FIRST EDITION

Title Page Art © Jon Bilous/Shutterstock, Inc.

Library of Congress Cataloging-in-Publication Data has been applied for.

ISBN 978-0-06-305168-3

23 24 25 26 27 LBC 5 4 3 2 1

For Emily

AUTHOR'S NOTE

The Raven Rock Mountain Complex and the secret emergency presidential powers described in this book are real, though certain details have been changed or omitted.

CHARACTERS

WHITE HOUSE

— James Kline: President of the United States

— Dr. Sarah Kline: First Lady of the United States

— Claire Givens: White House Chief of Staff

— Benjamin Chilton: Special Agent in Charge, U.S. Secret Service Presidential Protective Division

— Eric Hill: Secret Service Agent

— Michael Hardwick: Secret Service Agent

— Laura Leigh: Secret Service Agent

— Liam Walsh: Secret Service Agent

— Samuel Brimley: Secret Service Agent

— Amber Cody: Secret Service Agent

— Tim Navarro: Secret Service Agent

— Matt Byrne: Secret Service Agent

— Joe Cody: Secret Service Agent (deceased), Amber Cody's father

— Major Paul Eubanks: Military Aide to the President

— Will Maddox: President Kline's Personal Aide/Body Man

— Captain Nathan Chen: White House Doctor

— Alexander Braun: Secretary of the Treasury, major fundraiser

— Stephen Reinhart: Former President (fifteen years ago)

— Ellen O'Hara: Communications Secretary

— Thomas Searle: Congressional Aide

RAVEN ROCK MOUNTAIN COMPLEX

— Lieutenant Colonel Bruce Drumm: Deputy/Acting Commander of Raven Rock

— Major Ashley Moro: Executive Officer

— Major Rebecca Vaughn: Communications Officer

— Captain Kevin Foster: Security Officer

RAVEN ROCK
MOUNTAIN COMPLEX

N

NORTHERN ENTRANCE

NORTHERN BLAST DOORS

RESERVOIR

COMMS CENTER

CAVERN E — BUILDING E — CANAL

CAVERN D — BUILDING D — COMMS SHAFT

INFIRMARY

CAVERN C — BUILDING C — REAR TUNNEL

CAVERN B — BUILDING B — WAR ROOM AND PRESIDENT'S SUITE

CAVERN A — BUILDING A

PASSAGEWAYS

MAIN TUNNEL

POWER PLANT

SOUTHERN BLAST DOORS

SOUTHERN ENTRANCE

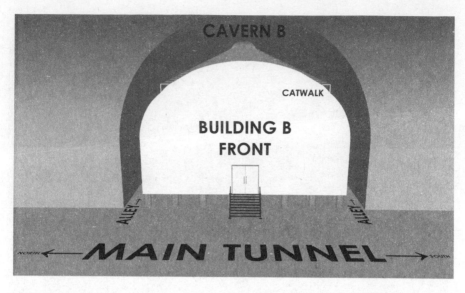

The view inside the main tunnel looking at the front of Building B in its cavern. The main tunnel ceiling liners and framing are omitted for clarity.

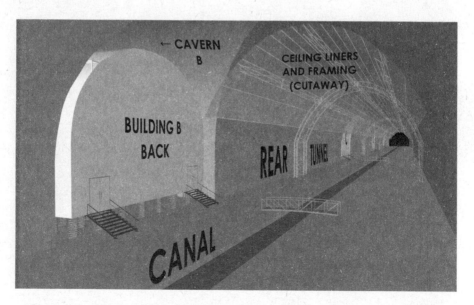

The view looking north up the rear tunnel from behind Building B. The ceiling liners and framing are shown in cutaway.

INSIDE THREAT

1

KILLER. TRAITOR. HERO. The man strolling toward the White House would be called many names by the time this operation was over, but among his accomplices he went by the alias Marcus. It was a nod to Marcus Brutus, the Roman assassin.

With his navy suit and crew cut, he looked like any other Washington bureaucrat, one of dozens on their rounds near Pennsylvania Avenue this evening, though his expression was a little brighter than most. He strode through Lafayette Park, eyes on the portico of the White House residence with its great black hanging lantern.

A group of protesters shook signs—"Tyrant" and "Killer-in-Chief"—and shouted slogans on the brick sidewalk, facing off with a row of Secret Service agents behind a steel barricade. One demonstrator stepped onto the barrier, and the agent shoved him back. The country was a tinderbox. All it needed was a spark.

Marcus surveyed the new thirteen-foot-tall black perimeter fence and the grounds just beyond it, noting the subtle variations in the grass—signs of pressure sensors beneath—and the well-hidden laser, microwave, and infrared motion detectors. Triggering any of them would bring out the black-clad emergency response teams and Belgian Malinois attack dogs.

He slipped across Pennsylvania Avenue, turning slightly to stay just out of frame of a school group's selfie, his eyes tracing the rooftops of the buildings surrounding the White House.

He picked out the sniper team on the eastern edge of the residence roof, a spotter and a shooter with a silenced custom Remington 700.

Glancing back to the office buildings towering to the northwest, he checked the parapet that concealed the Avenger system—a battery of eight Stinger missiles along with a computer-aimed machine gun firing six-inch-long bullets that could blow a plane out of the sky from a mile away.

As he neared the main guardhouse to the north of the West Wing, his heart drummed harder. His skin was warm despite the autumn breeze.

Marcus carried a SIG Sauer P229, two extra magazines, a SureFire flashlight, and a Benchmade folding knife. It was all he needed to bring this place down, to start a war.

He waited for a staffer to clear security and stepped up to the guardhouse window. The sentry inside, uniformed Secret Service, stared at Marcus as he pressed a blue badge to a scanner near the gate.

The guard's eyes went down. Marcus shifted his weight onto his right foot, his hand drawing closer to the SIG on his waist.

He knew what was on that guard's screen. Two words: Yankee White. It went beyond the normal security clearances. It was the highest access you could receive in the American government.

A green light flashed. The gate unlocked and Marcus pushed through with a smile and a nod to the officer.

He walked down Executive Avenue and passed the Marine guard standing at attention outside the West Wing's covered entrance.

The president was in the Oval Office, working late. Marcus moved on without slowing, turning past a copse of elms, the rolling grass of the South Lawn to his side.

The clouds stacked in the sky, bruised blue and purple with sunset. He walked slowly, his eyes on the windows of the Oval, six-inch-thick bulletproof glass. Behind them, the air in the room was kept at a slightly higher pressure than the outside to prevent biological and chemical attacks. A small wooden block marked with the presidential seal sat on the Resolute Desk, one of a half-dozen innocent-looking items—called knockdowns—that, when tipped over, would summon the counterassault boys with their heavy artillery.

President James Harrington Kline strode past the window, then stopped and looked out. He had dark brown hair, gray near the temples, and straight-line posture—he always held himself like he was having his portrait taken.

Marcus clocked his target and kept moving, wary of the three roving patrols. He knew their patterns down to the minute.

The government had invested hundreds of millions of dollars to protect that one man. The inner sanctums of the White House were unbreachable unless you knew their secrets. Marcus did. He was an insider. His orders came from the highest levels. Operation V was about to start.

The White House was just the beginning. Marcus knew where it would all end—fifty miles from here in a facility whose existence was one of the most well-guarded secrets in government.

His eyes went to the flag, twisting slowly in the night above the residence. To rebuild a nation, you must first destroy it.

Hero. Traitor. If he survived the next twenty-four hours, the world would understand which side he was on.

He pressed his hand to his jacket, felt the weight of the gun underneath, and marched toward the West Wing.

2

ERIC HILL BADGED into the West Wing and caught sight of a uniformed Secret Service agent on patrol. She gave him a reverent nod. Eric knew the look. It's what he got for saving a president's life, stopping the bullets with his own body, two in his vest and one in his shoulder. He'd never gotten used to it, never liked the way the Service paraded him around as a hero after that awful day.

He walked on and a political staffer glanced at him. Their eyes met, and the aide's quickly broke away, his face going a shade paler. Fright. That was a more recent look he'd gotten used to. Everything had changed. Eric wasn't carrying his service weapon. He wasn't running the presidential detail. He was stuck behind a desk on the ground floor. Some of the people he'd sworn to protect now feared him, and they weren't wrong to do so. He didn't have to worry as much about the hero shit these days.

He squeezed by a construction scaffolding and looked up, eyeing the crown molding, then took the stairs down to the ground floor. After he passed the door to the Situation Room, he ducked into the low-ceilinged suite that was the Secret Service's base of operations inside the White House.

His desk was in a cramped office in the back, out of sight by design, next to the armory cabinets. The surveillance tech monitored the security camera feeds. Eric looked over the bank of screens and watched POTUS pass from the Oval to the residence with two agents in tow.

Eric sat down to check the logs. As a patrol came off its shift and entered the suite, he took their weapons, made them safe, and locked them up. His hand lingered on the textured grip of the MP5 submachine gun. He missed its weight. He'd carried one for so long it became an extension of his body. It went in the safe, and he slammed and locked the door.

When he looked up, Benjamin Chilton was coming toward him. He was a Special Agent in Charge, known as an SAIC, or "sack." As the senior agent on duty, he was technically tonight's shift whip, the person who called the shots, though Chilton mostly avoided on-the-ground work. That left Eric to handle the lowlier aspects of getting the agents to their posts.

He wore a dove-gray suit, an oddly showy fashion choice even for the head of the presidential protection detail, but Chilton was always hustling to straddle the line between the agents and the politicians they protected. He'd only been in the top job for four months and still seemed a little insecure in the role.

"I like the beard," Eric said.

Chilton's hand went to it. "Really?"

"Sure. What's up?"

"How are you doing down here, Eric?"

"Every job matters."

A nod like a patient teacher from Chilton. "It should be temporary, you know. So long as . . ."

"As?"

"Just keep your head down and let this blow over."

"I'm here. I'm not out talking about it."

"And as far as Braun goes . . ."

"Yes?"

"Play nice."

Braun was Secretary of the Treasury Alexander Braun, a former presidential candidate. Eric had run his protection detail for a while. He was the reason Eric was behind this desk. Being busted down to administrative duty was, as Eric understood it, principally about optics. He would give up the gun for a while, but it was mostly to demonstrate to certain VIPs that something had been done and he'd learned his lesson. It hadn't even been processed officially through personnel. The bosses wanted to keep the whole matter as quiet as possible.

The other agents still looked to him for guidance and Eric often ended up informally whipping the shift from this glorified closet. The Service was short-staffed and they needed all hands and his experience.

Eric looked Chilton over, noting the vein standing out on his forehead, the left hand gripping the right. Stress.

A man in shining oxfords appeared at the door of the suite. It was Braun.

"Like I said," Chilton whispered. "*Nice.*"

Eric didn't respond, only stared past him at the former candidate. Braun wheeled toward them with his chin held five degrees too high.

"Eric."

"Mr. Secretary."

Chilton stood to Braun's side, pleading with Eric with his eyes.

"Well . . ." Braun licked his lips. "I was in the building and thought I would come down and say hello, face-to-face . . . man-to-man."

Eric held his hands out to the side: *here I am.*

"And I'm glad we were able to put that whole"—a glance to Chilton as Braun searched for the right word—"mix-up behind us."

Eric could handle being stripped of his gun and made to sit down here like a kid in a corner. He could handle putting his life on the line for professional liars. But he could not stand forced complicity in their bullshit.

"There was no mix-up," Eric said. Adrenaline surged up his spine. He loved this feeling, this hunger for the fight, for finally saying fuck it all. He had given into it the night he wrecked his career, the night he wrecked Braun, and it scared him how easily it could take hold.

A tight, desperate smile from Braun. "Now—"

"I know what I saw," Eric said. "I know who you are. How's the arm?"

His eyes stayed on Braun as the man appeared to try out a few responses in his mind and came up with nothing. He inched up from Eric, his eyes going down, his left hand cradling his right wrist.

"You were a good agent . . . once," Braun said, trying to hide the fear but not doing a particularly good job.

Chilton stared at Eric. One wrong step and he would demote Eric's ass for real, or try. Maybe this was some kind of test.

Eric moved fast, bringing his head and chest a half inch toward Braun, the slightest feint. There was five feet between them, but the politician blanched and flinched back, nearly lost his footing. A disgusted look turned into an extremely satisfied smile, then Braun turned and walked away.

Test failed.

Chilton followed, trying to placate him, and Eric returned to his desk, his duty logs and time sheets.

A few minutes later, he looked up to find Chilton standing in the doorway to the office.

"You couldn't let it go?" Chilton asked.

"I'm not going to lie."

"Listen. You eat shit for another month or so, show that you can stay in line, and then we go on like nothing happened. That's too much for you to handle?"

That fucking tone. Eric felt a rush of anger. "Tell you the truth, it may be."

"You're supposed to keep these people safe, and they're terrified of you. That doesn't work. I'm sorry, Eric, but I'm going to have to talk to the director."

Chilton stared at him, waiting. Eric didn't think he really wanted to go after his job. He wanted him to bow and scrape.

"Go ahead."

"What? This is serious. Demotion. Termination."

Eric smiled. "I'm done, Chilton."

"What?"

"You're right. It doesn't work. I'll save you the trouble and resign."

Chilton's eyes widened, and he started blinking quickly.

"You're joking. You're not far from being able to retire with the enhanced pension."

"That's fine."

"You're not going to quit. You're Eric Hill. You are the Service. We just need you to—"

"I'll get started on my letter," Eric said. "Watch your email."

"Don't fuck with me here, Hill. There will be consequences."

Chilton turned and left.

3

BACK BY HIS desk, Eric stood and watched the security cameras, breathing slowly as he let the anger subside.

Michael Hardwick stepped into the doorway. He was a big guy, thick black hair and brown eyes, a weekend rugby player and a machine of an agent, never tired, never complained. People often misjudged him based on his build, his black F-150, and his faded southern accent, but he had a razor-sharp mind. Eric had been working with him for seventeen years.

Hardwick gave him a knowing smile as he approached.

"What's up?" Eric asked.

"You went out with the number two from the French diplomatic mission?"

Eric rolled his eyes. "This town. It's like high school . . . yeah. She's great." He'd taken her to dinner at Fiola that weekend.

"Punching above your weight."

"Don't worry, I'll manage to fuck it up." He'd been distracted by everything happening with his job. He wasn't particularly good company these days.

"Speaking of punching above your weight . . . how's Ellie?" he asked Hardwick

"Don't change the subject, man. Where does a guy like you meet her?"

"The embassy. It was a lecture. EU security stuff."

Hardwick brought his head back, appraising Eric. "Do you speak French?"

"I get by."

"Huh."

"What?"

"We all thought you'd just been holing up at home recently."

"You don't have anything better to talk about?"

"Just sitting there drinking bourbon, cleaning your guns, and watching HGTV."

Eric played along, wincing at the HGTV mention, but he knew Hardwick was busting his chops. "I usually stick to *This Old House* and *New Yankee Workshop*, but there's only so many episodes, so . . ." He shrugged. "Though I manage to peel myself off the recliner every now and then." He'd spent most of his twenties working as a carpenter, and he was more inclined to drink too much bourbon, diamond-stone the chisels, and get into some hand tools and Japanese joinery, though Hardwick's larger point wasn't all that far off the mark.

"You're doing all right?"

"I'm good." Eric didn't feel like getting into a therapy session.

"Agent Leigh said you were yelling at one of the restoration guys last night?"

A laugh. "I wouldn't say yelling. I told him to sharpen his bit. You have to have some respect for your tools. He was mauling a nice piece of red oak."

Hardwick didn't quite seem to believe that version. The story was funny coming from Agent Leigh—she'd been in a surly mood herself recently.

Eric brought out an MP5, double-checked that the chamber was clear, and handed it to Hardwick with two magazines.

"We're on MP5s tonight?" Hardwick asked.

Normally the agents only carried pistols when they were working the presidential detail at the White House. The full-auto submachine guns and rifles were always stashed nearby, but out of sight.

"Chilton's orders," Eric said.

"The protesters have him spooked?"

"I think so. Could be an order from the big boss too," Eric said, meaning President Kline.

Hardwick slung the weapon. "Chilton still has you doing T and As?" Hardwick asked, shaking his head. Time and assignments were the most tedious paperwork in the service. "I'll never get used to seeing you back there."

"Every job matters."

"I'd be fucking dying."

Eric almost gave him another line, but he couldn't stand the taste of it. "I am, brother."

"This Braun thing?"

"It's been building for a long time. That's the last straw."

"Please don't tell me you're thinking about quitting." He must have heard part of the conversation. "You'd just be letting Chilton and Braun and all the other hacks win."

"I can't be part of the bullshit, Mike, the politics, the covering up the truth. I'm tired of it."

"You don't deserve to be behind that desk."

"I do, actually." Part of the reason he felt like he needed to get away from all this was that the anger was clouding his judgment. He had snapped that night. He went too far. He'd probably just gone too far again with Chilton and Braun. He was afraid that he couldn't seem to get himself under control, but he kept that to himself.

"What really happened?"

"Don't worry about it."

"What would you do?"

"Go back to New Orleans. Do some fine finish carpentry, custom wood-work, I don't know. I've got enough money socked away, partial benefits. You never thought about stepping back? It's a tough job on families."

Hardwick raised an eyebrow. He'd been dating a great woman, a nurse practitioner with two kids from a past marriage, for two or three years. Eric always wondered why he hadn't proposed to her yet. Hardwick was crazy about her, but they'd all seen plenty of marriages burn out from the long Service shifts, the constant time away from home, the missed holidays and anniversaries. Maybe that was it. It seemed like the job had been weighing on him too recently, though he wasn't one to complain.

Hardwick looked at him for a long time. He had a habit of thinking deeply before he spoke and saying little. "You'd die without this job," he said.

Eric thought back to when he was a kid, watching his dad buckle up his duty belt, slide a pen into his shirt pocket, and pin on his badge. He was a New York cop who'd fallen in love with a woman from New Orleans and ended up on the force there. Stop the bad guys. Protect the good ones. That's all he'd ever wanted to do. That's all he wanted now, but the lines get blurry in DC.

"You're the heart and soul of this place," Hardwick said. "You brought up half these agents. We need you, Hill."

The Service was Eric's family and working alongside these men and women a daily honor. That only made this more difficult.

Hardwick looked at him squarely. "If you had to do it today, would you step in front of those bullets again?"

"For Kline?"

"Yes," Hardwick said.

Eric didn't answer.

Hardwick shook his head. "This job . . . if you're not willing to die for them any given day . . ."

"Then what the fuck am I doing here?" Eric asked. It was a good question, and he let it hang in the air between them.

"I've got your back," Hardwick said, "whatever you need. Talk to Chilton, the officers' association, whatever. You tell me."

"I appreciate it, but I'm set."

Hardwick gave him a thumbs-up. "Where do you need me?"

"Northern colonnade."

He dipped his head, lowered the gun to the end of its sling, and set out.

4

AMBER CODY ADJUSTED her shirt and belt in the bathroom mirror until everything lined up perfectly.

Her hand slipped into her jacket pocket and came out with a presidential protection detail pin. Her fingers trembled as she fastened it to the lapel over her heart and looked at herself—her dark curls straightened and pulled into a tight bun.

She reached into her other pocket and came out with a small enameled disc—another presidential detail lapel pin from fifteen years before, her father's, the enamel cracked and metal pitted. The new pins had RFID chips embedded so they could be used for secure access, but her dad's was solid brass. She ran her thumb over it. They had cleaned it up before they gave it to her mother, but Cody would always remember it stained red on the day her father died.

Her chest tightened. She closed her eyes, shutting down any outward trace of feelings—not today, not a chance—and felt a shudder go through her. Relief and fear and God knows what else. She'd been trying to get to this place for fifteen years, for most of her life, and now it was up to her to prove she belonged in the most exalted—and dangerous—job in the Service.

She rolled her shoulders back, filled her chest, and straightened her suit. "Give 'em hell, Bear," she said to her reflection, turned, and strode out.

Eric stepped into the doorway of his office and saw Amber Cody in the bullpen talking with Chilton and the night shift agents—Laura Leigh, Samuel Brimley, and Liam Walsh—all of them drinking coffees from Swing's. Chilton and Walsh were laughing, and Cody was playing along with it, watching them carefully.

Eric felt a surge of emotion. He remembered her as a twelve-year-old sitting in front of her dad's grave while the head of the Service passed her mother a folded flag. But he put that thought out of his head and paid attention to the person standing before him now: five foot six, lean but strong, a meticulously put-together special agent.

His fingers went to his shoulder, the knot of scar from the bullet that made it past his Kevlar vest on the day an assassin came for the president. It was the same day that Amber Cody's father died. Joe Cody was on that detail, standing by the front of the presidential limousine when the ambush started. He engaged the shooter, took a bullet through the neck, and passed away before he reached the hospital.

Eric had been close with Joe Cody and kept in touch with the family after his death. Cody's widow moved out to be with her family in eastern California, a town called Mesa Springs that was surrounded by tribal lands. She was of Paiute and Shoshone descent on her mother's side.

He watched now as Chilton left and Cody and the others kept jawing. She tossed two paperboard coffee carriers into the trash. She was facing partly away from Eric, but he could still see the forced, eager smile, a slight forward lean toward the senior agents, almost a bow of deference. All pretty standard for a rookie on the detail.

"You should know Agent Cody had the highest range scores of any candidate for the past two years," Brimley said. He'd also known Cody's dad.

Agent Walsh ran his hand through his red hair, stepped closer to Cody, and took a sip of his coffee.

"Targets don't shoot back," he said in that whisper voice of his. "It's a different fucking story when you're on the wrong end of the gun."

He glanced around, met eyes with Leigh, and grinned.

Eric's impulse was to walk over and shove him back a foot or two, but he checked it. She was an agent now, not his dead friend's daughter, and he would treat her like anyone else on the detail. He'd met up with her when she first moved to town, and she made it clear she didn't want any special treatment, wouldn't stand for it.

"Let's give Agent Cody a chance," Brimley said. "I remember when you showed up after training with your suit pockets still sewn shut."

Walsh's jaw tightened, and he stared at the veteran officer. "And now I outrank you."

Brimley chuckled. Walsh was cocky and a bit of a mouth, but also one of the strongest agents on the detail. A good-looking guy, he still had a chip on his shoulder, maybe from barely clearing five foot seven.

"I'm just fucking around, Cody," Walsh said. "We do it to everybody. Welcome to the Show." Secret Service slang for the president's detail.

He punched Brimley playfully in the ribs. The other agent jabbed back, lightning quick with an old boxer's strength.

Walsh took a step and held his hand out to Cody. As she shook it, she finally noticed Eric. A hint of a smile, then she seemed to catch herself and put on a neutral, professional look.

Eric stepped closer to the bullpen. "Special Agent Cody," he said. "We're glad to have you at the White House." He kept his voice even. The last time he'd called someone that it was her father in the back of an ambulance.

"Thank you, Agent Hill."

"Let's get you set up with an MP5," Eric said, and she followed him to the gun safe. "What was Chilton talking about? His Brioni?"

"It is a beautiful suit."

He'd seen Chilton feeling the material on her navy jacket, which was fine, but basic, as an agent's should be, though the presidential protection folks had a reputation as peacocks. Seventeen years in the Service had trained him to absorb every detail in a glance—clothing, grooming, expression, body language—reading people, often hundreds in a row along a rope line, constantly scouring the environment for threats.

Cody's mom was in a nursing home, and she was the only one in the family with any money. He imagined that didn't leave a lot left over for the Italian wools, custom tailoring, and gold cuff links that Chilton and some of the other senior agents went in for.

"Was he ribbing you about your clothes?"

"No," she said, stiffening. "It's fine."

Eric thought about the coffees. He knew he should let it go. She didn't need a lecture and he didn't want her second-guessing herself, but the words came out of his mouth anyway.

"You brought coffees for the shift?"

She moved her weight from her left foot to her right. She could tell something was off.

"Yes. Sorry, I gave yours to Chilton. I didn't think he'd be down here. Agent Leigh had said it would be a good thing to do to start things out."

"I don't care about that," Eric said. The coffees were a small thing, but they bothered him tonight, something about the culture of back-scratching, of expecting perks, of taking advantage.

"You don't have to get them coffee. And you don't have to take their shit."

She narrowed her eyes and looked at him warily—a mix of *what is your problem, dude?* and a genuine concern that she'd misstepped.

"Sorry," she said, more to placate him than anything else. "First day and I'm glad to meet the team. Did I do something wrong here, Hill?"

"No." He held his right fist in his left hand. He didn't want her apologizing or trying to please him as her boss. That was the point. "Don't be, I . . ."

She wiped her hands down the legs of her pants.

"I've got some other stuff going on," Eric said, cursing himself. It had been happening more and more ever since the Braun thing—snapping at people, letting the bullshit get to him. He squeezed the fist. "Don't worry about it. But you don't always have to go along with whatever they say."

She looked at his desk, and his hip, where his service pistol should have been. She could see how that approach had worked out for Eric.

He wanted to explain, to warn her not to go along with whatever Washington asked of her, blind to the fact that the men and women in these high offices got there as often through vice as virtue. She put the Service and the Presidential Protective Division on a pedestal. She was a good person, so eager and hopeful it could easily shade into innocence. She didn't stand a fucking chance in this town.

But that was his protective instincts at work after all that had happened to her and her family. It was about Eric's own failings, his own bitter regrets. He managed this time to hold his tongue. It wasn't his place to tell her the full truth about the Service and its protectees, to tarnish what she believed in. She didn't need an unprompted rant and a patronizing old white guy projecting his shit onto her.

He was so bad at this kind of thing, never finding the right words, always pushing people away and putting them on edge, especially recently.

He didn't know what to say, so he handed her the MP5. She was still on guard and seemed a little nervous as she took it. Some stage fright was normal when agents first arrived to the Show from a field office. Eric had been no exception. It was like coming from a farm team to the majors.

She took it, checked the magazine—the MP5 was notorious for misfeeding when it had thirty-one rounds in the mag—loaded it, then slapped the cocking handle back, charging the weapon, all while pointing it down into the bullet trap beside the cabinet. Her left hand shook slightly at the beginning, then she grew more certain, forgetting herself in the familiar motions. The gun gave her comfort, the straightforwardness of steel and spring.

He looked over the security cameras, and thought of her wiping the sweat off her palms, her trembling hand.

"You're on the East Wing, B3." New arrivals didn't go on the front lines until they'd shown what they were capable of.

She glanced to the video feeds. "Third basement?" A trace of disappointment in her voice.

"You know how to find it?"

"Yes, sir," she said. She brought the MP5 to the end of its sling, waited for a moment to see if any further orders were coming, then turned on her heel and headed for her post.

5

TIM NAVARRO WAS the last agent to show up for the shift. He took his gun and drained his coffee in four long gulps. The dark circles under his eyes gave him a skeletal look.

"The twins?" Eric asked.

He nodded, crushed the paper cup, and tossed it into the waste bin.

"Lily figured out how to get out of the crib last night, and somehow she communicated that to Jake. Then they beelined to the cabinet under the bathroom sink at four a.m."

"God, were they okay?"

"Fine. Jake got into some Benadryl. A little sleepy, but fine. Twins, man . . ." He stared into the distance with a hollow look Eric was more used to seeing on combat veterans.

He glanced around the room and pulled Eric to the side. "Can I talk to you about something? Just between us?"

"Sure," Eric said, wary now.

Navarro lowered his voice. "Have you heard of anything sketchy going down around here?"

"Politics is a sketchy business. What's up?"

"Anything about an emerging threat? A power grab?"

"Are you talking about the usual political maneuvering . . . or a coup?"

"I don't know," he said.

"Navarro, Jesus, what are you hearing?"

The agent looked down as if he was weighing whether to say more. "Does the name Operation V mean anything to you?"

"V as in Victor." Eric frowned. "No, what is it?"

"I'm not sure. I'm just hearing things."

Eric leveled his eyes at the other agent. "From *who*?"

"Rumors. I wanted to see if you'd run across any of this. Could be total bullshit. I don't want to throw anyone under the bus." He looked at the desk. He probably didn't want anyone to end up in the doghouse like Eric.

Eric didn't press, just waited. He didn't want to scare off Navarro until he'd learned all he could.

"Citizen—have you ever heard that name?"

"An alias?"

"Yes. Supposedly it's someone high up in the government."

"That's where you're getting this info?"

Navarro looked down, ducked the question. *Supposedly*—it sounded like the information was coming to him secondhand.

"You know I'm always thinking about Rivas and Stiles," Navarro said.

Julian Rivas and Amy Stiles were veteran Secret Service agents. They had died earlier that year after their SUV crashed through a guardrail on the bluffs along the Virginia side of the Potomac River. Navarro and Hardwick had been the first to reach them. Rivas was killed instantly behind the wheel, and Stiles had been pinned down in the passenger seat. Navarro and Hardwick managed to get the protectee out of the burning car, but Stiles had been sealed inside by the mangled door. Navarro had to watch her die.

"Ever think that wasn't an accident?" Navarro asked.

"We all had questions, but the Service ruled out foul play." There had been a full investigation, though an attack on a candidate always inspires endless speculation.

"I know. I know. But this town is so crooked." He looked to Eric for assent, but Eric didn't bite. He was trying to keep that bitterness under wraps.

"The protests, these suspicions going around about Kline, everything happening in this country—I worry," Navarro said. "Sometimes it feels like the wheels are about to fall off."

"You believe those people?"

"There's twice as many out there tonight. I keep my eyes open."

"You think President Kline was behind the crash?"

"I don't know, but there's a logic to it. That wreck nearly took out one of his main opponents. You hear the talk. This idea that he's got some secret op going that's run by people only loyal to him. Off-book investigations.

He claims he's rooting out corruption but he's just eliminating anyone who might stand in his way. He'll get what he wants no matter what it takes."

"What does he want?"

"What does anyone want in this town? Power."

"Where are you getting this, Navarro? Who's Citizen?"

"I wish I knew," he said. "He could be trying to stop something even worse from happening soon."

"If you have intel, you need to pass it along, you understand?"

"I'm getting this as hearsay. It could be bullshit"—he gestured with his head to the floors above them—"and I'm sure as hell not going to write it up for the brass. I just wanted to know if you'd heard anything."

"I haven't, but listen, there's got to be a way—"

Navarro straightened up, and Eric looked back as Brimley walked in and checked something on a computer nearby.

"I'll think about it," Navarro said. "Where am I working?"

"Treasury tunnel." Eric stepped closer to him. "Find me after your shift," he whispered. "We'll figure this out. Nothing formal. No trouble. But if you're on to something, we need to run it down."

Navarro nodded and put his hand on Eric's arm. "All right, man. Thanks."

"And keep your eyes open out there," Eric said. "There's a rookie on B3."

6

ERIC SAT BEHIND his desk watching the cameras, sipping the bitter break room coffee, and keeping up with the team over radio. On the surveillance feed, a light flickered in an East Wing subbasement. The minutes turned into hours as a restless feeling grew in him.

At 9:17 p.m., he was tapping his foot against the thin gray carpet when, looking through his office door, his attention fixed on the monitor over the surveillance tech's workstation. The subbasement light had stopped flickering. The image was perfectly still. He moved closer to the screen and examined a duct fan in the top right corner.

He lifted his radio. "Navarro. Can you get over to T5? The camera feed is frozen."

"On it," Navarro's voice came back.

Eric stepped out and looked at the White House map on the wall. That section of subbasement ran beside a long secret tunnel for vehicles that allowed them to head out from an underground garage near the East Wing, drive under the Treasury Building, and exit the compound via a hidden ramp in an alley on H Street.

That exit, a block and a half from the White House, was how the commander in chief left the campus when he didn't want to be seen and it was notorious as the preferred route for presidential philandering. Agents called it the tunnel of love. It was also connected to emergency tunnels that led out from the residence and the Oval Office and another from the Presidential Emergency Operations Center, known as the PEOC, the bunker hidden under the East Wing.

The H Street entrance and its tunnel touched all the secret arteries of the

White House, but it was the least well-defended way into the complex, dark and on a public street with just one guard and a metal gate to stop ramming attacks.

Eric radioed to the guard booth at the mouth of that alley.

"H Street. Everything good?"

"Yes."

"No one came or went? No alarms?"

"Nothing."

He asked the surveillance tech to check the status on all the doors and gates that communicated with the Treasury tunnel.

A clatter of keys. "All closed," he replied. "Reporting normal."

"Can you operate the locks?" Eric asked.

More typing. "I don't see . . . wait." He stabbed at the key. "No. They're down. No response."

7

MARCUS LOOKED TO the cameras as he walked down a long corridor in the Treasury's third basement. They were down, but he took no chances and wore a thin black balaclava. Based on a glance at his G-Shock, it was twelve minutes until the next patrol. He held his SIG in his right hand as he eased open a heavy sliding door with his left. The low rumble of its wheels echoed down the passage.

These basement levels had been converted from the old Treasury vaults. He wasn't far from the emergency bunker, and many of the hallways were built according to a Cold War design, a zigzag pattern angling slightly to the left then the right every fifty feet as a way to dissipate nuclear blast pressure.

As he slipped through the door and closed it behind him, every sound threatened to give him away. A drop of sweat ran down his side. The lights on the keypad next to the lock were all dead.

The air was cooler here and the echoes came from farther off. He had entered an underground garage where the Secret Service always kept two armored SUVs ready behind locked doors for an emergency escape through the Treasury tunnels and the H Street exit.

The fluorescent fixtures overhead shimmered off the polished black paint of two identical Chevy Suburbans.

Marcus circled to the second Suburban, peering through the tinted glass into the cargo area. He moved on to the side wall of the garage, which was lined with tall locking cabinets that held gear for the counterassault team when they rolled out with the president.

He dialed in a combination and looked over the gear—rack after rack of heavy weapons.

His work in the garage took him eight minutes. He exited the way he had come, slid the steel door shut, and relocked it with a noise barely above a murmur. There was no trace he had ever been near those weapons and vehicles.

Marcus looked at his watch. Two minutes until the next patrol. He had to move.

Tap. Tap. Tap. Tap. The footsteps approached with the pace of a fast heartbeat. The agent on guard was early. Marcus slipped down the hall and pressed into the dark behind a steel support beam.

The nearest light was on the ceiling by the sliding door to the garage. He heard the agent pause, close to that door by the sound of his steps. The guard's shadow stretched toward him. Marcus pressed the button on his radio three times, slipped off his balaclava, and raised his pistol.

Navarro looked over the keypad beside the sliding door that led to the garage, then started down the corridor. "Passing the T4 junction," he radioed back. "Clear."

"Check the doors," Eric said.

"They're down," Navarro said. "They're all down. No lights on the keypads. We're wide open."

"Assume a breach," Eric said. "Clear for deadly force."

Navarro raised his gun in front of him as he moved forward. He halted, his attention drawn by a whisper ahead, breath or fabric brushing against something.

"Is T5 clear?" Eric Hill asked in his earpiece, but Navarro stayed silent as he walked down the hall, coming around the zigzag corner, trying to see into the darkness ahead, working against the strange design of these tunnels.

Navarro thought he saw a trace of movement in the distance by a pillar, maybe nothing more than shadow and nerves. He steadied the weapon and aimed straight at the pillar, staying close to the wall opposite as he came around it.

There was no one. He let out a long breath.

"Navarro!" a voice called out from ahead in the tunnel. He looked up, recognized the face, and lowered his pistol.

"Oh," Navarro said, with a relieved smile. "It's—"

The other person looked past him and gave a quick nod. Navarro heard someone approaching from behind. Before he could turn around, pain exploded in the side of his head. He staggered forward and crashed facedown on the concrete. His fingers rose toward his chest and the button on his radio mic as the blackness closed in.

"Navarro. Come back," Eric said, rising from the desk, the radio gripped in his right hand.

The line opened. A cry of pain. Then nothing.

"Navarro! Navarro!"

Eric spoke the code for officer down over the radio, calling for every Secret Service agent and uniformed officer to close in on that tunnel.

"T9 door is locked," an agent reported back. "Will not respond."

"Door T1," said another. "Same. The keypad's dead."

"Break them down if you have to," Eric said, then turned to the surveillance tech. "Ted, get those fucking doors open."

"I'm trying," he replied, glaring at the computer. "They're all offline."

Eric ran his left hand over the knuckles of his right, then stepped to the gun safe and dialed it open.

He pulled an MP5 off the rack, loaded and cocked it, then slung it over his shoulder. Reaching past the gas masks and riot shields, he grabbed a Remington 870 Magnum and a box of 12-gauge slugs.

"Hill, what are you doing, you're not—" The tech stopped talking as soon as he saw the look on Eric's face.

Hill walked across the suite, loading slugs into the shotgun. "I'm heading out. I have my radio. Eyes on the cameras and keep working on those doors."

"Will do," the tech said, his face pale.

Eric went through an exit in the back of the suite and climbed down a stairwell of white-painted cinder blocks lit by bare bulbs in cages. He hit the third basement and entered a tunnel with conduits and pipes along the ceiling. He ran, navigating the musty corridors. A threat to stop, a gun in his hand—the job felt right again.

He came to a door that led to Navarro's tunnel and punched the code into the keypad beside it. No lights. No movement.

Raising the shotgun's stock to his shoulder, he pressed the barrel against the door handle, faced away, and pulled the trigger. The Remington bucked against him, and the blast left him deaf for a moment. A bitter smell filled the tunnel as he reared back and drove his foot into the blown-out lock. Metal wrenched against metal, and he shouldered through, turning right, to the east.

"I'm inside the Treasury tunnel," someone said over his radio. "Approaching on the T3 junction."

The speaker was breathing fast, and Eric knew who it was before she identified herself at the end of the call. Amber Cody.

"Agent Cody. This is Eric Hill. I'm coming up behind you."

8

PRESIDENT KLINE SAT at the Resolute Desk, turning the pages in a book as reverently as if he were handling a Gutenberg Bible. The volume was bound in black leather and embossed with the seal of the Department of Justice above the title: Presidential Emergency Action Documents.

The PEADs were a series of laws and directives, drafted in advance, that could be put into place after a national catastrophe—a nuclear attack or coup takes out government leadership, a pandemic kills half the population, the grid goes down. The specifics were one of the most closely held secrets in government, but in essence they were orders to establish martial law through presidential decree, bypassing Congress and suspending civil liberties and the Constitution if necessary.

Reading through them was the stuff of nightmares, a glimpse of how America would attempt to survive its darkest hours since the Civil War. To his left on the desk lay a sealed red letter with the codes by which the president could invoke the emergency directives. Kline reached out and ran his fingers over the crimson paper.

A light flashed on the phone on his desk, and he pressed a button.

"Your wife is here, sir," said a voice over the intercom.

Kline closed the book and placed it and the letter into a portfolio. He walked to the study, where a wall safe was concealed behind a piece of paneling. After locking them inside, he went back to the Oval and opened its eastern door.

His wife stood outside, laughing and talking to Will Maddox, the president's body man, the aide who never left the president's side or close vicinity and handled, well, everything: phone calls, briefing papers, personal effects, schedules, and logistics. Maddox was from Gatlinburg, Tennessee, and had been a scholarship kid and star lacrosse player at Duke. That helped because half of the body man's job was blocking and checking—keeping people away from POTUS.

Sarah Kline wore a patterned shawl over a black dress and carried a stack of printouts under her left arm.

"The whole family's coming up?" she asked Maddox, continuing their conversation.

"That's right. I'm going to bring them around for the tour. Everything's been so busy I haven't seen my mom and dad in months," he said.

"Talk to my chief of staff and make sure I meet them."

"Thank you, ma'am," he said, and smiled. "But . . ."

"What?"

"You're sure? They don't get out of the Smokies much."

Another laugh. "Stop. I've heard so much about them. I cannot wait."

Kline stepped toward her, and she gave him a kiss.

"Sign me up for that too, Will," Kline said. "I can't believe I haven't met them yet. We'll do a lunch in the Mess for you all and I'll be sure to make time to say hello."

"Thank you, sir. I'm really grateful." His phone buzzed and he checked it. "The list of attendees for tomorrow's leadership meeting is ready. Do you want that in your packet for tonight?"

"Please," the president said.

Maddox nodded and took off down the hall toward the warren of offices that filled the West Wing.

Sarah watched him go. "He always moves that fast?"

"Always," Kline said. He gave a quick greeting to his military aide, Paul Eubanks, who had been standing at attention ever since Kline opened the door. One of them was always near, carrying the nuclear football, formally known as the "presidential emergency satchel," an aluminum Halliburton briefcase covered in black leather that held the nuclear launch codes.

The aide was posted here when Kline was working or sat just outside the entrance to the private residence while Kline slept. Eubanks was the regular officer on duty, Kline's enormous shadow, a six-foot-seven Kansan utterly dedicated to his duty. His former executive officer said that he took a while to warm up to people, but Kline hadn't really seen it. He appeared to be one of the most perfectly bland and humorless souls the president had ever met. But that was what the military was looking for in these aides, someone rock solid who would fade into the background like a piece of furniture.

Kline brought Sarah into the Oval and shut the door.

He looked at the papers under her arm. "Grant applications?"

"It never ends." Sarah Kline was an MD, an obstetrician. She'd taken a break from clinical work while her husband was in office, but she still taught a few classes and did research at Georgetown. "I talked to Jill, though." Their daughter, a senior at Princeton. "She can make it down tomorrow morning."

"Tomorrow?"

"I knew she'd want to see you before she left. I asked you to keep it open."

"I'm meeting with the congressional leadership."

"You can't change it?"

"It's really not a good moment to be imperious with them."

"She's been having a hard time. I think she really wants to see you."

"Have her come to Camp David."

"She can't."

"I'm sorry, hon. I can't get free. You know family comes first, but—"

"That's what you told me before you ran for this job." Dr. Kline looked down at the presidential seal woven into the carpet. "That was the deal, James."

"It is the deal, just not tomorrow."

"There's always a but. I've been trying, James . . . really trying."

"I know, but I'm fighting for my political life here. You see those people protesting. Half the Congress is scheming on how to impeach me, making me out as some kind of would-be despot. You can't imagine how far it's gone, the lies they're peddling. Politics is pure blood sport now. There are threats everywhere, Sarah."

"Is the cure worse than the disease?"

He waited.

"You're hunting down all these people who are supposedly conspiring against you. It can make you look worse. It only feeds the speculation. Trust that things will work out. Have some faith. What if you were more transparent?"

That wasn't how things worked. Kline had spent half his career at CIA. Trust wasn't one of his strengths. He knew the value of keeping your secrets close.

"We're investigating, not hunting anyone down. And it's deadly serious, Sarah. Believe me. I see the intel. I had no choice but to take these steps. I'm trying to clean up this town. That's the third rail, going after the real money. It's dangerous, but I'm not backing off."

"All right." She gave him a long, searching look, then pursed her lips and tapped the papers. "I'll be in the residence."

"I'll make it up to you both," he said.

A curt nod, and she turned to the door.

She opened it to see a group of four Secret Service agents striding toward them, their guns out.

Dr. Kline stepped aside to let Samuel Brimley, the lead agent, pass.

"Mr. President," he said, "we have a security issue. We're going to take you to the PEOC and lock it down."

"What's going on?"

"The cameras and access control system are offline. It's a potential breach."

Maddox appeared behind them, holding a folder.

"Let him through," the president called out, and the body man entered the Oval.

"Give me one minute," Kline said to Brimley. He walked Maddox to the safe in the study, dialed it open, and took out the portfolio with the red letter and the emergency action documents. He passed it to the younger man.

"This never leaves my side," he said quietly.

"Understood. Is this it? Operation V?"

"Be ready."

They walked back into the Oval and the agents surrounded them and Dr. Kline. As they were ushered out, Claire Givens, Kline's chief of staff, came down the hall.

"What is going on?" she asked. Nothing happened in this office without her knowledge.

"PEOC," Kline called out. "Givens, Maddox, you're with us."

"Sir," one of the agents said quietly, "there's a protocol and they're not on the list."

"They're on my list."

They all moved into the gallery and Eubanks followed with the nuclear football. Kline came up alongside his wife, and she took his hand.

9

AMBER CODY KEPT the stock of her MP5 tight against her shoulder, looking over the iron sights as she advanced through the tunnel. She cleared each of the zigzag corners in turn, the floor angling slightly down, taking her deeper under the Treasury Building. She had never set foot in these corridors and basements, but she knew every inch of them from long and careful study.

Her pulse throbbed in her neck and the tips of her fingers. Her index tightened on the trigger. She came around another bend, and her sight fixed on it, a man lying on his back beside a column: Tim Navarro. Agent down. She moved forward, fast but silent, and could make out in the darkness a figure standing over him, bringing a short-barreled rifle forward, pointed at Navarro's face.

She took aim as the figure turned, the head sheathed in a black balaclava, the gun rising to fix on her. It all happened in less than a second, yet it seemed to take forever. An image flashed in her mind of her dad's body collapsing after he was shot. The muscles in her hands shook, the fear taking over.

Give 'em hell, Bear.

She steadied the gun and ripped two three-round bursts as the attacker took cover. Cody kept moving forward, circling to the left to get a better angle on him.

Navarro was in full view now, lying facedown, blood on the floor around his head, barely breathing. He must have been injured before, because the attacker she had seen hadn't gotten a shot off.

The lights cut out.

She moved toward the wall for cover, weighing each step to stay silent.

Listening for any sign of the attackers, she could only hear her own fast breath.

With her right hand on the grip of the MP5, she reached her left into her pocket for her flashlight.

Her shoulder blade touched the cold wall, and she flinched away.

"Cody? What's your status?" came Hill's voice in her earpiece. Her mouth was dry. Her fingers rose toward the button on her mic, then stopped. Her voice would give her away; so would the light.

The soft rush of fabric came from her right. She slid six inches to the side, raised the gun, and took aim in the blackness, zeroing in on the sound.

Fingers pawed across her shoulders, and then shot toward her neck—a second attacker, just beside her. The hand gripped her trapezius and clamped down.

He pulled her against him, and she lowered the stock of the MP5 and drove it back with all her strength. It hit nothing. She was off balance now, and the man grabbed at her neck, his fingers closing on her throat.

She took her left hand off the stock, seized the man's wrist, and instead of fighting to regain her balance, she went with the fall, dropping onto her hip, hauling the man forward, adding to his momentum, and throwing him toward the wall.

He let out a grunt and fell hard as she rolled onto her side. The sling of her MP5 tugged across her arm—the man hauling it from her. She grabbed for it, but the weapon was torn from her grip. It fell and clattered somewhere off to the right.

On her hands and knees, she moved toward the sound, feeling along the floor for the weapon, her fingertips sweeping through the dust.

Her fingers jammed into the wall. She felt along it, but there was no sign of the gun.

A beam of light hit her, blinding white, and she flinched away. A second light switched on, just to the right of the other, and they flanked her, closing in.

She shifted her weight onto the balls of her feet and brought her hands in front of her. Rising to her full height, back against the wall, she faced them.

· · ·

Eric heard a grunt and clatter, and sprinted down the hallway, cutting left and right along the zigzagging walls. He came to a steel door, and another dead keypad. He set up at an angle to avoid ricochets and sent a load into the lock, wrenching apart the metal. He drove his boot into the door, but it didn't move.

A cry of pain sounded from within, a woman's voice.

Leaning to the side, he blasted it again. Pain arced across his temple, a hot sting from the shrapnel. He clapped his hand to it, then drove his boot into the door. The metal squealed. Another kick. The bolt wrenched free. He brought his hand down and glanced at it. Blood, but not much. He shoved open the door, switching the shotgun to his left and raising the MP5 in his right.

The tunnel was dark as he raced through the doorway and saw a woman rising from the ground. "It's Cody! Don't shoot," she called, and stood, hands up.

Her eye was already red and swollen on the outside corner, near the temple. Based on her expression, she was clearly in pain, but she was steady on her feet.

"I'm okay," she said, and pointed down the hall. "That way. At least two of them. They have my weapon and Navarro is down. It's bad."

She took him around the pillar, and went on one knee beside the fallen agent, feeling for his pulse. Eric's stomach dropped. Navarro had been smashed in the side of the head. More footsteps came up behind them, and Eric wheeled around with his gun to see a uniformed Secret Service officer rushing in.

"You," he said. "Get the first aid started on him. We need an ambulance and the medical unit."

Eric looked down the corridor, his face tight with anger.

"All right," he said to Cody. "You stay here—"

"I'm fine," she said. "*I* engaged with him and kept him from killing Navarro. I need a gun."

She reached her hand out, already moving past Eric. He watched her for an instant, unslung the MP5, and passed it to her as they strode down the hallway. The door at the end was locked, its keypad dead.

"Stand there," he said. She moved over and Eric pressed against the wall and blew apart the lock.

Agent Laura Leigh spoke over his radio. "We got through," she said. "We're a minute out from T5, coming from the east."

"How many agents?" Eric asked as he moved through the door.

"Eight."

"The attackers fled north through tunnel D from T5. We're coming up behind them. Cut off the exits. There are at least two of them."

He shined his light, running now, but the tunnel ahead was empty.

10

AMBER CODY BEGAN to describe what happened in the attack while they moved down the tunnel. He was nearing its end when he saw flashlights. "Don't shoot," Leigh said through her earpiece. "We're approaching."

The rest of the tunnel was empty, and they met with Laura Leigh's team at the next junction. They hadn't seen anyone either.

"Did you catch the faces on any of the attackers?" Eric asked Cody.

"No," she said. "One was wearing a balaclava. Male. Strong build. At least six feet tall. Right-handed. There was a second who jumped me in the dark."

Eric took another look at the injury to Cody's temple, then conferred with Leigh for a moment. He told Cody and another agent to check on Navarro and help get him safely to the medical unit.

"Get those injuries looked at while you're there, Cody. Strong work tonight."

"I'm good to go," she said, gripping her MP5 and looking down the tunnel.

"You took a hard hit. We have enough hands now. Go with them. See the doc and we'll get you back on patrol."

She started to protest.

"Agent Cody, please."

Her eyes met his and she nodded, then took off with two other agents.

Eric continued to the tunnels under the Treasury, coordinating the search over the radio as more backup arrived at the building—agents and uniformed Secret Service officers. Chilton established a cordon around the White House complex and Eric, who knew every brick in this building, guided the teams through the tunnels, leaving the attackers with no escape.

Eric was leading a search of another corridor that connected to the T5 junction when the surveillance tech radioed.

"Access control is back. All cameras are restored."

"What do you see?"

"No sign of them," the tech replied.

Eric checked with the other agents. Every tunnel and exit was covered. *Where the fuck are you?* he thought.

"A dozen uniforms just arrived," the tech said. "Where should I send them?"

"I'm coming back to you," Eric replied. "I'll handle them. Gather footage of all areas connected to T5 before and after the incident." He needed eyes on the whole building.

Back at the Secret Service suite, Eric sent out the uniforms, then looked to the map on the wall. He marked out the movement of every team he had. There was no way the attackers could have escaped.

Hardwick ducked his head in the doorway, the neck of his shirt ringed with sweat. "T1 to T4 are clear," he said. "Where do you need us?"

"Here," he said, pointing to the map. "Secure and search the basement access to the residence. I'll tell the uniformed division to put the freeze on the surrounding blocks. If—"

"I've got this, Hill," Chilton's voice came from behind Eric.

Hardwick looked from Eric to the supervisor, then back to Hill. It was clear enough who the agent wanted to hear orders from.

"Go ahead," Chilton said to Hardwick, insistently, and the agent obeyed.

Chilton threw a look at Eric as he came closer, checking out the shotgun in his hand and the cut on his neck. He ran his hand along his chin, then fixed his suit by tugging near the button. He didn't like any challenges to his authority, but he seemed to have cooled off from earlier. "You all right?"

"Fine. There were two attackers. They knocked out Navarro here"—he pointed to the map—"and Agent Cody engaged with them before they—"

"I talked to Cody in medical. I'm up to speed."

"How's Navarro?" Eric asked.

"Touch-and-go. Subdural bleed."

"The president?"

"In the PEOC." The emergency bunker under the East Wing. It was spoken as one word, pee-ock. "He's with the senior staff. Everyone is okay."

Another hard look at the shotgun. "You're not cleared for that, Eric."

"You're serious?"

Chilton's eyes went to Eric's waist. "Are you carrying concealed too?"

Eric had a SIG Sauer P232 holstered inside his belt at the four o'clock position.

"I have my backup. Always. I look out for my agents."

"*My* agents." Chilton shook his head and smirked. "Stay by your desk. We're surging every gun we have, and the Capitol and DC police are backing up on the freeze and street search. Whoever did this won't get away."

"We covered the exits immediately. Assume the attackers are still inside, armed."

"I'll handle this, Eric." He came closer. "I need people I can count on. I thought you didn't even want this job."

A few choice obscenities came to Eric's lips, but he held them back. Chilton was a prick, but he wasn't wrong. Eric had been ready to walk away. Now, with his blood up and a gun in his hand, he couldn't imagine leaving the watch. He was more concerned about finding the attackers than putting Chilton in his place.

"Listen to me. Look inside, and out," Eric said. "Canvass every inch of this building. Consider everyone a suspect. *Everyone*."

"I give the orders around here," Chilton said. Then he turned his head slightly—something coming in on his earpiece. His expression was grave. "Put that weapon back in the safe and remain at your post. We'll discuss your actions later."

He exited the suite.

11

OFFERING A RESIGNATION is not uncommon as a gesture of accountability in DC, but every so often someone accepts the damn thing and then you're out on your ass.

Eric didn't think Chilton was going to take any drastic actions against him tonight, though. The SAIC had been trying to threaten him into submission, and Eric called his bluff.

Eric had worked closely with the director back in the day, and that may have been why he'd been treated so carefully to this point—the quiet shift to desk duty until all this blew over. He didn't think Chilton could convince him to fire Eric, although there was a chance he'd succeed in shipping him to some field office where he would go blind tracking down Medicare fraud for the rest of his career. If that happened Eric would quit, but he could tell that the threat of resigning had scared Chilton, as he had intended. They didn't want Eric cut loose, free to talk about what had happened with Braun. They wanted him under control. That's what the pension threat was about.

Eric walked to the surveillance station and stood next to the tech. "Run me through everything you have before and after the attack. Start by the Treasury tunnel," he said.

The tech looked at the shotgun, then Eric, and started typing. He scrubbed through the footage and Eric studied every figure, every door.

"All the cameras went down?" Eric asked.

"Yes. The same thing you noticed. The images froze."

"But that tunnel was first?"

"That's right."

"Any sign of a hack? An intrusion?"

"None."

The tech focused on the exterior cameras, which made sense after a breach. Eric looked at the footage—the empty gardens, the protesters, the pedestrian and vehicle gates. He studied the time stamps, noting when the cameras had gone offline and come back, thinking about when he had heard Navarro call out in pain on the radio.

He considered the distances to the exits from the campus, and a sick feeling took hold of him. After the cameras went down, an attacker would have had to breach the perimeter and then sprint straight to Navarro's location to make it, with no time for stealth. It was impossible they came from outside the White House complex.

"Show me inside access to the tunnel. Anywhere we had employees working. Residence. East and West Wings."

The tech looked up at him, a trace of doubt in his eyes.

Eric rolled his finger in the air and the tech brought up the tapes. Eric watched over the cleaning and construction crews, the young aides leaving for the night, the butlers and stewards.

"Hill, you all right?" someone asked him. He turned to face the White House doctor, a navy surgeon named Nathan Chen. He was gesturing toward Eric's cheek and Cody stood to his side.

Eric wasn't okay, but it had nothing to do with the cut.

"It's not bad. A graze."

Chen looked to Cody. Her face said *I told you so.* Eric guessed that she'd brought Chen down to check on him. She was looking out for him as much as he was looking out for her.

"I won't slow you down," Chen said, and waved him closer. Eric stepped over and showed him his temple. After a brief inspection, the doctor got to work cleaning it.

"You're okay?" Eric asked Cody as Chen put a bandage over the cut.

"Fine."

"I wouldn't say fine," Chen said, his eyebrows rising. "That was a hell of a blow. But if she insists on going back to work"—another look to Cody, as if all these stoics were testing his patience—"she should be okay. Just be careful."

Chen was used to it. He'd come up as a Naval Special Warfare corpsman with the SEAL teams before becoming a doctor and joining the White House medical unit. He was close with the president and Sarah Kline.

He finished with the bandage and started walking out. Eric joined him and asked about Navarro, though Chen didn't have any more information.

At the door, he quietly double-checked with the doctor about Cody's injuries.

"No concussion. Maybe some shock from the scare. A bit of a flat affect. She's all right physically, but make sure she has someone to talk to."

"I will," Eric said. "Appreciate it."

After Chen left, Eric went back, filled two cups of water from the dispenser, and walked over to Cody.

"Thanks," she said, and took one.

"You want some coffee?"

"I'm wired enough."

"We can get you a ride home. I know it's a lot."

She finished the water.

"No. Seriously, I'm good." She rose and picked up the gun. "Where do you need me?"

"Listen," he said, searching for the right words. "If you got the impression before that I had doubts about you, I'm sorry. We start everyone out slow."

"It's fine. I'm the rookie."

"You don't have to prove anything. Wait for backup if something else jumps off. And it's fine to take a break."

"I know. I don't need it."

He studied her for a moment. The flat affect. It wasn't shock. It was calm or a perfect imitation of calm. He realized that she had been through her share of shit well before tonight.

"Don't you dare take it easy on me, Hill. I'm just another agent."

"I'm not. I'd be doing this for anyone who got banged up like you did. You saved Navarro," he said.

"We'll see how the surgery goes."

"That took real grit, Cody. If your dad could see you now, he'd be proud."

A smile. A touch of emotion in her eyes. "He can," she said, and cleared her throat. "Enough with the Hallmark stuff, Jesus." She adjusted the sling on her weapon. "Can we get to work?"

Eric went to the safe and swapped his shotgun out for an MP5.

She looked at the submachine gun.

"Are you supposed to—"

"Don't worry about it," he said, then loaded and cocked the weapon. "Now, I've checked all the footage, and the officers around the perimeter haven't found any sign of an escape."

"You think they're still here?"

"We have to be sure. We checked the tunnels, but now we need to search this place from top to bottom, every space big enough for someone to hide." He was still wary that an insider did the attack, but he needed to eliminate the other possibilities first, including that someone had breached the White House and was still concealed in the building. "I'll get some people."

"Shouldn't we check with Chilton?"

"Let me worry about Chilton," Eric said. "Come on."

She hesitated, thinking it through as he started walking away, then rushed to join him.

They'd gone about fifty feet when Chilton's voice came over the radio with a new order. The police and backup Service officers would continue the search in the city, but the threat might still be inside. "We're going to canvass every inch of this building," Chilton said. Eric could almost laugh. It was word for word what Eric had told him.

"Great minds," he said, and led them back into the tunnels.

The White House complex—the president's mansion along with the East and West Wing working areas—was eighty thousand square feet, with just under two hundred rooms. Add in the Eisenhower Executive Office Building and the Treasury, both inside the secure perimeter, and you can quadruple that. The graveyard shift stayed on even as they called the morning crews in early. By the time the Service had searched and secured every space large enough for a person to hide in, dawn was breaking over the Potomac, casting a rosy glow over 1600 Pennsylvania Avenue.

Eric and Cody were walking past the Kennedy Garden on the way back from the Treasury when another call went out from Chilton. "CASTLE is secure. There is no threat inside. I repeat. CASTLE is secure."

That was the Secret Service code name for the White House. Cody paused next to one of the oaks and looked to Eric.

"They escaped?" she said, surveying the black fences, the cameras, the guard booths. The emergency response teams were on patrol, the attack dogs roving unmuzzled now. "That doesn't make sense. They couldn't just slip away."

Eric looked at the windows of the West Wing, watching the staffers and agents move down the halls. "No."

The snipers were still watching, and the Stinger missiles rolled forward. Chilton may have declared the complex safe, but the higher-ups were still bracing for more threats.

They neared the colonnade, and Laura Leigh stepped out. "There you are," she said. Her eyes went to Eric's gun, then his face.

Eric waited.

"Chilton and the president want to see you in the PEOC." She looked to Cody. "Both of you."

"What about?"

"No clue."

Cody was staring at Eric, a bit of alarm showing now.

"Face time with POTUS," he said, and smiled, though he had no idea if they were in for praise or a dressing-down. "You're on your way."

She swallowed, her lips dry. "Are we in trouble?"

"Decent chance I am," he said. "You should be fine."

12

ERIC WASN'T TOO worried. Going to see Kline was a good sign. If Eric was on his way out, the bosses would keep him away from POTUS. Perhaps all of Chilton's threats had been bluffs, or maybe he was just waiting until after this crisis to try to demote Eric.

They went along the lawn to the East Wing and returned to the basement levels. Two turns brought them to a heavy steel door guarded by a pair of agents: Brimley and Walsh. Both carried M4 carbines with holographic sights. Usually those were reserved for the counterassault team, but the White House wasn't hiding the full military kit anymore.

"We need your weapons before you go in," Walsh said.

"Seriously?"

"Yeah. New rules."

Eric handed over the MP5 and Cody gave hers to Brimley.

"And the sidearm," Walsh said, his eyes going to Eric's waist.

Eric reached by his right kidney and drew the P232, a lean pistol chambered in .380. The older agents swore by it as a backup piece and for concealed carry, though special agents on the presidential detail were no longer supposed to have backup guns. Eric had always worn one—his dad never went to work without a Smith & Wesson on his ankle—but it was technically against the regs.

He took it out, looked it over, and passed it to Walsh with reluctance. The other agent examined the worn steel.

"This is the one?" he asked.

"That's right," Eric replied.

He nodded. "We'll take good care of it."

Walsh spoke into his radio and a moment later the door opened inward, the rumbling of its massive weight felt as much as heard. It was as thick as a bank vault's, and Eric could see where the heavy bolts on all sides would slip into the frame to secure it.

They entered the Presidential Emergency Operations Center. The main room was a nest of cubicles, each with a secure laptop and several phones. It was tight, the air stale, and felt more like a cramped call center than the current seat of the most powerful nation in the world.

At the far end, a last door stood, protecting the conference room that most people pictured when they imagined this bunker. The president was inside. He and the first lady had been locked down here for hours.

The door to the conference room opened, and Eric saw POTUS inside: jacket off, coffee in hand, standing at the head of the table.

Cody caught a glimpse of President Kline as she strode through the workspaces, keeping her posture as straight as when she was on the parade grounds at Fort Jackson.

She'd joined the army after college, served as an officer in the Third Infantry Division, then ground her way up the Service ranks. She rose from tracking down counterfeit twenties in the Fresno, California, office to doing presidential protection by never resting and volunteering for every shit detail.

She could feel the others' eyes on her. The only woman down here, the men towering over. Nothing new. She was used to being watched by others, always measuring—whether she was strong enough, whether she was some diversity hire, whether she was worth making a pass at in the bar after work.

She'd learned to brush it off, but this was a new kind of pressure, on the top job in a crisis, with the commander in chief thirty feet away, a famously demanding scion of the American elite ready to ask her how she managed to let two killers go free in his White House.

She felt like they could smell it on her—the dry dust of the Owens Valley shithole where she'd grown up, the mothball scent of the secondhand stores in Georgetown where she picked up her Eileen Fisher blouses, the fear sweat clinging to her skin.

She was scared, as much as she hated to admit it, of them and of doing or saying the wrong thing and botching years of work. A lot of that feeling was just adrenaline, still coursing through her body from the attack. Her mind kept replaying it, the fingers closing on her throat, the man's breath on her cheek, the pain exploding in her temple. She asked herself what she could have done better, cursing herself as she thought of the shots she missed.

It was habit by this point, this endless internal interrogation. She could tune it out, and hide it well, though she had come to appreciate it as you would a hard-ass coach. Because she had to be perfect. It was the only way to get from there to here, the only way to shut up the people who judged her with a look and quiet the voices in her head—be twice as good.

Fair? No. And was some of it maybe in her own head, a lifetime of *you're not good enough* that had worked itself deep into her psyche? Decent chance.

But she didn't care; she was glad for the fire it gave her. Because she wanted to be twice as good, more than that; she wanted to be the fucking best.

She marched straight ahead.

Eric watched Chilton step out of the conference room with the president, shut the door behind him, and press a button on the keypad to lock it.

The SAIC approached, rubbing his hand on the side of his neck, just above his loosened tie.

"You were still carrying? I told you before to put your weapon in the safe," he said to Eric.

"I did. Then I got a different one. I'm not walking around this place unarmed."

"The intruders are gone."

"You know it's an intruder?" Eric asked. He was surprised how much Chilton had come off his earlier power trip. Maybe he wanted Eric's experience to fix the mess taking place on his watch, and bureaucratic revenge would come later. Maybe he had nothing left now that Eric had called his bluff.

Chilton squinted at him. "What are you getting at?"

"It's an inside threat," Eric said.

Chilton stepped closer, raising his finger toward Eric. "Stay in your lane here, Hill. I don't need wild speculation adding stress to—"

The door behind him opened, and James Kline stepped out of the conference room.

He was younger than most of the men who had held the office recently, with dark brown hair cut short enough that you could barely notice the waves to it and eyebrows a shade lighter. It gave him the look of an outdoorsman—a sailor or angler—even with the grueling schedule Kline kept. He had an easy smile, though Eric could tell it was practiced, and his eyes were usually narrowed just slightly, always appraising.

A Yale Law grad, he'd worked at a white-shoe corporate firm before becoming an attorney with the Senate Select Committee on Intelligence, then the CIA general counsel's office. From there he'd moved on to the Senate, tapping into a long family legacy in politics.

"I need to get back in the Oval," he said to Chilton.

"Twenty more minutes, sir. Running some last checks."

The president turned to Eric and Cody.

"Agent Hill," Kline said.

"Mr. President," Eric said.

Kline's eyes remained on Eric's for a moment, and Eric had an odd feeling that Kline had brought him here to take his measure in person.

"And you are Agent Cody?" Kline asked, looking to the bruise on her temple, his face pained.

"Yes, sir."

"Thank you," he said, then reached out and shook her hand. "Are you all right?"

"Fine, sir."

He led them into the command center.

"Sir," Chilton chimed in, but Kline held his hand up to dismiss him.

They stepped into the conference room, a space the size of a school bus, its walls covered with screens and red digital clocks ticking the time off in a dozen zones around the world. The air felt close and humid.

Chief of Staff Claire Givens acknowledged Eric with a slight tilt of her head. She was standing in the corner with Will Maddox, the president's body man. Another aide, Paul Eubanks, stood stooped next to them, too tall for the space, carrying the nuclear football. Both he and Maddox carried MP5s, which was definitely not protocol.

Givens whispered something to Eubanks and they both kept their eyes fixed on Eric as if he was the threat. Eric noticed Maddox and Cody exchanging a look. It made it seem like they knew each other from before, even though this was her first day at the White House.

The first lady smiled at Eric. He had never worked with Dr. Kline, but she had a good reputation among the close protection details—treating them as humans, offering coffee or a place to warm up, kindnesses all too rare among the VIPs.

Chilton followed them in, and the door closed. "I wanted to thank you both for your work in stopping these intruders," Kline said, and he seemed to take note of Eric's reaction to that word.

The president turned to Cody. "What are we dealing with here? Two men attacked you?"

"One was almost certainly male, though he was masked. The other I struggled with was strong and large, but I can't make a conclusion as to sex, sir."

"And you were able to get away?"

"Yes, sir."

Eric looked to her, hoping she would go on. He wasn't going to speak for her, but he would find a way to make sure they fully understood and appreciated her bravery in those tunnels.

After a deep breath, Cody continued. "I came across the first figure standing over Navarro—about to execute him, I believe. He aimed at me, and I fired six rounds as the attacker took cover. I closed on his position. The lights went out. In the dark, a second attacker jumped me and put me in a choke hold from the rear. I was able to drop and throw him across the tunnel, freeing myself, though I lost my weapon."

The president and the other figures in the room listened, rapt, as Cody, nervous but not letting it get the better of her, calmly went on.

"The two attackers then cornered me. I fought back but one knocked me unconscious with what I assume was the butt of the rifle. I was out for a short time before Agent Hill breached the door and they fled."

Kline came over and put his hand on her arm. "Agent Cody, you answered the call last night. Extraordinarily brave work. Thank you."

"Sir." She dipped her head.

He asked both Cody and Hill for anything else they might have seen to identify the attackers, but Cody had told all she knew.

Chilton looked daggers at Eric, silently warning him to shut up. Kline seemed to notice, and looked at Hill, waiting.

"We can't be certain it was an intruder," Eric said.

Dr. Kline looked to him, startled.

"You're saying?" Givens asked.

"Given the amount of time from when the cameras went down to the attack, the entry and exit without being seen, and the system access, we need to consider and secure against an inside threat."

Chilton crossed his arms. "Sir—"

Kline waved his objection away. "Agent Cody, thank you again. Now perhaps I can have a word alone with Agent Hill?"

"Of course, sir," she said, and headed out.

13

CHILTON SHUT THE door. Eric was glad to have a chance to talk one-on-one with this crowd. He hadn't been able to stop thinking about what Navarro had told him. Operation V. Citizen. A power grab. He had a duty to share it and more than that, he wanted to see how Kline and his people would react.

The president sat at the edge of the table, a few feet from Eric, and crossed his arms. "You think it was one of our own?"

"I have to. I consider risks and defend against them. How else could two attackers breach the heart of the White House, then disappear despite a city-wide dragnet?"

"That's an excellent question," Kline said.

"Navarro talked to me before the attack. He was agitated," Eric said. "He wanted to know if I had seen anything suspicious happening. He asked me if I knew anything about a power grab."

Kline and Chilton exchanged a look.

"Operation V," Eric said. "What is it?"

The president took a long breath in through his nose, and Eric saw that his words had captured the attention of every single member of Kline's team. Will Maddox stood up straighter, his hand going to the sling of his rifle.

"You heard that from Navarro?" Kline asked.

Eric nodded. "And twenty minutes later someone nearly killed him."

"Have you mentioned it to anyone else?"

"No."

"What did Navarro say it was?"

"He didn't know, but it had him on edge."

"You're aware there are multiple threats against me," Kline said. "You see these deluded people protesting outside."

Kline's past with the CIA had brought out all the characters, waving signs saying he was part of every conspiracy since the Illuminati. But Navarro was no fringe paranoiac. Eric looked at Kline's face and all he could see was that burning SUV with Rivas and Stiles inside.

"We believe Operation V is a plot to remove me from power by force."

Eric's eyes fixed on a portfolio at the head of the table, between Givens and Maddox. Inside he could make out a volume bound in black leather, and a red envelope tucked beside it.

Eric stiffened. They were the Presidential Emergency Action Documents and the codes to invoke them—a blueprint for martial law.

When he looked back, the president was staring at him. "Does that track with what Navarro told you?"

"He didn't get a chance to tell me much."

The president examined his face. "You have your doubts, Agent Hill? A different theory?"

Eric looked around the room. Givens had been with Kline since his CIA days, and all the others owed their careers to him. Kline always surrounded himself with loyalists, a closed circle of people who had been with him for decades.

He was aloof, with no gift for retail politics, shaking hands at fish fries and county fairs. Yet his career had been one long, unstoppable rise, driven by old family connections and a mysterious talent for steamrolling anyone who got in his way. His political vision, modeled on Teddy Roosevelt and Dwight Eisenhower, was to restore America as a great power at home and abroad by breaking through the dysfunction in Washington.

The rumors about a power grab suggested that Kline would be the one to seize it.

He stared at the president, and thought of Navarro lying on that floor, of Rivas and Stiles dying in that burning truck. He knew why he couldn't leave this place, this job. Something was wrong. Someone was hunting down agents, and Eric wouldn't rest until he found the culprit.

Anger ran through him, the same feeling he'd had that night with Secretary Braun when he derailed his career, and he remembered that mood of being at the edge of control.

What if the president were involved? Eric had always made a distinction. The office of the presidency, its powers under the Constitution, and its importance to the nation were larger than the individuals, all too human, who occupied the White House for one or two terms. You do your duty to the office, no matter what you think of the politician holding it. That's what he had always believed, but if that politician starts fucking with Eric's people, it's a very different story.

He breathed slowly as Kline looked at him, holding eye contact in that unsettling way he was notorious for. Eric didn't have enough solid info to accuse Kline of any crimes or plots.

"I wanted to pass this information on," Hill said. "And see what you knew about it."

"I know there is a campaign against me, Eric. We aren't certain of where it comes from, exactly. Some of it would be worth laughing at if it weren't actually catching on. The gray cardinal, have you heard that one? The CIA put me in power so the spies could control the government, a quiet coup. Or I'm a tool of foreign interests, a Manchurian candidate. Or Wall Street's puppet." He laughed at that notion. "Or an out-and-out murderer, calling in hits on anyone who gets in my way. All very impressive for a paper-pushing attorney, I have to say."

"Why are they coming after you?"

He shook his head. "This is what happens when you try to cut through the graft, to set this country up to compete in the twenty-first century. Honestly, I could almost stomach the corruption on its own—that's DC—but we're going to be begging China for scraps if we keep this up, if the only bills we pass are kickbacks to our donors, if we don't start investing in American strength."

A smile. "Politicians and speeches, I know, I'll save you," Kline went on. "You start to go after the money and suddenly you have a target on your back. I can handle a little hardball, but this smear campaign has gone further than I could have imagined. These rumors are starting to cloud people's judgment on the Hill. Serious politicians. I still think we can work together, but after what happened last night, it will be ten times harder. Whoever is spreading these lies about me will twist this to fit their story."

"You have some sense of who is behind it?"

"It's all done from the shadows. There are certain figures pulling the strings, and they are gathering others, organizing, claiming I'm a threat to the Constitution. They're building a movement. It sometimes goes by the name 'The Order.' It appears to be taking commands from a single source, an individual or a small circle posing as an individual. We have the alias for one of the conspirators—Cassius."

"As in the plot to assassinate Caesar?"

"Yes. Not very reassuring. We're turning over every rock with a task force at DOJ to uncover his identity and see how dangerous he is."

"Citizen?"

The president's jaw tightened. "That's the code name we believe is being used by the leader of all this, the one spreading the misinformation and organizing The Order. That's from Navarro?"

"Yes, but that's all he knew." Navarro made Citizen sound like a righteous whistleblower, not the traitor Kline was making him out to be. "Is he highly placed?" Eric asked.

"He gives that appearance and does seem to have access to inside information."

"Why haven't you shared this within the Service?" Eric had a hard time swallowing what Kline was saying. He hadn't heard any of these specifics.

"We have." Kline looked to Chilton. "But it's need-to-know."

They weren't cc'ing the shit list, Eric assumed, which is why he hadn't been read in, or it was restricted to the president's innermost circle.

"What are you prepared to do to stop them?" Eric asked.

"I won't let some cabal threaten this government." The president considered him. "You're not buying this, are you, Hill?"

"I'm trying to make sense of the threat so we can stop it."

"There have been some doubts about you, Eric," Kline said. He cocked his head to the side and studied him again. "About whether you can be trusted."

"You can trust me to find and take down whoever did this to Navarro and Cody."

"Good," Kline said. "We were just discussing our options. You have the most on-the-ground experience here. What's your take?"

Chilton's mouth tightened into an asterisk as Kline asked *Hill* for advice, but Eric was the only one here who'd actually saved a president's life.

Eric looked at him squarely. "Assume the threat is someone close, with access, possibly the highest levels." Nervous glances around the room. "I saw we were still on high alert with perimeter and air defense even after the all-clear. Do you have intel on a continued danger to the White House?"

"We do," Kline said.

"We're getting chatter about another attack," Chilton added. "But we can't pin it down to anything specific."

Eric thought for a moment. "I'd put you on Air Force One and go to forty thousand feet."

Silence. Eric's warning carried weight.

"Until?" Kline asked.

"We understand what happened and find the men who did it."

"How about a weekend in the country? Chilton was thinking Raven Rock," Kline said. "We already had Camp David on the schedule."

Raven Rock was a massive Cold War bunker complex near Camp David, a refuge for the president if Washington were destroyed or the White House somehow taken.

Eric looked to Chilton. He seemed to now be entertaining the idea that those inside the White House couldn't be trusted.

"That could work," Eric said. "Not as clean, though." Planes had been preferred to bunkers as the go-to emergency refuge for the president ever since the Russians acquired the H-bomb, which could cut through even the thickest bunker doors. Air Force One could stay up for days with midair refueling. But Eric had a sense of why Kline would prefer the Rock. It would let him remain in control. When they sent President George W. Bush into the sky after 9/11, the comms broke down at forty thousand feet, and he was effectively sidelined during the most devastating domestic attack since Pearl Harbor. Raven Rock had a full war room where the president could wield as much power as if he were in the White House, possibly more.

"Thank you, Hill," Kline said. "I appreciate your input and your work on this."

There was a tone of dismissal to Kline's words.

"Sir," Eric said, and stepped out.

Chilton followed and cornered him once they were clear of the president. "You're way out of line, here, Eric. The insider stuff, practically accusing him. Whose side are you on?"

"I don't do politics, Chilton."

"I hope not."

"Just get him and his family to a safe place before something else goes down."

"He won't play scared."

"He wants to go back to the Oval?"

"He wants to do his whole schedule today before he considers heading out to Raven Rock. You know the kind of pressure he's under. Congress is going after him."

"It's an insider, Ben. Keep him buttoned up and keep the access down to a handful of people you absolutely trust."

"You should go then."

Eric patted him on the shoulder. "Now you're getting it."

14

ERIC WALKED UP to Walsh on his way out to retrieve his MP5. The agent handed over the submachine gun.

"And the P232?" Eric asked.

"We'll hang on to the pistol until everything settles down," Chilton said. "I'm locking down all concealable weapons. A precaution."

Eric glowered at him.

"You'll get it back at the end of the shift. Don't worry."

Eric didn't have time to fight over a gun and demanding an easy-to-hide pistol wouldn't have looked good given the circumstances.

Givens had stepped out of the conference room and was now talking on one of the landlines in a cubicle to his right. The chief of staff's voice was gentle, and he realized she was talking to one of her daughters, telling her to listen to her grandmother and that she would be home as soon as she could.

"Yes, if you're good I'll make biscuits tonight. I love you too, baby. Now put your father on."

He'd never heard her so quiet or seen her so rattled.

Eric left the suite and headed for the West Wing. He wanted the logs of everyone who was in the building during the attack. Moving down the corridor past the Cabinet Room, he stopped short, almost crashing into a man carrying a stack of binders clutched to his chest.

The other man startled and clutched his paperwork. He had been in the middle of a conversation, not looking which way he was going. ". . . we really need to keep the lines of communication open," were his last words before he nearly careened into Eric.

He stared at Eric's weapon and froze. The president's communications secretary, Ellen O'Hara, stood next to him, her auburn hair up in a loose bun. She'd been his partner in the conversation.

"Eric," she said, "do you know Thomas Searle?"

"Good to see you," Eric said, using the classic Washington line for when you can't remember if you've met someone before. Eric knew who he was, though, a senior aide to the Senate majority leader. He had the soft body and pale face of a Hill lifer, small and sharp eyes behind a pair of glasses, something owlish about him. These aides really ran Washington, and many lived the job like they had joined a monastic order. They often seemed like overgrown boys to Eric, awkward and nice enough, though behind the scenes they were bureaucratic knife fighters, not to be taken lightly, the soldiers in the political maneuvering he despised.

"Likewise," Searle said, with a little smile. "So the complex is safe now?"

"We're taking care of it."

He relaxed. "Oh good." He brought his fingers to his temple. "We have enough on our plates already. Thank you so much, Agent Hill." He turned back to O'Hara and touched her elbow. "I really appreciate you working with us on this. I'll call you once everyone is on the way."

"Perfect," she said, and Searle took off down the hall.

"Was that about this meeting with the congressional leadership?"

"Yes."

"Kline is going to the Hill?" Eric asked, the doubt plain in his voice.

"No. The Saint Regis. It's off the books. Neutral ground. A peace summit, really."

"He can't scratch it? We're trying to get him locked down."

"Dude, no way. Half of them think he's a dictator in waiting, and the other half think he's inches away from getting toppled in a coup. He's fighting for survival here."

"That's political survival. There's a difference. Tell him not to go."

"I'll do my best," she said. "Is this attack part of something bigger?"

"We don't know yet. Stick close to me or the other agents."

"I thought the all-clear went out."

"No. They're getting more threats."

"God. If this gets out, it's going to be a shit show."

"Is there any truth to it, these rumors that Kline is doing some kind of investigation, trying to root out enemies inside the federal government?"

"That makes him sound like McCarthy."

"Nondenial denial."

"He has been," she said. "But these are real threats."

"What kind of threats?"

"Beyond my pay grade."

"You're not spinning me."

"No."

"Have you seen Agent Cody?"

"A while ago. She was heading back to the East Wing with Agent Leigh."

"Geared up?"

She glanced back at him. "Yes."

"What time is Kline's meeting at the Saint Regis?"

Staring at her phone again, she just said, "Fuck."

"What?"

"They want everyone at the PEOC."

"He's heading out?"

"I don't know."

15

ERIC WENT WITH O'Hara as she rushed to the bunker. Hardwick and Walsh were working the doors to the PEOC. They let Ellen through, and Hardwick held up his hand for Eric to stop.

"Is POTUS rolling?" Eric asked.

Hardwick looked down and listened to his earpiece before he answered. "They're rounding up a counterassault team for a small covert package." That meant a motorcade with as few as four armored vehicles and the president in an unmarked SUV. It was the commander in chief's default travel mode for unannounced, low-visibility trips around the city.

"It's a go?"

"Maybe just preparing the option," Hardwick replied. "They've had Marine One on the lawn for the last ten minutes too."

"Cody's in there?"

"Yeah, Chilton brought her in."

"What for?" Eric asked.

"I don't know."

"What is this chatter coming in about a continued threat?"

"The intel boys can't get a handle on it, not sure if it's domestic or foreign, or the scale, but all the needles are moving."

The door opened, and Eric looked through to see Amber Cody and Ben Chilton in conversation at the back of the office area. Chilton looked to him, then pulled Cody to the side, out of view.

"I need to talk to Chilton," Eric said.

Hardwick shook his head, genuinely pained. "You can't. They're limiting access."

Eric looked down the hallway, toward the scene of last night's attack. Chilton and the others seemed to think that Eric and Cody had chased off the assailants before they were able to complete their job—going after the president, presumably—and now the threat was gone. But what if the attackers were scouting or laying the groundwork for a later strike?

"Did they search those SUVs in the garage?"

"Searched them, cleared the garage, and they're bringing in two fresh rides from the jock."

The JOC, or Joint Operations Center, was the Secret Service's main DC headquarters, located in an unmarked office building six blocks away on H Street. That's where they kept the presidential limousines and the full twenty-vehicle package.

"His detail shouldn't be near anything that was breached last night."

"Eric . . ." Walsh sighed. "I'm sorry, man. It's not your call anymore."

Cody stepped out and approached Eric. They'd let her bring her gun in.

"What's going on, Cody?" he asked, taking her aside.

"They're putting me on the presidential detail for the ride to the Saint Regis."

"Kline is definitely going?"

"Yes."

"It's a bad idea," Eric said, and quickly warned her as he had warned Hardwick and Walsh.

She looked from him to the doors. "Why didn't they let you bring a gun in before?" she asked.

"Because they're being careful, as they should. Chilton warned you about me?"

"Vaguely. Why would your own protectees be afraid of you?"

"I can explain later," he said, "But don't trust everything you hear, and you need to be watching everyone right now."

"My boss? My fellow agents?"

"It's not all black-and-white, good guys inside, bad guys out there and all you have to do is guard the line between them. You need to make your own calls."

"I need to do my job." She stared at him as if asking *what the hell happened to you, man?*

It shook Eric for a moment—the possibility that the bitterness had poisoned him, had him seeing ghosts.

Hardwick stepped up to them. "Cody, you're here. Hill, I've got to clear this hallway. Kline is coming out. Chilton only wants his crew around."

Anger surged in Eric, but he bit his tongue. "Let me back up the second team."

Hardwick fumed. "You know the position you're putting—"

"You need me."

"Fuck it, fine. I do. But stay out of Chilton's and Kline's sight."

Eric tapped his fist against Hardwick's shoulder, then dropped back down the hall. He would stay just behind them in case things went south.

He watched Cody take a position next to Hardwick by the door, all of them weapons up and ready as the president approached.

As he moved down the tunnel, closer to where Navarro had been attacked, it finally hit him—something that had been nagging at him all night, though he'd never managed to articulate it.

Navarro had suffered close-in blunt-force trauma. He'd never fired his weapon. He was a pro; there was no way an attacker could get that close without setting him off. Navarro knew the man who had put him down.

16

ERIC GUARDED THE approach from the rear tunnel as Kline stepped out of the PEOC with the other agents covering him in a box formation.

Cody trailed twenty feet behind them, guarding Dr. Chen, Ellen O'Hara, Sarah Kline, Will Maddox, and the military aide with the nuclear football. Eric followed, keeping his distance as they approached the entrance to the garage. The doors opened, the quiet rumble reverberating back from the cavernous space beyond.

Cody stood by the door, guarding the hallway as the protectees went in. Eric moved closer, peering into the garage.

She looked at him, on edge. "What are you doing? You're supposed to stay out of Chilton's and Kline's sight."

He held his hand up. "I've got this."

Two armored Suburbans were parked on the western side of the garage. The Service had pulled up four more SUVs on the eastern side, near the rolling door. It opened onto the vehicular tunnel under the Treasury that led to the H Street alley exit. Those four vehicles looked like fresh rides from headquarters. Eric checked the tags on all the trucks and realized that the SUVs on the western side, closest to him, were the ones normally parked down here—including last night.

He walked into the garage.

"Hill," Cody said, glowering at him, but his attention was fixed on those vehicles.

Brimley came to him, leaning forward, arms slightly out to the side, a hint of his Montana youth still showing in the rancher's walk.

"You shouldn't be in here, Eric," he said.

"They've searched those hard cars?" Slang for the armored vehicles.

"Of course," Brimley said.

"And the gear cabinets?"

"Everything."

"Why are the Suburbans from last night still here?"

Brimley looked at them, and his lips tucked in. "I don't know."

Something wasn't right.

Eric glanced to the other agents loading the president and his staffers into the four vehicles on the far side of the garage.

Footsteps. Cody coming inside the garage. "Watch the hall," he said to her. "The hall," he repeated, more insistent now. She went back to her post.

"Listen, Brimley. Go over and tell them to get the jammers going from the ECM truck."

An SUV full of electronic countermeasures always followed the president. It could block radio signals that would trigger roadside bombs.

"In here?"

"Do it," Eric said. Brimley looked at him warily, torn between his respect for Eric and Eric's persona non grata status. After an instant, he walked toward the president's detail.

Eric circled the SUVs, crouching down to look under the chassis.

He heard a quiet *thock*, like an electrical relay opening, coming from the rear of the second Suburban that had been here last night, near the gear cabinets. The faintest smell hit his nose—like an old penny or the electric scent of a model train engine.

"Bomb! Get behind the trucks!" Eric sprinted toward the president. The agents looked his way, shock on their faces. Walsh raised his gun toward him as the others moved instantly. The president reacted as quickly as any of them, pulling his wife toward cover as the agents surrounded both of them with their bodies, rushing in a diagonal to get them behind an SUV. As they slipped around the hood, white light filled the garage, and something pounded Eric in the back. The pressure slammed into him like a heavy shore break wave. It knocked him onto one knee as the sound came, a crack so loud it felt like it would break off his limbs. He rose and kept moving, reached for Ellen O'Hara, and pulled her behind one of the fresh SUVs.

Shrapnel flew and ricocheted off the concrete. Red light danced across the walls and the slow roar of burning fuel filled the garage as one of the SUV's gas tanks let go. Heat scoured his skin. He smelled gasoline and burning hair as he kept going, seventeen years of instinct driving him toward the president to get him and the others to safety.

The agents rushed Sarah and James Kline back to the door where they had entered. Eric brought Ellen forward to join them and slotted into the formation. They ran as a unit, Hardwick in the lead, the protectees in the center. Eric scanned left, then right, and met eyes with the president. Kline gave him a grateful nod as they reached the door.

Crack-ping. A shot. A rifle round ripped into the concrete to his right.

As they brought Kline into the hallway, another bullet buried itself in the door frame, coming from just behind the SUV near the western wall that had blown. Two more shots. One angled through the door, blowing a hole in the concrete of the tunnel that led back to the PEOC.

"Left!" Eric called out. "Get to the storeroom!"

A groan came from behind him. He looked back to see Agent Cody exiting the garage with Agent Brimley, holding him up. His neck was cut, and he held his hand to his chest, taking shallow breaths.

Eric let the president's crew go ahead and ran toward Brimley as more shots went off. "I've got him," Cody said, bringing Brimley forward.

Through the door into the garage, Eric saw an agent stagger in the smoke and fall to one knee. He ran over and pulled the agent, Matt Byrne—barely thirty and a recent addition to the detail—to safety behind one of the armored Suburbans.

The agent pulled back his suit jacket, and Eric saw that it and his shirt were soaked in blood. "There," Eric said as he took the agent's hand and pressed it over the source, a gunshot wound on his ribs near his armpit. It was close to where Eric had been hit fifteen years ago, just above the vest. "Press hard," he said.

Two gunners from the counterassault team ran through the doors into the garage and took cover beside them.

Eric glanced toward the sound of the gunfire, then heard another blast. Black smoke poured toward them.

"Jesus," said the counterassault sergeant beside him, an ex-Airborne guy. "How many shooters are there?"

Eric leaned out to look once more, watching the angles of fire from the far wall.

"None. It's our own ammo cooking off!" he shouted over the din. "The gear cabinets. Get your people out of here!"

The sergeant leaned out, scanned the space, and dropped back. "That's it. Come on."

He and Eric lifted Byrne, and Eric helped him keep his hand tight on that wound as they ran for the door.

Eric looked back through the black smoke as they exited. No attackers followed. They moved down the tunnel as a volley of gunfire sailed through the door.

17

SHOTS KEPT CRACKING behind them. Fifty-caliber bullets ripped through the concrete as they moved fast down the corridors, approaching a knot of agents outside an open door ahead. They waved Eric and the others through, and he and the sergeant eased Byrne down onto the concrete.

The gunfire from the garage had cut off the path back to the PEOC, so they had taken shelter here. It was a storage area that could double as a safe room until they figured out what the hell was going on.

The space was about twenty by twenty, with boxes on heavy-duty steel shelves lining both walls.

Dr. Kline came over and knelt beside Byrne.

"Gunshot," Eric said, pointing to the wound. The first lady nodded, gently pulled Byrne's hand away, and tore open the fabric around the hole. Eric looked across the room, where Brimley stood beside Cody, holding a bandage to his neck. He was still up and talking. She raised her palm toward Eric in a reassuring way—it must not have been too bad.

The president, looking stricken, took a knee beside Byrne. "You're going to be all right," he said. "We've got you. Okay?"

Byrne managed a weak, "Yes, sir. Thank you." Kline let the doctors work and came over to Eric, with Chilton and Claire Givens soon rushing over to join them. They clearly didn't want Kline close to him alone.

"Anyone else hurt?" Eric asked Kline.

"No," Kline said. "How did you know there was a bomb?"

"I didn't trust those trucks after last night, and I heard part of the pre-ignition sequence."

"And the shooters?" Kline asked.

"I don't think there were any."

"What?"

"An explosive took out the Suburban closest to the weapons safe and set off the rounds inside. The bomb could also have been inside the gear cabinets, which would explain why checking the SUVs didn't turn it up. Who did the garage search?"

Kline looked to Givens.

"I'll find out," she said.

"Who triggered the explosive?" Kline asked, then lowered his voice. "He had to have been in the room to know when to set it off."

"Or anywhere in the complex," Eric said. "Your moves get telegraphed."

"An insider," Kline said.

"That's right. What time were you supposed to leave this morning?" Eric asked. "On your normal schedule?"

"Seven forty-five."

"You should have been on the road when it went off. It could have been on a timer set by someone who knew your schedule, though everything still points to an inside attack. Navarro was assaulted from close up and he didn't even fire his weapon. That means he probably knew the attacker."

The president glared at Chilton.

"What are you hearing?" Eric asked the Secret Service chief.

"We're getting warnings over all the systems. Access control is still spotty. The radars have been glitching."

"What the fuck are we dealing with here?" Kline said, turning to Givens, who was reading something on her phone; the tenser things got, the more the chief of staff affected calm. "The Pentagon and NSA are looking into cyberattacks, state actors."

"And?" Kline asked.

She glanced at her cell again, and looked up, her mouth a flat line. "No one knows shit."

They couldn't tell if they had buggy software or World War III.

"Mr. President," Chilton said, "we are in the middle of a complex attack. We need to get you out of here."

"The PEOC?"

"Don't trust anything on the White House systems, sir," Eric said. "They've already been breached."

"We run?" Kline said, stiffening.

"This doesn't have to hurt you," Givens told him. "An attack can prove everything you've been saying about the forces against you."

"Assume an inside threat with full access," Eric said. "There's no choice but to go."

Kline looked slightly down and set his jaw. "What are my options here?"

"There are armored helicopters on the South Lawn," Chilton said. "We have F-16s in from Andrews."

"Up now?"

"Armed and ready for anything."

"We take you to the Rock with a handpicked crew," Chilton said "Very small. All cleared Yankee White. It's secure. It's a different system, completely air gapped. With the full war room, you will be as in control there as you are here. That will keep you and Dr. Kline safe until we determine what is happening."

Kline thought about it. "This is an out-and-out war on my government."

"Sir," Eric said.

"What?"

"Keep it small. Take the chief of staff and three agents you absolutely trust. Get on Air Force One. Go to forty thousand feet—"

"I appreciate it, Hill, but this may be the start of something much larger," he said. "I'm not taking myself out of the fight." He looked back to Chilton and Givens. "The Rock. Skeleton crew. Yankee White. Every name on the list goes through me. Understood?"

"Yes, sir," Chilton responded.

Kline stepped to the side and checked on Byrne. Sarah Kline and Dr. Chen had sealed a bandage on three sides over the gunshot to his chest. The plastic fluttered with every breath, a way to keep his lung from collapsing.

Chilton and Givens moved toward the door, quietly giving orders to a handful of agents, preparing for the cull.

Yankee White. Only those who could be absolutely trusted to take the president's life in their hands.

Chilton said something to Cody, and she nodded reverently. He moved away just as Eric approached.

"Are you all right?" he asked Cody.

"Fine," she said, and shook her head. "My God." There was more going on behind her grim expression, but she didn't say anything else.

"Did Chilton ask you to go to Raven Rock?"

"He did." She looked at his face. "I can handle it."

"I know. That's not it. Something's not right with all of this, Cody." Everything could be explained as an inside attack. But after what Navarro had said, Eric had to consider that all of it could be a provocation created by the president, the ultimate insider, a way to stage a crisis that would allow him to consolidate power and silence his critics.

"This is where I'm supposed to be, Hill. Protecting these people."

"My gut—don't go. Listen, I . . ." He had this same feeling the morning her dad was killed. Cody didn't know the full story.

She stared at him. How do you tell someone that what they've been living for is a lie?

"I'm going. This is the job."

As stubborn as her old man. "Eyes open, all right?"

"Always," she said.

Eric looked to Cody, to Hardwick, to Sarah Kline, and to Ellen O'Hara as Chilton whispered to them, getting them ready. That protective instinct pulled at him, so strong. This wasn't the kind of danger you could lock out with a steel door. And there was only one way he could guard against it—from the inside.

He couldn't leave the other agents. He'd bled with these people, and for these people, as they had bled for him.

He walked over to Chilton and tapped him on the shoulder. The chief turned.

"I'm going," Eric said.

"You?" Chilton raised an eyebrow, then came in closer. "You told me twelve hours ago that you were done. You don't trust him." Chilton glanced at the president. "So why should he trust his life to you?"

"Because I'm good at this, and you need me." He didn't have to mention the garage, the SUVs, the call he'd made that saved all of them. The smoke was still hanging in the air.

Chilton let out a laugh. "Unbelievable. Guard the tunnel outside, west end."

Eric wanted an answer. "Yes or no."

"West end."

Pushing harder against the SAIC would be counterproductive, would bring Chilton's ego into it; he was still uneasy as the new head of the detail. Eric would find a way—he'd just earned himself a lot of credit with the president and his people. He nodded and went fifty yards down the tunnel, where a set of access stairs went out to the South Lawn. He could hear the helo blades thudding overhead.

He kept his MP5 out and ready, standing in this tunnel, listening to the radio chatter, the breath of the other agents, and the soft sound of leather soles on linoleum. Five minutes. Ten.

He turned at the sound of a crowd coming. Chilton was at the head of a pack of six agents, the president and first lady at the center. Eric stepped to the side, by the door, ready to cover them on their way through.

Chilton marched toward him, staring straight ahead, as if Eric were invisible. Three feet away, he glanced at Eric and called out, "You're on Chalk Two." The second helicopter. "Take the six o'clock as we head out."

Eric shouldered the door open. He was in. It could have been due to his performance in the garage, or the director might have overridden Chilton because they needed Eric's experience. He doubted that they just wanted another body for the decoy helo but that was a possibility. There was no time to think it through, but it left Eric feeling uneasy.

They climbed the stairs and exited onto the South Lawn. As he rose, he scanned the grounds along the sight of his weapon. Four Marine helicopters stood on the grass, blades spinning, sending washes of air rushing past them. The president's crew would travel on two helos and the other two would serve as decoys, standard practice. The snipers were out with their fifty cals, and the Stinger batteries bristled from the rooftops surrounding the White House.

He covered the trees and fences as POTUS and his inner circle moved toward Marine One at the center of a diamond formation. The box was good for tight spaces, the diamond for open ground.

He was in the second group, with Dr. Chen and Eubanks the military aide at its center, heading for the second helicopter. The president had brought his body man with him onto Marine One—Will Maddox was carrying the portfolio that held the emergency action documents and the red letter to invoke them. Kline was keeping it even closer than the nuclear satchel.

Agent Cody was on the left side of the diamond, gun out, looking impossibly sharp for someone who'd been jumped and stayed up all night. Eric fell into his old spot and put his left hand on her shoulder to keep the formation tight as they climbed onto the Sikorsky.

18

Saturday. 8:43 a.m.

FORTY MINUTES LATER, the helicopters banked over the scrubby pines of Catoctin Mountain in Maryland, northwest of DC.

Eric pointed out Camp David in the distance to Cody, and they started dropping as they approached the border with Pennsylvania.

Raven Rock Mountain rose straight ahead, sparsely forested with a two-hundred-foot red-and-white radio tower rising from its peak. In the morning light, he could make out thick concrete structures dug into the side of the mountain, for ventilation or perhaps holding gun or missile batteries out of view. The helicopter descended toward the bottom of the round mountain, heading for a military base that looked like a small maximum-security prison. It flared and touched down gently on the helipad.

Cody studied the triple razor-wire fences that surrounded them and the massive tunnel drilled straight into the side of the mountain, large enough for a four-lane road.

"Raven Rock," she said. "I've been briefed on it, but seeing it up close . . ."

"Yeah, it's hard to imagine."

Raven Rock Mountain Complex was a continuity-of-government site that had been around since the 1950s. Designed to serve as an underground Pentagon, it was where the Department of Defense would relocate if DC were destroyed by a nuclear weapon, though the president could use it in an emergency.

A similar facility, called Mount Weather, was located in Virginia's horse country and would protect Congress from doomsday, but Raven Rock was the original, the first of the Cold War. Every time Eric got near the place, he thought of *Dr. Strangelove.*

Three black Suburbans rolled toward them from the base. Eric climbed down the stairs and led the helicopter's passengers onto the tarmac. Cody came up beside him as the president prepared to leave Marine One.

Cody stood perfectly straight, hands hovering near her belt buckle, the pride of protecting the commander in chief so clear on her face. He remembered that feeling, remembered it pure and untarnished once.

The crew in Marine One dropped the stairs, and the president stepped out and crossed the tarmac to shake hands with a lieutenant colonel in fatigues. Eric assumed he was the Raven Rock commander.

Benjamin Chilton, as the Special Agent in Charge of the president's detail, led Kline into the lead Suburban, along with the first lady, Kline's body man, the chief of staff, and Agents Hardwick and Leigh.

Eric would ride in the second SUV. The colonel and another officer walked toward Eric and his crew.

"Sir," Eric said.

"Lieutenant Colonel Bruce Drumm. With two *m*'s. Can't be beat," he said, extending his hand and letting out a laugh like a mortar burst. "Deputy commander of Raven Rock Mountain Complex. And this is Major Ashley Moro."

Eric and Cody shook their hands. Drumm had Mediterranean features, and a deep tan that surprised Eric given that he worked under seven hundred feet of stone, while Moro projected a quiet confidence.

"We're the landlords of the Rock," Drumm said, opening the passenger door of the SUV. "Welcome."

He climbed in. One of his officers was driving. Eric and Cody got in the back with Major Moro and the remaining agents from the helicopter climbed into the third SUV with another one of Drumm's officers.

Eric watched Drumm as they drove down the tunnel. His fatigues were fresh out of the plastic, fold lines showing. Each patch looked like it had been applied with a carpenter's square. He'd been waiting for this day his entire life. Staring ahead, the lieutenant colonel looked slightly stunned by everything that was happening. He didn't seem to have the command presence or the rank to be running this place during a crisis.

Drumm glanced his way.

"What is it?" he asked. "The tan?" Another laugh. "I get it all the time," he said, shaking his head. "They have beds in there, so we don't all go blind from vitamin D deficiency."

"The commander is inside?"

"In Italy on vacation. I'm running things while he's gone. Relax." He laughed again. "We'll take good care of you."

Eric nodded slowly, hiding any skepticism. They drove down an access road, through a pair of vehicle gates, and headed for the mouth of the tunnel that led under the mountain. It was an arch forty feet high and eighty feet wide at the bottom.

As the shadows closed around them, chatter came in on Eric's radio. It was Chilton.

"We're getting irregular air defense warnings from JADOC at Bolling," he said. "Assume the worst. Code Black."

"Copy that," Drumm said.

Code Black. The protocols to defend against a decapitation strike—an attempt to take out the country's leadership in a massive, coordinated attack. The last time they'd been triggered was a fateful September morning.

The SUVs followed a serpentine route around three vehicle barriers—a caution against ramming attacks—then continued through the tunnel with its rock walls.

The bunker entrance was protected by two nuclear blast doors, one after the other in the tunnel. The first loomed ahead, a solid steel wall slowly retracting, sliding to the side into a recess like a massive pocket door, leaving an opening large enough to drive four big rigs through side by side.

As the SUVs advanced through the door's frame, Eric looked up and saw the bolts that locked the blast door in place when it was closed, dozens of them, each the diameter of a telephone pole, all retracted.

They followed the lead vehicle toward an identical blast door a hundred yards farther up the tunnel. It was closed, another white expanse.

The sound of churning machinery came from the walls and the outer door behind them rumbled closed, shaking the vehicle like an earthquake.

"Each of the doors weighs thirty tons," Drumm said. "Together, they'll hold off a nuclear blast."

Only after the outer door had closed did the inner one slowly slide open.

Eric looked at the fans built into this section of tunnel between the two barriers. It could serve as an airlock in the event of a nuclear or biological attack.

They passed through the second, inner door, and once they were a hundred yards beyond it, it trundled back into place, closing with a clang.

Drumm's face grew serious, and he took a second handset from a clip on his waist.

He spoke into the handset. "We're going Code Black. Lock it down. Lock it down. Confirm."

A voice replied something that Eric couldn't make out. Moro handed Drumm a binder and he looked down a checklist, confirming every step the other engineers would follow as they sealed off Raven Rock. "Good," Drumm said, with a forced calmness. "Just follow the steps."

A grinding sound came from the blast doors, the bolts locking into place. Glancing back, Eric could only see a sheer wall of white-painted steel.

Drumm put down the radio. "We're secure," he said to Eric, and thumbed to the door behind them. "Nothing gets past those."

Eric checked his watch. Nine fifteen a.m. The start of the lockdown.

They drove on into a long, curving section of tunnel that appeared to have no end. The place was a fortress, and Eric thought again about the president and Chilton's insistence on coming here instead of going up in Air Force One. Being sealed in left him with a grim feeling. The air tasted different, with a charcoal smell to it, like he'd just put new filters in his truck.

They went on in silence, deeper into the mountain. After a minute, he could no longer see the blast door in the rearview. He set his jaw and swallowed and his ears popped from the growing pressure.

Drumm looked at one of the markings on the wall outside. "We're seven hundred and fifty feet below the ridge now."

White light spilled out ahead of them.

"There it is," Drumm said. The tunnel widened and ran in a straight section a mile long.

"We're driving through the main tunnel," Drumm said, pointing along the roadway. "It's six miles long and runs south to north from one side of the mountain to the other. The tunnel is gently curved at the north and south ends but here it runs for a mile straight. The northern exit has two blast doors like the ones we just passed through."

They were traveling and facing north. Along the right-hand wall of the straight tunnel section ahead, five giant arched openings had been carved out of the stone, each one as tall as the main tunnel. They looked like the entrances to long vehicular tunnels, all of them running perpendicular from the main tunnel to the east.

Just inside the entrances to those five long caverns, there were five gray facades—the fronts of three-story buildings, each with a set of metal steps rising toward their entrances. They'd been built inside the caverns, almost completely filling them. The buildings were shaped like long hangars or Quonset huts, and had curved roofs to match the curved ceiling of the caverns and fit neatly inside them.

The president's SUV drove past the first building and parked at the second, which had a giant letter *B* marked on its facade. Eric's vehicle pulled up behind them.

"The main element of Raven Rock is these buildings on the right," Drumm said. "There are five of them, A through E, from south to north. You are looking at the front entrance of B, which like the others runs two thousand feet due east in a space that was carved out of the stone to accommodate it. They are laid out perfectly parallel, long straight structures, each filling its own hollow in the rock."

Eric looked at the windowless facade next to them. BUILDING B. RAVEN ROCK MOUNTAIN COMPLEX, it said, and featured the seals of the units that operated here—engineering, communications, cryptography, and continuity-of-government specialists.

He'd been down here three times on drills with the Service, but he paid close attention to Drumm's briefing. They could be sealed in for days, and he wanted to know everything he could about his environment when under threat.

Looking east, he saw that Building B, like the others, didn't completely fill its cavern. There was a gap of about eight feet between its gray exterior walls and the space in the stone that had been bored out to house it, and a similar gap along the roof. Someone would be able to move in those dark and narrow voids down the entire length of the building.

Eric opened the truck door, and the sound of whirring fans—the bunker's ventilation system—filled the vehicle. He and the others got out, and they walked in a tight group up the roadway.

A scaffold-like system of metal framing was affixed to the ceiling and the upper heights of the tunnel walls. It supported taut white lining material that covered the bare rock overhead. Eric could hear the moisture dripping onto it like drumbeats.

Metal catwalks ran in the narrow spaces behind and above the liners. Some of the catwalks branched off from the main tunnel, allowing access to the roof of Building B.

"Each office building fills its own long hollow," Drumm said. "We call them caverns—Cavern A houses Building A, Cavern B houses B, et cetera, each running parallel with four hundred feet of solid stone between them. You'll be here in B." He walked them toward the entrance, where the president's SUV had parked.

Agents Hardwick and Leigh protected Kline and his crew as they climbed out of the lead SUV.

Eric and Cody fanned out, covering the main tunnel in both directions. Agents Walsh and Brimley had been riding in the third SUV, which parked behind them. That made for six Secret Service agents total inside the bunker.

Cody stared into the shadows under Building B. It didn't sit directly on the stone floor of its cavern. Rather, it was built on a bed of massive springs, each eight feet tall and spaced about ten feet apart, supporting the entire structure. There were hundreds of them, arranged in a grid pattern like the inside of a giant's mattress. Eric looked into the darkness. Someone could easily hide there and travel unseen as well.

"First time here?" Drumm asked Cody.

"Yes."

"Those springs protect the building from shock waves in the event of a nuclear strike," he said, and swept his arm down the main tunnel. "The curves at the north and south ends of this tunnel help dissipate any over-pressure or radiation from a blast, and if it gets this far it will just blow straight past the buildings since they are set off to the side."

He pointed to the exterior of the building, covered in dark gray plates. "More blast protection, as well as shielding from an electromagnetic pulse."

Drumm gestured with his hand from left to right, looking around the massive underground complex.

"We actually have more office space than the Pentagon, though most of ours is held in reserve." He put his hand to the stone wall of the tunnel.

"Raven Rock. She's really an underground city. The air is all filtered with countermeasures for chemical, biological, and radiological attack. When we're running at full capacity, we have police, fire, a convenience store, a barbershop, a power plant, gyms, racquetball, a surgical suite, crematorium, whatever you need."

"Not the last two, I hope," Cody said, craning her head around.

"Ready for anything!" Drumm replied, strangely chipper. He looked at her MP5 with something like amusement. "Though we're behind a hundred and twenty tons' worth of blast doors, so I don't think you'll need those."

That remained to be seen. Eric watched the president move alongside his body man and his military aide, both armed, one carrying the red letter and one the nuclear football. Drumm unlocked the door at the top of the steps, and guided them all into Building B.

Eric kept close to the president's people as the door clanged shut behind them and Drumm locked them in.

19

KLINE AND HIS team stayed together at the front of the pack. The president knew his way. He'd visited Raven Rock at least four times during continuity-of-government exercises.

On the inside, the building was surprisingly normal. With its gleaming linoleum floors and fluorescent lights, it looked just like the basement levels of the Pentagon, though the ceilings were lower and the corridors tighter.

Drumm walked beside him and Cody. Kline hadn't spoken to the deputy commander since that first handshake when he arrived, always pressing on by himself, leaving the deputy commander behind. Either Drumm had gotten the hint that POTUS and his team wanted to be left alone, or he was too nervous to insert himself in Kline's circle.

"Just like a movie," Drumm said to Eric as the agents and the president strode ahead. Eric gave him a polite nod.

"The suites for the executive branch, the president, and the war room are all straight ahead at the back of Building B," Drumm said.

"Got it," Eric said. "I've been through Raven Rock a few times."

"Oh good."

"Where are your people?" Eric asked.

"In Building E."

"And the other buildings?"

"Empty. We have a skeleton crew going per your people's orders. What happened up there?" Drumm asked. "All I saw was what was on the news, the cordon around the White House."

"Apologies," Eric said. "Need-to-know."

They traveled down one of the main corridors running the length of

Building B. Through doors to the left, Eric glimpsed a large open area that looked uncannily like a high school cafeteria, with the far end dedicated to Ping-Pong and pool tables and a small stage.

"Is that a karaoke machine?" Eric asked.

"You have to keep busy down here, or . . ." Drumm twisted his hand by his temple, suggesting threats to sanity, followed by another seal-bark laugh.

"The suites are straight ahead," Drumm called to the president's lead pack, though they clearly knew where they were going.

At the end of the corridor, Hardwick and Leigh led the president through a heavy steel door into an office area, and the rest followed. This suite had been set aside for executive branch staff, though it was far too much space for this small team: Kline, the first lady, Chief of Staff Claire Givens, the body man, the doctor, and the military aide hulking like an oak tree under the low ceiling.

Ellen O'Hara had stayed behind at the White House to handle the press. The national security adviser wasn't here either, which Eric found strange. He'd been traveling, giving a talk at the University of Michigan on the president's Asia policy, but there might have been enough time, since the attack last night, to fly him home on a government Gulfstream.

Eric watched Kline conversing with Chilton. Maybe he hadn't wanted to overreact by having his national security adviser rush home, but there could be other reasons. Kline hated being second-guessed in a crisis and with his CIA experience, he didn't feel much of a need for someone to hold his hand on matters of war and peace.

Claire Givens joined Kline and Chilton, all of them huddled close together, voices low.

Eric kept thinking about the possibility of an inside threat, and the warnings from Navarro and the president—Citizen could be someone at the highest levels of government, could even be locked in here with them.

Cody had moved toward one of the side doors, guarding it without even needing an order, showing strong instincts. She was now talking to the body man, Will Maddox. They were both former military. Maddox had been a lieutenant in the Eighty-Eighth Infantry.

The kid had an easy smile, and a way of getting people to open up. He'd spent so much time with Kline he could anticipate the president's needs without a word, pulling a politician's necessities from the shoulder bag that he always wore—hand sanitizer, Tide pen, Clif Bars, pocket packs of tissues.

He helped everyone. You would sneeze and he was so fast he would seem to materialize beside you, holding out that Kleenex. It was a strange transition for a guy who used to carry an M4 carbine and a plate carrier loaded with grenades and extra magazines, but he was proud to do it, and deservedly. No staffer was closer to the president, and body men went on to some of the most powerful positions in government.

Eric watched him checking out Cody's bruise, and from her gestures it was clear she was walking him through what had happened last night. They were the two youngest people here, and seemed to know each other from before.

Eric considered the portfolio Maddox carried that held the PEADs emergency documents and the red letter and started walking toward them. He had a few questions for the body man.

But Kline beckoned Maddox over as if he'd strayed too far, and the body man moved double-time to join the president's circle.

Eric approached Cody. "Solid guy," he said, and glanced to Maddox.

"The best."

"You know him?"

"Yes. Through the Tillman Foundation."

Eric pointed to the bruise on her temple. "First day and you already have a war story."

"He asked."

"I'm glad. You kicked ass back there." Eric looked at Maddox huddled with the president, holding the portfolio in front of him with both hands.

"Did he say what he's working on?" Eric asked.

"No," she said.

"Was he keyed up?"

"We all are, I think. And that's how fast he always moves." A laugh.

"He didn't seem nervous?"

Cody's mouth tightened. Something was on her mind.

"What?"

"Nothing out of the ordinary given the circumstances," she said.

Hardwick opened the door at the end of the office area, where a hall led to the president's suite and the war room. Chilton ushered Kline and his people through.

Eric walked after them, and Cody followed.

In the hall, the president's circle went through the door to his suite, then closed it behind them. They left Agents Leigh and Hardwick standing post outside.

Those two straightened up as Eric approached—guards' posture.

"They could use a few more agents in there," Eric said. Chilton was the only one from the Service inside with Kline.

Leigh shook her head. "We're watching it from here," she said, "and the other entrances. They wanted some time alone."

Eric nodded, outwardly cool. The president's suite had a small office and conference area for staff, an office for the president, and a private apartment and living area for Kline and his family. It was essentially a mini White House and West Wing, all connected to the war room. Together the presidential suite and the war room occupied the back end of Building B and formed a bunker within the bunker, protected by thick armored doors.

From the war room, the president could wield all the powers of the commander in chief even more easily than he could at the White House. The Situation Room was a capable op center, sure, but this was a full-scale alternate national military command center, modeled on the Department of Defense's own war room, a backup in case the Pentagon was destroyed. Eric wanted eyes on what was happening inside.

"No one goes in," Agent Leigh said. "That's the order."

20

AS ERIC STEPPED away, Leigh said "hold on" and listened to her earpiece. "Chilton wants you to check the exterior of Building B for any weaknesses or points of entry to the president's suite and war room."

Eric glanced to Drumm, who was standing farther down the hall. "They should all be known, right?"

"Yes. There are only four ways in, and they're all locked tight."

A shrug from Leigh. Eric wondered if Chilton was just trying to keep him occupied and at a distance. An order was an order, and Eric didn't mind a chance to learn the ways into the secure areas at the back of Building B from Drumm.

"Colonel Drumm, Agent Cody," Eric said. "You're with me. Nearest exit?" he asked Drumm.

The engineer started walking and waved them on. They left the offices and turned right down the hallway. A minute later, Drumm brought them to a heavy door that would let them exit to the exterior of Building B on its northern side.

"You know," Drumm said, clasping his hands together, "my team in Building E would be honored if POTUS might have a chance to make an appearance."

"That would be a stretch under the circumstances," Eric said.

"I understand."

He went through the door and onto a set of metal steps. Cody looked to Eric and shook her head like a hardened master sergeant. "Rookies," she whispered.

That got Eric. They followed him through the exit, which led out of

Building B into the cavern that housed it. They were in the narrow space between the exterior of the building and the rock wall of the cavern—eight feet wide though it ran two thousand feet east–west along the northern side of the building.

They descended the steep set of steps to the cavern floor, and started walking east, deeper into the tunnel.

Eric could feel the cold radiating out from the hard Pennsylvania greenstone. Water dripped down it like tears. They passed a small tunnel that had been bored through the cavern wall at ground level. It was the size of a hallway and ran north through the stone.

"That goes from Cavern B to Cavern C?" Eric asked.

"Yes," Drumm said. "We call them passageways. They are located a third and two-thirds of the way down each cavern so you can travel between them."

"They run north all the way to Building E?"

"That's right. You could go through there, cross under Building C to the next passageway, take it north to Cavern D, and so on to E."

"So your people could make it from Building E to here mostly unseen."

Drumm seemed puzzled by the suspicion behind the question.

"Well, yes. But they couldn't get inside Building B. It's locked and access-controlled, and the presidential suite and war room in B lock from the inside on a manual system."

Drumm led them on, farther east toward the very back of Building B. Cody peered ahead through the darkness. The cavern met a perpendicular tunnel ahead, lit by yellow overhead lights.

"All the caverns connect in the back?" she asked.

"Yes," Drumm said. "That's the rear tunnel. It runs north–south parallel to the main tunnel along the back of all five buildings. If you were to look down on all of it from on high, you'd see Raven Rock is laid out like a five-rung ladder. The buildings in their caverns are the rungs and the main and rear tunnels are the sides."

Drumm led them into it and looked to the north. The rear tunnel was as large as the main one and also lined with framing, liners, and catwalks up high.

"Not quite as nice as the main tunnel," Drumm said. "It's sort of our basement or garage."

They stepped out into the center of the cavernous space and looked west, back the way they had come. It gave them a view of the back of Building B in its cavern, and Eric noted the two entrance doors there, both accessed via steps.

"Both of those doors are secured from the inside," Drumm said. "And the fourth entrance is around the corner, just like the doors we took to exit, but on the southern side of the building. No one is getting in without the president's say-so."

Eric looked up and down the rear tunnel, a long, empty bore, far darker than the main one, lit only by sodium lamps every hundred yards. A canal, about five feet wide, ran north–south down the middle of the tunnel for its entire length, with water flowing through it like a stream between stone banks.

Eric climbed onto a low metal bridge that crossed the waterway.

"The canal carries water from a reservoir at the northern end of this tunnel." Drumm pointed that way.

The lights cast long, streaking reflections on the oil-black surface of the canal. The air was warm here, and he could hear the chugging of heavy machinery. Eric took a deep breath. It tasted liked exhaust. "The air. Is that normal?"

"Once we're buttoned up, yes," Drumm said. "It's from the diesel plant at the southern end of this tunnel. Some of the water from the reservoir runs down through this canal to cool it."

Eric looked at the tiebacks, threaded rods sticking out from the walls that held up the weight of the rock overhead.

"You worry about collapses?"

"I worry about everything. Fire. Running out of air. Choking on our own exhaust. The whole place slowly turning into an oven. People aren't supposed to live this deep."

He walked over and put his hand to the stone wall like someone caressing an elephant. "But if you take care of her, she'll take care of you."

Cody's and Eric's eyes met, and she raised her eyebrows. "How long have you been down here?" she asked.

"Twenty-three years," Drumm said, then let out a laugh that reverberated down the tunnel. "Though I get out sometimes! Need to keep Mrs. Drumm happy."

That was a relief. Eric had been starting to get the feeling that Raven Rock itself was Mrs. Drumm. Though he had a lot of respect for anyone so clearly dedicated to his job.

"As far as breaching the presidential suite," Eric said, pointing to the back of Building B. "What if you had a determined adversary? Even an insider?"

Drumm appeared to be mildly scandalized by the suggestion, then smiled, game to play devil's advocate for a moment.

"There are other ways," he said, looking over the catwalks that ran along the roof of Building B. "Secret passages. But only the president knows them."

"Only the president?"

"Well, I know everything about this place," Drumm said, and grinned. "But that's need-to-know."

"Seriously?"

"Yes. Kline would have to clear you himself."

Eric's radio came to life in his earpiece. Chilton's voice. "Hill. We need you back in the suite. We've got something."

21

THEY RETURNED TO the executive offices inside Building B. One of Drumm's comms staffers stood at ease in the middle of the work area while the rest of the president's people clustered around President Kline at the end of a conference table. He was holding a printout in his hand.

Eric and Cody approached, and Kline turned the piece of paper toward them. It was a personnel file showing a head shot of a man with graying hair and a goatee.

"Could this be one of the men who attacked you?" Chilton asked Cody.

She looked it over. "I didn't see the faces. Height and weight seem small, though."

"Everything is more frightening in the dark," Chilton said. Walsh smirked at the comment.

"It's possible," Cody said. "Who is he?"

"An IT contractor. Part of the renovation crew," Chilton said. "Headquarters traced suspicious traffic from the White House system to IP addresses associated with him. And his phone puts him six blocks from the intrusion last night before he turned it off."

Eric looked at his address. Penn Quarter. "He lives close. That could be his normal traffic patterns. Have we brought him in?" Eric asked.

"We don't know," Chilton said. "Communication with the top has been . . . tricky." He gave a hard look to the sergeant from Drumm's comms staff.

"Is there any word on Navarro?"

"He's out of surgery," Chilton said. "He's stable, but there may be brain trauma. Agent Byrne will be all right."

Eric looked at the IT contractor's hollow cheeks, the thin neck. He couldn't see this man taking down Navarro and he hadn't appeared on any cameras. "He wasn't inside when it happened."

"That we know of."

Eric looked over the others, their exhaustion now buoyed by some relief.

They wanted to believe that they'd found their man, an outsider. Soon enough they would be back to their lives and out of this hole.

"Just follow the checklist," Drumm said over the radio, his voice insistent. He called out to them across the office area. "The phones should be up any moment, ma'am."

"We need that *now*," Givens replied, her expression as polite as her voice was cold.

"We can't talk to the top?" Eric asked.

"No phones, no email," Givens said.

Drumm came over, holding his hands together in front of him. "I'm sorry about this. It's just a brief transition period while we link the two systems. Then everything will be seamless, as if you are still in the White House."

"Until then"—Chilton pointed to the paper—"the messages go through the comms folks here."

"You can't patch a call through?" Eric asked.

"Not at the moment," Drumm said. "You would have to physically be in our comms center in E. But any minute, sir! We're engineers. We fix things." A strained smile, and he walked back to the other comms folks.

"Unbelievable," Givens said. "There's a ninety-million-dollar war room about two hundred feet that way with phone lines that can survive an H-bomb."

"As long as you want to connect to the Pentagon command center or NORAD," Kline said.

Eric looked at Givens, who was standing at a workstation, alternately checking the computer on it and the landline. The politicos were all constantly glued to their cell phones. She still held hers in her hand like a broken talisman.

Being cut off only added to his uneasiness. Givens stepped away and approached Drumm and the comms officer. Eric took a step to the side to eavesdrop on the chief of staff.

"I have something that needs to go out," she said.

"We can take care of it over in Building E, ma'am," Drumm said.

The muscles in her jaw tightened. The "ma'am" really wasn't sitting well with her.

"The president of the United States doesn't play telephone."

"We are doing everything we can, ma'am. I am so, so sorry."

Givens brought him over to where Will Maddox was standing, holding the portfolio. The president broke away to join them. Eric followed, then Chilton crossed over to block his path.

"How was the exterior survey?" he asked.

"Good," Eric said, watching as Givens gave orders to Drumm and the body man, Maddox's face as solemn as if he were heading into D-Day.

"Cut short when we were called back here," Eric said. Drumm and Maddox headed for an exit. He assumed they were going to Building E to get a message out. But Eric didn't like that Maddox was carrying the codes and PEADs directives to declare martial law in that portfolio.

"I'll go finish up," Eric said, looking for an excuse to get outside and follow. "Or I can guard Maddox if he's headed outside the suite."

Chilton held up his hand. "No. That's fine. I need you here."

Maddox and Drumm disappeared through the exit.

22

SOMETHING WASN'T RIGHT, Eric knew it. Losing communications with the top left him troubled.

"I'm glad you have a lead on the attackers, but do not let your guard down," he said to Chilton.

"It's under control. We have our man."

"Navarro trusted his attacker. That's the only way he could've gotten close enough to inflict those injuries without Navarro firing his weapon. And now we're in here suddenly cut off from the outside world."

Chilton's brows rose. "You think . . . *they* have infiltrated Raven Rock? Have you seen this place?"

"Don't trust anyone."

"That's your problem, Hill."

"Have you checked on all of the comms staffers?"

"Yes. Security went through every one of them. All Yankee White. All beyond suspicion. We're good."

He leaned in closer and examined Eric's eyes.

"You and Cody have been on duty since yesterday evening, right?"

"Yes."

"Grab some chow from the mess hall you saw on your way in and get some rest too. I need you all sharp. And make sure Cody does too. I like her enthusiasm, but I don't want her to burn herself out."

"Sir, I—"

"It's not a suggestion. Now's not a good time to be doing your own thing." He glared at Eric. If Chilton was wary of anyone in here, it was him.

Cody walked up to them. "Where do you need me?" she asked.

"Chow hall, and there's a bunk room past that. Try to catch some sleep before the next watch. Hill will show you the way."

She looked to Chilton as if questioning if she was being dismissed.

"You're doing excellent work, Cody. Food and rest, and then report back, all right? You've earned it."

She nodded and started walking. Eric turned to go with her, and Chilton watched him with that hard stare.

Eric had some questions for Cody and a break from the chief would give him room to maneuver. It felt wrong to be watching his own people, watching his back, to have suspicion on him as if he were the damn inside threat.

They went into the main corridor, then turned into the mess hall, the Granite Cove Dining Facility, according to the sign. It was all linoleum floors, brown and white tiles, and eight-person tables with benches attached that could be folded up and rolled to the side when necessary. A mural of a mole wearing a uniform and rendering a crisp salute adorned the northern wall—the mascot of these officers who spent their working lives underground.

He peered through a door on the west side into another gymnasium-sized room that had been divided into bays and filled with row after row of bunk beds.

"How many people can stay down here?" she asked.

"Five thousand in an emergency, buttoned up for months."

"Canned food?"

"That or MREs," Eric said. Meals, Ready to Eat—the self-heating rations the military uses on deployments.

"That solves one problem," she said. "None of them will poop."

Eric cracked up. The MREs were notorious in that regard.

"You're hungry?" he asked, looking to the metal cabinets on the far wall that held the rations.

"I'm good. Grabbed something from the navy mess after the all-clear."

Eric had too. He pointed to a nearby bench, offering her a chance to rest. She took it and he sat down as well, with his left arm on the table. "How bad was Brimley hit back at the White House?"

"The cuts weren't pretty, but he'll be all right. Tough old bastard. He said, 'It'll take more than that to kill this hairbag.'"

Eric laughed. That was Service slang for an older agent. Brimley had worked with her father, and Eric could remember, after one of the inaugurations, Brimley showing Cody, in elementary school then, how the Service radios worked and letting her listen to his earpiece. Eric had watched her eyes go wide as she eavesdropped on the code names and secret language of her father's world.

"It's easy to get thrown off by that crusty cowboy exterior," Cody said. "But he's always looked out for me."

"The guy's a love bug."

"What?"

"He and his wife, they're like teenagers. You run into them in the Rose Garden after a few drinks at the Christmas party, they can't keep their hands off each other, baby talk, the whole nine."

"Brimley?" She couldn't believe it.

"Yup."

"That's really sweet," she said, and thought about it. "And a little gross."

"I don't know. Good for them," Eric said.

"What's this about you dating the French ambassador or something?" she asked, doing a decent job hiding her disbelief.

"You haven't been here one day and you're up on the gossip?"

She shrugged. "Got to know the grapevine."

"No comment. I saw you talking with Walsh before."

A faintly disgusted look from Cody.

"God no. Not like that," Eric said. "Was he giving you a hard time?"

"Nothing I can't handle."

Eric waited.

"I'm used to being underestimated," she went on. "You put your head down, do the work, and prove them wrong."

"I think you already have. On your first day."

Eric had caught it before from Walsh, hints that female agents were good at pleasing the bosses and checking off bureaucratic requirements for promotion, but couldn't be counted on when the bullets started flying. Walsh was always on some self-mastery, self-improvement kick—supplements, ancient texts, and elaborate workouts—willing himself into greatness through the discipline of the month and evangelizing to others about it. Eric got the sense the guy spent too much time on the internet. Cody was too polite and professional to say that he was full of shit, but she seemed to have arrived at the correct conclusion. He wasn't Eric's favorite, but at least he put that same intensity into being an agent.

"It's been a long one," Eric said. "You should get some rest."

A doubtful look. "You're going to sleep in the middle of this?"

"No." He was hoping she would sack out so he could go check on Maddox and the comms people without getting her involved in his insubordination.

"Me neither," she said.

"Maddox is working on something for the president. You're sure he didn't say anything about it?"

She didn't answer, just evaluated him for a moment.

"I see you watching all of them, Hill," she said. "Your mind going a thousand miles an hour. You've had your guard up against the cynics so long . . . it can turn you into one. You don't believe in your own people anymore?"

"You've got a good eye, Cody. You're giving me advice now?"

She shrugged. "I keep it simple. I shut up and color. And I sleep well."

"Shut up and color" was military slang for just doing what you're told. It was one of Joe Cody's credos.

"You got that from your dad?"

"Of course."

"When did you decide you wanted to join the Service, work your way back to the White House?"

A laugh. "The day we arrived in Mesa Springs, and I got a good look around. I remember the first time my dad brought me to the Oval Office. It was decorated for Christmas, and I saw him chatting and laughing with the president like it was no big thing. I couldn't believe it—then the president of the United States turned around and shook my hand. He gave me an ornament and whispered, 'Give 'em hell, Amber.'"

She paused, and Eric gave her a moment. Her dad used to tell her that, though he usually called her "Bear." Clearly he'd been bragging about her to the president.

"I'll never forget that feeling, like I was right in the middle of everything decent and good in the world. After Dad died, and we moved to California, things were tough. My mom took it hard, you know. I saw a lot of my friends, my brother get dragged down . . . a lot of temptations in that town. I mean fuck, it got me for a while."

She looked down and years of darkness passed behind her eyes in a moment. She swallowed, shoved it away.

"So I decided I wanted to get back here, to do this work."

"What'd your mom think of that?"

"She was pissed. Too dangerous. I get it. A lot of people told me I'd never make it, even people in my family—scrawny, just a girl, not some Div One football god like Dad. And it was hard—the army, then working my way up in the field office, so many dick jokes, so many dudes itching for me to fail."

"They were on the wrong side of that bet."

"Yeah, I used it. Revenge is great motivation."

"Your mom's doing all right?"

"She's happy. Doesn't quite understand everything that's going on, but good considering."

"You're taking care of her?"

"Sending money back. Can't be there as much as I'd like, but my sister's close."

"The nursing home. Can I ask what that runs every month?"

"I've got it."

He raised his eyebrows.

"Seven grand."

"Jesus." This was about more than proving herself. She needed the job.

"I know the Service isn't perfect, Hill. I'm not naive. But I like the clear path, I like the standards. You ace the exam. You practice your pistol until the webbing on your thumb bleeds and you're shooting perfect three hundreds every time. You go to the top of the list after protective detail training. No one can argue with that. I put my trust in the army, then the Service, I worked my ass off, and it saved me. I'm not doing it for them. I'm doing it for me. I like the discipline. I *need* it. So please don't tell me to start getting cute with orders from above."

She looked at him, and couldn't hide the hardness behind it, or didn't want to.

"What is it?" he asked.

Silence.

"You can level with me here, Cody. I'm not one of the bosses. I'm probably done after they finish needing me down here anyway."

She tightened her jaw, fighting her reflex against pissing off any of her superiors, a good survival instinct in any bureaucracy.

"He died for this job. I worked my ass off for it. And you don't even seem to care about it anymore."

It felt like a punch in the stomach, but it was a fair shot. "I take the duty as seriously as I ever did. But I'm careful who I trust. You see things. They change you."

"Like what?" she asked.

Eric wished he still had faith like hers. He thought of telling her the dark side of shut up and color. She had warned him not to try to protect her, not to patronize her. Eric thought back to the day her father died in the ambush, fifteen years ago, when the president's motorcade came under fire at a security conference in Kuala Lumpur, Malaysia. No. It was still the wrong move to tell her the full truth of that day. It would have been pure defensiveness, Eric trying to justify himself, or lash out like the bitter old prick he'd apparently become. They were in a foxhole, a bad time to shake someone's beliefs.

"You're right, Cody."

"About what?"

"I should give shutting up a try."

Again, that disappointment. He had no idea what she really thought of him. She'd looked up to him once, but that was years ago. He wouldn't fault her for resenting him for living when her father had died, for coming out of that tragedy as a hero. He wouldn't fault her if she blamed Eric for her father's death.

A bile taste at the back of his throat. She should blame him. If he'd just been willing to tell the bosses to fuck off back then, her dad would still be here. But no, he shut up and colored. He went along in blind duty. From that day on, he started to lose faith in the job, and himself. He was no hero, and it was a relief that others were finally catching up to that fact.

He looked at her, tried to really see her, not just the memories or his assumptions.

"What?"

"I'm not sure I've ever heard you curse before."

"I was infantry. I could make *you* blush. You're still thinking of that little girl." She shook her head. "I keep it pretty tight at work, but it's kind of necessary . . ." She touched her fingers to the skin on the back of her hand. "Some people judge you differently."

"You have to be twice as good." Her dad, a rare Black agent on the presidential detail, had once confided in Eric about it—how careful he had to be, never dressing too casually, never speaking too coarsely or in anger, never able to mention the double standard without people dismissing him as having an ax to grind.

"You said it, not me," Cody replied. "I'm as old as you were when you and my dad faced down that ambush. I can handle myself."

She was right. There were fifteen years between them. He had to work not to think of her as a kid, but he'd been a kid when he started out.

"You more than proved that." He glanced to the door. She was watching him when he looked back.

"But if you're hiding things from Chilton, or working around him, I won't be a part of it," she said. "I can't afford to be."

"You won't be. This is on me." Eric was a middle-aged white dude who'd taken a bullet for the president. He knew that the Service would judge her far more harshly for stepping out of line.

"What are you doing, Hill? Why did they take your service weapon and put you on that desk?"

She was wary of him, but he wasn't the one she had to worry about. He wanted to tell her about Navarro and all his suspicions. Chilton had been so set on taking everyone to Raven Rock, despite there being better choices. And the intelligence pointing to this IT contractor as a suspect was coming through Chilton as well, lowering everyone's guard, drawing scrutiny away from a highly placed insider. Chilton could be Citizen for all Eric knew.

But Cody was right. Getting caught up in Eric's suspicions could easily derail her career, this life she'd worked so hard to build.

"The less you know about me and my bullshit, the better off you'll be. You should sleep while you can," he said, stood, and looked to the bunk room.

"You'll be here?" she asked.

No. He was going to find out what Maddox was doing, what the hell Operation V was, and who was behind it, but he wasn't going to involve her.

"Don't worry about me," he said.

Cody stared at him and shook her head.

23

WILL MADDOX STRODE north through the main tunnel, looking at the facade of Building D to his right. He slowed, turning back to see where Drumm had gone.

The deputy commander race-walked toward him, trying to smile, pumping his arms.

"Too much time in Granite Cove, I guess," Drumm said, patting his stomach with a laugh.

"It's me, sorry," Maddox replied, smiling. "I'm always rushing."

"What sort of message do you have?" Drumm asked, and glanced at the portfolio.

"You can just show me the setup."

"I only ask because we have a half-dozen different comms channels down here, and we're tied into the military control system if it's national command authority–related."

"A standard level IV encrypted line will be fine."

"We've got plenty of those."

"And a SCIF?" A sensitive compartmented information facility— essentially a bug-proof vault for the government's most closely held secrets.

"All of Building E is secure. This whole bunker is better shielded than a SCIF."

"I mean a place where I can call direct without any operator or switchboard. Solo."

"Sure. Sure." A look of concentration. "We can do that."

He lifted his radio and raised someone in the comms building.

"Moro, can you get a level IV line ready in Conference Three? Yes. Just set it up so it's fire-and-forget. I'm on my way with the president's assistant. He'll have the room to himself. Exactly," Drumm said, and put down his radio.

He turned to Maddox. "Just dial 9 for an outside line."

"Okay."

"No, sorry. That was a comms joke."

Maddox gave him a polite half smile, then walked on. Sweat slicked his palms. He dried them on the fabric of his pants and gripped the portfolio. The president wanted to keep Maddox's mission as low-profile as possible. The fate of the country could be riding on this call. Twenty-four hours ago, his main concern was that his parents would embarrass him in front of the president and first lady, call him Willie or talk about how he insisted on wearing a jacket and tie in middle school. But everything had changed.

He could see the gray front of Building E in the distance, the building nestled in its long cavern that extended perpendicularly to the right from this main tunnel. It housed the only working communications in this hole.

He slowed, looking for Drumm again, who had stopped twenty feet back, his radio pressed to his ear. The lights flickered overhead.

"You have to be kidding me," Drumm said, looking up. "Today? Bring up the checklist. I'll be right there."

Maddox walked toward him. "What's going on?"

"Power surges from the diesel plant."

"That doesn't sound good."

"No, it's fine. This place needs a lot of attention. The plant acts up sometimes and we have auxiliary engines as backups."

Maddox looked him over, saw the stress in his narrowed eyes. He was downplaying it.

"I should get over there just to be sure," Drumm said.

Maddox looked to the E building. "What about the call?"

Drumm already had the radio to his ear.

"Major Moro. Yes. Can you stand by at the front door to E? The president's assistant will be there in a minute or two. You met him. Will Maddox." He spelled out the last name.

"There you go," Drumm said to Maddox. "My deputy will meet you, and I'll be there as soon as I deal with this."

"You have to leave now?" Maddox said, gripping the portfolio tighter.

"We never let anything go down here," Drumm said, turning away. "Keep small problems small."

His radio squawked, a call coming in. "Major Moro will be waiting for you," Drumm said, walking away, giving him a thumbs-up as he answered the call. "Yes. On my way."

Maddox turned and walked alone past Building D.

24

MARCUS SLIPPED OVER the stone floor, moving under Building D, passing between the springs that supported the structure from beneath, each taller and wider than he was.

He went west toward the main tunnel. The lights ahead flickered as the power surged. It was all beginning.

He had an MP5 hanging from his shoulder, but he wouldn't use that, not yet. Too much noise. For now everything was stealth.

He heard voices echoing toward him. As he moved closer, he could identify the speakers: Will Maddox and Bruce Drumm. Marcus couldn't let them reach the comms building, Raven Rock's last link with the outside world. He knew what Maddox carried in his hand: a death sentence for Marcus, for this nation.

He glanced down at his watch, the hands marked with a faint green glow. Everything was in place, but they couldn't pull the trigger yet. Marcus stopped at the edge of the shadows, looking out at the light of the main tunnel. Drumm was going south, back the way he had come.

That left Maddox alone. Marcus keyed his radio twice, an unspoken signal, then took out a collapsible baton. Silently extending the steel weapon, he kept his eyes fixed on his prey. The faintest *snick* sounded as it locked open. He halted. This place was an echo chamber, magnifying everything.

Maddox didn't seem to notice. He kept moving, fast, always so fast, toward the mouth of the tunnel. Marcus tightened his grip on the club and moved toward the light.

Maddox stopped. His head turned to the right, scanning under the springs, straight at Marcus.

25

MADDOX LOOKED INTO the darkness under Building D. Cold air drifted from beneath it as he moved closer and peered between the massive springs.

"Hello?" he called out.

His own voice echoed back from the cavern that housed D an instant later. He raised his radio. "This is Maddox."

No answer. Only static came back on a second try. He stepped closer to the foundations of D, crouching slightly. The building, and the springs beneath it, went on for as far as he could see into the darkness.

He shifted the portfolio to his left hand to free his right, then reached into his pocket and came out with a flashlight—bright enough to blind temporarily, and a decent striking weapon.

"Who's there?" he said.

He clicked on the light and shined it beneath the building. The springs cut the beam into spiral patterns as he swept it slowly, right to left.

Dust and grime covered the floor. The springs were mounted on heavy steel plates and the odd patches of clean stone between them lit up like gems when the light hit them.

He saw no one. He turned the light off, slipped it into his pocket, and stepped away.

Footsteps, hard and fast, came up behind him in the main tunnel, suddenly so close. He spun and drove the light toward the attacker, but he blocked Maddox's arm to the side as he lunged in.

A ball of pain exploded in the body man's temple. He staggered to the side, arms rising to keep his balance, seeing darting flecks of light as vertigo took hold.

Throwing his left leg out, he managed to stay up. Another shot toppled him forward, his vision tunneling as he groaned in pain.

He was only dimly aware as he crashed to the ground, his face against the stone. It slid over his skin, someone dragging him, no, two people, one on each leg. He forced his eyes open, even as his skull throbbed in waves, and felt nausea rising.

The light from the main tunnel receded. The springs passed by on his left and right, not much more than shadows in the dark as he was flipped and pulled under Building D. The grit on the floor scraped along his back.

They brought him into the passageway—a small tunnel running north through the cavern wall—and let his legs drop as he hovered near the edge of consciousness. A metal snick in the dark. A knife opening.

Maddox lay still, desperately wondering how much of his strength remained. The faintest glimmer came toward him through the shadows—a blade.

He drove his right leg forward with all his strength toward the approaching figure. The stacked wood sole of his dress shoe connected with flesh, and he heard a long gasp.

He turned over, crawling forward, somehow getting his legs under him, still unsteady.

There was faint light ahead, and he ran for it, supporting himself with a hand on the wall. Another blow, another bolt of pain through his skull. Maddox fell to one knee, and hauled himself forward, crawling, unsteady.

He'd made it four or five feet when the attacker stomped on his ankle, cracking bone, pinning it to the stone. Maddox ground his teeth together, reached forward, and dragged his fingers across the floor, trying to pull himself toward the light, his arms shaking with strain.

His ankle went free. He pulled himself forward, then saw the figure, striding ahead, standing over him, holding the portfolio in his left hand.

He drove his boot down into Maddox's head, slamming his skull into the stone floor.

"We know you were going to betray us, Will," the man said. "You picked the wrong side in this war."

The pain yielded to a spreading numbness. Maddox had only the vague sensation of movement, of being dragged on his back, then nothing.

26

IN THE DINING facility in Building B, Eric shouldered his weapon and headed for the hallway.

Cody's question stayed with him: *Why did they take your service weapon and put you on that desk?*

He was back there, sitting in a running Chevy Suburban outside of Braun's mansion in Alexandria. It was during the presidential primary, and the Service was stretched protecting the more high-profile candidates, including Braun, a party power broker and moneyman who had decided to make a run for the top seat himself.

All day Eric would stand ready, his back to Braun, listening to him spin out the same stories with Nora Braun, his high school sweetheart, now wife, by his side. Braun put himself out there as a self-made man, a devout Lutheran, a rare honest broker in Washington Babylon lecturing about a return to decency.

By night Eric would hear him shouting at Nora, his voice audible through the brick and lath of his four-million-dollar Colonial.

See everything and see nothing. That was Eric's job. Private life is off-limits. It's the only way to earn a protectee's trust, the only way to keep them safe. So you tune it out. You live with the dissonance. You disappear behind the suit and earpiece.

Eric had been doing it for seventeen years, protecting good men and hypocrites alike. It was the job. It was Washington. It was eternal.

He'd heard the fear in Nora's voice on those nights. In rare moments alone, he would see her, eyes downcast. He asked if she was okay, if she needed someone to talk to, if there was anything he could do for her.

It was always the same answer. "I'm fine, thanks, Eric." But one morning she'd paused for a long time before she said it, and she never looked up as she spoke. Then Braun came out and gave Eric a look, as if to say, "Women, right?"

That day, he felt complicit, the anger growing into something he couldn't control.

He brought them home from a fundraiser that night, with Braun showing the razor-sharp buzz he'd get after a few scotches, slapping Eric on the shoulder, cracking jokes, looking for trouble with that bored rich-kid grin. Nora was silent, staring out the window.

Eric stood watch outside, patrolling the sidewalk, moving to keep warm, listening for threats. Braun started up with the shouts, and Eric realized he was listening for something else—an excuse.

Braun screaming. Her crying. Silence, then a slammed door. Then Braun barked at her with rage like Eric had never heard before: "Put them back on!"

A thud came over and over again from inside the house—someone pounding on a door, followed by the sound of splintering wood. Eric ran up the front steps. He had his excuse. He didn't call for backup. He wanted Braun alone.

He crossed the foyer and the main hall with its low modern sofas. It was a museum house, a life on display. He took the main stairs up two at a time. Inside the master suite, he could hear Braun's low, growling voice, so different from the one he used at the podium it was almost unrecognizable.

Halfway up the stairs, that voice went silent. As Eric crossed the second-story hall toward the master, he heard footsteps coming toward the door of the bedroom, men's dress shoes clacking across the hardwood, then muffled on the Berber rugs.

Braun stood in the doorway to the master bedroom, his face red.

"You can go back to your post, Hill. It's nothing." He began turning back into the bedroom.

Eric moved closer and Braun faced him. "What the fuck are you doing?" Braun asked.

"Go downstairs," Eric said.

"Is this a joke?"

Eric walked up to him, and past. Braun puffed out his chest with a mix of indignity and drunken amusement on his face. Inside the suite, the door frame leading to the bathroom was cracked.

"Hill," he snarled. "Get out of my house. Now!"

Eric kept going. That gave him an angle on the bathroom mirror, and he could see Nora Braun sitting on the floor in front of the double sinks in a torn slip, arms crossed and head down, a pair of heels scattered across the marble.

"Are you all right?" he asked her, ignoring Braun's demands and shouts.

She shook her head, and Eric saw the red welts on her shoulders and upper back.

"She's impossible," Braun said, looking for an accomplice now. "*She* came after *me*."

"Go downstairs, and wait in the library," Eric said to Braun.

He laughed, like he couldn't believe what he was hearing. Eric wanted to separate them, to see what kind of help she needed, and if she had someplace she could go. A campaign is a prison of appearances. It would be hard, but there were ways to keep her safe. But it had to be her decision.

"Downstairs, now," Hill said.

"You work for me." Braun put his hand on Eric's shoulder. "Get out of here."

Eric looked at the hand.

"Now!" He pushed Eric back. Eric had managed to keep himself in check so far, but in that moment suppressed fury broke through.

He seized Braun's hand, bent it back until he heard bone snap, and shot his palm into his solar plexus, a few inches below his heart, knocking the wind out of him. Braun stepped away, cradling the broken wrist with his other hand, his mouth going like a feeding fish but taking no air as his diaphragm spasmed.

Eric stepped into the bathroom, where Nora looked on, stunned. "Do you have someone you can call? A safe place?"

She was shaking as she looked to her husband. "Yes, but please don't call the police. Don't tell anyone."

"Are you sure?"

"Swear to me you won't."

"I won't. But there are people who can help you. I can get it started. Just say the word."

Nodding, she stood up, then started walking out. Eric stayed between her and Braun while she got her cell phone and went downstairs. When Eric turned back, Braun was staring at him, a strange kind of fear on his face, as if he were enjoying this somehow. "You're fucking done," the candidate said. "You know that."

Eric did.

The incident never went public. Within the Service, he watched the slow process by which the truth gets melted down and recast to suit the needs of the politicians on high.

Eric was reassigned and eventually stripped of his service weapon and put on desk duty. Nora Braun stayed silent, quietly living apart from her husband, separate rooms, separate travel, though she was there beside him with a forced smile for the big speeches and rallies until Kline knocked him out of the primary.

Eric got a message to her, to make sure she was okay. Her only response was a request: tell no one what happened.

27

HILL'S RADIO CRACKLED to life as he neared the exit from the mess hall. A transmission came through. "This is Agent Leigh. I just heard something in the main tunnel."

"Me too. What the hell was that?" Chilton responded.

"Maddox's voice," Leigh said.

Eric stopped, and looked back to Cody. She was standing by the table, listening in as well.

"He sounded hurt," Leigh went on. "It came from the north. I'm on the move, just north of Building B in the main tunnel."

"I'm coming," Chilton said. "Be there in one minute." Walsh and Hardwick radioed that they were heading out from their posts.

Eric was already moving, gun in hand, with Cody up and flanking him now. "This is Hill," he said into the radio. "Cody and I are on our way."

They marched into the hallway, turned right, and followed it toward the main entrance of Building B.

"Was there something going on with Maddox that had you worried?"

The muscles in Cody's jaw tightened. "He seemed afraid," she said. "Underneath everything."

"Of what?"

"I don't know."

"During the attack?"

"Before it."

"Did he give you anything specific?"

She saw Brimley coming toward them from the presidential suite with his elbows-out stride.

"I shouldn't have said anything," she whispered. "I can't be your spy, Hill. I don't want any part—"

She stopped talking as Brimley approached. Eric thought through the numbers. It sounded like Chilton was already out in the tunnels—he'd said he would be at Leigh's location in one minute. It was odd he'd left Kline's side. "Who's watching the president?" Eric called out to Brimley.

"The military aide and Dr. Chen."

Both well trained, but not enough. "Stay back and cover Kline and the others," Eric said.

"You think it's a distraction?" Brimley asked.

"Could be," Eric said. "Tell POTUS to stay buttoned up in the suite. Chilton wasn't with you when the call went out?"

"No."

"Why not?"

"I don't know," Brimley said. "He was in the suite talking to the president and then he went out, well before Leigh's distress call."

"How long ago?"

"Six or eight minutes."

"Go," Eric said, and Brimley turned and walked toward the president and his people.

A minute later, Eric and Cody pushed through the front doors of Building B and exited into the main tunnel. As they climbed down the metal steps, the tunnel air surrounded them, damp and smelling of fumes. Far to the north, he could see the other agents moving along the route that Drumm and Maddox had taken to join the comms staff in Building E. He and Cody went quickly up the main tunnel, scanning under the buildings as they passed and searching around the vehicles and equipment that were parked along the tunnel's western side.

There was no one hurt along the route, no sign that anything was wrong except for the way the lights overhead would flicker every minute or two.

He and Cody eventually caught up with the other agents as they climbed the steps to the front entrance of Building E, which held the communications center. Chilton was pounding on the door when Eric came up beside him.

"You were outside when Maddox was attacked?" Eric asked.

The suspicion behind Eric's question brought shock, then a look of disdain to Chilton's face. "Yes, I was trying to raise him on the radio. The signal was shit inside the suite."

Eric studied the Secret Service chief—he didn't trust Chilton. Maddox could have been in an accident, but Eric had to assume that the attackers had somehow gotten inside Raven Rock and gone after him. Eric had been watching the body man, wary that he and the rest of the president's people were making moves to seize power. But Maddox had been afraid even before the attack at the White House. Eric had to consider every possibility—including that Maddox was a target because he was trying to resist or trying to blow the whistle on whatever the president was doing. Chilton was outside the suite, with the opportunity to get to him. He was a suspect in whatever happened.

Before Eric could press it any further, the door opened.

"You certainly took your time," Major Moro said, her hand on the inner door handle, then pulled back in surprise. She leaned out and looked down the main tunnel.

"Where is Maddox?" she asked.

"He never made it here?" Chilton asked, pressing inside.

"No."

"Where's Drumm?" Chilton asked.

"The power plant, at the southern end of the rear tunnel. He's working on the diesels with the other engineers. There was a power surge he had to deal with, so he sent Maddox ahead."

"Maddox was alone?"

"That's right, but just while traveling from Building D to E."

"In the main tunnel?"

"Yes."

Chilton stepped closer to her. "You are certain that Maddox never made it here?"

"One hundred percent. We've been waiting. Is he lost? Did something happen?"

"He's not fucking lost," Chilton said to her, the muscles in his jaw standing out. "Lock your people down in this building. No one leaves. Get Drumm on the radio."

"I've been trying. I can't. It must be the repeaters," she said. "The transmission range has gone to hell."

A system of radio repeaters strengthened and rebroadcast radio signals along the tunnels. Without them, they would only be able to communicate over short distances.

"Agent Leigh, you're with me," Chilton said, then turned back to Moro. "We need to search this building and see the comms setup."

"It's inside, straight ahead," Moro said, clearly rattled by his suspicions of her people.

Chilton turned back. "The rest of you search these tunnels going south toward Building A." He looked into each agent's eyes. "Find our man."

28

ERIC WANTED TO stay close to Chilton, to see what he was doing in that comms building, but there was no way Chilton would tip his hand while Eric was there, and Eric couldn't justify watching over the top man like he was a suspect.

The answers were with Maddox, and the old protective instincts pushed Eric to find him.

He broke off and descended the stairs with the others. Eric sent Hardwick and Walsh to the east in the cavern that housed Building E, searching through the springs under the building, while Cody, Eric, and Leigh started sweeping south through the main tunnel.

"Maddox," Eric called out. It was the first time he'd raised his voice down here, and the echo was astonishingly loud, the name coming back from the emptiness, again and again.

A moment later Cody repeated the call.

They walked on, their lights passing over the equipment along the sides of the tunnel and its green-black stone walls.

After they stopped at Building D, Cody peered into the darkness under its foundations—row after row of springs.

"I'll take Cavern D and search under and alongside this building," Eric said. "I'll sweep over to meet Hardwick and Walsh in the rear tunnel. You two go down and search Cavern C."

Leigh looked at him, and he wondered if she was worried about leaving him on his own, out of their sight with everything going on. Eric could see the distrust getting to everyone.

"That works," Leigh said.

"If the radios go down completely, I'll meet you at the main entrance to Building B. Shout if you see something."

He turned and shined his light to the east at Building D. It didn't completely fill its cavern, leaving an eight-foot gap between its exterior walls and the cavern walls. At ground level, the foundation made of springs also stopped eight feet from the cavern wall, creating an alley-like lane between the springs and the cavern wall. That alley allowed for easy passage down the length of the cavern without having to move between the springs that supported the building. There was one along the north side of the cavern and another one along the south.

Eric illuminated the northern lane, then walked into it.

He swept his light between the springs to his right, working methodically. Each footstep let off a soft grind against the stone.

After a few minutes, he neared the first passageway, a hallway-sized tunnel running north through the stone wall of Cavern D, and trained his light inside it. It ran to Cavern E, allowing access between caverns without having to return to the main tunnel. There were many of them, allowing anyone to slip hidden between the caverns.

This deep, far from the main tunnel, a sense of disorientation pressed in, the feeling that he was buried in some infinite labyrinth.

Fuck that, he thought, and pressed on to the east, toward the rear tunnel.

As he went deeper, he saw nothing but dust and spiderwebs wavering with the drafts. Soon the sound of machinery and fans could be heard from the rear tunnel, and a moment later he caught a distant echo of Agent Leigh calling Maddox's name.

The lights flickered far ahead. He looked back and could see that the lamps in both the rear and main tunnels were going in and out like dying fluorescents. A low boom sounded from the north, powerful but distant, muffled. Everything went black except for the long beam of his light.

An instant later, a flashlight appeared to the east, in the rear tunnel. Eric slowed, raising his gun as it approached the back of Building D ahead. A figure stepped into view. Eric took aim and the light turned toward him.

"Hill! It's me. Friendly!" It was Drumm's voice and Eric saw he wasn't armed.

"What was that blast?" Eric called out.

"I don't know. Power went down."

"This way," Eric said, and met him halfway, both standing in the alley between the springs under Building D and the cavern's wall. He led Drumm west, toward the main tunnel. He had to find the other agents and the source of that explosion.

"Where were you?" Eric asked.

"The diesel plant."

"And Maddox?"

"I sent him to E."

"He never made it."

"What? It was only a couple hundred yards."

The surprise seemed genuine. They traveled west through Cavern D and were two hundred feet from the main tunnel when light came toward them, the overhead halogens flicking on ahead.

"Emergency backup," Drumm said.

When they reached the main tunnel, Eric saw Amber Cody and Laura Leigh coming their way.

Drumm turned to him. "We need to figure out what the hell that blast was. From the comms center we can get an overview of any damage and if we're in trouble. Then we find Maddox."

Eric agreed, and they all walked north. As they got closer to Building E, garbled voices came from Drumm's radio. They only became clear when they were a hundred feet from the building's entrance.

Drumm held the handset to his ear and stopped. "What?" he said, his voice shaky.

Eric came up beside him. The engineer's face was white. "Comms are down," Drumm said.

"Which ones?"

"Everything. We're cut off."

29

ERIC FELT A cold touch along his spine. "I thought the communications could survive a nuclear attack."

"They can," Drumm said, "but we're trying to work this place with a skeleton crew because of your people's orders, and no one will tell us what is going on." He cooled down. "Don't worry. We'll get it back up."

Eric tried his radio again, attempting to raise the crew with the president in Building B, but there was no response.

A voice came through the static. "This is Chilton. All agents on the search for Maddox report to Building E. Now!"

Eric couldn't shake a sick feeling as he, Agents Cody and Leigh, and Drumm climbed the steps from the main tunnel to the Building E entrance. Drumm let them in, and they headed down a main corridor. The layout was similar to B, though the hallways were narrower here, and the suites and offices bunched together more tightly. The walls and floors were worn, and unlike the rest of the bunker, it had the atmosphere of actually being inhabited, with the faint scent of coffee hanging in the air.

Drumm pushed through a pair of double doors into a comms center. The place was all beige and gray, a low-ceilinged thirty-by-forty-foot bullpen full of cubicles. It had none of the grandeur of the ops centers on TV and in movies, with their cathedral airiness and omniscient view of the world.

Officers sat at desks, each one equipped with four monitors and two phones featuring more color-coded LED buttons than a piano had keys.

Massive binders rested on reading stands at each workstation, the volumes a foot thick, indexed and tabbed for all the worst fates America might face. Drumm's people and their predecessors had been down here 24/7/365 for seventy years preparing for the end of the world and now somehow they'd been caught out.

Eric noticed a lot of stuffed animals on the desks—moles. The commander's desk, currently vacant, featured a plush one wearing a fez and sitting on top of a brass plaque that read THE GRAND HIGH MOLE. It didn't inspire confidence.

Half of the comms staffers were standing, calling to each other in a jargon Eric could barely understand.

Chilton was already here, barking orders at Major Moro, Drumm's number two.

"It can't all be down," Chilton said. "Get me a goddamn line."

Drumm walked toward them and interceded. They spoke in lowered voices, and Eric moved closer. Chilton was talking about a message that absolutely had to go out, and Drumm replied with something about low-frequency transmissions. Chilton's body language tightened up as he saw Eric approaching.

"What about cameras?" Chilton asked, changing the subject. "Why don't we have eyes on these tunnels?"

"They went down during the surge."

"Are these all of your people?"

"Some are checking on the comms lines and any damage from the blast."

"They're out there?"

"Of course."

"I want them here under watch."

"What are you implying?" Drumm asked.

Chilton glared at Eric. "What?" he asked.

Eric pulled him aside. "We need to get out of here. This is an attack. They're inside. Forget the comms. Get the doors open. Get the president in the air."

Behind his anger, Chilton seemed to be listening. He held his hand up to Eric. "We don't know that for certain."

"We have a man missing and we're being systematically isolated. Surely you—"

"There's no need to panic or overreact."

"You have to see it. You want the president taken down on your watch?"

Chilton didn't answer. He walked over to Drumm and said, "Open the doors."

Drumm looked up from a monitor. "What?"

"Open this place up and get three vehicles ready."

Drumm crossed his arms. "The blast doors are sealed. It's not like ducking out to check the mail. There's a protocol for everything in this place. That's how we survive down here." His hand went to one of the massive binders on the desk beside him.

"This is not a discussion," Chilton said.

"There may be damage to the systems and it's a very complicated—"

"We've been out of contact with the government for two hours. I can get the president and let him know you're keeping him locked down here, or you can open those fucking doors."

Drumm's lips pressed together and disappeared into a line as he looked over the comms center. He nodded. "All right," he said to Chilton, then called across the room.

"Major Moro," he said. "Bring up the perimeter controls in SCADA."

"Sir?"

"We're going to open the blast doors."

"You're sure?"

A glance to Chilton. "I'm sure."

Moro dropped into a chair and started working the keys on a terminal at the front of the room.

"Can you talk to the military command centers, *anyone*?" Chilton asked Drumm. "We need to coordinate with Marine Helicopter Squadron One."

Drumm chewed his lip. "Those systems are down at the moment. We are working on—"

Eric stopped paying attention to him when he noticed Moro at her desk, suddenly breathing faster, punching the keys with a desperate force. She paused, then tapped out another drumbeat on the keyboard.

Moro walked toward Drumm and stood to his side. Drumm turned her way, stepping away to get her alone out of the agents' earshot, but Chilton was having none of that.

"What is it?" Chilton demanded.

"We're having an issue with the doors," Moro said. "Both exits. North and south."

"The blast doors?" Chilton's voice was like ice. He ran his hand through his hair. "Is there any possible innocent explanation for those explosions we heard? An accident?"

Drumm beckoned him closer and the three of them huddled. Eric took a few steps to hear them better.

". . . in theory it could be a malfunction. The bottom line is they're not responding," Moro said. "We're running the hydraulics to retract them, but they're not moving."

"You're sure?" Chilton said.

A somber nod from Moro.

"What does that mean?" Chilton looked from one officer to the other. "We're fucking locked in here?"

He stepped to Drumm. "I don't know what you people are trying to pull."

"What?"

"The comms, the doors . . ." Anger got the better of Chilton, and he just shook his head instead of filling in the rest of the accusation.

Eric watched him carefully, trying to gauge whether this could all be part of an elaborate act. It could justify the president invoking the emergency directives while holed up in a place that would allow him complete control of the military once comms were reestablished.

"How do we get them open?" Eric asked. They turned toward him. "Manually? There has to be a way."

Drumm's and Moro's eyes met. "The hydraulic gear?" Drumm said.

Moro called to another officer two desks over. "I need the schematics and protocols to pull the blast doors manually." The woman rose and walked past a panel of status lights to retrieve them from a cabinet.

Drumm got on the radio and began making commands to the engineers, his voice loud as the reception went in and out. Moro handed him a binder, and he started walking toward the exit.

"Let's go," he said.

Chilton followed. Eric brought his gun up and went out with them, joined by Agents Cody and Leigh. They left Building E through its front door and descended the stairs into the main tunnel.

Eric went up to Chilton as they walked. "What about the president? Have you heard from him?"

"No, but his suite in Building B is unbreachable. We'll check the blast doors at the northern end of the main tunnel while we're close to them and then go back to him."

Chilton's priorities didn't seem right, unless he was in on this and certain that the president was safe. Or he was simply scared to bring POTUS bad news—a common failing in politically minded bosses in the Service. He'd dropped the search for Maddox too, which left Eric asking if he knew what had happened to him, possibly even played a role in it. Or—and this seemed like a reach, but he had to consider it—Maddox was out there doing the sabotage.

A pair of headlights bore down on them, a work truck driven by Drumm's engineers. Their boss waved it down. As they approached it, Cody stepped closer to Eric.

"This is an attack?" she asked.

This place was seventy years old, a Cold War money pit. He'd been in enough exercises and crises over the years to know to expect chaos and broken systems when a real emergency hit, but this was too many.

"It is."

"You trust Drumm's people?"

"I don't trust anyone, remember?" he said, watching Chilton and the other agents. The threat was in the White House and now it was here, which led him to suspect those who had been at both places—the insiders.

Eric stared at Chilton as he climbed into the cab of the truck, and the chief turned and met his gaze, his brows rising slightly, as if to say, "What?"

Another truck pulled up, an F-350 with two men in fatigues in the cab. They were hauling a generator, a compressor, coils of hose, and two gear boxes in the bed.

Eric climbed onto the bed, followed by the other agents—Cody and Leigh, Hardwick and Walsh. He kept his hand on the grip of his MP5 and looked to the north. The main tunnel continued on past Building E, then started gently curving toward the sealed blast doors.

He pounded his fist on the cab, and they took off.

30

ERIC PICKED IT up long before they reached their destination—the acrid smell of explosives and behind it the reek of burning plastics and oil.

The first of the two northern blast doors came into view as they sped along the curving tunnel, the air rushing past them, Cody holding on to the truck's bed rail. The vehicles stopped thirty feet from this inner door, and they climbed down.

"This is no accident," Eric said.

"No," Drumm replied, his head turning, searching for threats.

Eric signaled to the team, pointing Cody, Hardwick, and Leigh to cover the main tunnel to the south. He went over to the east side of the door, where a machine room had been carved into the rock.

Chilton approached him with Major Moro and another engineer from the truck. Eric took the Secret Service chief aside and said, "This is clearly sabotage."

"I've got it under control," Chilton replied, and walked on. Eric couldn't tell if he was scared to admit he made the wrong call by bringing the president here or if his denial was part of something more sinister.

Drumm and Moro went inside the machine room, which held the electronics and controls for the blast doors. Drumm drew a multimeter from the pocket of his fatigues and looked at the damage, his face pained by what they had done to his bunker.

Eric tightened his hands on his gun and looked down the main tunnel to the south, the way they had come, ready for a secondary attack from whoever had set that blast. The engineers carried the generators and hoses into the machine room.

Eric heard a motor rev behind him as one of the engineers hauled on a generator's pull cord. It chugged to life, throwing out smoke. Eric kept watch as they worked, running hoses into the machinery, one man climbing halfway inside the wall.

"Starting pressure!" Drumm called out.

The compressor spun up with a high droning sound.

"That's good," Drumm said. "More."

Eric heard a clank from deep in the wall.

"More!"

Drumm's face was red. Sweat ran along his temple as he stared into the machinery. "What are we at?"

"Four fifty," Moro said.

"Keep it coming," Drumm called out, waving his hand toward himself like he was directing traffic.

"Five hundred."

A creak from deep in the wall.

"Hold up!" Drumm shouted.

Eric glanced at the door, a white expanse like the side of a barn. It seemed as permanent and immobile as the stone walls to his right and left.

"All right! More!"

The compressor struggled, its engine groaning. Eric stepped away from it, and waved Cody to follow him.

A grinding noise came from inside the wall. "That's it!" Drumm said. "Come on!"

The engineers dialed up the compressor. The sound from inside the wall pitched higher in tone, almost a scream.

"Come on!"

Tink! The sound was loud and high, like a cable snapping under pressure. A great crashing noise came from inside the wall, and something ricocheted out of the machine room and skittered off the stone.

Eric took aim by instinct as Drumm reeled back, clapping his right hand over the back of his left. A line opened up on the skin, and a drop of blood welled, then fell from it.

Drumm looked at it in disbelief.

Eric ran toward him, calling for the others to get back. They retreated, clear from any other shrapnel as the engine raced. He reached the deputy commander and looked him over, checking for other injuries.

"Are you hit anywhere else?"

Drumm looked down and shook his head. He wiped the blood away. The cut went through the skin, but no deeper, and Drumm seemed steady enough on his feet. He looked across the floor at the gleaming pieces of metal, and his face fell.

Chilton came over, his expression a mix of fear and anger. "Are you all right?" he asked.

Drumm shook his head and looked at the door. "That's it."

"What does that mean?"

"We can't move it."

"What about the blast doors at the southern end of the main tunnel, where we came in?"

"We had an officer check them. They're down too."

"So how do we get out of here?"

Drumm took a deep breath and looked him in the eye.

"We don't."

Chilton's face went white, and Drumm pulled him aside. Eric approached them and heard Chilton saying, ". . . you're telling me you've buried the fucking president under seven hundred and fifty feet of rock?"

"We can try to dismantle them, but . . . the whole place is built around those doors."

"There has to be another way."

"There is an emergency pedestrian exit, a long tunnel just wide enough for one person. It's all manual locks. It'll take some work to get it open."

"Where?"

"In the main tunnel across from Building C."

"Where exactly?"

"It's a black door on the west side marked M-27. Thirty feet south of the entrance to C."

Chilton nodded. "Okay. Get it ready."

A low boom came up the tunnel from the south. Eric spun. It sounded far off.

He grabbed Chilton. "We're under attack. We need to get the president and the others." The boom was still reverberating from the depths of the complex.

Chilton swallowed, then lifted his radio. Pure static.

"You won't be able to talk to anyone in B without the radio repeaters," Drumm said.

Chilton's eyes narrowed. "Keys," he called to Drumm, but the deputy commander was frozen in place.

"What?"

"Give me the keys to the truck. Now."

Drumm nodded to one of the engineers, who walked them over.

"You drive," Chilton said, passing the keys to Eric and working his radio futilely. Eric circled his finger in the air and the other agents came over.

"Hardwick, Walsh," he said. "Stay with Drumm's people, watch them, and see if they can get any of these exits open."

He had the other agents—Cody and Leigh—get into the bed of the F-350.

Chilton climbed in the passenger seat. Eric jumped in and started the truck. He backed it into a K-turn, then took off, his heart pounding and the overhead lights strobing past as he raced toward Building B and the president's suite.

31

"THERE," CHILTON SAID, pointing to the west side of the main tunnel as they drove. Eric pulled over on the right, across from the entrance to Building C.

A heavy steel door frame was set in the stone. It looked like the mouth of a narrow mine. The door bulged out, the steel bent. Chilton stepped out to look at it.

Even from his seat, Eric could see rubble spilling out from the wrecked door. He felt a pit in his stomach. The blast they'd heard was this emergency exit being blown.

Another truck pulled up behind them. Drumm stepped out and joined Chilton. He moved close to the comms chief, and Eric could see that they were talking about the doors, but also looking back under Building C, with Drumm pointing and explaining. It seemed like he was gesturing to indicate something deep in the cavern that housed C, or even behind the building in the rear tunnel.

Eric walked up to Drumm. "Is there any way we can get out through that exit?"

Drumm held his hand to his cheek. "We'll try. It doesn't look good. God. The damage to this place. We don't have the budget, the paperwork . . ."

"Paperwork?" Eric let out a dark laugh. "The only thing you need to worry about right now is keeping your people alive."

Drumm looked back at him, his eyes empty as the gravity of their situation sank in.

The attackers must have been planning this for months. They were prepared to cut off the communications and exits and had wired Raven Rock up like a giant trap. The attack at the White House was designed to get the president in here at their mercy.

A nauseous feeling rose in Eric. He didn't trust Chilton's assurances that the president's suite in Building B was secure. He wanted to make sure they were safe, and to see what Kline and his people were doing in the middle of all this.

"Is there any way you can get the southern blast doors open?" he asked.

"I'll send a larger group to check."

"And see what you can do here," Eric said, then turned to the other agents. "We're going to B. Come on."

Chilton hesitated, then gave a few final orders to Drumm. Eric noticed Chilton looking back at Building C as the chief walked toward the truck.

"What's going on with C?" Eric asked as they loaded into the vehicle.

An instant of hesitation. "Nothing," Chilton said.

Eric drove south down the tunnel, then pulled up in front of the B building. The agents climbed out. They were all on guard, with tight defensive postures, shoulders rolled forward and guns held tight.

They went inside B and walked down the main corridor.

Chilton stopped them just outside the entrance to the executive office area. "Hill," he said, pointing down the hall. "You're here. Guard the approaches."

He put his hand on the door and Eric stepped to him. "I should be inside."

"You're here." Chilton was puffed up, overcompensating to cover his nerves.

The other agents watched them facing off.

"Sure," Eric said. Going straight at Chilton would get him nowhere. The supervisor opened the door, and Agents Cody and Leigh lingered near Eric, with concern on their faces.

"Keep your eye on Chilton," he said to them. "Something is going on."

Eric watched them disappear into the executive offices, then started a patrol of the hall. He needed a moment to think. He was in the middle of a goddamn coup, but there was no way to tell whether it had been launched by the president or his enemies.

As he patrolled the corridors, the suspicions ate at him. Kline and his people had to be watched.

He turned around, went back to the door to the offices, and punched in the access code. The red light flashed. A second try gave the same result.

He lifted his radio and made a call to anyone in range. "This is Hill. I'm locked out."

32

ERIC POUNDED HIS fist on the door and made another call.

A second later Cody responded, "On my way."

The door opened and she stood just inside.

"Did they change the codes?" he asked.

"They must have," she said. "Locking it down."

"And not tell the agents on watch?" he asked.

"Maybe they tried. Radio reception is basically nothing."

Eric stepped through and noted a bit of wariness in the way Cody was looking at him.

He scanned across the tops of the partitions and cubicles. The office area was empty. "Everyone else is inside the president's suite?" he asked.

"Just Chilton and Kline's staff. The agents were all posted outside of it, on guard in the hallways. You're sure we're locked out?"

Eric marched through the office area and exited into the hallway that led to the war room and the president's suite. He turned south and came to the door that led to Kline's private quarters.

"Go ahead," he said, looking to the keypad for the lock.

She seemed leery of taking direction from Eric rather than Chilton, but went ahead and entered the code.

The red lights flashed. She tried the radio. No answer.

"The system could be down," she said, her optimism straining against the grimness of their situation.

"It doesn't look down to me."

"What is this?" she asked.

"Seems like Kline doesn't trust any of us, or he's doing something he doesn't want us to see."

She considered him for a moment. "Why did you have a concealed weapon at the White House?"

He'd given her enough reason to be cautious about him, but he wondered if someone else—Chilton? Givens?—had warned her not to trust him.

"Don't read too much into that," he said. "I always carry a backup."

"That SIG, the P232, was it the gun you used when you outdrew that guy and saved the senator?"

"It was what I used that night, but I didn't outdraw him."

The story had become legendary around the Secret Service, and like most legends, it had strayed from the truth.

It was eight years ago. Eric had responded to a call for backup from an agent. The guy had been on what was supposed to be a quiet detail, but a man in the middle of a psychotic break had jumped him and knocked him out, then grabbed Senator Miller—a long-shot presidential candidate—and put a gun to his head, yelling about how he knew the end of the world was coming and the senator wouldn't listen to him.

Eric was the first on the scene, facing off against the shooter in the front yard of the senator's place in the Palisades.

"I heard the attacker pulled on you, but you managed to shoot him first," Cody said.

"No," Eric replied. "He already had the gun to Miller's temple. I drew as soon as I got to the scene, but it was a standoff. He was well trained, a survivalist type. The orders from the command were not to take him until the snipers and hostage unit arrived, and I didn't have a shot anyway. He was using Miller as a shield, and he said he was going to kill him if I didn't drop my pistol.

"The attacker pressed the gun in—a big 1911 Colt—and from the way his knuckles were going white I could tell he was serious about the threat, just about to fire. So I tossed my weapon."

"Your primary?"

"Right."

"I stalled him, but he was getting more erratic. When the sirens sounded, he turned. I pulled my backup piece—the P232—and shot him when he wasn't looking, missed Miller by a couple inches."

"You shot him in the back?" Cody asked, that disappointed look returning. The idea of hiding a gun and taking someone when they weren't looking clearly didn't sit right with her.

"Let's call it the side. Through his ribs. It put him down. It wasn't a gentleman's duel at twenty paces, but anything's fair game. That's why I always carry a backup gun. I'd rather be a crafty son of a bitch and save the principal than a Boy Scout watching him die."

"By disobeying a direct order?"

"I got the job done. I understand why they changed the story. They didn't want it going around that I had ignored the commander and used an off-the-books weapon in such a high-profile save. The Service needs its heroes."

"Apparently. Anything else you want to tell me?"

"What are you asking, Cody?"

She looked at him with a flash of unguarded anger, then closed her eyes and pushed a breath out through her nose. Back in control.

"Forget it. And now the Service wants you disarmed and locked out."

He could see her mind going, weighing whom to trust.

"I can understand their logic," Eric said. "But that doesn't do much to put me at ease. And they've locked everyone out."

Cody crossed her arms and looked at the keypad, deep in thought for a moment.

"What's a PEADs?" she asked.

"Where did you hear that?"

"From Chilton."

"Presidential Emergency Action Documents. They're a raft of laws that have been drafted in advance to be invoked in case of massive disaster like a nuclear attack."

"Martial law?"

"No one knows what's in them besides the president and two or three of his advisers."

Her eyes went to the doors.

"But yes," Eric said. "Something like martial law. The president could act without congressional or judicial oversight, suspend the Constitution if necessary. His designees could even take over the states and major industries. There have been different rumors about what's in them over the years."

"But they would be justified in a situation like this, right? The president under attack?"

"It depends on the scale, and down here we have no way of knowing that."

"I think Agent Leigh heard Chilton talking about the PEADs too. It startled her. 'Once CIA, always CIA,' she said. That was about Kline?"

"Yes."

"He could rule the country from a place like this? A military command center."

"Easily."

"Do you think it's possible the president is behind this somehow? That it's a power grab?"

"You were right before. You don't want to be involved."

"It's too late for that." She took a deep breath.

"You asked me before if I'd seen anything off with Maddox."

Eric waited.

"He had four cell phones, two of them with tape on the back. I noticed them when he was working on something in the study off the Oval Office, but I think he was trying to keep them hidden. I've only seen that with people working undercover, making sure to use the right names for each line. Why would a presidential assistant have that set up?"

Kline had said there was a hidden faction working against him. He'd called it The Order. But what Cody was describing made it seem like his closest aide was part of the conspiracy.

"That close to the Oval," Eric said, "you have to assume he was acting on Kline's orders."

"So the president is running his own secret operation or is somehow behind all of this?"

"We have to consider the possibility. These threats could be a provocation he created to give him an excuse to seize power or eliminate his enemies, or he allowed the attackers to go on, maybe even encouraged them, for the same reason. Did you ever talk to Maddox about it?"

"No, but I could see he was afraid last night and today before he went out into the tunnels. I'd never seen him scared before."

"You're sure you want to know?"

A steady gaze. "I am."

Eric told her about his conversation with Navarro before he was attacked, how he had warned him about a power grab and something called Operation V, how someone highly placed named Citizen was trying to warn others and stop it. He explained the president's claim that there was a secret network that had sworn an oath to take him down, and how he was committed to rooting it out at any cost.

"We're in the middle of a war?" she asked.

"We need to act like it, and find out who Citizen is. Depending on who you ask, he's either the threat behind this whole thing or our savior."

"The Secret Service agents who were killed, Rivas and Stiles. Were they part of it?"

"Navarro was worried it was foul play. A lot of people are."

"I've heard the rumors, that Kline was behind the crash somehow, to take out a politician who had dirt on him."

"Who did you hear that from?"

"I see the protesters. In the field office we would keep track of all the conspiracies people cooked up about the president."

"But not from anyone here?"

Cody hesitated, touched her earlobe with her thumb and forefinger. "Just one agent. Nothing about foul play but I heard her mention Rivas and Stiles when she was on the phone."

"Laura Leigh?" She was the only other female agent on duty.

"That's right." Cody wrung her hands. "Killing fucking agents."

Eric imagined there was no greater sin in her world after what happened to her father.

"What's the theory?" she asked. "That Kline is staging all this so he can seize power and shut down his critics? And he went after Navarro first for knowing too much?"

"That's one theory," Eric said. "Or this is all being done by the network conspiring against the president. They are planting the rumors about Kline to justify a coup and bring others to their side. They orchestrated the White House attacks to get him here, where they could trap him."

"And the person leading it all, Citizen—he, or she, is an insider?"

Eric nodded. "Yes. Kline said Citizen has access to high-level information and Citizen would have to be close to the president to pull this off."

Cody looked up and down the hall.

"He could be in here with us now?"

"Absolutely."

"Who is it, Hill?"

"Could be an agent, or a staffer. It could be anyone."

"Kline is locking himself in there because there's no one he can trust."

"Or he's about to take control. If this is all a provocation from Kline, Citizen could be one of his people, or the president himself."

"What do you believe?"

It was the same question the president had asked him, in a different form. *Which side are you on?*

"I believe we need to watch everyone right now."

"And if Kline *is* behind it?"

Eric swore his oath to the Constitution, not to the president, but the idea of taking arms against the office he had spent his life protecting made him sick. It would force him to go against the other agents, brothers and sisters, if they were involved.

But as he thought of Navarro lying there in a pool of his own blood, a dark feeling took hold of him, decades of anger from seeing those in high office abuse their power. He remembered the last time it got the best of him, that night with Braun, remembered the satisfying crack of bone. It might end with people calling him a traitor, but he would do whatever it took to keep his promises and protect this country.

"Then there's no map except the Constitution," he said, "lawful orders as best you can judge, and your own conscience. And maybe both theories are right. They're all crooked, and it's us against the world. How's your first shift going, Cody?"

She pinched the bridge of her nose, then put on a mock-eager smile. "Aces. I'm really learning a lot."

Eric remembered the first time he had to confront that truth. You want to follow orders and do what's right, then you figure out you have to choose one or the other.

A strange silence settled over them. Eric realized it was the vent overhead.

The hum of the fans deep in the HVAC system slowly died. The air was still.

"Why did you insist on coming here?" she asked.

The main reason, when he really thought about it: he didn't want to leave her or any of the other agents alone with the president's people. "Everyone needs someone watching them at all times now, either to protect them . . ."

"Or to stop them."

She looked at the locked door, then back to Eric, a new sharpness on her face. Of course she was suspicious. He was talking about possibly going up against the president.

Eric stepped toward the door and keyed his radio again. The air grew warmer.

Clank clank. The sound came muted from down the hall. It had a long echo to it: a door to the outside opening.

33

ERIC LOOKED TO Cody, and they started moving without a word, heading north toward the sound, covering the hallway with their weapons. A pair of doors opened to an interior corridor with beige walls and a drop ceiling that ran along the northern side of Building B. Eric moved through first and held his MP5 tight against his shoulder.

"Leigh was supposed to be posted here," Cody said. "And Brimley at the far end."

Two agents gone. There was a door ahead to their left that exited to the outside: the cavern housing Building B. As they came closer, Eric picked up a faint odor. "Diesel fumes," he said. The air was slightly cooler here.

"Someone came inside," Cody said.

Eric checked the exterior door: still locked.

He keyed his radio. "Brimley, Leigh. Come back." He tried again, but a wash of static was the only answer. He put out an open call. Nothing. "President's suite, come on."

He and Cody continued down the hall. A light sweat broke out on his neck, a product of the rising temperature and his body readying for a fight. He pounded on a pair of steel security doors that led toward the war room and the president's suite at the back of B and tried the combination again. The red LED flashed. He banged his fist against the steel once more, the boom of flexing metal echoing down the hall.

His radio came to life. "Hill, is that you outside the war room?" Agent Leigh's voice.

"Yes, near the northeast corner of B. We have a breach."

A moment later, the door creaked open.

Leigh stood just inside. She looked down at his gun, held up and ready.

"Where's Brimley?" Eric asked.

"In here," she said. "Everything's fine."

Eric edged forward to look through the door and glimpsed a conference area that stood next to the war room.

"Why aren't you at your post?" Eric asked, peering around as Brimley came up beside Leigh.

"Chilton called us in here," he said.

Cody and Eric exchanged a look, then he stepped closer to the door.

Leigh stiffened, her hand going to the gun.

"We can only let people in on Chilton's say-so," Brimley said. "I'm sorry, Hill. Direct order."

"Get him out here. Someone came in those doors where you had been on guard."

Leigh looked to Brimley, alarmed, lifted her radio, and raised Chilton while Eric kept watch on the corridor. He glanced back to see Brimley walking off to find the chief.

A minute later, Leigh received a call back on the radio. Eric couldn't make out the transmission.

"Chilton's not here."

"What?"

"He was in with the president, and now he's gone."

Brimley came up beside her and nodded in assent.

"Where did he go?"

"We don't know," Leigh said.

"The president's okay?"

"Yes, we just saw him in the suite."

Eric looked back down the hall to the door that had been opened to the exterior. The answer wasn't in here. It was in the tunnels.

"Keep your eyes open," he told Leigh and Brimley. "Something is going down. Don't trust *anyone*."

He turned and moved down the hallway. Cody walked by his side.

"What's going on?" she asked.

"Chilton pulls them off their post, then the exterior door opens. It wasn't someone coming in. It was him leaving and making sure that no one saw him go. He and Maddox could be out there."

"Doing what?"

Eric remembered Chilton and Drumm's conversation, and Drumm pointing to Building C, or past it.

"I'm going to find out," Eric said, and shoved the door open.

"*We'll* find out," she said. "Everyone needs someone watching them."

She was right. Eric could use the help, and someone to back up his story if anything went down. He'd rather have her by his side than on her own in this viper pit.

"Let's go." They slipped through the door that led out of Building B into the cavern surrounding it. Climbing down the steps, they moved quickly but quietly.

Eric led them through the narrow alley between the exterior of the building and the stone wall toward the rear tunnel.

The way that Drumm had been gesturing when he talked to Chilton, and the location of the exit Chilton had taken made Eric suspect that Chilton was heading for the back of Building C or beyond it in the rear tunnel. Eric and the others hadn't had a chance to search that area before the comms and doors went down.

Turning the corner from Cavern B into the rear tunnel, Eric led them north, keeping his gun ready as they moved through a dark stretch between the overhead lights.

The water lapped beside them in the narrow canal that ran down the center of the tunnel for its entire length. Eric surveyed the back of Building C in its cavern, then noticed as Cody went ahead, her light trained to the north. He followed her toward the back of Building D.

There Cody stopped and shined her light on fine bits of gravel that had been scattered over the stone floor in the rear tunnel, the specks glinting. She looked to her left, slipping into the labyrinth of springs that supported Building D.

Eric moved into the dark behind her, pulse quickening as he studied the patches of grime and dust on the floor. By Cody's light, he could barely make out twin tracks of clean stone about hip width apart, as if someone had been dragged. They ended under the building, about forty feet in.

"Someone was pulled out of here," Eric said.

The evidence of violence braced him, sharpened his senses. There were no tracks indicating a fight, but that didn't mean anything. Much of the stone floor was clean enough that no traces would have remained if someone had been attacked there.

He followed the tracks back to the rear tunnel. They searched the floors, the metal walkway that bridged over the narrow canal, and the water, but there were no other signs.

Eric climbed the walkway, and wrapped his hand around the steel railing, covered in a faint oily sheen. He looked up and down the rear tunnel, listening in silence, but all he could hear was slow-moving water.

Cody fixed her light on something drifting in the canal, then crouched down and grabbed it, troubling the black mirror surface.

He came closer to her as she lifted it: a pocket pack of tissues swollen with water.

34

"MADDOX," ERIC SAID. He was always carrying packs of them for the president.

Cody's hands tightened on her weapon. Eric tried the radio. There was no reception. He toed some dirt off the edge of the stone and watched it flow with the water south toward Building B.

He turned in the other direction and walked upstream to trace where the tissues had come from. They moved to the north, ready for an attack at any moment. Eric peered into the shadows, straining to hear footsteps, but only caught the gentle movement of the water beside him as they passed Building E.

There the rear tunnel and the canal that ran down its center continued straight to the north, but ahead a small waterway branched off to the right at a ninety-degree angle. It entered a smaller tunnel, about fifteen feet high and ten feet wide, that had been bored through the eastern wall of this rear tunnel.

Eric approached it and shined his light to his right, down that smaller tunnel. He remembered from the facility map that it led to the reservoir that had been carved out of the stone to the east.

A faint shiny patch in the smaller tunnel caught his attention.

He looked back and met eyes with Cody. She'd seen it too.

He led them over the canal on a low metal bridge and approached the mouth of the smaller tunnel.

Cody covered their rear. "If you get in close with anyone," she whispered, "go for the face so they can't blend back in later."

Eric nodded. Brutal and smart. She had probably been thinking about what else she could have done in her fight against the attackers at the White House.

Holding his light along the barrel of his MP5, Eric went into the smaller tunnel. A stream of water flowed down the middle of it, like a sewer tunnel, leaving him a narrow space to walk. It wouldn't give him much room to cover the angles or dodge if someone came at them.

He knelt and examined the spot he'd noticed before, a wet streak through the dust as if someone had smeared drops of moisture with a boot. He touched his finger to it and examined the color under his light—a blackish red.

The skin prickled on the back of his neck. "Blood."

"Covered up?"

"Looks like."

Another try on the radio. No response.

He waved her forward and pressed deeper into the passage. The air was damp and musty, growing cooler with each step as they advanced. The sound of water lapping came from ahead, echoing as if in a great space. Eric trained his light on another smear of blood, then looked back to the mouth of this tunnel where they had first entered, far behind them now.

Cody glanced at him, her face pale in the blue-white glow of his flashlight, and they continued. He could make out the end of the tunnel. He shined his light through and glimpsed where it opened into a much larger space—a wide stretch of water like an underground lake.

They reached it and stepped into a massive, dimly lit cavern. It was rectangular in shape, about the size of a high school football stadium. The sound of every footstep reflected off the tall stone walls.

This was the reservoir. Pumps churned in the background. Concrete pillars rose from the surface of the water every forty feet, climbing toward the ceiling, where they supported vaulted arches. The place felt to Eric like a flooded cathedral.

They were on a stone walkway that ran along the edge of the water, beside the walls of the reservoir's cavern. Grated metal walkways extended from it over the surface of the water, allowing access to pumping equipment closer to the middle of the reservoir.

Cody looked to him, and he pointed to the right along the walkway. Keeping close to the wall, he circled the edge of the cavern.

Drip.

Eric brought up his MP5. The sound was faint and not surprising in a place with millions of gallons of water. He scanned for its source but couldn't place it, then kept on along the edge, searching the greenstone below his feet and the concrete walls for further signs of a blood trail.

Drip.

The sound was closer as they reached the back of the reservoir, the eastern wall. The walkway was wider along this edge, and to his right a set of wide pipes and valves with twenty-inch-diameter wheels ran along the wall. Water coursed through them, and he trained his light on the junction boxes and machine room doors.

Drip.

Looking forty feet ahead between the pipes, he caught it: a red glimmer along the base of a panel, and at the bottom, a drop growing fatter.

He came close to Cody.

"Did you see it?" he whispered.

"No."

"There. Blood."

He moved forward, working his way around the machinery, his heartbeat a fast murmur in his throat and ears. The drop fell, and he came closer. As he approached the source of the drip, he cut to the right and aimed his gun behind a tall metal enclosure. Clear.

He squared up to the panel, MP5 trained on the worn powder coating. It was about three by five feet, a vertical rectangle set in the wall.

He pointed Cody to his left, to open the latch while he covered whatever was inside, then stood, gun ready.

She reached for the latch.

He nodded.

She pulled it open, and he lit it up, his flashlight filling the crypt-like space. A body lay crumpled on the concrete floor: Will Maddox, his throat cut. Eric stepped in, crouching through the entrance. He heard Cody taking short breaths behind him.

It was a crawlspace about twelve feet deep, with a set of valve controls and narrower pipes running in conduit racks along one wall.

He knew Maddox was gone, but the training automatically took him through the next steps: feeling the still arteries in his neck and pulling back the lid to reveal a dilated, glassy eye. He worked methodically, even as rage burned under his skin at seeing this young man's life splashed out on the dirty floor.

There was no sign of the portfolio he'd been carrying when he left the president's side or the red letter that could be used to invoke the emergency laws. Eric checked his pockets quickly and found only a wallet, an energy bar, and a White House pen.

He touched the back of his hand to Maddox's cheek. Warm. Whoever killed him might have just left or was still in the reservoir.

He turned, and saw Cody looking in. Her throat worked, but her face showed no reaction as he climbed out.

"He's gone," Eric said.

"Chilton did this?" Her voice was cold. The anger surged through Eric again, a desperate need to act, to move, to answer this crime.

"He was out in the tunnels. He would have had time." Eric thought through the motives. Maddox and Chilton could both have been involved in the president's power-grab plot. Maddox tried to back out or blow the whistle, and Chilton took him down. It tracked. But so did the possibility that the attackers were simply taking out the president's people as part of a coup. Eric stepped out and scanned the reservoir.

He pressed the button on his radio. Nothing.

Eric searched with his light, left to right through the cavern. There were blind spots, places to hide behind the pillars and pumping equipment. "The killer could still be here."

He glanced back at the blood, how far it had spread, figured the timing. "They're close."

Cody's eyes widened, and Eric continued north along the wall, looking behind every possible source of concealment. He went around the corner, along the northern wall now. Fifty feet later, he paused. Cody was hanging back, staring across the water.

He trained his light in that direction and saw nothing.

Cody gestured to her ear as she came closer. She'd heard something. Eric strained to pick it up but caught only machinery churning and their own breath.

Then footsteps, coming from the tunnel that had led them here.

It was the only way in and out.

35

AGENT CODY STARED at him, her face half-shadowed. He pointed two fingers forward, and they continued, moving silently and slowly. They advanced toward the entrance, rounding the last corner to walk along the western wall. That brought them all the way around the edge of the cavern and back to the smaller tunnel that had brought them here.

Eric stopped just beside its rough-cut entrance, listening for another sign of the attacker. Cody put her left hand on his shoulder, keeping the gun up in her right. That was how they had been taught to stack when breaching buildings or fighting in close quarters. They could move by touch through any darkness or chaos.

Eric went fast into the tunnel. The walkways on either side of the running water were only a few feet wide, and his shoulder brushed the damp stone with every step. There was no room to hide or evade an attack.

They scanned left and right, but the tunnel was empty. He trained his light through the water—clear.

They walked on, the air growing warmer, sweat soaking into his clothes. He slowed before they reached the end of the passage.

White light spilled toward them from around the corner, where this tunnel joined the rear tunnel at a ninety-degree angle. It came from the south and looked like the beam of a flashlight held low to the ground, but it was perfectly still.

As they neared it, he caught movement, a shadow shifting along the floor of the rear tunnel ahead.

Eric sprang forward, aiming his gun and light around the corner to command the space. Cody followed, low and to his left.

Chilton lay on the stone floor of the rear tunnel beside the canal, eyes wide to the ceiling, his hand and arm dangling in the water, swaying with the current, throwing a shadow onto the wall. The flashlight rested between him and Eric, its beam illuminating the fallen chief.

They both took aim, pure reaction, but he didn't move. Chilton's face was serene. Two thin red lines, like straight quotation marks an inch tall, stood on his shirt over his heart. Two well-placed stabs would have bled him out in seconds.

Eric swept his gun up and down the rear tunnel, but there was no one, no sound, no light. The water was clear.

He crouched and reached for Chilton's throat while Cody covered them. No pulse. Eric checked his watch, then pointed south down the rear tunnel and started racing in that direction, the only way the killer could have escaped.

He peered into the distance as he ran, but could only see a few hundred yards in the dim light and hazy air. Advancing with Cody, he tried to spot the attacker before he could make it south to Building E, where he could disappear under its foundations.

As he moved, Eric thought through the people who had come from the White House capable of this kind of violence. It could have been any of the other four Secret Service agents besides him and Cody. The president was perhaps physically able, but it was almost impossible to imagine him doing this. Nate Chen, the doctor, and Paul Eubanks, the military aide, certainly had the strength and experience. And there were two dozen officers on Drumm's staff.

They soon neared Building E in its cavern, and he scanned to his right to search beneath it.

Footsteps sounded to the south, far down the rear tunnel. They took off toward the noise. The attacker was heading toward Building B, where the other agents and Kline's people remained.

They kept a fast pace, their guard up for ambushes as they passed the dozen places a killer could hide. Eric caught a figure darting along the side of the tunnel far ahead near Building B.

He sprinted after, his feet pounding the hard stone as he passed Building D, then C. He was closing the distance but there were no more signs of the attacker.

He slowed as he reached the back of Building B in its cavern.

Sweat dripped down his temples. He spun slowly, looking along the barrel of the submachine gun. He could see all the way to the southern end of the rear tunnel now, where the power plant was located. There was no one.

He and Cody looked under the foundations of Building B.

"Why come this way?" she asked. "They're going after the president?"

Eric looked up at the back of Building B, three stories tall, the sheer gray façade of the structure that housed the war room and the commander in chief's suite.

"Or returning to their post."

36

ERIC TRIED TO raise the president's people on his radio. He had to stand close to the back of Building B to get through.

"Hill, where are you?" It was Agent Leigh's voice.

"Rear tunnel. Just outside B," he said. "Lock it down."

"What's happening?" Leigh asked.

"There's a threat loose. Let no one in or out."

He ducked into the alley between the north side of Building B and the stone cavern that surrounded it.

"Meet me at door T-2 on the north side," he said to Leigh, "the door Cody and I left through."

He and Cody scanned the springs under the building with their lights as they approached the steps to the exterior door.

"We'll get the other agents and search?" Cody asked.

"After we confirm where they were."

She stopped short. "You think one of them was the killer?"

"We can't rule it out," Eric said.

"What the hell is happening?"

"One explanation: the attackers are going after the president. They killed Maddox and Chilton to stop Kline from getting a message out."

"Or?" she asked.

"Chilton and Maddox were trying to stop a power grab by the president and Kline's own people took them out."

"Which people?" she asked as they climbed the steps.

"Could be other agents, or the military aide, even the doctor. They all have the training."

"Or it could be one of Drumm's comms people."

The lock slid back, and the door opened.

Leigh stood there, her gun angled across her body, and Brimley came up beside her. "Hill, what's happening?" she asked.

Eric looked past her to see Givens, keeping her distance, watching Eric warily as she pulled her shawl tight around her shoulders.

"We found Maddox's body," Eric said. "He was killed. Chilton too. We tracked the threat back to this area."

"What!" Leigh said, her face stricken.

Brimley took a step toward Cody. "You all right?"

"I'm good."

"Where did this happen?" Givens asked.

"Maddox's body was in the reservoir past E," Eric said. "It looked like he was attacked under D and dragged there. Chilton was killed in the last ten minutes at the northern end of the rear tunnel, just outside the entrance to the reservoir."

"Jesus Christ," Brimley said.

"Tell me everything," Givens said.

"We don't have time," Eric replied. "The threat is here. The killers came toward this building."

"You don't have time?" Givens's flash of indignation passed quickly. She was calculating, the risk sinking in.

"Who is inside?" Eric asked. "And did anyone leave?"

Givens simply blinked at him. "Are you implying that one of our own people might be responsible?"

"I need to know. We're in here with a killer."

"No one went anywhere."

"Who do you have inside?"

"The president, the first lady, Eubanks the military aide, and Dr. Chen."

"And Brimley and I were patrolling the perimeter hallways," Leigh said.

"Separately?"

"At times," she said. "With radio checks every minute or two, and we saw each other every . . ."

"No longer than five minutes," Brimley said.

Eric looked to Givens "You talked to them too?"

"We heard it," Givens said. "We were close enough to get snatches of radio reception."

Eric watched all of them. There was no hesitation, no mutual glances of fear or coordination.

"No one came or left?"

"One of us would have heard it," Brimley said. Eric thought back to how he had caught the sound of the door opening when Chilton headed out.

"You can lock yourselves in?" he asked Givens.

"Yes."

"I could use Brimley and Leigh on the search. Are you good with that? We can arm Chen and Eubanks with the backup MP5s for the president's protection."

Agents Brimley and Leigh exchanged a look.

"We already have," Givens said, and then added to the agents: "Go get them. We'll be all right."

"The president and the first lady are okay?"

Givens nodded. "They're locked in the living quarters."

"Do not let any agents in the suite alone," Eric said. "Don't let Drumm or any of his people in until we've cleared them. Stay in the suite until we come back."

"It's one of us?" Givens asked.

"It could be. Caution is how we keep our people alive."

She remained inside as Brimley and Leigh stepped out of B onto the metal steps. The door closed and locked behind them.

37

ERIC AND CODY climbed down to the floor of the B cavern and started walking west in its alley, toward the main tunnel. Cody came up beside Eric. He slowed to let the others go ahead so they could talk without being overheard. "They're all clean," she said.

"Or they're covering for each other," he said. "But that doesn't track." He glanced at Leigh.

"What is it?" Cody asked.

"Agent Leigh's been acting strangely recently. Did you notice her fingernails?"

"Cut to the quick."

"Much shorter than usual. Maybe biting them and covering it up. Stress, well before all this started. Keep an eye on her. We need to check out where Hardwick and Walsh and Drumm and his staff were too."

Eric had never seen eye to eye with Agent Walsh, and his inflated sense of self-importance could make him susceptible to being drawn into a plot.

He stepped into the lead, and they continued west in the narrow alley between the building's springs and the wall of Cavern B until they reached the main tunnel.

They went north. Across from Building C in the main tunnel, Hardwick patrolled near a group of comms staffers and engineers at work on the emergency exit tunnel that had collapsed in the second blast.

Hardwick and Drumm approached Eric and he told them about the killings. Their reactions struck him as genuine.

"Are we safe?" Drumm asked, now wearing a small bandage on the hand that had been cut.

"No," Eric said, looking over the crew. It was about half of Drumm's people.

"Any progress here?" Eric asked.

"No. The whole damn thing collapsed."

"Your other staffers are with Walsh?"

"Yes, checking on the southern blast doors."

"Which buildings are occupied?" Eric asked.

"We have a handful of my staff in Building E, the comms center, and some of yours are in Building B, and that's it. Since we're on a skeleton crew, the others are shut down except for the infirmary in Building C. That's always ready."

"I want you to get your people here. All of them."

"The radios can't make it that far without the repeaters," Drumm said. "But I can use the public address." He pointed to a PA call box on the wall just north of them. "It's for emergencies . . ." Eric's eyes opened wide. This certainly fucking qualified.

"Right," Drumm said, and strode toward it. Eric had noticed similar call boxes located throughout the bunker.

Hardwick confirmed that none of Drumm's people had left this area since they started working on the exit. A moment later, Drumm's voice spoke out over the public address, filling the tunnel, calling Walsh and his crew back.

Eric noticed Agent Leigh glancing at him as she talked to Brimley. He went over.

"What's up?" he asked her.

"We should be on the move, finding whoever did this," Leigh said. "This buddy system stuff where we're all watching each other is too slow."

"We sit tight until we account for everyone."

She gave him a hard look. She didn't like the suspicion of their own people.

Three minutes later, headlights approached from the southern end of the tunnel. Walsh and Major Moro pulled up in trucks with the rest of Drumm's crew in the cabs and beds. Eric did a quick count. It was all of them. Drumm went over to explain the situation to Moro while Eric pulled Agent Walsh aside, told him about the killings, and asked whether all these people had been with him for the last hour.

"Every one," Walsh said. The news of the deaths left him with a hard, angry look, and he shifted his weight from foot to foot. The guy looked like he wanted action, revenge. They had made no progress on opening the southern blast doors.

Eric and Cody went to Cammel to double-check that no one else was missing. He confirmed it based on the rosters and entry and exit logs. Cammel's security officer, a tall captain named Foster who listened carefully and said little, explained that there was no way he could conceive of someone getting in without being cleared and on those lists.

Eric quietly asked them whether Agents Walsh and Hardwick had been with them when Chilton was killed. Foster said they had been close by the entire time. Eric took the logs from him and stepped away with Cody.

"There has to be someone else inside," she said to him.

"Or someone is lying."

There were thirty-five people now locked in Raven Rock. Eleven had come from the White House and twenty-four, Drumm and his staff, were already down here when they arrived.

Eric looked over the list:

- James Kline: President of the United States
- Sarah Kline: First Lady of the United States
- Nathan Chen: White House Doctor
- Claire Givens: White House Chief of Staff
- Paul Eubanks: Military Aide to the President
- Will Maddox: President Kline's Personal Aide
- Benjamin Chilton: Special Agent in Charge, Presidential Protective Division
- Eric Hill: Secret Service Agent
- Michael Hardwick: Secret Service Agent
- Laura Leigh: Secret Service Agent
- Liam Walsh: Secret Service Agent
- Samuel Brimley: Secret Service Agent
- Amber Cody: Secret Service Agent

With Maddox and Chilton killed, only eleven of the White House thirteen remained. He scanned down the names of the Raven Rock personnel, all of them officers, including Bruce Drumm and Major Moro.

He was trapped in one of the strongest vaults in the world with a killer, or killers. They could easily be standing within feet of him. They'd already sabotaged the exits and all communication and murdered two people. Given that there had been an attack at the White House as well, he was more suspicious of the agents and the president's people.

Eric studied their faces, calculating, accounting for who had backed up whose story.

He started breaking them into groups. He and Agent Leigh would be in one team, Agents Walsh and Brimley with Cammel in the second, and Agents Hardwick and Cody with Moro in the third. The comms staffers he split between the three groups. He and Leigh would take half of Cammel's crew from the southern door to search the reservoir and do evidence and body recovery.

Only the Secret Service agents had weapons. The president would remain locked in his suite in Building B, under guard by Chen and Eubanks.

If the killer was here, he was working with others to back up his story. He made sure that no one was with someone who could have lied to establish his or her alibi during the Chilton killing, and that he had two agents watching each of the comms crews.

Eric ordered them all to stay in their groups, with no one going off on his own, and for everyone to account for everyone's movements at all times.

The implication was clear enough: the attacker was one of them. He saw a lot of uneasy faces as he spoke.

No one would be able to stab anyone in the back. It was a grim ops plan, but he had no other choice.

38

ERIC SENT THE other teams, one led by Brimley and one by Hardwick, out to sweep the tunnels with instructions to meet back in front of Building C. Then he took Agent Leigh and his crew of comms staffers toward the bodies.

He set an hour for the search, and they saw no further traces of the attackers as they navigated through the tunnels to the reservoir. Eric and Leigh, like all agents, had done turns in the law enforcement sections of the Service and were trained in forensic recovery. They looked for any trace of the killer—fibers, blood under the nails—but both victims were remarkably clean.

Drumm had retrieved two body bags from the infirmary inside Building C and given them to Eric before he headed out.

The handles of the bag dug into the calluses on Eric's palms as he and three comms staffers brought Maddox's body back to the infirmary, with Leigh and three others carrying Chilton's corpse behind him.

The other crews returned within a minute of the rendezvous time, watching the body bags solemnly. Hardwick and Brimley reported to Eric—no sign of the attackers, and all was well with the president and his people in Building B.

Eric had Drumm lead them through the corridors of Building C to the infirmary. He called Agents Cody, Hardwick, and Brimley in with him to examine the corpses—the latter two had the most forensic experience. Moro and the other comms and engineering staffers would remain outside with the other agents watching them and come up with next steps on how to get doors open or find another way out.

Eric and his team moved through the infirmary waiting area into a treatment room, and laid the bodies down on the one operating table and a lab bench against the wall. Eric unzipped them both for Hardwick and Brimley to examine.

Brimley started with Chilton, lifting his head slightly to show scraping along the back of his skull. Hardwick looked at the face of his dead chief, subtly crossed himself, then pointed to faint bruising along the side of his mouth.

"Someone gets a hand over his mouth, slams him to the ground on his back, then two stabs to the heart. He'd be done in a few seconds."

"Shouldn't our attacker be covered in blood?" Cody asked.

Brimley examined the stab wounds. "Not if he hit the vena cava and laid him back. The blood pressure is lower there." He shook his head. "We're dealing with a pro. This is surgical."

"He'd have to be strong. And quiet to get that close."

"Or Chilton knew him."

"Or her," Cody said.

The older agents looked up, and Brimley nodded. She was right. Eric didn't know if she was just reminding them to keep an open mind or pointing a finger at someone specifically. There was only one woman down here with the experience to do something like this: Agent Leigh.

Eric thought back to when Maddox had been attacked. Leigh and Chilton were the closest agents and Leigh had seemed defensive about the precautions Eric had been taking against an inside threat. She'd been stressed recently where once she had been the most easygoing agent on the team. He would have to question her about it, carefully.

Eric walked over to Maddox's body. He glanced to Cody, staring at her friend's face, her look of pity slowly giving way to anger.

"Maddox was most likely attacked near Building D around 1030 hours," Eric said. A little less than five hours ago. "That's when we heard him call out over the radio. Assume at least two killers, given his weight and the fact that they appeared to carry and drag him at least part of the way. We noticed the drag marks starting near the back of D and they led us up the rear tunnel to where the body was stashed in the reservoir."

"Killed there or under D?" Hardwick asked.

"In the reservoir, based on the volume of blood and body temp."

Hardwick looked back and forth between the two corpses. "What were they both doing out there on their own?"

"Maddox was carrying a message from the president to transmit through the comms center. He had a portfolio with him, now gone, that could have held the PEADs and the red letter," Eric said. "We don't know what Chilton was doing, but he went to some lengths to keep it secret."

"We need to talk to Givens and the president," Brimley said. "See if Chilton was acting on their orders and what he was tasked with."

Eric had noticed Chilton talking to Drumm and pointing to Building C shortly before he went out in the tunnels. The engineer probably knew something about what Chilton was up to out there. "Would you get Drumm?" Eric asked Cody.

She stepped out and came back with Drumm a moment later. He swallowed when he saw the faces of the dead. Eric took him aside.

"What did Chilton talk to you about, right before we left you at the emergency exit tunnel? I saw you two gesturing toward Building C, as if you were giving him instructions."

Drumm kneaded his right hand with his left. "I can't say."

Eric leveled his eyes at him. "People are dying, Bruce. What was he doing back there?"

"I'm sorry. He had me swear to keep it in confidence."

"For the president?"

"I really . . . he was very clear."

Eric needed those answers. He turned up the pressure. "With everything happening, I would counsel you against withholding evidence. You were the last one to see Maddox alive?"

"What?" Drumm said, staring back stunned.

Eric heard footsteps coming up the hall. He readied his weapon and stepped out to see Dr. Chen coming his way, the MP5 hanging from his shoulder. He moved with it so naturally, but the president's doctor shouldn't be armed for battle. It troubled Eric. So did the fact that Eric didn't have his pistol or backup gun. Chilton had limited everyone to MP5s so there would be no concealable weapons in the bunker.

"What's going on?" Eric asked Chen.

"Givens and Kline sent me. We need you back at B."

39

THE BODIES WOULD remain in the infirmary. Eric left Brimley and Walsh at Building C to watch Drumm's people, and each other. He gathered the other agents—Leigh, Hardwick, and Cody—and started walking with Chen to B, scouring for threats, searching behind every parked truck and mechanical structure along the main tunnel's western wall.

Chen brought them inside B and back to the executive office area, where he radioed to Givens inside. "We wait here," he said, and stood beside the door to the president's suite like a sentry, seemingly guarding against the agents.

Leigh hung near the back of the offices, watching the exits with her gun down. She stood there, picking her thumbnail against the edge of her MP5's grip over and over. A minute later, she slipped out the door.

"Stay here," Eric told the others, and went after her, tracking her toward the mess hall. She went inside and Eric stepped through the door as it closed. He approached her quietly. She was standing in front of one of the open cabinets, her gun slung over her shoulder.

When she turned around, an MRE in her hand, she flinched at the sight of him and dropped it to the floor.

"Jesus, Hill," she said. "Not a good time to be sneaking up on people."

Leaning down, he picked up the packet and handed it to her. "You all right?"

"Fine," she said, and held up the pouch. "Starving."

"Go ahead," he said.

"Did you eat?"

"Grabbed something before," he said. "I thought I saw some instant coffee in there, though. You want one?"

"Sure," she said.

He wanted her at ease. Sharing a drink would help. She opened the meal—Chili and Macaroni—and took out the crackers while he poured a plastic envelope of coffee crystals into a Styrofoam cup, filled it from the hot water tap on the water dispenser to her right, and passed it to her.

"What the hell is happening, Hill?" she asked as the crystals turned from mud into smooth black liquid.

"I don't know. You didn't see anything suspicious when Chilton left? Anything since?"

"No," she said, and nodded back toward the offices. "You mean besides the president and his people hunkering down in there with their own armed guards?"

"Chilton didn't say why he called you in or where he was going?"

"No."

He let the silence work on Leigh as she picked at the crackers.

"Chilton and Maddox," she said. He watched her, waited for her to go on. "How does anyone knife two people in *here*?" She shook her head. "I saw them huddling with the president, before Maddox went out. Maddox was on edge. They were in on whatever Kline is up to and now they're dead."

"What do you think happened?"

She shut her eyes. "I don't know. But this whole thing is so sketchy. That's an alternate military command center. They can do whatever they want from there."

"You think that's part of it?"

"His crew is so tight. They go back years. Have you heard that Kline was more than some paper pusher at CIA?"

Eric just raised an eyebrow and let her talk.

"That some of his official bio is a cover story and he was actually part of the directorate of operations?" she asked.

"He's dangerous?" Eric replied. The idea that the president was a secret agent sounded like more conspiracy nonsense, but Kline had been remarkably calm during the attack at the White House.

He wanted to hear her take on all this. If she had evidence that Kline had staged the attacks or taken out Maddox and Chilton as part of a power grab, Eric needed to hear it. And if she was part of a clique trying to stop the president and his people, Eric had to know that too. They might be traitors or heroes, depending on how far they would go, their methods and justifications. She could be part of the group that the president warned about—The Order. She could even have played a role in killing Maddox or Chilton as part of the maneuvering against Kline.

With two of the president's people dead, it was hard to believe Kline was behind the violence, but it was possible. For now Eric would listen, play along, keep her trust until he understood what part she played. The danger was being drawn into sedition.

"He has the PEADs down here," she said. "Martial law. Absolute power. The plans are all in place. All he needs is a crisis."

She held her hands out, indicating everything around them, and looked straight at him: the crisis was here.

"So he's been planning this for a long time?" Eric said, dropping his voice, playing the conspirator to keep her talking. "He was behind everything that happened at the White House to get us down here?"

"It's a perfect setup," she said. She seemed to be restraining an agitated energy. Her wide eyes and close talk made him increasingly on guard that she was part of an attack on the president. "Look at what happened to Rivas and Stiles. The crash."

He waited. She glanced around the room and came closer.

"You know there's evidence, right?"

"Evidence?"

"That Kline was behind the death of those two agents. The candidate they were protecting wasn't the target. Agent Rivas was. He'd seen something he shouldn't have."

That notion chilled Eric. He thought of the suspicions Navarro had shared just before he was attacked. "You think the same thing happened to Navarro?"

"I don't know."

"You've seen this evidence?"

She hesitated. "We can't trust Kline and his people, Hill."

"What is it?"

"We shouldn't talk here," she said.

"Where are you getting all of this, Leigh? What's your source?"

No answer.

"Citizen?"

He watched her eyes, blinking too much. Nerves. Was it because she was afraid of the threats against her, or fearful of incriminating herself as part of a plot?

Eric stood there as the steam rose from her coffee, waiting for her to give up something real in all these endless suspicions and countersuspicions.

"Who's Citizen, Leigh? Are they in here?"

He could be talking to Citizen right now. Her chest rose and fell. She went to say something, then stopped.

Eric leaned in. "Are you part of—"

The door banged open, and Chen stepped in. He watched them for a moment before he spoke. "Hill, you're up."

40

ERIC LOOKED FROM Chen to Leigh. Had he come in to stop them from talking, from coordinating?

"What's going on?" Eric asked the doctor.

"You're on with Givens."

The chief of staff wanted him alone; Leigh gave him a warning look.

"Sure thing," Eric said. He wasn't going to get anything else out of her with Chen hovering nearby.

The doctor escorted them back to the executive offices, seeming uncomfortable in his role as armed security. The other agents were posted near the doors. Eric looked around, his concern rising. Cody was missing.

When they were halfway across the suite, the door opened and Claire Givens stepped out, with Agent Cody walking beside her. The scene had a post-interrogation vibe.

Cody's eyes met his briefly. She had let her off-the-job personality show more with Eric, but she was still very buttoned-up around the others.

The chief of staff seemed to be taking statements from people separately. On the face of it, that was good procedure. It meant that Eric was a suspect, but he should be. He'd found the bodies.

Givens brought him to an empty office on the side of the suite and shut the door. She laid a pen and small leather-bound journal on the desk. She always carried them, though she took notes sparingly.

"We need to get this under control, Hill. What is happening?"

That was Givens's style. Everything could be managed. The woman could turn three separate political crises into opportunities in one day and still be home in time for a perfect family dinner. But the strain was showing in her hollow look and drawn shoulders.

"Everyone has an alibi," Eric said. He explained the circumstances of Maddox's and Chilton's killings and how their bodies were now being refrigerated in the infirmary storeroom in Building C. Then he walked her through everything he'd learned from questioning the other agents and Drumm and Moro's people.

"Someone is lying," she said.

"Or the attacker got inside without us knowing it."

"So now it's an outsider."

"The bottom line is we're in here with the killers. Assume at least two and they have had time to turn this place into a trap. Everyone's a suspect until proven otherwise. But we need to regain the initiative—"

"How did you find the bodies?" she asked.

Eric stared at her for a moment, then explained the tracks he'd found, the blood trail, and the sounds that brought him to Chilton.

"Chilton ordered you and the others to guard this area. You disobeyed that and went out on your own."

"I did. That's the only reason we found him. With respect, if you and he had listened to me at the White House, those two men might be alive right now."

Her lips tightened. "And where were you when Maddox was attacked?"

"In the mess hall with Cody."

Givens nodded. "You've known her for a long time, worked with her father, yes?"

Eric could have laughed at the idea that Cody was in on it with him. "Yes, I have. But I saw two other agents within a minute. So count me out on Maddox, but it is possible I could have gotten to Chilton, and Cody is the only one to confirm my story about finding his body, so you can keep some suspicion on us as a pair."

"You seem to be going out of your way to incriminate yourself."

"We need to think straight here. Now, what were Chilton and Maddox doing out there on their own? What orders were worth their lives?"

"That's enough for now," she said.

Eric bristled. "What are you hiding, Givens?"

"Nothing, but you should pose those questions to the president."

"I will. Get me in there."

A contented smile. "Sure thing. He wanted to talk to you one-on-one," she said. "Wait here."

41

GIVENS SLIPPED THE pen into her notebook and walked out. At the office door, Eric watched her return to the entrance to the presidential suite, where Dr. Chen ushered her through.

Eric approached Cody, who was standing by the corner to his right. She tracked him, a bit of wariness in her eyes.

"It's all good," he said. Clearly Givens had asked her to confirm Eric's story. He didn't want Cody thinking she'd ratted him out. "You holding up?" he asked.

"I should have slept when I had the chance. There's no way now."

"We can figure something out."

"I'm all right," she said.

He nodded, but his eyes were on Hardwick, who kept glancing back to Agent Leigh on the far side of the room, watching her without letting on. Eric excused himself from Cody, then walked over to Hardwick.

"Did you see anything before the killings went down?"

Hardwick thought for a minute. He was the last guy on earth to talk shit. "No," he said. Another pause. "Did Leigh say anything to you? Anything off?"

"Like?"

Hardwick frowned, but didn't answer.

"Something about evidence against Kline? The crash?" Eric asked.

"She talked about it with you?"

"Yeah," Eric said. "Did she read you in on any of it?"

"No. And with everything going on . . . it doesn't sit right with me that she's bringing that stuff up . . . putting people against the president. Do you buy it? That Kline could be orchestrating all of this?"

"If I could see this evidence, I'd consider it, but two of his confidants were killed. Maybe they were part of something and got spooked." Eric sighed. "But that's a farther leap for me than the idea that someone's out to get him. What's your read?"

He patted his hand on the barrel of his gun. "This I understand. It's the fucking politics that's lethal. Be careful."

Eric peered down the hall and saw Agent Leigh watching them. Her eyes broke away as soon as she saw Eric looking.

"POTUS wants to talk to me," Eric said to Hardwick. "One-on-one."

"That doesn't sound good." A faint smile. "You missing desk duty yet?"

"Swinging a hammer somewhere is sounding better and better."

Eric heard a door open and turned. Givens stepped out, and waved him over.

Hardwick gave him a *good luck* look, and Eric went to the chief of staff.

Givens brought him down the corridor in silence and waited outside the steel door to the president's suite. Chen stayed with them and radioed to be let in.

The door opened a moment later. Eubanks stood just inside, carrying an MP5 in his right hand and holding the nuclear football in his left.

"Your weapon," Chen said. Eric looked to Givens.

"Every precaution," she said.

Eric moved closer to Eubanks and both he and Chen raised their guns slightly.

Eric looked over the two men, then unslung his MP5 and handed it over. They led him through a small reception area, though the desk where an assistant might have sat was empty.

Givens gestured for Eric to go ahead, and the two armed men walked just behind him on either side, doing a good job staying out of each other's lines of fire if they had to light up Eric.

The doors ahead were matched oak. They stepped through them into a large open room, with a conference area set off behind glass, and a few workstations to his right. Coffee cups and water bottles littered the desktops.

Givens approached a door on the right, decorated with the presidential seal, and knocked. A lock slid back, and Kline opened it.

"Come in," he said, and waved Eric through. Givens and the two others started to follow him, and Kline held up his hand.

The armed men paused, unsure, looking to the chief of staff for guidance.

"It's fine," Kline said, his frustration with his minders showing.

Eric stepped inside and Kline shut the door behind him.

This part of the suite looked like a dated, squared-off version of the Oval Office. A pair of silk sofas faced each other across a coffee table and a massive mahogany desk stood at the end of the room. Eric's eyes lingered on the corner, where a barely visible door in the paneling allowed the president easy access to the war room.

"Have a seat." Kline pointed to one of the sofas as he walked toward the desk.

"I'll stand if it's all the same, sir."

Kline turned around in front of the desk and crossed his arms, his usual pose in meetings. Something felt off to Eric about sitting there while Kline stood over him.

"Whatever you like."

Eric stood at ease beside the sofa and looked over the desk.

The red letter lay just to Kline's right.

42

KLINE FOLLOWED ERIC'S eyes to the document. "Everything all right?"

"Fine, sir."

"Givens caught me up on your work since the bodies were found." A deep breath, and he went on, all old-school stoicism. "So we have multiple insiders covering for each other, or this place was somehow infiltrated by an outside threat?"

"Or both. Though Drumm and Moro tell me an infiltration is impossible," Eric said.

"Unless someone helped them get in."

"True."

His eyes bore into Eric, but he showed no emotion about the news. "There could be collusion between agents and Drumm's staff?"

"It's possible."

Kline shook his head and laughed darkly. "Maybe it's everyone. You. Me. Have you ever read *The Man Who Was Thursday*? By Chesterton?"

"A long time ago."

"It's the same approach no matter what's happening: we trust no one."

"Exactly."

He ran his fingers along his jaw, and Eric noticed his eyes going toward the door behind Eric that led to the living quarters. They had brought him here to keep him safe, and now he and his wife were under threat.

"How do we find them?" Kline asked.

"Stop the bleeding first."

The president waited.

"This is an ongoing attack. They appear to be targeting you and your people, and in particular trying to stop them from whatever mission you had sent them out on."

Eric couldn't question the president as a suspect, but there were other ways to get the information he needed.

No response. Eric went on. "What were Chilton and Maddox doing out there alone?"

"They were trying to communicate with the national security adviser or the Pentagon."

"How?"

"Drumm suggested to us there might be other ways to talk to the top."

"They worked?"

"I don't know. They never came back."

"What was the message?"

"First was a question. Was the government still standing? We've been locked down here incommunicado for hours. The VP must know something is wrong. Has he taken charge? Are the attacks here part of a broader campaign to seize power in Washington?"

"You had instructions for Maddox and Chilton to pass on if you could get through?"

"That would depend on the situation. The least we could do would be to give the authorities evidence about the conspiracy against us."

"What evidence?"

"That the attackers are inside Raven Rock, which narrows down the list of potential suspects dramatically. We wanted to get out any information we could, help find who else the plotters might be working with, anything to help the people up top head this off."

"Did you send Maddox and Chilton out to invoke the presidential emergency directives?"

"No."

"The red letter was here the whole time?"

Kline gave him a withering look, as if the answer was obvious. "Yes."

It also could have been taken from Maddox's body and brought back here, though if that was true, Eric doubted Kline would have left it out in the open.

"Why all the secrecy?" Eric asked. Chilton had gone to great lengths to escape the president's suite unseen.

"I sent them solo because I didn't know who would stab them in the back and I couldn't risk the attackers discovering and eliminating our last means to talk to the top. I wasn't careful enough."

"What are those means?"

Kline looked at him knowingly. "Trust no one, right?"

"Right. Do you know why Will Maddox might have been acting out of character recently? Fearful? Edgy?"

"Look at what's happening. It would have been strange if he hadn't been."

Eric nodded, but he could see that the question had gotten to Kline. He was holding something back.

"You said we stop the bleeding," Kline asked. "How?"

"Bring everyone together, in one place. Everyone watches everyone. No room to maneuver. Then we find a way out or a way to get a message to the top to tell the Army Corps of Engineers to blow the doors off Raven Rock."

"We simply sit here eye to eye with the killers? They just stabbed two men to death. We're in their trap."

"You stay locked down in this suite. We can question the others one by one, find those we trust, and sweep the whole bunker sector by sector. There may be some way to close off sections after we clear them. Then we can hunt the attackers down and eliminate them."

"You've given this a lot of thought."

"It's the only way forward I see."

"You were the first to find both bodies."

"Yes." Eric had told his story. He didn't need to launch into a defense.

"We talked to Cody."

"Good."

"A lot of people told me not to trust you, Eric." Kline stared at him. "There was talk about how you ended up on that desk."

"That's fine. You shouldn't be trusting anyone."

Kline didn't say a thing. It was like he was waiting for Eric to explain himself, but what happened that night with Alexander Braun, the Treasury secretary, wasn't Eric's story to tell, and he assumed that Kline knew everything anyway.

"All right," Kline said, and pressed a button on his desk. He took a step toward Eric as the door opened, and Chen walked in, his gun hanging by his side. Givens stood in the doorway.

"Hill is in charge of security now that Chilton is gone," the president announced to the chief of staff. "He'll give you next steps."

That threw Eric for a moment. He looked to the president.

"I trust you on this, Hill. Find them."

He was being brought into the president's inner circle, where Maddox and Chilton had once stood. The one thing more unsettling than Kline's suspicions was his trust.

43

GIVENS AND CHEN led him out. Based on her facial expression, Chief of Staff Givens was furious that Eric was being put in charge, but she was diplomatic about it. "Let me know what you need," she told him in a clipped tone.

The doctor gave Eric his gun back as they walked down the hallway and returned to the executive offices where the other agents were waiting.

Cody pulled him aside. "Kline tapped *you*?" she said.

"I know."

"I felt like a damn witness at your trial when Givens talked to me."

"Don't sweat it. I want you to go outside into the main tunnel and radio to Walsh and Brimley. It's a straight shot and they should be in range. Have them bring Drumm, Moro, and all their people back here to the mess hall. No exceptions, no objections. Everyone."

"Understood," she said, and moved out.

Hardwick walked over and Eric explained the plan to gather everyone here in Building B.

"Do we have any gear down here to check hands and clothes for explosives residue?" Eric asked.

Hardwick shook his head.

"Okay, when the comms folks get back, I want you and Brimley to patrol the hallways around the presidential suite and the war room."

Hardwick glanced across the room at Leigh. "For people trying to get in or trying to get out?"

"Both," Eric said.

A long look from Hardwick at the door that led to the presidential suite. "He puts you in charge after everything that happened?"

"Yeah. I'm glad he's listening to me, but I don't like it."

"I don't even know why you're in here . . . no offense."

"None taken. I assumed it was because I proved myself during the attack at the White House. Who made the call to bring me? Chilton?"

"I don't think so. He was pretty against it."

"Givens is no fan."

"And there's no way you charmed anyone."

"Maybe Brimley put a word in for me. Or O'Hara before she stayed behind at the White House." The press secretary was Eric's closest ally among the president's people.

"Or Kline wanted me down here the whole time for some reason."

"I don't know, but sidekick to POTUS . . ." Hardwick shook his head. "You'd be safer clearing mines."

44

AGENT CODY RETURNED ten minutes later with Drumm's people and the two agents, Brimley and Walsh, who had been guarding them at Building C. Eric grabbed Agents Leigh and Hardwick and brought everyone into the mess hall.

"This is all of them," Drumm said. Eric did a quick count to confirm all twenty-four officers were present.

The Secret Service agents walked them over to the tables in the dining facility, doing a fair job concealing the fact that they were essentially prison guards.

Eric paced across the linoleum, met eyes with a bearlike comms officer chewing a ballpoint pen, then addressed them all.

"You know by now that there is a security breach and two people from the executive branch have been killed. We are locking down for everyone's safety until we find the suspects." He tried to use some bureaucratic army-speak to keep the officers at ease. "The process here is to eliminate the risk by treating everyone with an appropriate level of caution, an inside-threat protocol."

Murmurs from a few of Drumm's people. Eric made a note of their names and faces. "You're all Yankee White. You're the most well-trained, well-trusted professionals in government so know that this is not an accusation or a reflection on you. We're going to look out for each other. Simple as that. Anyone needs to leave this room, for any reason, you talk to me. Sit tight and feel free to get some coffee and chow."

He beckoned Drumm over and took him out of the others' earshot by the karaoke machine.

"We need a communication channel to the outside and we need an escape route. What's realistic?"

Drumm seemed hesitant to speak.

"Kline put me in charge here," Eric said. "He told me Chilton was trying for an alternate way to talk to the top. What is it?"

"We were going to try tapping into the comms lines closer to where they lead to the surface."

"You were going to meet him?"

"Yes, I was going to show him a couple of places behind Building C in the rear tunnel where you can access the lines directly. I was waiting for him to radio so I could help with the technical side of it, but he never called."

"Could we still talk to the top through those lines?"

Drumm shook his head. "I had my people check. They were all taken out at the same time as the emergency exit tunnel."

"Who could have gotten to it?" Eric asked, looking around the room.

"Anyone. It was a small explosive charge. It could have been planted five minutes ago or hidden for weeks."

"That kind of knowledge points to one of your people."

He pressed his lips together. "It does."

"And escape?"

Drumm walked him through the status of the blast doors. They had been sabotaged, with the massive bolts securing them stuck in locked positions. The emergency pedestrian exit across from C in the main tunnel was hopeless, completely caved in.

"We're sealed in here," Eric said.

"They spent billions to make sure no one could breach this place. That works both ways."

"But."

Drumm put his hands on his hips and took a deep breath. Eric could tell that whatever he was about to propose was a reach.

"There was an old tunnel from the original excavation in the fifties, very rough and unreinforced. It was filled in, but getting through that would probably be easier than trying to cut through the blast doors or dig out the emergency exit. Even if it did work, it would be barely wide enough for one person to get out."

"What will it take?"

"Some demolition through thick concrete."

"Do you have explosives down here?"

"No."

"Weapons?"

"Some pistols in a safe in Building E. I'm the only one with the code."

"So the attackers sneaked in explosives."

"They must have."

"Then we should assume they have weapons too. What about getting out through air intakes and exhausts?"

"They all run through a pattern of narrow holes, each about four inches wide and hundreds of feet long, drilled through solid rock. Picture a honey-comb."

"We're good on air?" Eric asked. He could taste the exhaust even inside the building, and the temperature was at least in the high seventies.

"We should be. The venting systems appeared to have taken some dam-age. They were never perfect, but it will be livable for days."

Days, Eric thought. *This could go that long.* They'd only been down here for eight and a half hours.

"I want you to scout that old construction tunnel and any other system that we might be able to use to communicate," he told Drumm, "even if you have to jury-rig something."

Eric looked over the crowd. Most were still standing, talking quietly in small groups, the agents eyeing Drumm's men with suspicion and vice versa.

"Give me the names of a few men and women you absolutely trust," Eric said. "We'll clear them and get you a small work crew. Is there anyone we should be wary of? Don't point."

Drumm thought about it. "No one jumps to mind."

"Who's your biggest pain in the ass?"

Every unit had one, and they were nearly impossible to get rid of in the big army bureaucracy. Drumm told him to check out the officer chewing gum at the second table from the back.

"How bad?"

"Garden variety. Shirking, always complaining. Nothing on the order of this. Who's the pain in your crew?" Drumm asked.

Eric looked over the officer, then faced Drumm. "That'd be me."

He studied the comms staffers, noting who clung together and who was watching him too closely. The intensity of the situation was good. It would force reactions, get them to drop their guards.

"I want schematics for the entire facility and personnel files on everyone."

Drumm nodded. "Moro brought a laptop over from the comms center. I can pull them up."

"Good, thanks," Eric said.

Drumm walked off toward his deputy.

Eric brought Cody to a table far from the others and started briefing her on the next step, mapping out everyone's location at the critical moments—comms going down, Maddox's attack, Chilton's murder, and each explosion. He was already going through it in his head for those he knew, watching the individuals in the mess hall as he retraced their movements, building a map of the entire day in his mind.

He paused as he noticed a figure in the doorway: Givens checking on them, her eyes darting around like she'd stumbled into the lion's cage. As soon as Eric looked her way, she stepped out of view.

Moro brought the laptop over and showed Eric the maps and staff dossiers.

Eric looked across the room. He'd need Drumm's list of those he trusted, but the deputy commander was gone.

"What's up?" Cody asked.

"Drumm, where'd he go?"

"I saw him walking toward the doors," she said.

"Did Givens bring him to the presidential suite?"

"I don't know."

"Stay here," he said. "You and the other agents are on watch." He headed for the president's quarters, passed through the empty executive office area, and a minute later was standing outside the door to the Klines' suite.

Hardwick came around the corner.

"Did you see Drumm and Givens?" Eric asked.

"A minute ago. They went inside."

Eric knocked on the door, then radioed in.

A moment passed. He tried to raise them on the radio once again, then lifted his fist to pound on the door, but it opened first.

Givens stood just inside.

"Eric," she said, with a smile that put him on edge. "I was just coming to get you. The plans have changed."

45

GIVENS BROUGHT ERIC to the president's office with the same weapons protocol—Eric handing his gun over before Eubanks and Chen escorted him through the suite.

Drumm was already inside, seated on the sofa to the right. The president was leaning back against the desk, arms crossed.

"Eric, good," Kline said. "Apologies about the change-up. There was one possibility I wanted to check in with Drumm about and I think you should hear it."

Kline looked to the deputy commander and gave him a nod.

"There may be a way to get a message to the top. Very-low-frequency radio, VLF, for an over-the-horizon communication."

"You both knew about this before?"

"Drumm had mentioned something."

They had been holding back. "How does it work?"

"It was originally installed to be a survivable means of communication after a bolt-out-of-the-blue attack. Cold War, really, but it was never decommissioned."

"Is it in the communications center or here in the war room in B?"

"They're both cut off. We would have to access where the lines lead to the surface, inside the comms shaft that rises from the rear tunnel."

"Is that what Chilton was after when he was killed?"

"It's the same idea," Drumm said. "We were thinking of trying to tap into the normal communications lines then, but they are all totally down now. For this we'd actually have to climb the shaft. At the top we can tap into the cables that lead to the radio antennas at the peak of the mountain. It's a last resort.

"The downside is that it links directly to the National Military Command Center in the Pentagon through a very specific protocol. It was designed to be used only in the event of a nuclear strike or other catastrophe. It should still function, but we would have to spin up OPLAN PEADs to use it. It's all tied into the national command authority authentication."

"The Presidential Emergency Action Documents?"

Drumm nodded. "Just to prove the president's bona fides and get through. It's preferable to using the nuclear authentications." He glanced to Eubanks and the satchel in his right hand. "We do not want this place cleared hot to authorize nukes given everything going on."

Eric looked to Kline. "What happens after you trigger the PEADs?"

"I would only use it to authenticate. Then we call in the cavalry, as you suggested, to get those blast doors open from the outside, also pass on what we know about the attackers, and revoke my authority until I'm out of this."

"Sir?" Eric asked.

"I'm in a national military command center and the line of succession may have no idea I'm under attack. I need them to invoke the Twenty-Fifth Amendment if they haven't already and transfer my powers to Vice President Sutherland. We're down here with the nuclear football, a war room tied into Strategic Command, and a threat we don't fully understand. The codes are at risk of seizure and I'm at risk of coercion. That puts my wife in danger. She will be a target for hostage-taking and God knows what else until we revoke my authority."

Kline's face was solemn. Eric had never known a commander in chief to give up power. The Service had dealt with presidents near death's door—most famously Reagan after the 1981 assassination attempt; he was in a far graver condition than the public ever knew—and the first instinct was always to minimize the incident and hold on to the office.

"Where do we tap into the VLF line?" Eric asked.

"It's at the top of the comms shaft, off the rear tunnel behind Building D," Drumm said. "You have to climb the vertical access shaft to reach a crawlspace carved into the rock. I doubt anyone besides me and Moro even knows it exists. That's what I'm banking on."

"Sounds good," Eric said. "I'll go check it out."

"We should bring Drumm too, to handle the technical side," Kline said.

Eric still hadn't fully ruled out Drumm as a suspect. "We?" Eric asked. "You're not thinking of going."

"With respect," Kline said. "I'm not giving anyone these codes until we find out who is behind the attacks. I need to be there."

"You shouldn't leave the suite."

"I've decided, Eric. The order has to come from me."

"The last two men you sent on a comms run are dead."

"I can handle myself. We'll bring Chen and Eubanks as extra security."

"We have everyone under watch. We can find the attackers. There's time."

"They have this place wired up with explosives, and who knows what other means they've prepared to come after us," Kline said. "We need to act now. I won't risk being coerced or having these codes falling into their hands."

Eric didn't answer for a moment. This was what everyone who was suspicious of Kline feared. He was about to put the U.S. on a war footing and invoke absolute authority, then supposedly give it all away. It could be part of the setup, the final step in Operation V.

"When do you want to go?"

"Now," Kline said. "The sooner we get word topside, the sooner the rescue starts and the sooner we take the worst possibilities off the table. Then we only have to worry about our own survival."

46

ERIC WATCHED KLINE, taking his measure.

"Why do you trust me on this, sir?"

Kline gave him a half smile. "I don't trust anyone, but you're the best gun we have."

If this was happening, Eric wanted to be close to Kline, and armed. "Let's go," he said.

"Make sure the agents out front guard the entrances to the suite," Kline said, "but don't tell them we're leaving."

"Which way are we going out?" Eric asked.

"Leave that to me," the president said.

Eric held his hand out to Chen for his gun. He looked to Kline, who nodded. The doctor handed it over with a watchful expression.

Drumm mapped out the path to access the old VLF radio line. They would go north through the rear tunnel to where it intersected with Cavern D. From there they would climb into a tall vertical shaft that ran up from an opening in the roof of the rear tunnel. It carried cables toward the top of the mountain, where the radio towers stood.

Givens came back a few minutes later. "Everything's set up front."

Eric double-checked the action on his weapon. Drumm was looking around, probably for his gun. "We'll handle security. You deal with comms," Eric said.

He wasn't letting any of Drumm's people near a firearm. Eric pointed to the leather valise Eubanks carried. Many imagined the nuclear football having a red button or trigger inside that would start World War III, but it was much less dramatic than that. It held a binder featuring various launch options and their codes along with a satellite phone and other backup communications tools. They would let the president select and call in a nuclear response no matter where he was. Unless he was sealed underground.

Simply gaining access to the codes in that valise wasn't enough to order a nuclear strike. The president always carried a second set of codes on his body, in a thin plastic wallet-like device known as "the biscuit," which had to be cracked open to reveal the ciphers within. With the codes from the biscuit—called the gold codes—and the valise he could call in a launch.

"You're not bringing that," Eric said. "We can't have the codes and POTUS vulnerable."

Eubanks stiffened and gave Eric his Frankenstein's monster stare.

"Sir," he said to Kline in protest.

"He's right," the president said. Eubanks gave him the valise and Kline brought it into the living quarters. The military aide watched it go like someone had taken his child.

"There's a safe in there?" Eric asked Drumm.

"Yes. In the bedroom."

"Who has the combination?"

Eric stepped to his right for a better look inside. He saw Kline exiting the bedroom and pausing in the doorway, and he caught a glimpse of Sarah Kline's face inside. She looked as strong as always, but there was something in her eyes—sadness or fear. James Kline's head dipped slightly as he left her, then shut the bedroom door.

"Everything all right?" Givens asked.

"It's fine."

"Does she have the combination?" Eric asked.

Kline looked at him guardedly.

"I'm thinking about her safety, whether she's a target for coercion."

"No."

"Good," Eric said.

Kline led everyone into the living area of his apartment, which was decorated in late 1980s or early '90s florals and pastels. The president's quarters had been nicknamed the Lucy and Desi suite because its style had been stuck in the 1950s for decades and was always behind the times.

He stepped to the side and touched the chair rail near the corner of the room. He slid it to the right, with part of it disappearing into the wall. It revealed a small keypad, which Kline covered with his body as he entered a code. He pressed on the paneling and it swung outward, a hidden door in a thick steel frame. It led into a passage just tall enough for an adult to walk through comfortably. Conduit ran along its white walls and LEDs illuminated the space from above.

"Where does it exit?" Eric asked.

Kline pointed to a trapdoor set into the floor ten feet into the passage. "That hatch will let us drop underneath the building, where the springs are. We can go through them to the rear tunnel."

Eric stepped in to check the other side of the door. It was keypad-protected coming into the suite as well.

"All right," Eric said. "We'll set up in a diamond around POTUS once we're in the tunnels. Have you two done any close-quarters work?" he asked Chen and Eubanks.

They both nodded, Eubanks more hesitantly. Eric knew that Chen started out as a corpsman with the SEALs.

"Watch your muzzles," Eric said. "I'm in the lead in the diamond, Chen on the left, Eubanks in the back, and Drumm on the right." Drumm, unarmed, would mostly be facing a stone wall as they moved north in the rear tunnel. He carried a small bag of gear to start the transmission.

"We'll go silent," he said. "Stay close."

Everyone nodded, even Kline. Eric would rather have his own agents, but he wasn't even sure if he could trust them. He didn't like that the president's two men during all of this just happened to be well trained. But Eubanks and Chen had also been inside with POTUS and multiple other witnesses during the killings, which took some suspicion off them.

Eric stepped into the passage, still nagged by the idea that he might be riding along on a mission to give Kline absolute power. Eubanks and Chen followed like kill-house pros—never sweeping the others with their barrels.

Ten feet in, Drumm crouched down and unlocked the trapdoor. Eric stepped beside him, readied his weapon, then gave him the nod. The engineer pulled the hatch open, and Eric moved to the left, scanning through it. Clear.

Drumm took an escape ladder—rungs suspended on lengths of chain—from a box on the wall. He hooked it over the edge of the trapdoor as Eric slung his rifle over his shoulder.

Hill was the first man through, dropping quickly to the cavern floor. He scanned left and right, peering through the tall springs all around him, arranged in a grid under the building, spaced ten feet apart. They supported it from below and protected it from shocks.

The others climbed down and closed the hatch as Eric took a few steps to the east between the springs, toward the rear tunnel. It was two hundred feet away and Eric could make out its emergency lights at the far end of the forest of springs.

He heard careful footsteps behind him and the brush of MP5 slings over wool suit jackets. The others' breathing seemed so loud in the dark.

It was an eerie space, just tall enough for all of them to stand. They formed a close diamond around Kline and moved east between the springs toward the very back of the building's foundations. There the cavern that housed Building B met the rear tunnel, which ran perpendicular to it.

This space under the building was open on all sides, and Eric paused before he stepped out from among the springs to enter the rear tunnel, his last moment of cover.

He leaned out, and looked to the south in that tunnel, leading with his MP5. He saw no one.

He moved into the rear tunnel, an empty bore over a mile long. It carried the faint smell of exhaust, but felt so open compared to the cramped confines under B.

The strangeness of this place struck him again. The tunnel ran straight north and south as far as he could see, obscured by darkness in the distance. It was just as high and wide as Cavern B and all the other caverns, forty feet tall and eighty across at the floor. A long vehicular tunnel through a mountain was the most similar space he could picture from civilian life, though these bores were twice as big as the largest car tunnel he'd ever seen, and this one had the narrow canal running down the middle of it like an open sewer. The floors were smooth stone.

Eric glanced in the other direction, north, as Eubanks and Chen moved that way to guard that approach.

He stepped farther into the rear tunnel and thought he heard something behind him, far under Building B. He turned to see the mouth of Cavern B looming above and behind him.

It was like someone had taken the Lincoln Tunnel and built inside it a gray, windowless office building with a curved roof, filling the tunnel from entrance to exit while supporting the entire edifice on a foundation of springs. All five buildings, and the five caverns that housed them, were two thousand feet long. The buildings were a little over sixty feet wide, and three stories tall.

The sound again: a loud click. Eric raised his weapon.

Whoom. The noise boomed from deep in Cavern B.

Whoom.

Again. The sound hit him in the chest, like the pressure from an explosion. A red glow flashed through the cavern and the heat tightened his skin. A wall of churning fire raced toward them between the springs.

Eric grabbed the president as the flames moved closer with the sound of a jet engine.

Eubanks and Chen moved to the north, to escape that way in the rear tunnel. Eric rushed south with Kline. Drumm stood not far from Eubanks and Chen, mouth slightly open, staring as the flames closed in.

"Run!" Eric yelled.

47

THE FIRE BLOOMED from the back of Cavern B into the rear tunnel, rising to the full height of both bores.

Drumm and the others ran to the north in the rear tunnel, while Eric and Kline continued south.

The heat was unbearable. The air choked Eric with the smell of burning plastics.

The tunnel's ceiling liners ignited and dropped, twisting through the air toward them, the debris falling closer and closer.

"Get in the water!" Eric yelled.

He grabbed the shoulder of Kline's jacket and hauled him to the five-foot-wide canal as a steel bar dropped toward them. Eric shoved Kline out of the way, but it caught the president's arm. A grunt of pain came from his lips as Eric took a long step and pulled him over the edge.

They plunged into the warm, dark water. He stayed down, eyes closed as muffled crashes broke out all around him. Red light pressed through his eyelids.

Eric counted: one, two, three. Panic is the enemy when you're underwater, and marking the passage of time keeps it at bay. Even jacked on adrenaline, anyone could hold their breath for twenty seconds. He took three strokes to the south. A wave of pressure hit him as something crashed into the water. Heat pushed down from the surface.

He pulled Kline forward, ten or twenty feet by now, the count climbing to ten, then fifteen, his lungs shrinking into a hungry ball at the center of his chest.

He opened his eyes and felt the freshwater sting. It was clearer than he thought it would be, and looking up he could see the flames were behind them. He put his arm around Kline and kicked for the surface.

They broke through, and he saw the collapsed rubble, still burning, blocking off the rear tunnel to the north. The framing and liners had fallen in a towering pile behind Building B.

The building itself looked intact, though some if its shielding had been broken off to add to the wreckage.

Kline took a long breath, then coughed from the fumes. Eric reached for the edge of the canal, dragged himself out, and pulled the president from the water. He was breathing fast but able to stand on his own.

Eric cleared his weapon, drew the cocking handle back, and tilted the MP5 to drain any water from the chamber and barrel.

"Are you hurt?" Eric asked Kline, and started walking them to the south, away from the choking fumes.

Kline nodded, feeling along his left upper arm, wincing.

"Broken?"

"No. Bruised, maybe burned. I'm good. Where are the others?" he said. "Did anyone else make it out?"

Eric shined his light northward, looking through and past the wreckage behind B.

"Anyone?" Kline asked.

Eric paused, then walked to the north until the smoke stung his eyes, pushing him back.

"Eric," Kline said as Hill took a step to the side, looking for any signs of life. He couldn't leave them. A hand gripped his shoulder.

It was Kline, pointing to the flames crawling toward them from the north along the ceiling of the rear tunnel. They had to move before another collapse took them. Eric cast a glance back as the rubble behind B settled, sending out a plume of flame and sparks, then he turned and went south in the rear tunnel with Kline.

He scanned the path ahead with his light and gun as they advanced, then lowered the light so he could grab his radio.

"Keep your eyes open," Kline said. "I'll call."

Eric passed him the radio. Kline tried to raise anyone. On his third try a voice came back, distorted through the static.

"Mr. President. Are you okay?" It was Agent Leigh. She broke off cough-ing at the end of the transmission.

"I'm all right," Kline said. "I'm with Eric Hill. My wife, is she okay? The others?"

A burst of static. ". . . she's safe . . . we're okay. B is intact, but there's a lot of smoke . . ." More static. ". . . we're inside B . . . evacuating . . . the main tunnel is clear . . . where are you, sir?"

Eric ran his hand across his own throat.

Kline looked puzzled.

"Don't say it over an open line," Eric said.

Kline nodded. The fire may have been a way to flush him out, to give the attackers an opportunity to strike. Still, there was a flicker of distrust, as if he was worried Eric was trying to get him alone.

Agent Leigh went on, the reception getting worse. ". . . we are moving out of range, to the west, sir . . . need to clear this building . . . we'll be in the main tunnel . . ." Then her voice broke up.

Kline called out, tried to get her back, but she was gone.

"They're all right," the president said, holding the radio in disbelief.

Eric looked back. The fire had slowed its advance along the ceiling of the rear tunnel and appeared to be mostly behind them, but he wanted more distance. The path ahead, to the south, was clear.

"Was that a bomb?"

Eric nodded. "Incendiaries or gas." It didn't have the crack and sharp pressure wave of conventional explosives.

They had almost reached the back of Building A. Someone's voice came from behind them, a man's shout of pain to the north in the rear tunnel. Eric turned. It was coming from the far side of the rubble behind B. He focused his flashlight that way. The flames on the debris had died down.

Another cry. It didn't sound like a call for help from the injured. It sounded like someone being beaten.

He waved the president behind him, so he stood between Kline and the threat.

"Who is that?" Kline asked.

"It could be Eubanks, Chen, Drumm," Eric said.

"Separated from us by that wreckage?"

"Right. They probably made it clear to the north side of it."

"They're under attack," Kline said.

"We need to get you safe."

"What does that mean?"

"The diesel plant at the southern end of the rear tunnel. We can lock it. It's fireproof, a vault."

Kline shook his head.

"Sir, listen—"

"No. We can go under Building A and work our way north, through the passageways or the main tunnel, help those other agents and the people inside."

Eric looked at the wreckage. The pile behind B had settled. He might be able to make it through now, though the rear tunnel was still thick with smoke. But there was no way he was bringing the president toward the attackers.

Kline glared at him. "Sarah is back there." His voice was hard as slate.

"You have the codes," Eric said. "The authority. You can't get taken. They would have all the leverage. I'll take you to the diesel plant. You'll be safe there. The country will be safe with you there."

Kline glanced south down the tunnel, then back to Eric.

"Find my wife. Protect her and the others. I'll go to the plant and lock myself in."

Eric wanted to save those people as badly as Kline did, but the decades on the job had inculcated a basic rule: never leave the principal.

"Just go!" Kline said. "If you're worried about me, give me a weapon. Do you have a pistol?"

"No."

"Nothing. A knife?"

Eric had managed to get his inside even after Chilton tried to keep out any concealable weapons. Kline must have been able to tell Eric was carrying from his reaction. The president held his hand out.

Eric hesitated for a moment and then passed him his Benchmade. Kline flicked the blade open and weighed it in his hand.

"Here," Eric said. "Take my vest."

Kline held up his palm to stop him. "I'm good."

"You need it."

"Not as much as you do," he said, backing away. "Go. They're out there. There's no time."

Eric tried to convince him to take the body armor once more, but he refused, and headed south to the power plant.

Eric turned and started moving fast in the other direction.

48

ERIC HEARD THE pained voice once more as he moved north in the rear tunnel, approaching the wreckage behind Building B. The flames were now red embers glowing along the broken framing and shreds of liner. He held his breath as a black plume of smoke drifted past him.

He examined the wreckage where it had fallen across the narrow canal that ran down the center of the tunnel. Shining the light in, he saw that if he crouched under a fallen section of framing, he could pass to the north along the stone bank of the canal.

He moved in, staying low, the metal radiating heat, stinging his back as he stilled his chest and pressed on through the smoke. He rose on the far side, watching the embers near the ceiling for any further collapse. His light looked like a solid beam through the fumes.

He caught the contours ahead of an armed man, stooping down over another, dragging him along the ground. They were farther north in the rear tunnel, almost behind Building C. Eric ran toward them, raising his gun.

As Eric's light fixed on him, the figure turned and took aim with his MP5. Eric's finger tightened on the trigger. "Drop it!" he called.

"Hill?" the man shouted back. It was Eubanks.

"It's me," Eric said, moving forward, the smoke clearing.

Eubanks pointed the gun away, and Eric lowered his slightly, though both kept them at the ready. The military aide's uniform was soaked, and his lower lip was split.

"Chen is down!" he called out.

"From the collapse?" Eric asked, dropping to a knee beside the doctor, who was lying on his back on the stone. Eric kept his gun ready in case Eubanks had been part of the plot.

"We were attacked."

Chen's hair was matted, blood mingling with the water from the canal. They had jumped in to escape the fire too.

"Where's his weapon?" Eric asked.

"They must have taken it. We ran here from the fire, and they jumped us in the smoke."

"You didn't answer the radio call."

"We were moving. We could barely breathe."

"They went north," Chen said, his voice a whisper. The doctor closed his eyes, grimacing in pain.

Eric moved in close and spoke quietly enough that Eubanks wouldn't hear him: "Did Eubanks have anything to do with this?"

Chen shook his head. "No. He fought one off. He saved me."

"Did you see who it was?" Eric asked them both.

They shook their heads.

"Two attackers, maybe more," Eubanks said.

The knee of the doctor's pants was torn, the skin abraded underneath. "Can you move?" Eric asked.

Chen held his hand up, and Eric took it and helped him to his feet. He was shaky on his legs, but he could stand.

"Let's get them," Chen said.

A doubtful look from Eric.

"We need to find these bastards," the doctor said. "I'm good."

Eric waved Eubanks closer, and they each took one of Chen's arms over their shoulders. Eric shifted his rifle to his left hand. He was trained on both sides.

"Where's Drumm?"

"He went that way," Eubanks said, pointing west to the springs under Building C in its cavern. "He was going to get the emergency lights working and help the people from Building B."

They moved north up the rear tunnel past Cavern C. The attackers were close. Eric wanted nothing more than to find who was behind this and take them down before they could kill again. It pulled him forward, an overpowering physical need like hunger.

He caught a figure in the shadows a hundred yards up.

49

ERIC SHINED HIS light that way, but the man was gone.

There was decent cover ahead, a carve-out in the tunnel wall for a stand-pipe.

Eric brought them to it and they all stepped into the space, like a shallow open closet three feet deep, eight feet high, and spanning eight feet north to south along the tunnel wall. Chen put his hand to the stone to steady himself, touched his head where he'd taken the blow, and cursed.

"Stay with him," Eric said to Eubanks. "Back me up if I take fire." He killed his light so it wouldn't give him away, then moved out, hugging the left-hand wall, gun up, listening carefully, the rear tunnel lit only by the dim red glow of the flames behind him.

A faint scratching sound came from ahead. He hit his light and took aim as a figure ducked around the corner into Cavern D to the north.

Eric kept his aim steady, taking a few steps to the right to get a better angle.

"Friendly!" he called out. "It's Eric Hill. Secret Service."

Motion in the dark near the corner. Eric saw a barrel emerge, steadied the submachine gun, and took aim. As the man's shoulder appeared, Eric pulled the trigger.

Hill's gun bucked twice, then stopped in the middle of what was supposed to be a three-round burst. He was still seeing white from his muzzle flashes when he hauled on the cocking handle. It wouldn't move. Jammed. The goddamn water. That was why Eric always carried a sidearm and a backup gun, but Chilton's orders had left him with nothing.

Eric sprinted back—wide open and unarmed, advantage lost. The first crack of gunfire came for him. Three bullets hissed past, then sparked along the wall. He cut to the right, then leaped for cover beside Eubanks in the carve-out as more shots sailed by, just feet away.

Eubanks leaned out and laid down two bursts of suppressive fire.

"The bolt on this is frozen," Eric said, and glanced to the military aide's weapon. Eubanks handed his MP5 to the more experienced operator, took Eric's submachine gun, and pulled back on the cocking handle. Nothing.

"Pull the mag and try again. Harder," Eric said, and slipped to the front of the small carve-out, pressing against the stone to stay out of the line of fire. He inched to the side, ready to hit the shooter with a burst, but three shots thundered down the tunnel, exploding against the rock just beside him. He pressed back.

A light hit them. Pinned down.

"What the hell do we do now?" Eubanks asked, still trying to fix the malfunction.

Eric heard movement. They were closing in. He didn't have the angles to defend them, and this spot was so tight he would take a bullet as soon as he edged out.

Footsteps. Closer. He looked around for anything he could use for distraction or cover. He thought of trying to shoot down the lining material along the tunnel ceiling, intact here, but that would take dozens of rounds.

He fixed on the greenstone wall of the rear tunnel across from him as the man's movements grew louder. Eric squeezed past Eubanks and Chen to the southern side of the carve-out. That gave him a better angle as he sent three rounds across the tunnel, hitting the far side at a slant. Sparks flew as the bullets spalled and ricocheted off the rock wall.

No more sounds of movement. He sent another burst at a sharper angle, then heard a snarl of pain.

A rattle behind him. An ejected bullet casing skittered past his feet. Eubanks clicked the mag back in and shouldered the other MP5. He'd cleared it. Eric pointed ahead, leaned out with the gun. Eubanks backed him up.

As someone moved near Cavern D, they each shot at him. They heard retreating footsteps.

Eric emerged, pressing the advantage while Eubanks covered him from the carve-out. He crossed toward the water, getting some protection from a gray metal box—pumping machinery next to the canal that ran down the center of the tunnel. He advanced, looking for movement in the curls of smoke.

A beam of light shot toward him from the south. He turned and took aim.

"Hill! It's Hardwick! Friendly!" The other agent walked toward him out of the haze, gun up but aimed away. "You good?"

"Good!" Eric shouted back. "Shooter to the north."

Hardwick tracked toward him in a crouch, then took a knee beside a matching metal box to Eric's right, on the other side of the canal. He was just across from Eubanks and Chen, and dipped his head to acknowledge them.

"You came from the south?" Eric asked.

"Yeah. I made it out of Building B and then circled back to the rear tunnel under Building A."

"You saw POTUS?"

"No," Hardwick said. "He's solo?"

"Making for the diesel plant. It's secure."

"He must have already passed me by the time I hit the rear tunnel from A. Agent Cody is searching that way."

"Did everyone make it out?" Eric asked.

"Yes. A few injuries, no deaths. The smoke was bad inside B. We evacuated in the dark, looking for any exits we could."

"Where is everyone?"

"We tried to keep Drumm's people under watch, but we lost them in the chaos. They scattered toward the main tunnel, running for their lives really. Walsh is going after them."

"Dr. Kline and Givens?"

"Agents Brimley and Leigh are with them."

"Leigh?"

"Yes," Hardwick said. "We were cut off from them and the president's people by the fire, but we managed to connect over the radio. They told us to look for you all and POTUS back here."

Eric still had his doubts about Laura Leigh, but at least Brimley was with her.

"They need to find a secure place to hole up," Eric said.

"That's what they're doing, heading north in the main tunnel, looking for a safe spot in one of the buildings, C, D, or E. Brimley's been down here before. He'll take care of them."

Hardwick looked across to Chen, resting in the corner of the carve-out.

"I can get him someplace secure," Hardwick said.

"Building C?" Eric asked.

Hardwick glanced in that direction and shook his head. "The door to it from the rear tunnel was locked. I'll take him south. That way I can be certain POTUS and Cody are covered on their way to the power plant. You and Eubanks want to clear the rear tunnel to the north, then make sure the first lady and the others are all right?"

"That works," Eric said. He didn't want Kline and Cody back there without an experienced gun like Hardwick and he didn't want to give Leigh a chance to get Sarah Kline alone.

"You and Cody can take care of Chen and the president in the power plant," Eric said to Hardwick. "Stay there and once I get the lay of the land we'll figure out where to get everyone together. The radio still works over short distances and line of sight, and we can use the public address as a backup."

He gave him code words that they could call out over the PA to tell each other where they would meet—at the diesel plant or in Building C, D, or E.

"Nice work on that MP5," Eric said to Eubanks. "Ready?"

"Good to go."

Eric leaned out from behind the junction box, covering the tunnel ahead as Hardwick crossed and helped Chen to his feet. He came out supporting the doctor on his left, the gun in his right hand.

"Can you make it back through the wreckage behind B?" Eric asked him.

"I'm set," Hardwick said, then turned and started down the rear tunnel to the south.

"Come on," Eric said, and he and Eubanks moved north, hunting for the shooter. After a moment he glanced back, but Hardwick and Chen had already disappeared into the smoke.

50

AGENT CODY ADVANCED south through the dark rear tunnel, sweeping left and right with her MP5. She waved the president forward, and he followed. She still couldn't get over the surreal image of the president walking by her side with a knife in his hand, or the fact that she was guarding him solo.

"You're holding up okay, Agent Cody?"

"Fine, sir. Thank you." She'd never heard him speak so informally.

"Good. You're doing excellent work down here."

"I appreciate it, sir," she said, on edge nearly as much from being alone with him, solely responsible for his safety, as she was from the threats in these tunnels.

They'd been locked in since nine fifteen this morning, and she'd been up the whole night before, on duty at the White House. Her bones felt as heavy as lead from the fatigue, but the adrenaline kept her going.

She had spotted him moving south in the rear tunnel past Building A soon after she and Hardwick split up. Hardwick headed north toward the voices and the fire while she went south to search for survivors or more attackers. Cody came up to him with her gun pointed at his chest—he'd only been a silhouette ahead—and had apologized for it repeatedly. Taking aim at the leader of the free world seemed like a bad career move. Kline ultimately succeeded in reassuring her that it was okay; she was just doing her job.

The rear tunnel south of A was rough stone with no ceiling liners. The lamps overhead were still out.

She shined her light around her. It reflected off the water in the narrow canal that ran down the center of the tunnel, and she swallowed as the image of Maddox's corpse took over her mind. Now that she was one-on-one with Kline, she couldn't stop thinking about Eric's suspicions that the president was somehow behind all of this. It warred with her natural reverence for the man and the office.

She found herself slowing, and stepping to the side, always trying to keep Kline in her peripheral vision, lit by the reflected glow of her flashlight.

He stopped and started with her, watching her stride, and she wondered if he could pick up on the trace of fear. Her hand ached from squeezing her weapon so hard. They were trapped in the bowels of this mountain, in the dark, up against an unknown number of assailants.

The stone under their feet started to shake as they came closer to the diesel plant, and then the air itself vibrated with the sound.

Crack.

She spun and fixed on the noise. Gunfire. It had come from behind her, far to the north in this rear tunnel.

Br-r-rap.

She stepped toward it, her gun rising, aiming her light. All she could see was smoke and the glow of embers where the wreckage had piled up behind Building B. Eric Hill and Hardwick were that way.

Br-r-rap.

Kline faced the same direction. He looked to her. "You should go."

She glanced to the south, then back north.

"I can't leave you, sir."

He lifted the knife. Was he weighing coming with her?

"I'm fine," he said. "We're almost to the plant."

She licked her lips. Dry. "I'll stay with you, sir."

She beckoned him to follow her south to the diesel plant, where he could take cover, but he stood on that spot.

"I understand if you need to go back up the other agents."

She wanted nothing more, but the first duty was protecting the president.

And she had to wonder whether Kline would be happy to be alone, un-watched. Eric's wariness was getting to her, the fear and suspicions taking root so easily in her sleep-deprived mind.

"Thank you, sir. But this is the job. Please." She looked toward the plant. Kline nodded and they started moving.

51

THE POWER PLANT was a two-story steel structure housed in a smaller cavern that had been carved out of the stone to the east of the rear tunnel, to their left as they moved south. It still seemed strange to her, these edifices tucked into their stone alcoves, the hollow space and building inside it almost perfectly matched.

They crossed over the canal on a short steel bridge and approached the plant's double sliding doors. Kline punched in a code and told Cody to keep watch while he hauled back the right-hand door. Distant voices echoed from the north, but she couldn't make out what they were saying.

She went in first to clear the plant. Four diesel engines, each the size of a train car, shook near the center of the warehouse-like space. It was about forty feet wide and eighty feet deep.

She had expected it to be claustrophobic and full of exhaust, but the floors were spotless, painted a pale yellow like the walls, and the air was much cleaner than the tunnels outside with their drifting smoke.

"We're good, sir," she called out. Kline closed the knife, a thick Benchmade folder, with one hand, impressing her with his facility with the blade. He clipped it in his pocket and pulled the door shut, dropping low and using his legs to shift its heavy weight.

The chug of the engines shook her body, the sound almost disorienting her as it pounded her ears. Kline closed the latch on the door, then twisted a mechanism that drove locking rods into the floor and ceiling.

His shoulders fell after he secured it and he stood there, hand on the latch, breathing deeply, finally letting his guard down.

She noticed him favoring his right arm as he walked away, his lips tight with pain.

"Are you hurt?" she asked.

He flexed the left arm. "It's fine. A little well done, perhaps."

The emergency lights flickered, then came on.

"That's a good sign," Kline said.

Cody let her MP5 drop to the end of its sling and pointed across the floor to a small office area with a glass window that looked over the plant floor.

He walked to it and went inside. She expected him to rest in one of the chairs, but he leaned against the front of the desk.

She had seen photos of him standing that way in the Oval, and something about him using the same pose while in this diesel plant, still wet from his plunge into the canal, made her smile.

He looked down at how he was perched and let out a quiet laugh. "Just another day at the office. You said Leigh and Brimley were with my wife?"

Dr. Kline was the first thing he asked about when they had met near Building A.

"Yes, sir," she said. "And they are guarding Claire Givens too."

He nodded, but seemed unhappy with the arrangement. "And Walsh?"

"He's rounding up Drumm's people to get the lights back on and check the damage—"

"And watch them?"

"Yes, sir."

He touched his left arm and inhaled sharply.

"I can help with that, sir," she said. "Take a look or dress it."

"That's all right," he said. "But thank you. This is your first shift on the detail?"

"Yes, sir," she said, keeping her voice loud and steady.

"You would never know," he said. "I met your father a few times when I was in the Senate. One of the best agents we've ever had. He was an equestrian, right?"

"His favorite thing." They would ride together when they used to go visit family in California. Mesa Springs was a no-hope town, so hot and dry your lips would crack, but get ten miles out into the Sierra, on horseback among the pines, and the beauty would steal your breath. She hoped to see it again one day, to ride again, to make it out of this.

She couldn't believe Kline remembered him so well. He must have met hundreds of agents since her father served.

Kline nodded and smiled. "You'd have made him proud, Cody."

The compliment warmed her, but she was so exhausted she was still nervous about saying the wrong thing, uncomfortable under the president's gaze.

He pointed to her temple where she had taken the blow at the White House. "How is that?"

She brushed it with her fingers. Pain radiated out. "I barely notice it, sir."

"You were friends with Will Maddox?"

"I was."

"What a tragedy." He shook his head. "Did he talk to you about his work?"

"No specifics, sir." She rubbed her hand along the side of her neck. "What was he doing out there?"

The question came out before she'd had a chance to think it through.

"He didn't tell you anything? You didn't notice anything off about him?"

She thought of Maddox's nerves, the cell phones. It felt almost physically difficult to withhold from Kline. Those who haven't worked in the White House, or next to the president, couldn't understand the effect he had on people, the gravity of that power.

"You can trust me, you know," he said.

"Sir, no . . ." she said insistently. He looked at her hand, still on the grip of her gun. She relaxed it, let it fall.

"I know there are a lot of rumors out there. Have any of the other agents talked to you about me?"

"Sir?"

His eyes were on the gun now and she watched his hand. Was it closer to the pocket where he had put the knife?

"It's fine, Cody. You're not in trouble. Did anyone show you anything? Any kind of evidence?"

"Evidence, sir?"

A quiet laugh, as if it weren't worth mentioning. "That this is all a power grab." He held up his hands. "Or that I had something to do with the crash that killed Agents Rivas and Stiles?"

She shook her head. That felt less culpable than an outright no, a spoken untruth. Eric had talked to her about all of this, but she couldn't throw a fellow agent under the bus. Nor could she lie to the president. She had no idea what to do if he pressed.

"It's fine, Agent Cody. One of the reasons I brought you here is because you come from the outside. No one could have gotten to you . . . almost no one." He must have been thinking of Eric. "Who's passing this stuff around?"

Another noncommittal shake of her head. She couldn't deceive him, so she stood there, the words stalled in her throat.

"I realize this is all . . . terrifying," he said. "Though you don't seem very terrified. I may have gotten too relaxed with the protocols. I'd feel more comfortable, given everything that's going on, if you put down the gun. Over there."

"Sir, I don't doubt you. If I said anything—"

"It's a precaution," he said firmly. "You're fine, Agent Cody. I'm simply being careful here. Please."

She looked down at the MP5.

"If anyone comes after you . . ."

"It'll be close," he said, and his eyes went to the cabinet along the wall of the room.

Some part of her questioned it, and her training made it hard to put down her weapon, but obeying the command came automatically. She slipped the sling off her shoulder, walked over, and laid it on top of the gray metal.

"Thank you," he said. "Now—"

Three clangs echoed through the space. A barely audible voice came through the main doors to the outside. Her eyes went to the gun, as did Kline's. He'd even moved toward it.

The president hesitated, then nodded. She retrieved the weapon and led him out of the office.

As they came closer to the front, three more bangs sounded, and then a muffled voice.

"It's Hardwick!"

Kline stepped to the side. She looked to him, and he nodded, pointing her to a spot on the right that would give a good angle on the door.

"Is it clear?" Kline called out.

"Yes. I have Chen with me. He's hurt," Hardwick answered.

Kline listened intently, seeming to verify the voice, then pulled back the locking rods and opened the latch for the doors. He slid it open, peering out. The tunnel looked pure black now that their eyes were accustomed to the lights inside.

Hardwick stood supporting Chen, the doctor's head down, blood matting his hair.

"Nate!" Kline said.

"I'll be okay," he said, his voice weak. "Concussion. Bleeding's under control."

As Hardwick brought him inside, Cody scanned behind them. Kline shut and secured the door.

"What was all the shooting?" Kline asked as he helped carry the injured doctor toward the office. "Anyone down?"

"No. Eubanks and Hill took fire from the attackers. They're all right. They're closing in on the shooters."

"They need backup?" Cody asked.

"Yes. Cody, you go north up the rear tunnel and link up with Hill and Eubanks. Help them find those gunmen and make sure the first lady and the others are secure."

"On it," she said. Her time with the president had left her shaken, unsure what exactly just happened, whether she had seen through him or simply ruined her credibility and even her career by revealing her suspicions of Kline. She felt more comfortable facing down guns than politicians.

"I'll set up security here," Hardwick said, easing Chen down so he could sit on the ground with his back to the wall. Hardwick crouched and checked the doctor's injury. "We'll get everyone together under one watch once it's safe."

Cody looked to Kline for assent.

He gave her a nod. She tried to see if she'd angered him by withholding before, but he seemed fine. He was just being careful about everyone and everything.

"You all right on your own?" Hardwick asked.

"A hundred percent," she said as she raised the bolts on the door and opened it. Hardwick put his hand on her shoulder. "Excellent work, Cody. Stay safe out there."

"I will, thanks," she said, and stepped into the dark. The door clanged shut and locked behind her.

52

HARDWICK SECURED AND double-checked the latch on the door as Kline walked back to the office inside the diesel plant.

The president went to the doctor, his eyes closed now, his chest slowly rising and falling. "Is it okay to sleep?" he asked softly. "With the concussion?"

Chen opened his eyes wide. "My pupils. Dilated?"

"No."

"I'm good," he mumbled, and closed them again.

Hardwick came back and watched Chen as he drifted off, his head resting to the side.

"That's okay?"

"He said so."

"I don't love that, but . . . doctor's orders."

Chen stirred slightly, and that seemed to satisfy Hardwick.

"My wife is safe?"

"Yes. She made it out."

"Leigh and Brimley, how do you know we can trust them with her?"

"They both have decades in the service."

That wasn't enough for Kline.

"And Cody, Hill, and Eubanks will back them up," Hardwick said.

"I want those three to go to her and Givens straightaway. Can you radio Cody to make that clear, while she's still in range?"

"Yes, sir. I'll check these other doors too."

"Cody already did."

"Peace of mind," Hardwick said.

He stepped out, turned right past one of the massive diesel engines, and disappeared.

Chen let out a faint sound of pain, and Kline crouched down and put his hand on his shoulder.

"You all right?"

A "yes," not much more than a sigh, came from Chen. Kline waited with him for another minute until he fell back to sleep, then walked into the main area of the power plant. He went by an engine, with its massive flywheel spinning, then a generator, wired up with power cables as thick as his thumb. He could hear steam and water churning through the cooling pipes around it. The heat pressed through his clothes and stung the burnt skin on his shoulder.

He looked to his right, but Hardwick wasn't there. He passed a second engine and saw him on the far side of the warehouse, the radio up to his ear. Hardwick turned with a start when Kline came closer, his free hand moving toward his gun.

A smile. A raised hand. "Apologies, sir," he said as he lowered the radio.

Kline could barely hear him this close to the engines. The noise had covered his approach and let him startle Hardwick.

The president led him away from the diesels, where they could talk without yelling. It seemed odd that Hardwick had radioed over there among the roar of the engines.

"Cody will grab Eric Hill and check on Dr. Kline, sir."

"You got through?" Kline asked. Cody hadn't been able to raise anyone.

"Barely."

"Good," Kline said. "Thank you." He should have felt relieved, but he wasn't. "We're lucky to have you, Hardwick. Are you doing all right?"

"Fine, sir."

"How are Ellie and the girls?"

Hardwick had been dating her for perhaps two years as Kline recalled, a nurse practitioner with two daughters from a past marriage.

"Doing well, sir." There was something businesslike about his manner, not what Kline expected. Usually the agents appreciated a moment to lower their guards and talk guy-to-guy.

"Well good. We'll have you back home soon."

Hardwick glanced down at the president's pocket, where the clip of Hill's knife was visible.

"Eric sent you out on your own, sir?"

"I wanted a gun, but there were none to spare."

"You shoot?"

"I do all right."

Something was off about Hardwick's manner and that radio call. Kline shouldn't have left himself alone with just one agent, but he had been focused on getting help to his wife and the others. He was suddenly very conscious of the gold codes he carried in his pocket.

"You went to Hill and Eubanks after they took fire, and then came back here?"

"Correct. I wanted to get Chen to safety and make sure you were set."

"We're secure?" Kline asked.

"Absolutely."

Kline's eyes went to the MP5. "Then you can put the gun over there," he said, pointing to a console near the wall.

Hardwick didn't answer. Kline took a step toward him, and he tightened his grip on the gun.

"I'm afraid I can't do that, sir."

53

AGENT CODY FELT the air getting warmer as she walked north in the rear tunnel. Bands of smoke drifted past her and the emergency lights that had come on overhead weren't able to provide much illumination.

She kept her gun up, and held her flashlight parallel to the barrel, sweeping the space as she continued on.

She scanned under the foundations of Building A in its cavern and saw nothing. The fires ahead had died down to embers among the wreckage, though the fumes still hurt her lungs.

She stepped back to take a few last clean breaths before she went through the smoldering debris behind Building B. Looking back, she could still hear the thrum of the power plant where she had left the president, Hardwick, and Chen.

Something was nagging at her. Hardwick had walked away from a firefight, and then sent her into it. She thought through the sequence. It made sense he would want to get Chen to safety. She could see him wanting to take the lead on the president's security, but she couldn't imagine Hardwick sending her into action in his place.

She looked north through the smoke. An order was an order. Just go. But as she stood there, a tight feeling grew in her stomach.

Eric's words came back to her: *Trust no one.*

She turned around.

Her nerves grew worse as she tracked back toward the plant, and she didn't know whether it was from being alone among these threats or from going against an order. Her heart was pounding by the time she neared its doors.

She took two deep breaths as she approached them and tried to think of what she would say. If she told them that security dictated keeping two agents with POTUS, it would sound like insubordination and an insult to Hardwick. She would simply start by saying she needed clarity on the orders, whether to go straight for Hill or—

A crack sounded from inside the plant, loud even over the engines' racket. It was a gunshot—a blast and a *tink* of metal on metal as a round hit the wall inside. She shouldered her weapon and ran for the door.

54

HARDWICK'S FACE WAS apologetic as he said he couldn't give up his weapon.

"It's fine," Kline said. "It'll be right there."

"Not with what we're facing. I . . . can't. It's hard to convey the connection between a soldier and his weapon under the circumstances."

Kline had been under guard for a long time now. He'd grown completely accustomed to having Secret Service agents by his side or outside his room night and day. Now he only noticed when they weren't there. He was trying to articulate to himself what was off about Hardwick's manner, and then he realized it. Hardwick had been facing him, keeping him in view the entire time. Kline was used to having the agents surrounding him, between him and the threat, always looking at their backs. But Hardwick had eyes on him as if Kline was the threat.

"I understand that, Agent Hardwick, but go ahead and put it over there."

"No. I'm sorry, sir."

Kline felt a warm rush pass along his skin, the hairs rising.

"I get it," he said, lifting one hand in a reassuring gesture. He could feel the heft of the knife in his right pocket and turned that side slightly away from Hardwick, concealing the motions of his hand as he inched closer.

"Stop there," Hardwick said.

"What?"

"Don't come any closer. It's for your safety."

So much for the dance, Kline thought. Hardwick knew he knew.

"Why did you do it, Michael?"

Hardwick played confused, even as his hands tightened on the gun.

A leaden sickness grew in the president's belly as he watched the MP5 rise, not aiming at him yet, but close.

"Why would you betray your oath? Turn on your own government?"

Hardwick stood as straight as a Marine guard, took a breath in, then spoke in an authoritative tone.

"Sir, we can do this calmly and peacefully. I am relieving you of command until such time as the Congress may by law provide—"

"Peacefully?" Kline said, the anger twisting his face. "You've killed two people down here. You left Navarro to die. How could you do this? Are they threatening Ellie? We can help."

"I swore an oath to the Constitution, not to you. If that means I have to sacrifice my career, or my life, to stop you from violating the supreme law of this nation, so be it. But I'm asking you, for the good of this country, not to resist and to ask the other agents to stand down. And I will need the codes you carry."

Kline raised both palms and took three steps away from Hardwick, moving closer to the main door though it was still twenty feet off. No way he could escape in time.

"Where are you getting all of this, Michael, this poison?"

"Don't lie to me, sir. Give me that much respect. You know what you did."

"You're a good man, an exemplary agent. I can't understand it. Who got to you? What did they tell you?"

"You ordered the death of Julian Rivas, because he was too close to the truth."

Rivas and Hardwick were like brothers, Kline knew. He had nothing to do with his death, but it must have put Hardwick on tilt, corrupted his judgment.

"I did no such thing. What truth? Honestly. I just want to know what delusion is driving all of this."

"You're going to take control. Rule by fiat. Round up anyone who suspects what you did. Anyone who stands in your way. If I weren't here, you would walk down to that war room, invoke some secret law, and just like that"—he snapped his fingers—"America as we know it is gone. You and the others will not be harmed. But you have to tell me the truth."

"The truth is you're a traitor, and worse, another man's tool. So this is Operation V? You lure me here and lock me up, start a coup. Citizen—do you even know who he is? Who's spreading this garbage? Whose orders you're following?"

Hardwick looked to the door. He had probably radioed out to his accomplices to help him take Kline—the repeaters that boosted radio signals must have still worked for those in on the plan—but now he was out of time.

"You have politicians on your side?" Kline asked. "Members of Congress? What is happening in Washington?"

Hardwick raised the MP5.

"Get on your knees. You're going to lie on your stomach, cross your ankles, and put your hands behind your head."

Kline just stared back. "What exactly are you planning to do?"

"We're going to the command center in Building B. The people need to understand what's happening. There will be an orderly transition."

"You want to do a broadcast from the studio in the war room?"

He nodded. There was some small relief in knowing that Building B was intact enough that the war room still functioned.

"A fucking show trial?" Kline said. "At the point of a gun? Look at yourself."

"Get down."

"How many of you are there?"

Hardwick aimed the gun at his face. Kline stared down the black hole of the barrel.

"You won't kill me," Kline said, stepping to the side.

"Get down."

"No."

Hardwick came closer, left hand tight on the stock of the submachine gun. Kline moved back until his shoulder blade hit the shaking steel of the diesel engine.

"Down!" Hardwick shouted. Kline had nowhere to go. He looked over Hardwick's shoulder, as if he saw someone coming.

A glance back from Hardwick. Kline lifted his right foot, then drove it down onto a hose leading from the base of the engine. A cloud of steam and water droplets blew out, the heat swallowing his foot for an instant as he lunged to the side. No shots. He heard Hardwick groan as the vapors hit him.

Kline ran for the exit, pulled the bolts and the latch open, and shoved the heavy steel door to the side.

Hardwick stepped out of the cloud of steam, stalking toward him, his teeth gritted in pain, MP5 leveled at Kline's chest.

"You won't," the president said.

Crack. The gun spat fire. A bullet rang against the steel door to Kline's right. The blast forced his eyes closed for a second and when he looked back Hardwick had the sights fixed on his head.

"I will."

Kline forced himself to focus solely on Hardwick and show fear, but he could see that Chen had gotten up and was slipping behind Hardwick while carrying a fire extinguisher, straining to keep his balance.

"All right," Kline said, and raised his hands. Hardwick heard the doctor approaching, but it was too late. Chen was already driving the extinguisher through the air. It connected with Hardwick's temple, a *thock* like a good break in billiards.

Hardwick stumbled to the left, and Chen tried to move in, but his balance was off from the blow. Hardwick caught himself and stayed upright, dodged another swing of the extinguisher, then threw the stock of the MP5 into the side of Chen's head. He dropped, instantly unconscious. His head hit the floor with a sickening crack.

Hardwick aimed the gun at the fallen doctor. Kline ran for the door, for the narrow black opening. He lunged through, banging his shoulder against the metal, nearly losing his balance.

Agent Cody stood outside, twenty feet away, her gun aimed straight at him.

55

CODY STEPPED BACK, tracking the figure that banged through the open door to the plant. It was President Kline, scrambling toward her, shielding his eyes from her light. She aimed her gun away and he moved closer tentatively, his hands out to the side as if to show he was no threat. He was acting like she might shoot him at the slightest provocation.

"Sir, what's happening?" she called out.

His eyes went to the door, then to her, calculating. She turned her weapon toward the opening as a shadow crossed the light within the plant.

"It's Hardwick," Kline said, moving to her side, looking for protection. "He took a shot at me. He's one of the attackers."

"Hardwick?" she asked in disbelief as she caught the silhouette through the door—a man carrying a gun.

"Yes," Kline said, still putting distance between them, moving up the tunnel.

"Halt there!" she called out to Hardwick. "The exit is covered."

"Do not listen to him, Cody!" Hardwick shouted. "He's behind all of it. He went after Chen to keep him from talking. I tried to stop him."

The president's fear. The two men, one with a gun and one without. She understood what was happening, but still Hardwick's voice had power over her. Her superior. The badge she had known and respected since she was a child. Her teeth ground together.

"Put it down, then we can talk," she called out, then looked back to the president. He waved her toward him and she nodded, slipping backward and to the side so that she could keep her eye on the door and Kline at the same time.

"You're covered!" Kline yelled. "Drop it!"

The shadow grew in the doorway. Hardwick was coming.

Kline gestured to her: pull the trigger, then go.

She nodded, glad the order was for covering fire instead of having to hold ground and go head-to-head, even kill a fellow agent.

She put three rounds into the door frame, holding the stock of the MP5 tight against her shoulder as it kicked. Sparks flew out from the steel ahead. The shadow pulled back.

She and Kline took off north up the rear tunnel, and she kept herself between him and the threat.

Hardwick shouted again, but she couldn't make out the words over the din of the power plant. She and Kline were fifty yards from Cavern A, from cover and escape. She looked back and saw light spill from the power plant door as it opened wide, and Hardwick emerged.

She moved with Kline toward the back of Building A in its cavern.

A figure emerged from the smoke to their north in the rear tunnel. It was Liam Walsh, carrying an MP5 and picking his way through the wreckage behind Building B.

"Walsh!" Kline called out. "We need backup. Hardwick is coming. He's part of the attack!"

Shock on the young agent's face. He looked to Cody, and she nodded to confirm it.

"I got you. Hold there!" he yelled back, picking up speed toward them.

Hold there? she thought, and her eyes met Kline's. The president kept moving, making for the turn around the corner that would let them escape from the rear tunnel west into Cavern A. He didn't trust Walsh's order either.

Her mind raced through every minute of this endless day, who went where when, who vouched for whom.

Walsh's gun was up, still pointed down the tunnel toward Hardwick.

"Just wait there," he called. "Cavern A isn't clear."

The president slowed as they approached the intersection with A and Cody came up beside him.

"Hardwick and Walsh were both out when Maddox and Chilton were killed," she said. "They vouched for each other. We can't risk it. Come on!"

They went for Cavern A with Cody sprinting ahead to cover him. Walsh called for her to stop, but she ignored him. His face changed: eyes narrowed, brow down, mouth tight. His gun turned her way.

She raised hers.

"Put it fucking down!" Walsh barked, taking aim as she and Kline cut into the southern side of Cavern A. Moving in the blackness, they entered the alley that ran along the southern edge of the cavern between its stone wall and the foundations of Building A. The springs supporting the building gave her some cover from Walsh, coming down from the north, but that wouldn't last.

Kline kept going and angled to the right, heading under the building, sliding between the springs. His speed and confidence in the dark surprised her.

He could have ordered her to kill Walsh, but he hadn't.

They were now fifty feet into the cavern, going deeper, west away from the rear tunnel. She followed Kline into the springs, moving through the shadows, feeling for those metal coils, each as thick as her calf, tracking him by the quiet sound of his footsteps scraping across the floor.

A beam of light shined into the cavern from the rear tunnel, illuminating the alley that ran along the cavern's northern side.

It started tracking toward them, filtering through the coils. Fear tightened the muscles along her back.

"Here," Kline whispered from ahead under the building. She went to his voice and kept her gun aimed at the source of the light, though at this distance she had no chance of sending a bullet clear through that forest of springs.

She heard Kline's breath, coming and going fast, and pulled up beside him. He had brought them behind something that blocked the light of the pursuers. It was a sheet metal box about eight feet wide on every side and eight feet tall, a housing for some kind of equipment, with wires and ducts leading out of the top of it and running up through the floor of Building A over their heads.

She leaned out to the side to look around the housing. A second light was searching through the coils, coming toward them along the southern edge of the cavern. She assumed it was Hardwick joining Walsh.

The two attackers were getting closer, moving west, sweeping the foundations, one along the northern side of Cavern A and one along the south. The southern light turned toward them. She ducked back as it passed over the housing where they had taken cover.

The beam of the flashlight came back and fixed on the housing. The other beam soon joined it. They started moving faster toward her and the president.

Kline looked in the other direction, west to where Cavern A met the main tunnel. It offered an escape, but it was still a thousand feet away through the springs under this building.

"Ready?" he whispered.

"You first. I'll be right behind you and will give cover if they spot us."

"Cody . . ." Protest in his eyes.

"Move, sir. I've got this."

Kline looked at her, then dipped his head. He stayed low and started racing west between the springs. She ran after.

The southern beam angled toward them, and she cut right to stay out of its way. The other light turned toward them from the north, and she could hear the heavy pound of boots racing closer. The flashlight's beam passed over Kline as he darted between the coils ahead, then it fixed on him.

Cody spun, taking aim at the source of the light, looking for a clean shot through the springs.

Hardwick called out to her. "Cody, listen to me. You don't know the truth about Eric Hill . . ."

56

ERIC AND EUBANKS raced south in the rear tunnel, drawn by the shouts and gunshots.

"Did the shooters get around us somehow?" Eubanks asked.

Eric thought it through. There were paths through the caverns and passageways to do it, but the attackers they'd been chasing north wouldn't have had time.

"No," Hill said, striding over the stone floor toward the wreckage piled up behind Building B, his light piercing the lingering smoke. "It's someone else."

Eric took a deep breath and ducked into the haze. Picking his way through the fallen metal framing, he found the path he had taken through the debris the first time.

Once through, he pointed his flashlight south down the rear tunnel, and could just make out the entrance to the power plant in the distance, light coming through its open door.

That should have been locked, with Hardwick, Cody, Chen, and the president inside.

He shouldered his MP5 and continued along the western wall of the rear tunnel, scanning for movement.

Light spilled from the cavern to the south that housed Building A. From the patterns, he took it for flashlights moving inside. They appeared to be pointed away from him, deeper into Cavern A, under the building within. He continued on with Eubanks in the rear tunnel until he reached the corner that would let them turn right into A.

Eubanks stacked behind him, his eyes wide and wild with adrenaline, but he was staying disciplined with the gun.

"You take the northern edge of this cavern. I'll take the south," Eric whispered. "Lights off until you need it. Don't give us away."

Eubanks nodded, and Eric rolled out, scanning the narrow alley that ran between the northern wall of Cavern A and the spring foundations of Building A. One man was moving far down in that space, armed and only visible as a silhouette from the light he carried. He was facing and heading away from them, west toward the main tunnel.

Eric waved Eubanks in after that man and headed for the southern edge of the cavern, where another light was moving, searching under the springs. Once Eric reached the south side of Cavern A, he turned down the alley there and moved toward that light.

He was about fifty feet from it and closing in when the man ahead of him in the alley spun around, fixing on him. Eric shined his light back, taking aim, squinting to see who he was facing.

Through the glare, he could make out Michael Hardwick, his MP5 trained on Eric. With the hand holding his flashlight, Hardwick raised a finger and put it across his lips. He approached along the alley, aiming his gun away, no threat. He walked with pain, and his hand looked burned.

"What's happening?" Eric asked.

"Walsh and I chased two attackers under A," he said, pointing to the moving flashlight to the north.

"Were you hurt?"

"From the fires," Hardwick said. "It's fine."

"What happened to the president and the others?"

"They're back at the diesel plant."

"The door was open."

"What?" Hardwick said, looking to the rear tunnel. "Walsh and I will take these guys. You check the plant. Who's with you?"

"Eubanks."

"Good," Hardwick said, and started turning away.

"I'll go with you," Eric said.

"We've got it. Check on the president and Cody."

Hardwick's reply was too fast, too insistent.

Eric looked ahead through the foundations of A, where Agent Walsh's light was tracking along the northern side, and caught a glimpse of Agent Cody slipping between the springs, gun up and aiming toward Walsh. She had her flashlight on him, fully aware of who she was pointing that gun at.

Eric trained his weapon on Hardwick. He had lied about where Cody was. Hardwick brought his MP5 up a split second later. "What the hell is going on, Mike?" Eric asked.

"Hill, Hardwick is bad!" Cody shouted. She must have seen him or heard his voice. "He and Walsh came for me and the president!"

Hardwick shook his head. "She doesn't understand, Hill."

"Where's Kline?" Eric asked, keeping his voice even.

"It was him and his people the entire time. They took out Navarro because he knew too much, and now they're after us. I can prove it."

Eric wanted to trust him, the most loyal of his men, but he had already lied, and he and Walsh had raised weapons against Eric and Cody.

"What are you doing, Michael? Put that down."

"It's all true. He was behind the crash that killed Rivas and Stiles. I fucking watched them burn. These attacks are a provocation so he can seize power." He lowered the gun slightly. "Eric, I need your help. I wanted to keep you out of it, but I believe you'll do what's right here. We need to protect this country from men like him. You know that as much as anyone. We have support, powerful people up top. Hear me out. I'll show you."

"Put down your weapon, then we can talk. I don't know what you heard or who got to you, but this is not right."

"If you only knew."

"The Order. You're part of it?"

"I swore, Eric. I'll lay my life down if I have to."

"Citizen? Cassius?"—those were the two conspirators' aliases that Eric knew of—"Who the fuck are you?"

Eric tightened his grip. Hardwick brought his gun level between them. Eric might have imagined a situation where Hardwick had discovered something damning enough about President Kline to take action, but none that would justify turning his weapon on Eric or a fellow agent.

Eric knew what it was like to be pushed to the breaking point by corruption and hypocrisy. He had felt the dark pull, had given into it one night and nearly lost everything. But seeing his friend's eyes, now cold and lethal, he knew he wouldn't go along with this.

"You're going to kill me?" Eric asked.

"I don't want to. Put it down."

"We know it's you, Mike. You're trapped in here, outnumbered. It's over."

A cold look on Hardwick's face. It unsettled Eric more than the gun. They were so close that Eric would only have one shot.

"Put it down."

Hardwick only stared back. Eric didn't want to telegraph. He kept everything relaxed as he eyed over the front sight, aiming at the bridge of Hardwick's nose.

Anger filled Eric, tinged with grief. It felt as bitter and wrong as the smoke in his lungs. Hardwick had been a good man who had his people's back no matter what. Somehow that unquestioned faith had been used to turn him against his brothers. Two men were dead. Now Eric had to put him down.

Eric tightened his finger on the trigger. "Mike, please."

Light shot from behind Eric, somewhere under the springs, throwing his shadow forward toward Hardwick. Eric cut right, spinning toward the source of the light. A muzzle flare flashed, red blasts in the distance, and three bullets skipped off the springs beside Eric.

He felt a slash of pain across his shoulder—frag, he hoped, though a gunshot can feel like nothing until you collapse—and tried to line up a shot on the light, but the springs were too dense.

"Eubanks!" he called to his ally to the north. "Attackers coming in from behind!" Hardwick must have had more shooters backing him up, coming in from the rear tunnel to corner Eric here under Building A.

He turned to cover Hardwick. A blow rocked his skull. Eric fell, his gun hand exploding in pain as Hardwick kicked the MP5 from it.

Hardwick had attacked him from behind and now stood over him among the metal coils, his submachine gun aimed at Eric's head. "You're on the wrong side of this, Hill."

"Look at yourself," Eric seethed, climbing to his feet. "Look!"

Hardwick ordered him to stay down as another light fixed on Eric. "What are you waiting for!" Walsh called out from the north.

Gunfire broke out on that northern side of the cavern, the shooters distant from each other. No shouts of pain. Eric assumed it was Walsh and Cody trading shots, or perhaps Eubanks engaging with someone closer to the rear tunnel. How many attackers were flooding into this cavern to trap them under Building A?

Hardwick aimed the gun at Eric's head. Eric noticed a tremble in Hardwick's left hand, a pained look on his face. The other agent tightened his fingers on the barrel, and it went still again. "Call them off!"

"No," Eric said, noting the empty look in Hardwick's eyes, ready to kill. Eric shifted his weight forward. He would go down fighting.

57

FOOTSTEPS SCRATCHED TOWARD them from the west, behind Hardwick. The agent turned, but the other person was already in too close. It was Kline. The light hit his face as he lunged forward with a knife in his hand. Hardwick knocked it away, the blade missing him by inches. The knife fell from Kline's right hand as he seized on the barrel of Hardwick's MP5 with his left. They struggled over the gun, standing side by side until Kline drove his right elbow into Hardwick's throat.

The agent let out a strange, breathless gasp and reeled back and Kline stripped the weapon from his hands. It all happened in a second as Eric moved toward them, his legs still unsteady from the blow to his head.

A light from the north—where Walsh had been—fixed on the president. Eric picked up the knife from the floor and pulled Kline out of the way as a three-round burst ripped toward him through the springs.

Kline raised the gun to his shoulder, steadied it, and shot back as he moved, remarkably controlled fire for a civilian.

Two figures were coming straight at them under Building A from the west, the main tunnel. It was Drumm, with Moro ten feet behind him. As Eric moved to meet them, he caught the glint of his own dropped weapon just in front of Drumm.

The engineer slowed, crouched, and lifted it from the floor. He looked at it, eyes wide, then to Eric, who had his hand outstretched.

Drumm tossed it the five feet between them. Eric grabbed the MP5 out of the air, pulled it to his shoulder, turned, and sent two volleys of gunfire to the north, toward Walsh.

Sweeping his light under the springs, Eric caught a glimpse of Hardwick, now unarmed, escaping toward the rear tunnel under the foundations of Building A. "Go back!" Hardwick called out, and the other attackers' lights retreated with him to the east.

Eric keyed his radio. "Cody, Eubanks, you all right?"

"Fine," Cody's voice came back. "Walsh is making for the rear tunnel."

"In pursuit," Eubanks said.

"Keep on them," Eric said, picking out his allies' lights to the north. Hardwick and his crew were retreating east through Cavern A to the rear tunnel, while Eric and his people—Kline, Eubanks, Cody, Moro, and Drumm—were pursuing them from the west, closer to the midpoint of Cavern A.

He looked to Kline, stalking forward between the coils. "You okay?" Eric asked.

"Set," Kline said, and kept moving. *Paper pusher, my ass*, Eric thought.

Eric told Moro and Drumm and Kline to stay well back, and went after the attackers as they fled between the springs under Building A. Kline ignored him and kept moving.

Eric picked up the pace. He wasn't going to restrain the guy. His best option was to get far ahead of him and make the fight with the plotters short. He had three spare magazines on his belt.

The attackers emerged from under the back of Building A in its cavern and entered the rear tunnel. They turned to the north, their lights illuminating a pall of smoke still hanging in the air.

He raised his weapon, trying to find a shot through the building's foundation as he ran toward them. The maze of springs under A ended twenty feet ahead. Beyond it was the rear tunnel where he would have a better line of fire on Hardwick's people heading north. The wreckage that had fallen in it behind Building B would slow them down.

One of the attackers paused and threw something his way as he reached the rear tunnel. Metal skittered over stone.

"Get back!" Eric shouted to his team.

A ball of fire filled the rear tunnel—*fwooom*—driving him onto his heels. It was another incendiary bomb, cutting across the rear tunnel just north of where he had entered it from the back of Cavern A. The flames spread across the stone surfaces, a sure sign of a gelled fuel explosive.

They forced him back under Building A. There was no way through the fires. Kline came up beside him, gun in his hand, red light dancing across his face as the killers escaped.

58

THE OTHERS GATHERED around Eric. They kept their weapons up, squinting against the smoke.

"Where is Chen?" he asked.

"In the power plant," Kline said. "Hardwick knocked him out, may have killed him."

"What happened?"

"Hardwick sent Cody to you and Eubanks, then tried to take me in the plant and force me to make a statement or confession. He had a gun in my face. I didn't know how far he would go. Chen helped me escape but Hardwick put him down with a gun butt to the head. It was brutal."

Eric looked to Cody, without thinking, and realized he was looking for confirmation of the president's story. He still couldn't fully believe Hardwick would do this.

She nodded. "I'm sorry. Hardwick gave me the order and I went. Something seemed off about it, him staying there and sending me out, but by the time I went back to check he'd already gone after Kline." Her face went tight.

"It's okay, Cody. None of us saw it. Chen could still be alive?"

"Yes," Kline said. He looked to the south, the path toward the doctor.

"Where are the first lady and the others?" Eric asked.

"After they escaped the fires, they went to Building C," Drumm said. "The infirmary. They can lock it from the inside."

"And your people?"

"The officers I was with all went north to Building E, the comms center, to make sure the ventilation systems are all right and see if there were any other ways to get the doors open and get out of here. We were able to get the emergency lights working."

"Good, thank you," Eric said. He had everyone change the encryption keys on their radios so that Hardwick's people wouldn't be able to listen in. "Cody, Eubanks, Moro— check on Chen and bring him to the infirmary. We'll make sure the others already there are okay." He wanted to get Kline locked up safely too, but didn't say so explicitly. After seeing Kline with that gun, he had a feeling the president might object and try to take a more active role.

"Everyone set?" Eric asked.

They were all ready.

"Let's go."

59

ERIC COVERED CODY, Eubanks, and Moro as they exited the cavern and headed south in the rear tunnel. The burning debris still blocked the way to the north.

He stepped back under Building A, and Drumm brought him and Kline all the way to Building C using the north–south passageways between the caverns.

They went into the building through a side entrance. Only the emergency lights were on inside C, bright floods at the corridor intersections. Eric moved carefully. Mounted on springs, the floors amplified every step. Drumm led them to the infirmary via a side hall and Eric tried the door. Locked.

He raised his weapon to cover the hallway, then brought his fist up and knocked. After a moment he could make out the sounds of movement inside the medical suite.

"It's Eric Hill," he said, just beside the door. "You can open up."

"It's all right," Kline added. "It's me."

A scratching noise came from above the handle, and the door opened in. Agent Leigh stood there, gun raised.

"Where's Sarah?" Kline asked as he marched inside.

Leigh pointed down the hall to a doorway.

"What the hell is happening out there?" she asked.

"I'll fill you in," Eric said, and saw Agent Brimley emerging from the door ahead, still wearing the bandage on his neck from his injuries at the White House.

"You two cover the ends of this hallway," Eric said to Leigh and Brimley. "Both entrances. No one comes in or out without my approval."

They split up, and Eric walked with Kline to the door. He left Drumm outside the infirmary, with instructions to watch the two agents and not to tell them what had happened. He wanted to see their reactions himself when he told them about Hardwick and Walsh. The president led him into a small waiting area where the first lady and Claire Givens approached him.

Dr. Kline looked unhurt. She went straight for her husband and wrapped her arms around him, her eyes shut. It was a moment of such pure emotion that Eric looked down. There was something almost improper in witnessing it.

He kept checking on the door, looking for any warnings from Drumm.

"What is this?" Dr. Kline said, gesturing toward the gun. "And why are you two wet? What in God's name happened out there?"

Eric took a step and waved them closer. "Leigh and Brimley: Did they do anything sketchy? Try to hide any communications from you?"

"No," Dr. Kline said.

"They took us straight here and locked it down," Givens said. "They brought us through that damn fire."

"And you didn't see them talking to anyone else? You didn't get any sense of threat from them?"

"No. It was all quiet until about ten minutes ago, when we heard gun-shots."

"That was us," Kline said, "taking fire."

"From whom?" Dr. Kline asked.

"Hardwick, Walsh, and two others we couldn't identify."

The first lady and Givens exchanged glances, sickened looks on their faces.

"You're saying that two Secret Service agents shot *at* you?" Dr. Kline asked. "You're certain?"

"One hundred percent," the president said. "Agents Hardwick and Walsh are part of the plot, if not the leaders. We have to assume they're complicit in everything—the White House attack, locking us down here and cutting us off, and killing Maddox and Chilton."

"We needed to make sure the other agents, Leigh and Brimley, aren't part of it too," Eric said.

"They had us unarmed. They had every chance to take us and did nothing," Givens said. "You can trust them."

Static came through on Eric's radio, then Cody's broken-up voice.

"Hill . . . coming . . . main tunnel . . . C . . . clear . . . Chen."

"We're in the infirmary," Eric radioed back. "Meet you at the door to the main tunnel, west entrance to Building C."

"Copy . . ." More static.

"They should have Chen," Eric said to Kline.

"We're going to need you, Sarah," the president said. "He's hurt."

Eric went out to the western door and met Cody, Eubanks, Chen, and Moro. Cody and Eubanks stood on either side of the doctor, his arms draped around their necks, barely able to walk.

They brought him to the infirmary and Sarah Kline rushed through the door to meet them. After checking his injuries, she guided them through the waiting area into a doctor's office and treatment room, where they laid him on a table.

"Nate," Dr. Kline said to Chen in a loud, clear voice as she checked his pupils. "Can you hear me? Do you know where you are?" Chen only mumbled. It pained Eric to see him this bad, but Sarah Kline moved with total confidence as they got Chen settled on the table.

As they finished, Eric caught sight of Agent Leigh out of the corner of his eye by the western door. He went to her.

"Talk to me for a second," he said, and she followed him into the hallway outside the infirmary. He shut the door behind her and kept a few feet between them, his hand hanging close to his gun.

"You all right?" he asked.

"Fine," she said.

"Good." Eric leaned in. "When we spoke before, you said there was hard evidence against Kline, something that would show he was making a grab for power and implicate him in the crash that killed Rivas and Stiles."

She drew back, wary.

"What is it, Laura?" Eric asked.

"Nothing."

"Then you can tell me where you are getting all this?"

She crossed her arms.

"You saw what happened to Chen," he said. "You saw Chilton's and Maddox's bodies." He stepped closer.

"It came from Hardwick."

Eric let out a breath. "All of it? Him alone?"

"There were others."

"Who?"

"Walsh."

"What did they say?"

"Some of their past protectees, high-level people, were sharing information with them about what Kline was doing." Her gazed drifted downward. "Supposedly there was proof, rock solid, that he was involved in ordering Rivas killed, and that he had already begun invoking the emergency directives in secret to give him the power to eliminate his enemies. When the attack happened at the White House, and he took us all here, it fit with what they had warned about. He was seizing control. He'd taken out everyone who tried to stop him." She looked up. "What happened out there, Eric? Do you trust him?"

She'd had her chance to go after Dr. Kline and the others. Her only resistance would have been Brimley, twenty years older, injured and unsuspecting. But she hadn't.

"Hardwick and Walsh attacked us fifteen minutes ago, under Building A."

"What?" Her hand went to her mouth. "No."

"I was ten feet from Hardwick. He was ready to kill me. *He* did that to Chen. Walsh tried to shoot Agent Cody."

"Could they be trying to stop Kline . . . I don't know . . ."

"Nothing justifies going after a fellow agent. They're behind this attack, Laura. They had incendiaries just like the ones that went off in Cavern B. They used them to get away. They orchestrated all of it. It's a fucking coup. Hardwick must believe he's doing the right thing."

"He's so solid."

"I know. I tried to see his side, tried to make some sense of it. Maybe if Kline were behind all of this and he was trying to stop him, but no. Hardwick and his people wired this place up, plotted this out. It's treason. It's murder."

"Are you sure?"

"I am. Cody, Eubanks, Drumm, Moro, Kline—all of us saw it firsthand. Hardwick and Walsh are killers, and now they're desperate. Tell me everything they gave you about who they're working with."

"That's all I know. I asked to see the evidence, but once we were sealed in here, they said they couldn't, because the comms were down. God, if they can get to Hardwick, they can get to anyone. Who would be able to pull that off?"

"I don't know, and I don't know what's happening up top, if the government is even standing. He didn't give you *anything*? No names?"

"No." The color went out of her face, and she covered her mouth with her hand. "I could have been one of them. I trusted him."

"I did too."

"Was anyone else suspicious of Kline? Working against him? Brimley? Eubanks? Even Cody?"

"You were the only other one who mentioned anything."

A strange out-of-body sensation gripped Eric, like the feeling that comes just before a car wreck, when you know you're going to hit, and time slows down.

He could have followed Hardwick into the darkness. Knowing that his friend was behind this left him with the unsettling knowledge that nothing and no one he believed in could be counted on anymore. The only consolation was that he finally understood who the killers were, and which side he was on.

"Hardwick came up to me after you and I talked," Eric said. "He may have been trying to feel out if I was receptive, if he could bring me into the plot."

"Were you?"

"Not enough for him to tip his hand."

"I should have warned you or Chilton. But I had no idea who to trust."

He looked at her. "You've been acting strangely for weeks, Leigh. Not yourself."

She reddened and looked down. "Trouble at home."

"With Greg?" Her husband.

"I don't want to talk about it. I know I've been . . . off, but it has nothing to do with any of this."

"Are you all right? Is he?"

She raised her hand. "I'm good. It's the last thing I want to think about right now, okay? So let's just take it one shit show at a time. How could Hardwick go against his own people?"

Eric rubbed his thumb along his index finger. "If you could've seen his face."

"He was going to kill you?"

"He had the chance. He didn't."

"He couldn't?"

"Not in that moment. If it had gone on another minute . . . who knows. He watched Rivas and Stiles die. They were like brother and sister to him. Loyalty to them is driving him. He's trying to get what he believes is justice, trying to protect others from Kline, to protect the whole country. His sense of duty is so strong, however warped. I don't know how far he'll take it. But this isn't going the way he anticipated. I can try to talk to him, get him under control, before . . ." He took a long breath. *Before I have to put him down.*

"Did you do anything to help him?" he asked her. "Even something small: advice, whatever. The end of this will be ugly, and I have to know."

She looked down and thought it through. "I listened to him. I asked questions. I talked to you about it. There was so much happening. I didn't know which way was up."

"You're all right. You took care of these people."

"They vouched for me?"

He nodded. "You'll be okay."

"Fuck," she said, and again, drawing it out.

"I know. Come on."

60

ERIC AND LEIGH went back inside the infirmary. He had her stand guard at the western door, and he returned to the waiting area, with its country doctor decor—Norman Rockwell paintings and Windsor chairs along the wall.

Kline looked at him through the door frame of the treatment room. The president was still carrying the MP5. It was as odd an image as Eric had seen in his career with the Service, yet Kline seemed perfectly at ease.

He waved Eric in, and they went into a combination storage room and lab off the back of the treatment area, all polished steel and bright overhead lights.

Kline shut the door. "Where were you?" he asked.

"Questioning Laura Leigh and the others," Eric said.

"And?"

"I don't believe she has anything to do with it."

"Sarah said it was just the two of them in the tunnels for a while on their way here. Leigh had the opportunity to take her and didn't use it."

"Hardwick has been trying to turn everyone against you, sowing doubts."

"Including you?"

"Yes."

"Did you bite?" Kline asked.

"You saw for yourself under that building which side I'm on."

"I did."

"I've worked with Hardwick for seventeen years." He'd saved Eric's ass more than once.

"I'm sorry it took seeing that in order for you to believe me, but here we are."

"What could possibly have turned him? What is happening?" Eric asked.

The president's eyes were on the MP5, Eric's hand tight on its grip. He hadn't noticed it himself. He was still on guard against Kline. He relaxed his fingers.

"You're angry, Eric. Angrier than you realize. I understand you and Hardwick were close. I understand how hard this is. But are you asking me to explain myself after everything you've seen?"

The Service was in many ways closer than family. Agents spent more time with each other than they did with their wives and husbands and kids. They gave everything to the job, including their lives. Some of them missed the births of their children. They lived together, ate together, counted off endless hours driving through the sticks, standing in the rain, staked out in cars, and holed up in hotels. And Eric protected his people like family. Hardwick had been one of the best, most loyal agents he'd ever known.

"No," Eric said. "I'm trying to understand what is going on, what we're up against, and how far it has gone. He said there was evidence. He wouldn't betray everything he dedicated his life to for no reason."

Kline considered that for a moment, a hint of anger showing. It almost sounded like an accusation, like *he* had to justify *himself* after Hardwick had come for him and his family.

"There is a reason. He was lied to, manipulated. Did he show you anything?"

"No, but he had evidence, or claimed to. He was using it to turn the others."

"What?"

"Something tying you to the crash that killed Rivas and Stiles. And a way to show that you were trying to seize power, suspend the Constitution, and eliminate anyone who could implicate you in those crimes."

Kline dipped his head like he'd heard this story before.

"You know about them?"

"I do. They're tapes. They're good. I might be persuaded if I didn't know personally that they were bullshit.

"It's audio," he went on, "supposedly of a conversation between me and Givens, discussing the plans to order Rivas's death. There are other recordings about the emergency action documents, some suggesting that I already signed them in secret, and just needed a crisis to take full control. It's all faked, but if you were primed to believe, it would be all you needed. How far gone do you think Hardwick is? Can we reason with him?"

"He didn't kill me when he had a chance. That's not to say he wouldn't if forced. Where does all of it come from? If we can prove it's all false, then we might be able to end this without more violence."

Kline watched him carefully. He probably suspected that Eric wanted to not only convince Hardwick, but also see the proof himself. Hardwick was out of control, no doubt, but Eric wanted as much clarity as he could find. Even after all he had seen, some part of him had trouble siding against his friend.

"So we have the pseudonym for the leader, Citizen," Kline said. "We know it's one person or a small circle of conspirators running the show, giving orders, and disseminating this false evidence to build a movement against me. We know they have been targeting politicians, Yankee White personnel, and Secret Service, trying to turn them. Citizen pretends to be a whistleblower, trying to save the republic from me. Everything we do to find him and root out his coconspirators they hold up as evidence that the rumors are true, that I'm on a witch hunt against all opposition. It's an impossible position."

"The Order. I asked Hardwick about it. He didn't deny being a part of it. Could he be Citizen?"

"It's possible," Kline said. "I don't figure him for a political type. More a soldier. If they convinced him I had Rivas and Stiles killed, his sense of loyalty did the rest, I imagine. It's vile, preying on a man's sense of honor like that, exploiting those agents' deaths."

"How did they die?"

"An accident, just as the investigation found. Citizen seized on it. Everything serves the lie."

"What kind of strength does The Order have?"

"We don't know. They've been recruiting, quietly, using this doctored evidence. Will Maddox made contact with them. He played along, feigned that he was susceptible as a way to find out who was behind it."

"He infiltrated them?"

"Yes. A former squad mate of his approached him. Will pretended to be interested to try to contact the higher levels and learn more about what they were planning. He was able to learn the name of the plot—Operation V—and move a couple of rungs up the ladder. He was the one who found out that one of the conspirators was going by the name Cassius."

"Gaius Cassius was an insider. Close to the emperor."

"Exactly."

"Which means there's probably a Marcus Brutus too."

"Brutus was even closer to Caesar, like a son."

"You think that's Hardwick and Walsh?"

"Possibly. And either one could be the leader, Citizen. Or Citizen could still be sitting in here under our fucking noses. We don't know. That was as far as we got. Everything The Order does comes through anonymous encrypted communications, always changing codes. We were tracing them, waiting for Maddox to hear more, and then we evacuated here."

"Is that why Maddox was trying to communicate with the top?"

"Yes. He was trying to reach Washington. We have people at the Department of Justice that we trust who are investigating them. Maddox was supposed to receive more messages from his contacts in The Order, but they switched codes on our way here and we were shut down before Maddox could pass the fresh codes on to the folks at the DOJ and FBI. If we can get that info to them, they can access the new communications coming in and combine that with what we now know—that the attackers are down here and that Hardwick and Walsh are part of it. They should be able to track down the whole ring with that, including Citizen. It's why we took the risk to send Maddox out to communicate and then Chilton.

"We were trying to head The Order off before they could make a major move in DC and we wanted to find out what was happening in the capital. We don't know how far this goes and who's behind it. We assume it's my political opponents, but it could be an op by an enemy nation. There could be a full-scale military putsch happening right now and we're completely in the dark." He looked at Eric. "I'd like to know if there is a government left to lead up there."

"Hardwick said that he had politicians on his side, made it sound like he was part of a larger movement."

"I'm sure. I pray the guardrails worked. He used specific language like he was part of a formal impeachment or an invocation of the Twenty-Fifth

Amendment, some kind of orderly military transition. His political allies are making moves. He wanted to bring me to the war room in B, the small broadcast studio we have there."

"And force a statement out of you?"

"A show trial or confession, something to justify all this. It could work. All that white marble in the capital—they designed those buildings to seem timeless, unassailable, because they knew how fragile those institutions are, only as strong as the men and women inside them."

Kline ran his hand along the steel lab bench to his right. "We need to get Maddox's information to DOJ, so they can track down who's behind this. And we need to cancel my codes and any military commands that might come out of this bunker."

"You want to give up power?"

"No one does. But I can't risk being coerced down here or having live codes in a live military command center."

"They're after *you*, aren't they? Do you think they would really attempt to do something with the codes, order a strike?"

"We don't know what they want, or who they're working for. They might try to get the codes for political leverage. There are protections in place against unauthorized use, but they've never been tested. They could hold the nation hostage with that power, or the threat of it, until their demands are met. Or there could be a madman controlling them who would really try to launch a strike. Assume the worst. There's too much at stake not to. How many people are working against us down here?"

"At least four. Hardwick, Walsh, and two other shooters, who we should assume are from Drumm's staff. But everyone is a suspect now. If they could have gotten to Hardwick . . ."

Kline nodded. "They've been planning this for a long time. Imagine the level of coordination you would need to cut off all the comms, sabotage the doors."

"And they must have been behind the White House attack as well."

"The injured agents there, and Chilton's and Maddox's murders. Jesus Christ. How many people does Drumm have down here?"

"Twenty-four. Every one of them could be in on it for all we know. And there are six Secret Service agents. Two of them are definitely bad— Hardwick and Walsh."

"What about the other agents: Cody, Brimley, and Leigh?"

"Don't forget me," Eric added. "I trust Cody, and I've been with her. Agents Brimley and Leigh didn't join the attack on Building B or go after the first lady when they could have, so I'm inclined to trust them. Though we should watch everyone. The only other people down here are Chief of Staff Givens and your wife."

"I can vouch for them."

"Can we destroy the codes?"

A dark laugh from the president. "You need to use the codes—both the biscuit and the football—to cancel the codes and take Raven Rock out of the loop. I would use them to authenticate myself and make that order to the Pentagon. I can't shut down a national military command center without them."

"The football is in the safe in your suite in Building B?"

Kline nodded.

"How do we make contact with the top?"

"Our only chance is to climb up and use the VLF system in the comms shaft that Drumm told us about."

It was in the rear tunnel behind Building D. Eric thought about the damage from the incendiaries. "We don't know if it's accessible after the fire."

"We have to try."

Eric still didn't like any of it—using the codes to make commands from this place while the attackers were on the loose, or having those codes out in the open.

"It's the only way," the president said.

Eric looked over Kline for a moment, studying his dark, sharp eyes.

"Why am I here?" Eric asked.

A quiet laugh. "I know you thought I was crooked, Eric. I'm sorry to disappoint you. You're here because you can handle yourself. I saw that in the White House attack, and you've proved it every moment since." Kline cocked his head slightly. "You think I'm setting you up somehow?"

"Why else would you allow someone down here who wasn't trusted by your head of security and chief of staff, someone who the Service busted down to desk duty, and then put him in charge of everything?"

Kline stared back at him.

"I need an answer."

The smile came, the one that so many found unsettling on Kline, like a guy turning over pocket aces.

"I brought you down here for the same reason they didn't trust you."

"*You* picked me for this detail?"

A slow nod. "I know what you did, Eric. Attacking your own protectee. I'm glad. Braun is a piece of shit and I wish you'd broken both his arms after what he did to his wife. I only wish I'd known about it before he got the Treasury job. Forget about the rules or your own self-interest—you did what was right. And that's what I need now. I am setting you up, in a way, because this is going to be brutal. Hardwick, Walsh—I know what I'm asking by putting you against your own brothers. You seem to be one of the rare ones who give a shit about the truth in this town, so I wanted you close. I know you may have your doubts, but I need to know if you're willing to go all the way with this, to go against your own people. You saw what they did, what they're capable of."

"I'm low on trust these days."

"That's their weapon, you know. Cynicism. You believe that everyone's crooked, that there is no truth, and they win. You don't like the bullshit. That's why you went after Braun. Good. Then push back against this garbage before it rots the country from the inside out."

"I'll do what's right."

"That's all I'm asking."

After a knock on the door, Givens stuck her head in.

Eric reached for his gun by instinct, then let it go.

"Is everything okay?" she asked Kline.

"Fine," he said. "How's the doctor?"

"I think he's coming to."

61

GIVENS BROUGHT THEM into the treatment room, where Dr. Kline was craned over Chen, checking an oximeter on his finger. "Nate, can you hear me?"

Chen said something so quietly that Eric couldn't make it out.

Agent Cody was in the corner. She stepped toward Eric, looking uneasy. He cocked his head at the door, and she followed him into the waiting area.

"What's going on?" she asked. Eric told her all he had learned from Laura Leigh and Kline, explaining the doctored evidence, Citizen, and the conspiracy against the president.

"Will Maddox was afraid because he was going inside The Order?" She rubbed her hands together. "That accounts for the multiple phones he had. You believe Kline?"

"I do. I was resistant at first. No one wants to be betrayed like that, to have to go after another agent. Did you see Hardwick attack Chen?"

"No. I arrived after." She shook her head and peered back down the hall. "What?"

"I don't get why he put you in charge, why he trusted you."

"I'm that bad, huh?"

"The fucking worst," she said, and threw a playful jab at his ribs. "No. I found out why you were on that desk."

She'd been doing her homework on him, figuring out who could be trusted. Good.

"Braun deserved what he got?" she asked.

"Yes."

"If it was justified, why didn't you take him down, tell everyone what happened? That could have gotten you out of it."

"Don't be so sure of that. More important, it wasn't my story to tell. She didn't want to be seen as a victim. Maybe she was still protecting him. I don't know. It doesn't matter. I promised her that."

"It's not right."

"I crossed a line. The anger got the best of me. I didn't need to hurt him that badly. I don't regret it. But I also don't regret standing up for what I did and accepting the consequences."

"Braun is still out there making speeches. He's running the Treasury."

"He's the moneyman. Untouchable. That's how it goes. The story changes. The excuses get made. The bullshit gets peddled until they're telling me not to believe my own eyes."

"That's the job?"

He thought about what happened to her dad. She didn't deserve to have her dream ripped apart by the truth, especially now, in the middle of all this. Her faith had saved Eric, made him think twice about the anger that could have turned him into Hardwick.

"Part of it. You go behind the curtain. You see the mismatch between the public and private faces. You keep your mouth shut. It's not always pretty."

"You don't trust any of them in the end?"

"It can go that way, but there are plenty of good people in this town trying to do the work. You were right to temper my suspicions about Kline. Thank you."

"You believe him?"

Eric thought about it. "I believe what I saw, back under that building. And I still want to hear what Chen has to say. Could Hardwick or Walsh be the man who attacked you at the White House?"

She thought for a moment. "Hardwick," she said.

Another jolt of anger had him balling his fists.

"So we're doing this, going against him and Walsh?"

She had grown up with her father's code—that the job was as much about getting your teammates' backs as it was about protecting the principal. Eric knew how hard it would be for her to go after a fellow agent.

"Yes," he said.

Raised voices came from inside. They went back and saw Sarah Kline leaning close to Chen. "What did you say?" she asked him. "Do you know where you are?"

He opened one eye. "Still in this fucking bunker, apparently," he said. "First time seeing an obstetrician, though." A raspy cough. He laid his hand on his belly. "Boy or a girl?"

She looked at him with concern. "Chen, you were hit in the head—"

"I know. I'm good. Bad joke. I'm in Raven Rock. It's Saturday, September fourth, and"—he looked to Kline—"the president, God willing, is James Kline."

The first lady smiled, eyes welling with relief. She ran him through a battery of questions and had him follow her finger with his eyes. Eric approached her, standing to the side, waiting.

She looked his way. "I need to talk to him," he said.

"Sure."

Eric came closer to the table. "What happened in there, Doc?"

He licked his lips. "Hardwick. He was trying to kill Kline. I tried to intercede and he . . . hit me with his rifle. The stock."

Eric nodded. "Thank you. We're all in your debt."

"You're going to stop him?" Chen asked.

Eric put his hand on his shoulder. "I am."

62

KLINE WENT TO the infirmary waiting area to get Drumm and Givens, and Eric walked over to Eubanks, who was standing guard near the door.

The guy had dark circles under his eyes, but his posture was still straight as a yardstick.

"You holding up?"

"Fine, thanks."

"When's the last time you slept?"

The military aide took his phone out of his pocket and checked the time. It was a quarter to eleven at night, but the hour seemed meaningless in this windowless underground complex. You never saw the sun and all light was artificial, like the world's grimmest casino.

Eubanks didn't wear a watch. The leash that he normally wore, attached to the nuclear football, usually sat on his wrist instead, though now the football was locked up in the presidential suite in Building B.

Eric noticed the photo on the lock screen—Eubanks with his arm around a woman with short brown hair holding a dog that couldn't have weighed more than ten pounds. It looked particularly tiny next to Eubanks. The photo seemed odd to Eric, who mostly saw the military aide standing still outside the Oval and imagined him just being propped in a closet when he was off shift. He'd tried to draw him out a couple of times, but it didn't get very far.

"Thirty-three hours," he said. "I've done longer. I'm good."

"Cute dog," Eric said. "Yorkie?"

"I don't know."

That threw Eric for an instant.

"Kelly and I found him under a car out in Brookland, half-starved. He'll probably be a wreck tonight." A sweet, pained look in Eubanks's eyes. "Thunder in the forecast. I wish I were home."

"We'll get you back. What's your first name, Eubanks?"

He laughed. "Everybody calls me Eubanks."

"One name, like Sting?"

"Exactly like Sting." He paused a beat. "It's Paul." He held out his hand.

"Eric," he said, and shook it. He already knew his first name, of course. He knew the full name and background of everyone who came in the White House during one of his shifts, but they'd never been formally introduced, and it felt like the right time. "Good work out there today."

"Thanks," he said. He pointed to Eric. "So what's this I hear about you and a French diplomat?"

"You all seriously don't have anything better to talk about?"

"Well, yeah, but it's all pretty dark, so . . . anyway, don't mess that up."

Eric held up his hand. "Good talk, Eubanks."

"How are you holding up?" the aide asked him.

Eric looked around the room. "Time of my life. And we haven't even broken out the karaoke machine yet."

Cody, standing on the other side of the waiting room, looked his way with a half smile.

"What's your go-to?" he asked her.

"'Friends in Low Places.'"

"Classic," Eric said, and noticed Drumm coming back in. "How about you?"

"'Born to Be Wild.'"

"Makes sense. Eubanks?"

"'Tiny Dancer.'"

That took everyone by surprise.

"Been in chorus since I was six," the Kansan said, and checked the magazine on his MP5. "I'll break your heart."

"Sounds good. We'll do a round once we mop up these assholes," Eric said.

The door opened and Givens and the president walked in. "Follow me," Kline whispered to Eric.

Hill, Kline, Givens, and Drumm went into the combination lab and storage area behind the treatment room.

Drumm looked uncomfortably at the chest freezer in the back where Chilton's and Maddox's bodies were stored as Kline walked to the end of the room and stood, his arms crossed.

"We have to get word to the top to disregard any orders coming from this bunker," Kline said. "Pass them what we know and try to find out what's happening. Drumm, your plan to use the very-low-frequency communication system in the comms shaft, is it still viable?"

"It should be. The fire damaged the ceiling liner framing in the rear tunnel, but the area behind Building D looked intact."

"The plan is to go from here in C to my suite in Building B to retrieve the football, then go up the rear tunnel to the comms shaft and try to make contact," Kline said.

"Is Building B still secure?" Eric asked Drumm.

"The cavern it's in is a mess, and there's a lot of wreckage behind it in the rear tunnel, but the building itself is sound. The presidential suite and war room are more secure than we are here."

"We could lock them down and defend them?"

"Now that the smoke has cleared, yes."

"You want to move these people?" Kline asked.

"Yes," Eric said. "The incendiaries under B are already blown. It's the one area we know isn't wired up any longer, if it's clear of enemy."

"Good," Kline said. "We need a place where we can make a stand, and I want it back. You don't let a national military command center hardwired to the nuclear authority fall into a traitor's hands. And it has the broadcasting suite. Hardwick clearly has propaganda wins on his mind. We need to deny him that."

"Let's start with the low-frequency comms plan," Givens said, "then check on B."

Kline shook his head. "I need the codes in the football to shut this place down as a military command center. That's in my living quarters in the suite in B. The Pentagon won't authenticate an order like that without them."

"Eubanks and I can go and retrieve it from the safe," Eric said.

Kline shook his head. "It's biometric. I'm the only one who can open it."

"Lord help me," Givens whispered. "You two are going to carry the nuclear football and the biscuit in the open with these gunmen running around. How many are there?"

"At least four," Eric said. "Hardwick, Walsh, and two other shooters. If they took the codes, could they give a launch order? There has to be some safeguard."

"There is," Kline said. "There are ten gold codes printed on the piece of plastic in the biscuit. Only one will authenticate me."

Eric had heard about this system. The decoy codes were there in case anyone ever stole the card or attempted to coerce the president. The correct code always appeared in the same position on the card, known only to Kline and the director of the National Security Agency, which printed new cards regularly and handled the cryptography.

"One in ten," Eric said. "That's unacceptable. We can't let them get their hands on it. And you know and I know these Cold War systems are buggy as hell and break down under duress." Drumm bridled at that. "An insider might be able to find some way around it. Or they may have an accomplice in the system up top. There's no other method to shut down military orders from this place?"

"No," Kline said. "As long as Raven Rock is live, I'm in danger, Sarah is in danger, and the country is in danger. If they took her, tried to coerce me . . ." He fought back a shiver as he contemplated it. "We need to shut this place down."

His voice was rough, the most emotion Eric had ever heard from him. It made sense. Duty could force him to choose between his country and his wife.

"The comms shaft is in the rear tunnel behind Building D?" Eric asked.

"Yes, off the east side of the tunnel. We'd have to climb the framing to gain access. It's a vertical shaft, about six feet in diameter, going up through an opening in the rear tunnel ceiling. Picture looking up the inside of a very large chimney."

"How high?"

"Forty stories."

Eric shook his head. "It doesn't rise all the way through to the surface?"

"No. It runs straight up about four hundred feet and stops. There's a ceiling. The wires go through four-inch-diameter holes bored in the ceiling and rise another three hundred and fifty feet to the peak of the mountain and the antennas on top."

"No way we can get through there somehow?"

"No. That last three hundred and fifty feet is all stone."

"We're going up on ladders?"

"Rungs set in the stone in the shaft, yes."

"What are the odds this will work?"

"Let's say eighty percent. They cut the other channels to communicate out, but this is a relic. I only know about it from the cold warriors because I've been here so long."

"It's staffed on the other end?"

"All the VLF systems are monitored because some aircraft and missile silos have them as backups. It would put us in direct contact with the Pentagon's war room."

"I still don't like having the president and the codes out in the tunnels," Eric said.

The others looked to Kline. He thought for a minute. "It's a go," he said. "We have to make contact, neutralize the risk, and get what we know to the top so they can stop this from going any further. Washington could be hanging in the balance right now."

Eric nodded. *Shut up and color.* "We'll go out with me, Eubanks, Drumm, Cody, and you," he said, looking to Kline.

"Cody stays. I don't want to leave my wife and Claire undefended." He gestured to Chief of Staff Givens. "And Cody's the only one I trust."

"Why?" Givens asked.

"She had a chance to shoot me in the back and didn't take it. Same as Drumm. That's my love language these days. We need her here watching the other agents, just in case."

It wasn't a bad idea.

"You're all good with this?" the president asked.

Everyone agreed.

"Let's get started," Kline said.

63

ERIC BRIEFED THE other agents on the plan in the waiting area—Brimley, Cody, and Leigh would remain here on guard while he, Kline, Drumm, and Eubanks made a run to check on Building B. He didn't mention the plan to make contact with the top. He wanted to keep their last comms option a closely held secret. After he'd given the orders, he pulled Cody aside.

"Kline wants you here," he said. "He trusts you. No one can get to the first lady. She's Kline's one weakness."

"I've got it."

Eric glanced at Leigh and Brimley.

"Any threat, you take it down. It doesn't matter who it is. You all right with that?"

Cody looked from face to face. Her lips pressed together. "Yes."

Eric, Kline, and Eubanks cleaned themselves up and changed into dry clothes—army fatigues in camo that Drumm provided.

Sarah and James Kline had stepped into the storage room to talk for a moment, and Eric caught a glimpse of them through the small window in the door. He'd been holding her, and it looked like she had been near tears, though she betrayed no sign of it when they came out and Eric met them in the treatment room.

The president double-checked that the nuclear biscuit was in his pocket.

"The red letter?" Eric asked.

"For this we have to authorize ourselves with the codes in the biscuit and football. They supersede everything."

"But you have it?"

"I do."

The president stepped out and Dr. Kline took Eric aside to check on the blow to the back of his head, now a solid lump. She finished, then crossed her arms.

"Watch out for my guy, okay?"

Her language was casual, but there was real vulnerability behind it.

"I will," he said.

She looked at him for a long moment, as if deciding whether to believe him. Then she leaned in and checked his pupils.

"Were you ever married?" she asked.

"No."

He thought about that instinctual need to protect family, so strong that someone would lay down her life without a second thought to protect those she loved.

"Close?"

"Once," he said. It was a woman he'd known since they were kids in New Orleans. They'd gotten serious and she moved to Washington. They lived together in a little two-bedroom bungalow in Del Ray, but ultimately the job and the endless shifts put too much strain on the relationship. She wanted a life like they had when he was back home—talking with friends till all hours, drinks on the porch, music every weekend—and there just wasn't time.

That's what he always told himself, at least. But it wasn't long after Joe Cody died, and dredging all of that up now, Eric realized that part of it was the bitterness beginning to seep in, to shut him down. He'd never loved anyone like that, never felt so at ease with another person. She was married now, with a son and daughter in elementary school, living in the Garden District, five blocks from where she grew up. Eric would look at the family snaps she posted online every once in a while to torture himself.

Dr. Kline nodded, and started checking the cut on Eric's neck, cleaning where it had opened a little in the action.

"Not this French woman?"

Eric let out a surprised laugh. "Jesus."

She shrugged. "People talk."

"It's only been a couple dates."

"You like her, though?"

"She's amazing." Funny, wry, and surprisingly down-to-earth.

"I hope it works out for you, one way or another." A bittersweet smile. "At the end of the day, nothing else matters." She paused. "But I guess we need to get out of here first, huh?"

"We will," he said.

He realized he'd given up on finding the real thing, or pulled back from it. He started thinking that if he made it out of here, he would get his shit sorted out, and stop giving up before he even started.

Eric had no wife. No kids. But he knew something about that willingness to sacrifice yourself for another. For seventeen years he showed up at his shifts willing to die for his fellow agents and his protectees. He missed that simple faith in the job. The corruption and dishonor he had seen in high office had stolen it from him. He wanted it back.

He looked Sarah Kline in the eyes. "Don't worry. I've got him."

"Good," she said, and patted him on the shoulder twice. "You've got a few miles left in you. Get going."

64

DRUMM, CARRYING A nylon bag of comms gear, led Eric, Kline, and Eubanks out the back exit of Building C and down a set of metal steps into the rear tunnel.

They moved south as a squad, spaced out so they couldn't be taken in one blast or burst of rifle fire.

He could still taste the smoke in the tunnel, the fumes growing stronger as they approached the back of Building B in its cavern leading off to their right.

The broken framing had collapsed in a tall pile against the rear facade of the building, the wreckage spilling down and across the rear tunnel, the steel discolored with rainbow streaks from the heat. Some of the ceiling liners—thick plastic material—hadn't completely burned, and had fallen stretched over the debris. Eric thought, somewhat absurdly, of the barricades from *Les Misérables*.

Drumm looked over it all. His face fell, and he reached out and touched the stone wall like someone caressing an injured animal.

Surveying the wreckage, Eric saw a way through it that would let them enter Cavern B along its northern side.

They followed him and Eric led them around the corner from the rear tunnel into the cavern, with Eubanks sticking close to his left. The president and Drumm were in the rear as they walked down the alley between the north cavern wall and the springs that supported Building B.

He brought them to a set of steps that led up to an entrance on the northern side of the building. Weighing each footfall, he climbed to the door. The metal still radiated heat from the fire. He gestured for Kline to stay back, while Eubanks stacked beside him, his free hand on Eric's back.

Eric reached for the door handle and felt it give. He turned it and pushed the door open, a faint squeal sounding through the tunnel.

He went in fast and quiet, covering right while Eubanks took the left. The hallways inside the building were empty. Emergency floodlights filled the corridor with a harsh glare.

He moved forward, to check the next corner—clear. He listened for a moment. Nothing. Then he gestured for Drumm and Kline to follow.

They moved down the hall to the presidential suite, Eric taking shallow breaths because of the fumes. He and Eubanks rushed through the door into the reception area—it had been left unlocked—and cleared it.

The door to the president's living quarters was open, and Eric and Eubanks made straight for it, each covering half the space. There was no one inside.

Eric told Drumm and Eubanks to check on the other entrances to this area and the war room while he stalked toward the living quarters with Kline just behind him.

Eric held his hand for the president to wait while he stepped into the apartment, but Kline followed him soon after, turning through the doorway, his gun raised.

He moved silently, his pulse loud in his ears, expecting an ambush, the quiet simply a trap to get him to lower his guard.

They moved through the living area of the one-bedroom presidential suite, the homey decor somehow accentuating the sense of threat.

Eric swept into the bedroom and the president tracked with him. It was clear. Eric relaxed, though he would never grow accustomed to the sight of Kline moving so confidently with that weapon.

The president caught him watching.

"You were always just counsel at CIA?" Eric asked.

"Dotting *i*'s and crossing *t*'s," Kline said, and moved farther into the room, aiming his gun around the bed. "They train everyone they send downrange."

Eric looked at him doubtfully. A call came in from Eubanks—the rest of the suite and the war room were clear.

The chair rail had been torn off the wall of the apartment, and the paneling—beautiful cherry millwork—had ripped away, revealing a wall safe, the metal gouged near where the bolt would lock. But it was still closed.

"It's welded to the framing," Kline said, walking around the bed toward it. The president stopped and stared down, his chest slowly rising and falling.

"What is it?" Eric asked.

Kline didn't answer. Eric came around and saw a canvas weekend bag upended, his wife's clothes spilled on the floor.

Shards of broken glass glinted among them. A framed photo lay on the ground, smashed. It showed Kline, with his wife and daughter, Jill, smiling in hiking gear, perched on a narrow peak in what looked like the Rockies.

Kline reached down and pulled the photo from the frame. He stared at it, running his thumb over the torn paper. He turned to face Eric, deep breaths coming in and out of his nose, the anger barely contained. They had come for his wife, chased her out of here, fearing for her life.

"Were Hardwick and Walsh close with anyone on Jill's detail?" Kline asked.

Eric thought for a moment. "No."

"But any of those agents could have been turned."

"We have to assume."

Kline tightened his fist until the knuckles cracked.

"The sooner we talk to the top, the sooner we can warn them," Eric said. "The safe."

Kline only nodded, his jaw clenched. He put the photo down and walked to the safe. After covering the keypad with his body, he entered a combination and pressed his thumb to the reader. The bolt pulled back. Kline opened the door and hauled out the black valise holding the nuclear codes.

Eubanks was waiting just outside, covering the door. Kline called the military aide in. He walked over and took the satchel from the president. A cord—leather over steel—ran from its handle to a metal bracelet. Eubanks's face was somber as he locked it to his wrist and brought the case down by his side.

He exchanged a look with Kline, and they all headed back to the living area. Drumm entered a moment later.

"Well?" Kline asked.

"The war room and the suite are secure."

"The locks still work? Can we trust them?"

"The lock on the outer door to the president's office was forced, but all the others are fine, so you can't get from his office into the rest of the suite or the war room. I can disable the electronics so we can only operate them manually from the inside," Drumm said.

"Fire damage?"

"Some near the roof of the war room."

"Does that give them a way in?"

"No. They'd have to put a massive charge on it to blow their way through. We'd still be twice as safe here in B than we would be staying in C."

"Good," Kline said. "We'll gather everyone here."

"Once we have them secured, we can go after the shooters, clear this place sector by sector," Eric said.

Kline nodded, then led them into the conference room to the north of the living quarters. He drew back the drapes on the rear wall to reveal a wide window with a view of the war room. It was empty, with stark shadows from the emergency lights. The screens were black. The place was the government's nerve center for the gravest crises imaginable, and now it was dead.

"You checked the comms in there?" he asked Drumm.

"Cut off. All of it."

Eric surveyed the war room. "They were here. Why would they give this up?" he asked. "It's the most secure spot in the facility. It has the command and control. They cut the comms. Surely they have a means to bring them back when they need them."

"What are you saying?" the president asked.

"They're planning something else."

Kline looked over the dark screens. "What?"

"I don't know. But we should get moving."

65

THEY EXITED BUILDING B the same way they had come in, walked to the back of the cavern that housed it, then turned north up the rear tunnel. Eric kept the pace fast. The shorter they were in the open with the codes, the better.

They passed the carve-out where Eric had been pinned down in the gun-fight earlier. He could make out the sheen of Chen's blood on the stone. Ten yards up, Eric caught a beam of light coming from the northern end of the tunnel, shining toward them. He backed the others against the wall and raised his gun. The light passed, disappearing somewhere north of Building E from the looks of it.

"What now?" Eubanks whispered.

"We go," Kline said.

They continued north until Drumm stopped them behind Building D in the rear tunnel. He pointed across the tunnel to the framing near the ceiling. Eric hadn't noticed it before. There was a square opening in the lining near the east side, and behind it blackness. That must have been the opening in the ceiling at the bottom of the comms shaft.

They stayed low as they crossed a bridge over the narrow canal that ran down the center of the rear tunnel, then they slipped a few yards north along the eastern wall.

Drumm stopped and put his hand on a vertical piece of framing standing a few feet from the cavern wall. It was made of tubular steel around three inches in diameter. The metal framing ran along the walls and across the ceiling of the tunnel, like construction scaffolding. The overhead liners were stretched across the frames connected to the round tunnel ceiling, to stop drips, Eric assumed. He could hear the drops drumming against the plastic every so often.

The liners only covered the arched ceiling, and started about twenty feet off the floor. Here the frames were exposed, with horizontal bars every four feet.

"We usually use a cherry picker to get up and reach the shaft," Drumm said, "but we can climb."

Eric looked to Eubanks and the leash connecting his wrist to the nuclear football. "Is that cord long enough to wear it across your body?"

He gazed upward. "I've got it."

"You're good with this?" Eric asked the president.

Kline reached up, grabbed a bar overhead, set his foot on one near his waist, and started climbing.

They soon reached the edge of the liner material as it began its arc along the upper walls and ceiling. Eric climbed up behind it. The air here was close and warm, the fumes thick. The tunnel wall began to curve toward the ceiling. Drumm led them onto a catwalk about twenty inches wide, running horizontally in the narrow space between the liner and the eastern wall of the tunnel. Eric leaned to fit as he went forward, his shoulder brushing against the cold stone. Odd drips of water ran down the walls, and every ten feet, he had to duck under a horizontal support bar.

They approached the square hole in the lining that Eric had seen earlier. Kline stopped just before it and Drumm pointed up. A round shaft about six feet in diameter ran up through the tunnel's ceiling.

Craning forward, Eric could make out the smooth interior walls of the shaft and a set of rungs bolted into them. Water dripped down the northern side.

Eubanks had made it this far while carrying the valise in his left hand. He unlocked the cuff from his wrist, ran it over his shoulder and across his body, then reattached it to the handle.

"Don't look down," Drumm said.

Eric let out a quiet laugh.

"Seriously."

Eric met eyes with the president for a last gut check. Kline grabbed a metal rung—each was only about a foot wide—and stepped off the catwalk. Hanging thirty feet above the stone floor, he started climbing.

Eric went second, then Eubanks, then Drumm. It felt like he was at the bottom of a well. The space was small and dark enough that Eric could ignore the growing vertical drop below him and focus on the next rung, each hand, each foot, settling into the rhythm, his gun bouncing on the sling over his shoulder.

The air grew dirtier as they rose. The smoke seemed to have settled here. The damp left the rungs increasingly slick under his hands.

He glanced down after what felt like a long time climbing, and saw the shaft dropping away below, and the faint circle of light near the bottom like a shining coin. He quickly looked back.

A moment later, Drumm let out a series of low coughs from the smoke, and Eric watched him, body shuddering, hands tight on the rungs.

The long stone well magnified the noise. It sounded loud enough to bring the attackers if they were anywhere near the bottom.

He paused, listening, watching for a change in the light below. Nothing. They kept moving. They were in almost total blackness now, and Eric turned on his flashlight, holding it in his left hand, and hooking that palm and wrist over the rungs to keep going. He shined it up to guide the others and caught the glimmer of greenstone—the ceiling high above them.

He could hear the other men's breath as they climbed. Slowly, the roof came closer, and Eric could make out bundles of cable running out from the wall and vertically through narrow holes in it.

"Unngh."

Kline's foot shot toward him. Eric braced for impact, grabbing the president's ankle, but Kline stopped inches away. He'd fallen two feet and hung from one hand, dragging his other foot against stone, searching for the rung and finally finding it.

Eric watched his calves shaking, heels going up and down like sewing machine needles. He'd seen it before, a combination of nerves and exhaustion when climbing.

"Keep moving," Eric said. "You're good." Freezing up would only make it worse.

The president was breathing fast.

"Kline, are you all right?"

Kline lifted one foot off and flexed the ankle that had been burned by steam in the power plant. He put it back on the rung and rose. Another step. Faster now. Eric followed and they fell into an even rhythm despite the smoke so thick it stung Eric's eyes. He peered up to see the president a few feet from the ceiling of the shaft with nowhere to go.

His upper half seemed to disappear into the wall, followed by his legs. Eric watched his foot leave the rung. When Eric neared the top, he saw it: a horizontal crawlspace going off to the left that had been drilled and blasted out of the rock, its eastern wall covered in thick bundles of cable and junction boxes. Eric took hold of one of the rails near its entrance, then pulled himself inside.

66

THE SPACE WAS five feet high and five feet across and went on horizontally for twenty feet, crowded with wires and full of smoke. Eric and Kline moved in to make room for Drumm and Eubanks. Drum squeezed past the president with an awkward nod and crawled forward.

He took a small headlamp from his kit and studied the wires, tracing them to one of the metal junction boxes on the wall. He unlocked its cover and peered inside, his lips drawing tight with concentration.

After pulling a multimeter from the nylon case, Drumm tested the circuits with a pair of red and black probes. He fought back a cough, opened another panel, took out a lineman's handset, and connected it.

The veins in his neck stood out as he put the handset to his ear, reached into the panel, and flicked a switch. Eric could make out the faint sound of static on the line. Drumm toggled another switch, put his hand to the wall, and waited.

A series of loud clicks came from the phone, then silence. Kline inched toward Drumm, listening.

"Raven Rock," said a voice from the handset. "This is NMCC One. Go ahead." Eric could hear the surprise in the speaker's tone as this Cold War relic spoke from beyond the dead, broadcasting by VLF from seventy-five miles away. How long had the other end of that line sat silent on some desk in the lowest reaches of the Department of Defense next to a weary duty officer? They had reached the National Military Command Center, the main war room at the Pentagon.

"This is Raven Rock." Drumm read out a short alphanumeric code. "I have the commander in chief."

Kline reached into the pocket of his fatigues and took out a thin beige plastic box. He dried his palms, then gripped both ends and bent it until it cracked in half. A piece of printed plastic the size of a playing card stuck out like the fortune from a cookie and Kline removed it, his hand shaking for an instant before he tightened his grip.

Eubanks unlocked the valise and pulled out a black leather binder.

Drumm passed Kline the handset.

"This is CINC actual," the president said. "Invoking the national command authority."

"Confirm, please."

He looked at the card and began reading slowly, "Echo Hotel X ray Zero . . ." As he went on, Eric slipped back toward the entrance to the crawlspace and peered down the four-hundred-foot drop. Kline finished the sixteen-character code.

The voice came back in a storm of static, unintelligible to Eric. He hoped the lack of clarity was just because he had moved away, but then he saw the disquiet on Kline's face.

"Repeat. Did not copy. Repeat," the president said, gripping the phone so hard his knuckles were white. Out of the static came four words. ". . . go ahead, Mr. President."

Kline pumped his hand holding the card. The system was still standing. He was still in power, for now.

"We are locked in, unable to open the doors, and under attack," Kline said. "Breach Raven Rock using any means necessary. Cancel the gold codes. Disregard any further military orders from this command." Static sounded from the handset. Kline pulled it back from his ear, then went on in a clear, even tone. "This is an inside attack. The Secret Service and likely the Raven Rock staff are compromised. Agents Michael Hardwick and Liam Walsh are coordinating the assault. Have the SecDef convene the cabinet and invoke the Twenty-Fifth Amendment. Contact the attorney general. He and his team need to view the files TEMPEST and OPERATION V on the executive office of the president compartmented system. The new code to access the messages in them is Charlie India Nine Two Mike Lima Six Zero. Repeat that back."

A voice came over the line, but it was washed out.

"Repeat. That. Back," Kline said, his voice rising, loud enough to echo down the shaft. Eric tightened his grip on the gun and gestured for him to keep the volume down—he didn't want him to give away their position—but Kline was staring straight forward.

A broken-up voice came from the handset:

". . . president authenticated . . . Raven Rock command . . ." More interference. ". . . Contact the attorney general . . . Tempest . . . Two Mike Lima." Then pure static.

"Did he only get the first half?" Eubanks asked, and raised the valise. "He should need these codes to finish cutting off Raven Rock from the command authority."

Kline began to repeat the message from the beginning, his hand tightening on the biscuit until it shook.

". . . cancel the gold codes. Disregard any further military orders from this command. Do you copy? Add extra protection for my daughter from the FBI Hostage Rescue—"

A click came over the line. The static was gone.

Kline looked to Drumm, who was already checking the panel with his meter. The president repeated the order again, speaking slowly, the strain in his voice rising with every word.

Drumm passed his hand across his throat. Kline lowered the handset and looked to Drumm and Eubanks.

"How much did they get?"

"It sounded like they received the evidence you were trying to pass on," Eubanks said. "That will give them the latest files on Operation V and the communications Will Maddox was working on when he infiltrated The Order. They probably heard about Hardwick and Walsh too."

He turned to Drumm. "Did the orders to cut off Raven Rock and invoke the Twenty-Fifth go through?" The amendment allowed the vice president to temporarily take over as commander in chief if Kline were unable to discharge his duties.

"I don't know."

Kline put his hand to his temple. "Fuck."

"What is it?"

"The Pentagon knows I'm alive. I'm here. I authenticated this command. If the order to cancel the codes and disregard anything coming out of Raven Rock didn't go through—"

"Jesus," Drumm said.

"Raven Rock is live."

"What does that mean?" Eric asked.

"We can't know without understanding how much they heard, but they could be primed to take orders from this command center now."

"Do you think the attackers overheard the transmission and cut off the line?"

"It's possible," Drumm said.

"Could they trace it here?"

Drumm looked at the panel, then back to him. From the way he knit his brow, Eric could tell it was bad.

"Can you reconnect?" Kline asked.

He shook his head. "The lines are dead."

"We need to get out of here and destroy all of these codes," Kline said. "If the attackers have a way to communicate, if they're controlling that line now, they absolutely cannot get their hands on them."

"Is there anything else you can do here?" Eric asked Drumm.

"No."

"Let's go," Kline said, and gestured to Eric.

Hill led them back to the shaft. He swung his legs out, gripping the rail with his right hand and feeling through the empty space for the rung. His foot slipped across the steel, then he got a firm step, leaned into the open shaft, and started climbing down. His muscles were fatigued from the long trip up. Surely the others were hurting.

Eubanks was just above him, the valise secured across his body. Eric moved quickly. The heat and the potential for an attack had him sweating, his hands slick.

The circle of light at the bottom of the shaft kept growing. The way down seemed so much shorter than the way up.

"Hold," Eric whispered, stopping the men as he studied the tunnel beneath them. He had a narrow view where the bottom of the comms shaft opened out through the tunnel ceiling. There was no threat he could see.

"Come on." He advanced.

A shadow moved below.

"Hold," Eric whispered again. They were eighty feet from the ground, with forty feet to climb until they reached the bottom of the shaft. A man appeared in the rear tunnel beneath them.

Eric reached for his gun. The figure glanced up and Eric recognized him as one of Drumm's men, Foster, the captain in charge of the security screening. He vanished to the left.

"Move," Eric said. "Steady." He didn't know if Foster was enemy or friendly, or if he had seen them, but either way Eric didn't want to be hanging from these rungs, easy targets in this goddamn stone barrel.

He climbed down, eyeing each step.

Three cracks boomed up the shaft—rifle rounds. They ricocheted, glinting off the wall, and he pulled tight against the rungs.

A quiet breath of pain came from above. He looked to see Eubanks bring his hand to his neck, his whole body tightening. "Paul," Eric said, taking aim down the shaft, "just hold on, okay, I—"

"I'm—"

Eubanks's feet slipped off the rung, and he dropped. His plunging weight tore free his grip. Eric wrapped his arm around a rung and braced as the soldier slammed into him. He let his gun fall to the end of its sling and grasped for anything to stop Eubanks's fall. He seized the lapel and collar of his jacket and gripped it with all his strength. The fabric went tight, wrenching Eric's fingers as Eubanks plunged past him.

It tore. Eric's arm flew up, holding a ripped section of cloth. Eubanks was gone, twisting slowly as he fell down the shaft into the rear tunnel. He hit flat on his back on its stone floor. Eric would never forget that sound. He started racing down the rungs at the edge of control.

A shadow moved below again. Eric stopped and took aim, but all he could see was a hand emerging for a split second, then Eubanks's still body sliding across the floor to the south until it disappeared.

The climb to the bottom of the shaft felt like a lifetime. Eric heard a muted crack from below, then fast footsteps. He came to the bottom. His feet dangled free, searching for the bars of the catwalk in the rear tunnel, blind and exposed for the moment that it took to support himself and climb down onto the framing and tuck behind the liner. He crouched low, gun up and ready, scanning what he could see of the tunnel. Eubanks lay on his back on the floor, his skull broken by the fall, the case torn away.

The shooter was gone.

67

ERIC CLIMBED DOWN the framing, searching for the gunman. His attention kept returning to Eubanks's still form. A red streak trailed over the stone, painted by the military aide's hair when the attacker dragged him out of sight. His left shoulder was dropped down three inches at an unnatural angle. The crack Eric had heard must have been Eubanks's collarbone breaking so Foster could strip the nuclear football from him. A shudder of rage ran through Eric.

He dropped the last four feet to the stone floor of the tunnel, went to the body, and felt for a pulse. Nothing.

He glimpsed Foster darting around a piece of equipment in the rear tunnel, past Building C about three hundred yards ahead. Eric dropped to one knee to steady the shot—still far too long for any guarantees on the MP5—and laid down a three-round burst, the stock pumping against his shoulder.

He sprinted south after Foster. The traitor carried the black valise under his left arm. As Foster neared the wreckage that had fallen in the rear tunnel behind Building B, the beam of a flashlight shot toward Eric from inside the pile of debris. Eric narrowed his eyes and kept moving as the light fixed on him.

A second light flicked on. The illumination from the two beams showed three figures besides Foster. He glimpsed Agents Hardwick's and Walsh's faces in the blue-white light.

Walsh dropped to one knee, readying a shot, mostly protected by a fallen piece of steel. The other men took aim from cover as well. Eric made out the weapons in their hands. They had honest-to-God rifles, what looked like M4 carbines firing high-velocity rounds, not the 9mm submachine guns that Eric and the other agents carried. The rifles had six times the range of his MP5.

Eric was running into an ambush, and Kline and Drumm were coming toward him. Any farther and he would be an easy target for that firing squad, two guns against four. Kline still had his codes on him. He couldn't let them take the president.

Eric halted, his feet skidding against the stone.

"Go north!" Eric shouted to Kline as the first rip of gunfire came from the attackers. A round skipped off the wall to his left, flashing red.

Kline and Drumm turned and ran to escape from the rear tunnel into Cavern D. Eric raced toward them and saw more lights fixing on them from the north in the rear tunnel. He cut left and jumped inside Cavern D just as shots rang out from the northern gunmen.

Kline and Drumm slipped through the springs under Building D to meet him.

"He got the valise," Eric said, leading them to the west, deeper under D. "There's four coming from the south, more from the north."

"Jesus," Kline said. "How? Are they multiplying?"

"Captain Foster was the officer in charge of security for Raven Rock," Eric said. "He could have brought others in."

As they tried to circle back to Building C, more lights appeared, more attackers searching along the main tunnel, cutting off their potential escape routes. A third of the way down Cavern D, another gunman ducked out of a passageway and opened fire with hurried shots. Eric calmly put two rounds into him from fifty yards—catching him in the body armor and the shoulder. He dropped his rifle and fled south down the passageway and Eric grabbed the weapon as they advanced. He, Drumm, and Kline tried to get free using another narrow passageway out of Cavern D, but soon after they entered it, they saw lights moving at both ends. Surrounded. A nauseous feeling took hold of Eric. There were probably a dozen attackers coming for them, maybe more.

As the shooters closed in, Drumm was able to use a panel for the fire and breach enunciator system to trigger an alarm far to the south, near the rear door of Building A. That drew the attackers away, and he, Eric, and Kline were finally able to make their way back to Building C to rejoin the others.

68

THEY WENT INSIDE Building C and tracked through its empty halls. The place was quiet, by all appearances just an after-hours office building, which only heightened the sense of strangeness, of menace.

Eric kept his steps quiet as they headed for the infirmary. He rounded a corner into the hall, and saw Agent Cody, gun up, aimed straight at him.

"Friendly," he said, but her barrel was already lowering.

"I heard shots. Are you okay? Anyone following?"

"We're clean, but we took contact."

Her eyes went to Eric's hands, still stained with blood.

"Eubanks is gone," Eric said.

Pain in her eyes as she nodded slowly. Kline approached her and they all went in through the open door to the infirmary.

Agents Leigh and Brimley were guarding the hall. Kline walked into the waiting area. His wife was standing by the door to the treatment room, talking quietly with Claire Givens.

The first lady turned as Kline entered, and he went straight to her and took her in his arms. She held him, eyes closed, an ophthalmoscope gripped in her hand.

Givens looked over the three men who had returned and then checked the waiting area. "What happened to Eubanks?"

Kline breathed in, then said, "He was killed."

The first lady's hand covered her mouth.

"Who did it?" Givens asked.

"Captain Foster, the security officer from the communications crew, but there were other attackers."

"How many?" Givens asked.

Kline looked to Eric.

"There were at least three separate groups of attackers," Eric said. "They seemed to be patrolling the hallways, searching, then they tried to corner us. Minimum eight attackers, easily twelve."

"My God." A stunned expression on Givens's face. "Were you able to get through to anyone in Washington?"

Kline waved Drumm and Cody in and gestured for them to shut the door behind them.

"Yes," Kline said. "The Pentagon." The first lady exhaled in relief. "But the connection was shaky, and we were cut off. I was able to authenticate myself, but I don't know that they got the order to cancel our codes and sever this bunker from the national command."

"What about Jill?" she asked, rubbing her thumb across her palm at the thought of her daughter.

Kline put his hand on her shoulder. "I tried to order extra protection for her."

"Did they confirm it?"

"The transmission was broken up. I don't know."

"Hardwick. Walsh," she said. "We can't trust the Secret Service anymore. Anything could be happening up there."

She moved in closer, whispered something to him. Eric could only just make out part of Kline's reply.

". . . so sorry. I had to start with the codes. The whole country is at stake."

From Kline's pained look, Eric had to assume she had asked why his first order hadn't been about their child.

The first lady stared at him for a moment, then shut her eyes, focused through the emotion. She was used to wearing a mask, hiding herself. It was the only way to survive the glare that comes with the most powerful office in the world. "The Pentagon knows we're here," she said. "Under attack.

They'll come for us. With everything going on they won't listen to some wild order from this bunker."

"If all they got was that the president is still alive, they might not transfer power," Givens said. "Raven Rock is still active." She turned to Kline. "Did they get the football?"

"Yes."

"Fuck," she said. "Where is the biscuit? We need to destroy it. It doesn't matter if they have the satchel: without the gold codes, it's useless."

Eric noticed Drumm looking down, a worried expression on his face. "What can they do with the football codes alone, Drumm?"

"We should be fine," the engineer said.

Eric had his doubts about that. The doomsday command-and-control systems wired up to Raven Rock were a seventy-year-old patchwork that had been tested only once or twice in true emergencies and come close to failing every time. He didn't know what a dedicated insider with the codes might be able to get away with.

"If the codes are useless, why did they take them?" Eric asked. "Can they use them to send direct commands to the bombers or silos?"

"They shouldn't be able to, but we've never run into anything like this before. Your people and my people have turned. They know those systems. We can't lower our guard."

"But everything would have to go through the Pentagon and the Strategic Command," Givens said.

Drumm looked nauseous. "Not everything."

The others turned his way.

"This bunker is part of the defense shield over Washington," Drumm went on. "There are two batteries of surface-to-air missiles built into the top of the mountain."

"Patriots or NASAMS?" Eric asked. He'd seen the concrete structures housing them on their way here.

"Patriots. Sixteen of them. Their presence here is a tightly held secret."

Eric cursed under his breath. That gave the missiles a range of up to a hundred miles. "Can someone take control of them from inside the bunker without going through the Pentagon?"

"Theoretically, no. But if they knew the system and had the codes from the football and had enough time, they might find a way."

"Jesus," Givens said. "Only a lunatic would try for a nuclear strike, but I could see them launching a Patriot against a target to prove they were serious. They'd have fifteen more to force us to meet their demands."

"Or they could use them to fight back a military attempt to retake Raven Rock," Eric said. "Given everything they've done so far, the attackers would absolutely pull that trigger."

"But you did get through," Dr. Kline said. "What do they know?"

"They definitely received the part of the message that will lead them to Will Maddox's evidence about The Order," the president said. "That should help them track down whoever is behind this up top."

"They'll know it's a coup, then. I mean, God, we've been held down here for eighteen hours. What's happening in Washington? Is the government still standing?"

"The system was working. They recognized my authority. The NMCC at the Pentagon was online and the authentication all went according to procedure. Everything is still in place. I need something to destroy the gold codes," Kline said.

The first lady waved him into the treatment room, took out a metal tray, and switched on an overhead fan. Eric went to the door and smelled alcohol as she leaned over the workbench. Flames rose from the tray. The plastic card with the codes blackened and curled into ash.

Chen's face was pale. Eric had to watch closely to see his chest moving on the table, barely rising and falling.

"How's he doing?" he asked Givens.

"Dr. Kline thinks he may have some bleeding and pressure buildup in his brain."

A sound like a sigh came from the back of Chen's throat. Eric could see a fresh dressing behind his ear.

"She did what she could down here," the chief of staff said.

He looked at Chen. "Would we be able to move him?"

She shook her head. "You think they're coming here?"

"They're looking for us," Eric said. "Eventually they'll look here."

"What do they want?" she asked.

As Eric thought about how to answer, Kline spoke up. "They want me to confess."

"To what?"

"These conspiracy theories that I'm going to seize power." Eric could hear the disdain in his voice. "That I killed anyone who tried to stop me or tell the public. That I murdered Agents Rivas and Stiles. Hardwick talked about it when we were one-on-one. He wanted to drag me into the broadcast studio in the war room and do a show trial."

"So they must still have a way to communicate out?" Givens said.

Kline nodded.

"Is there a way to talk to them?" Givens asked. "To reason with them?"

Eric looked at the doctor on the table and thought of Eubanks, his body broken on the greenstone floor.

"They're shooting on sight," Eric said. "I thought I could get through to Hardwick under the right circumstances, possibly talk him down. I thought I saw something in him . . . ambivalence, doubt, but I don't know. There are so few of us. We can't risk getting drawn into an ambush."

Givens looked at the others. "We're outnumbered now. How could they have turned eight, ten, twelve of the most trusted people in the government against us? And gotten them all in here?"

Eric looked to Drumm. "Captain Foster handled security, yes? Background screens? Physical access?"

Drumm nodded, a nauseous look on his face.

"Then the plotters only needed him, one man to bring the others in."

"Could they have sneaked in more people we don't know about?" Givens asked. "Weapons? Equipment?"

Eric put his hand to the barrel of the rifle he'd taken from one of the gunmen and held it up to Drumm. "SIG MCX. Do you have anything like this down here?"

"No. Only pistols and they're safe."

Eric checked the holographic sight. "The only units who get this stuff are special operations and counterassault. So yes, they have brought in their own gear. That explains the incendiaries and explosives too."

"There could be dozens of attackers down here," Givens said. "People they brought in who are not on any roster?"

"We don't know," Eric said. "Assume the worst."

Silence reigned for a moment. They were not dealing with some rogue attackers. They were outgunned on the enemy's turf.

"You let this happen," Givens said to Drumm.

"So did we," Eric said.

"What now?" she asked. "Are we safe here?"

"For now," Eric said. "But they don't need to hide their numbers or actions anymore. They are going to come for us, search every inch of this place. I want to get you all to Building B, the president's suite and the war room. It's the most secure spot we have."

"We can't move Chen," Sarah said.

"Can you get him stable?" Eric asked. "Relieve the pressure long enough to get him there?"

"Possibly," she said. "But that has its own risks."

Eric nodded. It would put the others in danger too, as they moved slowly, exposed and vulnerable.

"We're not outnumbered," Drumm said. "We have my people."

"Like Captain Foster?" Givens said sharply.

"No. The others. I have twenty-two officers down here besides him."

"They could all be against us."

"All of them?" Drumm said. "Come on. I was with seven of my staff after we fled the incendiaries that went off under Building B. Moro was with nine. They were all out there working to evacuate, put out the fires, or keep the air flowing. They had a chance to go after Kline or his team and they didn't. Most of them I've known for ten years at least."

"I've known Hardwick for seventeen," Eric said. "You can't underestimate how insidious this shit is, the lies, how they get their hooks into people."

"But they proved out in the moment. That's the same reason any of us trust any of the others in this room," Drumm said.

"You'd stake your life on that?"

A long pause. "I would."

"Where are your officers now?"

"Most went north to Building E, the comms center, after the fires broke out to try to keep this place running and see if there was another way to get the blast doors open or find another way out. Others are working in the tunnels."

"Major Moro headed out a half hour ago to check on your officers in E and see if she could help," Givens said.

"Who backed up Hardwick's and Walsh's alibis when Maddox and Chilton were killed?" Kline asked.

"Captain Foster," Eric said.

"Good," Givens said. "We know he's bad now. That doesn't cast doubt on the others."

"We have the pistols in Building E," Drumm said. "We can arm my staff—the ones we can absolutely trust—and even the playing field."

"Drumm knows this facility," Eric said. "He can use it against them. With that and more people, we could retake it."

"They have explosives," Drumm said. "If we get our hands on them, we could blast the old construction tunnel for an escape route."

Eric wanted Drumm's numbers. He wanted his guns. He wanted a fucking hunting party after what these traitors had done to his people.

"What are the chances you can get that old tunnel open for us to escape through?" Eric asked.

"We can't be certain it goes through to the surface anymore, but it should. It was part of the original construction, filled in when they were done. It's unreinforced and has a couple million pounds of stone sitting on top of it. There's no way to know if you can open it up without collapsing it on whoever tries."

"Odds?"

"Sixty–forty for success. I can't in good conscience order men and women in there."

Eric shook his head, the frustration rising.

Drumm clasped his hands together and looked down at them for a moment. "But I would try it myself . . . if we get the explosives."

Eric looked at the engineer with a newfound respect. "Thank you, Colonel."

Eric looked around the room. No hiding. No negotiations. They might have the strength for a counterassault. "All right—"

Drumm's radio came to life with a woman's voice barely breaking through the static: "Drumm. Come back."

The engineer lifted his radio, and Eric gave him a nod.

"This is Drumm. Go ahead."

More static, then Eric heard the words: ". . . progress on the door. We think we can get it open." Eric recognized the voice. It was Major Moro, Drumm's deputy.

69

MORO WAS JUST outside Building C. Eric and Drumm met her at a side entrance and brought her in. As they walked back to the infirmary, she briefed Drumm. His crew had continued working on the blast doors at the far ends of the main tunnel and made a breakthrough on the ones in the north, creating the possibility of an exit. Moro was all bright energy, talking fast as she rushed through the technical details—bypassing the SCADA computer control system, overvolting, running electricity straight to the bolt draws.

"Did you get that?" Drumm asked.

"It sounds like running the starter of a truck engine straight to the battery," Eric said.

"Analogous," Drumm replied.

Eric didn't mention that the last time he tried that, with a Toyota Tacoma in Baja, the engine had burst into flames.

"Bottom line?" Eric asked.

"We almost have the northern doors unlocked, and then we can draw them back with a hydraulic press and winches."

"This is different than your first try?"

"Vastly. We were trying to pull back the bolts then, but they didn't budge. They're unlocked now, and should be easy to retract."

They met with Givens and Kline just outside the entrance to the infirmary, and Drumm and Moro updated them on the doors and went over the plans.

"This is real?" Givens asked, hesitant as if she didn't dare say it aloud. "A way out?"

Drumm nodded solemnly. "It's our best chance."

Eric put Agents Cody, Brimley, and Leigh on security, giving each a post around the infirmary. Kline looked at him expectantly, ready with his weapon, and Eric tried to figure out how the hell you give the president of the United States an order.

"Stay inside with Dr. Kline, Chen, and the others. Don't let your guard down for anyone."

"Good luck," Kline said.

"Thanks. Anything jumps off, you raise us on the public address. There's a box—"

"I saw it. What's the call?" Kline asked.

"Use *reveille reveille reveille*," Eric said. "Then I'll know to come back here."

He slung his rifle and stepped out with Drumm and Moro, then watched as the president's people locked the door behind them. If Drumm's people were going to get those doors open, they would need protection.

Drumm, Moro, and Eric exited on the north side of Building C into the cavern, then used the passageways to head north without being seen by the attackers.

As they moved through the cavelike passageways, Eric heard Moro's breath—fast and shallow, gripped by fear.

Eric let her go ahead a little and whispered to Drumm. "Is she okay?"

He nodded and spoke into Eric's ear. "It's getting to her. But she's solid. She came on duty Friday morning, and was supposed to leave Saturday, but then we went into lockdown. She should be waking up to take her daughter to a swim meet right about now. Hasn't seen her kids in forty-eight hours." He paused. "Doesn't know if she will again."

It was Sunday, 5:10 a.m. They'd arrived Saturday morning, and been trapped down here for a full day and overnight. It would wear anyone down.

"And you?" he asked Drumm.

"I'm good." A bittersweet smile. "Could use a bit of fresh air, though."

Eric nodded. It felt like he'd been trapped on the bottom level of an underground parking garage for a week. He walked faster to catch Moro solo.

"Good work on the doors, Major. How are you holding up?"

"Fine," she said. "Not something we train for."

"You're doing great."

"Thanks," she said. "It's funny. You know, Drumm's been thinking about this moment his whole life—a true crisis, wondering how he would do. He doesn't want to let you down. You should see his basement, big home theater, racks and racks of movies. *Band of Brothers, Clear and Present Danger,* he loves that stuff. He found out you all were coming and that got him started talking about *In the Line of Fire,* you know, Clint Eastwood running with one hand near his gun and the other on the presidential limousine."

Eric smiled. "You know why we put the hand on the car?"

"No."

"You're looking elsewhere. If you're not touching that car, it turns and you keep going."

"Has that happened?"

"A guy from my training class was fifty feet down the block before he realized what was going on, the crowd shouting at him and pointing that he lost the ride."

She laughed.

"You all should be damn proud of yourselves for keeping us alive this long," he said.

"Thank you."

Eric separated briefly from Moro and Drumm and headed for the rear tunnel to check the spot where Eubanks had fallen. Only a red patch on the stone floor remained. The attackers must have taken his body away.

He returned to the passageways. Five minutes later, he reached the cavern that housed Building E and the comms center within it where Drumm's people were working.

"Drumm, it's Hill, where are you?" he said into his radio.

"The main tunnel at the front entrance of Building E," the engineer replied. "There's a truck here for us. My staff are all headed up to the northern blast doors."

"Progress?"

A breath. "They're open."

"What?"

"Get here. I'll tell you on the way."

70

ERIC MET DRUMM in the main tunnel in front of Building E. The engineer stood beside a running F-350 with one of his officers behind the wheel and Moro in the passenger seat.

Drumm climbed into the bed of the truck and gestured for Eric to follow. Hill got in, slammed the liftgate shut, and they took off.

He kept his gun ready in case the noise drew out the shooters. They drove north in the main tunnel, leaving behind the long, straight section that ran along Caverns A through E and allowed access to the front of the buildings within. Here the tunnel began turning slightly to the left.

The hair on Eric's neck bristled. This gently curving two-and-a-half-mile section of tunnel north of Building E had no exits. It was just smooth stone walls until it reached the blast doors at its northern end. The attackers could easily cut them off from the south and corner them in here if those doors remained shut.

"They've got the outer blast door open," Drumm said. "One hundred percent open."

"And the inner door?" Eric asked. There were two thirty-ton doors up there, one after the other, sealing off the tunnel.

"They've drawn the bolts on it, but the machinery to pull it back is dead. The only thing holding it shut is its own weight, so we can haul it back manually."

If they managed to budge that inner door, they would have an open path to the outside.

"Your staff initiated all of this?" Eric asked.

"They've been hitting those doors with everything we have."

"What changed now?"

"It's hard to say."

As the emergency lights flashed by overhead, Eric could almost imagine he was simply driving through a regular vehicle tunnel, like the one that ran under Baltimore Harbor on 895. But every so often, he would catch that lingering smell of smoke.

"Could it be Hardwick and his people, trying to escape?"

"It's possible. But we've had a crew up there and they haven't seen anyone. It could also be someone breaching from the outside . . . The president's VLF transmission may have worked."

"The military can open it from out there?"

"The Corps of Engineers can do anything."

Three minutes later, the inner blast door came into view. Its white wall sealed off the tunnel to the north. Seeing their exit cut off so completely gave Eric a twinge of claustrophobia.

They parked and all four exited the truck. Most of Drumm's people had gathered at the western edge of the door, where it would first open, retracting from west to east, slowly disappearing into the eastern wall of the tunnel like a pocket door. Moro rushed over to the group.

The drive to see the sun again was a mania affecting all of them. His own body felt lighter at the thought of it after twenty hours locked down here in the dark. He wanted out.

A massive clang reverberated down the tunnel. A sergeant hauled back on a sledgehammer and slammed it into something—Eric couldn't see it behind the other workers—driving it into the western side of the blast door.

"Easy," Drumm said. He pointed to the western edge of the door. "We wedge and force it open there, which will let us hook up the cables and haul it the rest of the way."

Another set of officers were laying out a system of steel cables, pulleys, and winches on the ground just in front of the door, running parallel to it.

Three more blows rang out, and the workers moved in, forcing a jack in at the western edge of the door. It looked to Eric like an oversize version of the jaws of life, a hydraulic spreader-cutter press that could be wedged into crevices to force something open.

"It's in!" someone yelled. "Steady!"

The sounds boomed down the tunnel. There was no stealth here. Eric surveyed the approach from the south.

The engine on a compressor roared to life, growing louder and louder.

"Hold!" Moro yelled by the press. "Hold!"

A high squeal rang in his ears, metal grinding against metal.

Moro shouted for everyone to join in on the western side of the door.

Drumm ran toward her, while Eric remained on guard. A crowd surged there around the press, a dozen of them holding it in place against the building pressure. If something snapped it would take heads with it.

"Hold on!" Moro shouted, pushing in with the others.

The metal shrieked. Someone holding an open binder in one hand tried to wave down Drumm, shouting about deformation and pounds-force.

"Fuck the checklist," Drumm said, and drove in with the others. "You've got it! More!"

The blast door inched back, with a low shudder that shook the stone under Eric's feet. Shouts of relief came from the crowd. Eric looked at the door, as big as his first apartment building in Falls Church—a two-up two-down—and probably heavier. He couldn't believe they had moved it, but there it was along the western edge—a black gap an inch wide.

"Set the cables!" Moro yelled. "It's open!"

She put her hand to the painted steel and looked up at it as if giving thanks.

Standing in the infirmary treatment room in Building C, Dr. Kline pressed two fingers into the clammy skin along Chen's carotid and felt only stillness. She brought her ear next to his mouth, straining to feel a touch of breath.

"Brimley," she said, waving him over and pointing to Chen's chest. The agent laced his fingers together, placed them on Chen's sternum, and looked to the first lady.

"Press, press, press," she said in a steady rhythm, and Brimley pumped Chen's chest. She pinched the doctor's nose and breathed into his mouth, his two-day stubble scratching her lips as she tapped with her foot to keep Brimley on time.

"Harder," she said.

One pump, a second. The dry twig crack of a rib. Brimley winced. "It's normal," she said. "Keep going."

Another breath.

She pulled back and whispered, "Come on, Nate. Come on."

71

MORO GUIDED THE crew at the western side of the blast door. They had set up the winch system, strung with steel cable as thick as Eric's thumb, and hooked it into the edge of the blast door where they had forced an opening. The other ends of the cables were attached to steel shackles bolted into the stone on the eastern wall, at the far side of the door. It would let them force the whole barrier to retract.

Moro stepped back, raised her hand, and brought it down. The winch came to life—a hydraulic system run off another compressor—drawing the slack out of the wires.

"Watch the angle!" Drumm shouted. "No shearing!"

"More!" Moro yelled. The motor revved higher. Eric eyed the straining cables.

The door shuddered back, eight inches, two, another four, the whole tunnel trembling with its weight.

Moro ignored the danger of the taut steel, walked up to the gap, and looked through.

Eric watched her face, the eyes wide with awe. He studied her hair. It was still, as was the dust at her feet.

There was a sudden heaviness in his chest. That wasn't right. If both doors were now open, air should be moving.

He crossed to the side so he could look straight through the gap as Moro aimed her light through.

"What . . ." she said.

A hundred yards down her beam of light hit white-painted steel. The outer door hadn't moved since they had sealed themselves in twenty hours ago.

"What is it?" someone called out.

"The north door," she said, her voice hollow with shock. "It's closed."

The others crowded in, their voices a disappointed murmur. Moro raised her hands, handing out orders, trying to keep calm.

Eric went to Drumm. "What the hell is going on? You said it was open."

Drumm lifted his shoulders. "The SCADA was wrong. But we're through one," he said, the relief still showing on his face. "The bolts on the second should be drawn back too. We just need time."

"Who gave you the readings that it was open?"

"What?" He thought for an instant. "Major Vaughn."

Eric had seen her file. Rebecca Vaughn. She'd been at Raven Rock for eight years—shoulder-length brown hair and the look of a dedicated runner. He scanned for her. "Where is she?"

Drumm looked around. "She was working on the cables. I don't know."

Eric started moving south, away from the sound of the engines.

The trucks were still there. There were no other exits or places to hide that he could see.

He listened, straining to hear over the engines and the voices. He caught it, faint but there—retreating footsteps.

He turned back to see Drumm walking toward him. "She took off. This is all wrong."

"It's open, Agent Hill. We're so close."

Eric looked at the MP5 hanging on Drumm's shoulder.

"You're with me," Eric said.

"My people are here," Drumm said, pointing toward the blast doors.

"Your people could end up dead if this is a trap," Eric said, and started walking. Drumm hesitated for a moment, then followed.

Eric kept them at a trot, moving south and keeping to the eastern side of the main tunnel, which gave them the longest view around its gradual curve.

He caught movement ahead—a retreating shadow, cast by one of the emergency lights farther down.

As he advanced, he saw three figures, all armed, disappear around a front-end loader parked along the eastern wall ahead. The person in the back looked like Vaughn.

He shouldered his rifle and proceeded, ready for the shots. The attackers had the advantage, both in numbers and weapons and by firing from cover.

No one shot back. He moved forward to see farther down the tunnel, every muscle in his body primed for the crack of gunfire.

Nothing. *Where the fuck are you?*

More shadows in the distance, far beyond the loader. They were retreating. Why flee when they had the advantage? Eric's stomach tightened. This was all wrong.

Tss tss tss tss tss tss.

A string of pops sounded from the main tunnel ceiling behind Eric, like a bundle of Black Cat fireworks going off, only twenty times louder.

He turned and looked north up the tunnel. Drumm was fifty feet to Eric's north and Moro was two hundred and fifty feet past him. Both had been moving his way.

The ceiling liners, stretched over framing, started to shake halfway between Drumm and Moro. A piece of metal clanged against the floor along the side of the tunnel there. The attackers were blowing the ceiling and it looked like the collapse would start between the two engineers.

"Get clear!" Eric yelled, his voice booming up the tunnel. "Moro. Go north!" She was on the far side of the explosions. Her best chance was to run away from Eric, toward the blast doors. "Drumm, to me!" Eric shouted, waving him closer.

Eric covered the tunnel to the south as the lining material overhead beat like a drum, the sound moving closer as the collapse spread toward him. Another piece of metal tore through it and fell on the ground behind Drumm. It was the end of one of the tiebacks—the threaded rods driven into the ceiling to support the weight of the stone overhead.

Drumm saw it too, and slowed for an instant, his mouth opening.

"Come on!" Eric called as he ran too, a flat sprint to escape the falling debris.

A fine shower of what looked like sand streamed down to Eric's left where two sections of liner met. He didn't look up, just kept moving as a creak sounded from the ceiling ahead. Sweat ran down his face.

He heard a sound like a sail snapping—stone hitting the lining. Then another. And another. The individual noises gathered into a rush, a sudden downpour. Eric risked a glance back and saw Drumm running toward him and Moro sprinting the other way, shrinking in the distance, a long tendril of hair loose from her bun, twisting in the air. He prayed she would make it far enough north to escape on the far side of the cave-in.

The liner over her tore. Mailbox-sized chunks of stone fell from the ceiling and crashed beside her. She ran faster, then disappeared behind the cascading debris as the tunnel collapsed.

A cloud of gravel and dust blew toward them. Squinting, Eric could see Drumm's shoulders tightening up as the shock of what had happened to Moro took him. His steps grew clumsy, slow.

Eric stilled his breath and went back, chunks of rock pelting him as he gripped Drumm's upper arm, steadying him, pulling him forward, racing against the falling stone.

72

THE DUST SWALLOWED them. Eric closed his eyes and kept moving. After five or six feet, he opened them, just barely, and could see the emergency lights ahead through the gray. He kept the rifle level, chest high, ready for fast shots from one hand.

The swirl thinned and Eric slowed to a trot with Drumm by his side. The engineer gritted his teeth and put his hand to his lower back. It looked like he'd taken a hit from the stones.

"You all right?" Eric asked, and scanned the main tunnel ahead. He led them to the eastern side for the better perspective around the curve.

The engineer didn't respond. He was still handling his weapon, but as the dust settled Eric could see the deadness in his eyes. They stared ahead, focused on nothing.

"Drumm." The other man took two steps but didn't respond. Eric touched his arm, and his head came around slowly. He was so out of it that Eric pulled him behind a parked scissor lift for cover.

"They're gone." Drumm's voice was faint, disbelieving.

"It wasn't the whole tunnel. They're cut off, but most of them are probably—"

"Moro," he said, and looked back to the rubble. "She's dead. There's nothing you can do."

"She might have made it far enough. She could have survived."

Drumm closed his eyes. Three long breaths, then they opened again.

"The attackers wanted to change the odds. Now we're outnumbered. Trapped where they want us."

"They wanted us in there," Eric said, cocking his head toward the collapse. "To take us out of the fight. They're making a move."

"The others."

"They could be going after the president and his people right now. Innocents. Leverage. They need us, Bruce. There's work to do."

Eric watched the anger filling in on Drumm's face, the brow drawing down, the lips pressing together. The life came back into his eyes.

"You ready?"

Drumm brought up his weapon.

"Let's go." Eric leaned out around the lift, swept the tunnel with the barrel of the SIG rifle, then moved south.

As they walked between the curving walls of the main tunnel, the quiet set Eric on edge. It was as if the attackers had vanished. Every corner, every obstacle was a waiting ambush. He was almost glad he'd had to rally Drumm, because he'd needed the boost himself. Seeing Moro in that tunnel collapse and knowing that they were outnumbered left him feeling hollowed out, sick. The only choice was to keep moving, answer it with action, and protect the others. He was glad for the way stalking through this space occupied every sense, fixed his mind on the present only.

They soon entered the straight stretch of the main tunnel. It ran due south with the openings of the five caverns and the buildings inside them spaced at regular intervals along its eastern wall. They ran from E to A, north to south, all on Eric's left as he walked south.

He and Drumm worked methodically toward Cavern C, scanning under the foundations of the buildings inside their caverns. They encountered no resistance. Eric climbed the steel steps to C's main entrance.

He lifted his radio and tried to raise Cody. Only static came back. He reached for the door handle, expecting it to be locked.

It turned freely. Eric stayed silent, but his focus sharpened. He waved Drumm up and directed the engineer to stand just beside him. Eric put his left hand on the door lever and held the SIG in the other.

He threw open the door and charged through, sidestepping, clearing the hallway then sweeping to his right as Drumm followed him and took up the other sectors. No one. Not a sound. The agents he'd put on guard were gone.

They moved down the main corridor inside the building toward the infirmary, where they had left the president and the others. The door to the waiting area was unlocked. Two empty water bottles and a paper coffee cup sat on the table, the coffee lukewarm—they hadn't been gone for long. There was no blood. No gunshot damage. No tossed furniture. Nothing to indicate a struggle.

The treatment room was empty, the paper on the table still crinkled from Chen's weight, but he was gone. Eric led Drumm into the storage room. The air was cooler than Eric expected. He walked up to the chest refrigerator and opened it. Three body bags now.

Drumm came up beside him. Eric reached out with his left hand and gripped the cold brass of the zipper on the top bag, then pulled it down.

Chen's left eye looked back at them. Eric spread the bag open. There were no other obvious injuries.

Drumm lowered his head and shook it slowly as Eric closed the bag and brought down the lid.

"We left six people here. Three armed," Eric said. "I don't think they could have been taken without a fight."

He'd feared the worst, but the absence of any signs of violence reassured him.

"They just left?" Drumm said.

"The doors are unlocked. That's consistent with them fleeing. Maybe they heard the chaos. Or saw the threat coming."

"Or they could have been outnumbered or coerced."

Completely surrounded and forced to give up without a fight. It was possible.

"Come on," Eric said. If they had been rounded up, he knew where they would be taken. He walked out and turned left, headed for the nearest exit.

73

AGENT CODY STEPPED through an exterior door into Building B and entered the executive office area, sweeping the space with her MP5 as Agent Brimley came in behind her.

"Clear," she said.

Kline and Laura Leigh ushered Sarah Kline inside the building, followed by Claire Givens. The president took a last look around the cavern outside, his gun up, then came in and locked the door behind them.

They had all been in the infirmary in Building C, shaken by Chen's death, when the first shots rang out.

Brimley was on patrol, just inside the main entrance to Building C, when he heard the gunfire. He risked a look outside in the main tunnel and heard the sounds echoing from the north, far up the tunnel near the blast doors.

After the sound of a massive collapse thundered down the tunnel, he saw a crew of gunmen heading their way. With Kline, he made the call to evacuate out the back of Building C into the rear tunnel and return to the war room and presidential suite that occupied the back of Building B—the most secure location in Raven Rock. The president's people were able to move easily now that Chen had passed, and Kline wanted to retake the war room in Building B before the attackers could.

Now inside B, they crossed from the executive office area into the hallway that led to the rooms of the presidential suite and military command center. The Secret Service agents stayed in front, clearing the path to the president's living quarters.

Kline unlocked the door to his apartment and stepped back as Agents

Brimley and Cody went in. Cody looked at the chairs thrown across the room, the gouges on the walls. Her pulse rose, knowing they had been here.

The president studied the room. "That's all from when they were here the first time."

It took ten minutes to sweep the war room and double-check and secure all the doors that led to it and the presidential suite.

Cody threw the last bolt, and she and Brimley joined Agent Leigh, the president, Sarah Kline, and Chief of Staff Givens in the conference room. The first lady and Givens were standing next to the window that looked out onto the war room next door. Dr. Kline had her arms crossed, her fingers worrying the skin near her elbow.

"We're locked down," Brimley said.

It was as if some electricity that had been coursing through all their bodies suddenly shut off. Givens's shoulders relaxed, and the first lady sat down and rested her head in her hands.

Kline put his hand to Brimley's arm. "Thank you," he said. "Thank you all."

He excused himself, went to Dr. Kline—she still looked haunted by having Chen die under her hands—and walked with her to the door to the living quarters.

Cody hitched the sling of her MP5 up on her shoulder and went to Brimley, now the ranking agent.

"I'm going back out," she said.

Brimley didn't answer at first, just thought about it. Clearly the idea troubled him.

"What?" Leigh said, just over Cody's shoulder.

"There were shots fired," Cody said. "Hill, Drumm, and Drumm's people are still out there. They need help. They could be under attack by the plotters as we speak."

Leigh looked to Brimley. "She can't go alone."

"We have no idea what's going on in those tunnels or if anyone is alive," he said. "Have you heard anything over the radio?"

"Nothing," Leigh replied.

"They can't all have been taken out," Cody said.

"That was one hell of a blast," Brimley said. "It sounded like the whole bunker was collapsing."

"I'll find Hill and Drumm and whatever reinforcements they have . . ." Cody stopped herself from saying *have left*. "The suite here is locked down. Now we need a scout, eyes on the tunnels outside."

Brimley rubbed his chin.

"I can't just leave them out there," Cody said.

"Leigh is right. You shouldn't go alone," the older agent said.

Leigh looked toward the conference room and then the president's apartment. "We're thin. We can't lose two people."

"I'll be fine," Cody said. "I'll stay hidden until I can link up with Hill."

"How will you find him?"

"The radios work pretty well on line of sight. I can check the two tunnels in five minutes without sticking my head out."

The two older agents exchanged a look and Brimley sighed. "All right."

"You need extra magazines for that?" Leigh pointed to Cody's gun.

Cody patted her hip. "I'm set."

"You see anything," Brimley said, "don't engage. Come back here. You're a shadow. Got it?"

"Got it."

74

TWO MINUTES LATER, Cody was stepping out of Building B through an exit on its northern side into the cavern. The door clicked shut and locked behind her. She went down the steps and headed east in the cramped alley-like lane between the cavern wall and the spring foundations under B, picked her way through the wreckage that had fallen in the rear tunnel behind Building B, and started tracking north in that tunnel.

It was more than a mile long, still hazy from the fires, with yellow emergency lights overhead every two hundreds yards barely able to penetrate the murk, leaving stretches of darkness in front of her.

Again, the sheer size of this place struck her, the buildings in their caverns stretching two thousand feet to her west. With their high curved ceilings and fluorescent lights, these bores kept reminding her of the stations and tunnels of the DC metro, endless miles connected deep underground, as if she were wandering through its abandoned system, taking shelter from a ruined city.

Fifty feet up, she stopped, scanned in every direction, pressed her back to the cold stone wall, and lifted her radio.

"Hill. Come back. Hill." She kept her voice low.

Another click on the button. "Drumm. Come back."

She double-checked the frequency and encryption keys Hill had given her and started moving north. She was about to try again when the radio came to life.

"This is Hill," said a voice through the static. "Cody, is that you?"

"Yes." A sudden lightness filled her. "Are you all right?"

"Thank God. Yes, we're good. You?"

"Fine. We got the president to the safe spot. The place we talked about before you left."

"Casualties?" Eric asked, his voice growing clearer. He must have been getting closer.

"Chen, from the past injuries. The rest are okay." She remembered the White House doctor's lifeless face, like a plastic mask, as they zipped him into a body bag. Hardwick and the other plotters had now murdered four people inside Raven Rock.

"Thank you," he said. "Where are you?"

"The rear tunnel, moving north from Building B."

"We're in Cavern C, heading for the rear. Any sign of threats?"

"None."

"There was a crew of attackers," Eric said, "at least three, heading south in the main tunnel. Keep your head up."

"How many people do you have?"

"Two. I'll explain when I see you."

Just two? Her thumb touched the key to reply, but her eyes were fixed to the north. A shadow moved along the wall in the rear tunnel ahead of her—it looked like a person. She lowered the volume on her radio and kept going, keeping her attention to the north, watching for Eric Hill to emerge from Cavern C.

The shadowed figure darted from the rear tunnel around the corner to disappear into that cavern, under the back of Building C, carrying what looked like a large duffel. She raised her gun and keyed the radio. Eric had said "we," but this was only one person.

"It's me," she whispered. "Did you just run from the rear tunnel into C?"

"No," Eric said.

"Someone's coming for you, heading west, just entered Cavern C near its southern side."

"One person?"

"That's all I could make out. He was carrying a black bag, didn't see me. I'll follow, keep my eye on him. Watch your shots. Looked like a big guy, six foot plus."

"Got you."

"Out," she said, and clipped the radio to her belt. She could have ducked back into Building B, but after seeing Maddox and Chen killed, she was done hiding from these bastards. She raised her MP5 and slipped over the stone.

75

ERIC AND DRUMM had been walking in the northern alley of Cavern C between the springs and the wall when Cody's radio call came through. They'd nearly reached the rear tunnel, but now Eric looked through the foundation under Building C, searching for the figure Cody had seen.

"How do you get into the building from the south side of this cavern?" he whispered to Drumm.

The engineer pointed through the springs to the far side of the cavern. "Steps there that lead up to a door."

Eric nodded and they slipped between the metal coils. He focused on the far wall, looking for any sign of the attacker.

Three gunshots burst from the south—red stars exploding in the dark. Eric shot back as he hauled Drumm behind a section of vertical housing for cover.

His chest pumped in and out, a rush of adrenaline coursing through his body. He took a long, slow breath in through his nose. The attacker had seen them first and had the advantage.

Eric looked out on the far side of the housing, then back to Drumm, a grim look on his face. The unrelenting attacks on Raven Rock and Moro's fate had hardened him. Eric could barely recognize the awkward deputy commander he'd met twenty-four hours ago.

Eric needed a distraction. "Shoot that way," he whispered, pointing off to Drumm's side. "Stay behind the cover."

Drumm nodded and brought his gun up. Eric gave him the sign and inched forward, ready to move as soon as Drumm fired.

Shots from the attacker hit the housing on Drumm's side the instant the barrel of his gun emerged. Eric lunged out, taking aim at the man, his face red, lit by his own muzzle flares.

Squeezing the trigger, Eric sent three rounds at him, aiming center mass—heart and lungs. The man, turning, shuddered with each shot and staggered back, his left hand rising to his chest and his gun hand dropping.

He didn't fall. Eric moved toward him and made out the bulk of the plate carrier—body armor. Eric brought his aim up twelve inches, fixing on his face.

"Drop it!" Eric shouted as the man straightened up, the gun by his side. He whipped it forward and Eric took the head shot, the triple tap finding home, the man's movements slowing in an instant before he collapsed to the floor.

Eric sprinted toward him and swept the gun from his hand with his left foot. One look and he was certain: the shooter was out of the fight forever.

He stepped back, aiming toward the rear tunnel, ready for more.

"Coming around the corner," Cody radioed. "Are you hit?"

"I'm good," he said as she appeared under the lights of the rear tunnel and walked toward them. They met near the back of Building C.

"North and south," Eric said, gesturing for Drumm and Cody to guard those approaches in the rear tunnel.

They moved forward with Eric in the lead. He leaned out from under the springs and scanned the long, straight expanse of the tunnel.

He stood there, the dirty air coming and going from his mouth and lungs, his pulse thumping in his temples. No movement. No follow-up. Ten more seconds felt like ten minutes, but no one approached.

Eric walked back and took a knee beside the man he had just killed.

The rounds had centered on his right cheek just below the eye, but he could still be identified. A high forehead, creases along the side of his mouth, brown eyes open to the ceiling.

Eric had never seen this man before, nor his photo.

"Drumm," Eric said, beckoning him over. The duffel lay beside the dead man. Eric felt it, then zipped it open—it was empty. He started going through the attacker's pockets as Drumm approached. The engineer stared at the shooter, his blood pooling on the greenstone floor, pushing away the dust.

"One of yours?" Eric asked.

"No," Drumm said. "Goddamn. They brought in others." The shock was plain in his quiet words. "That confirms it. Captain Foster handled security. If he can get in one man, he can get in dozens," Drumm said.

"What was he carrying?" Cody asked.

"Nothing. The bag is empty."

The man had fallen close to the steps leading up to the entrance to Building C. Eric searched him and found a flat piece of metal in the left pocket of his fatigues, a key. He pulled it out: brass with six bits.

"He was going to get something," Eric said, and handed the key to Drumm. "Where does this go?"

76

THE ENGINEER TOOK the key and angled it to catch the light from the rear tunnel.

"Inside," Drumm said, moving toward the steps. Cody and Eric followed him up and through the entrance into Building C.

He brought them north then east toward the increasingly loud sound of fans running. Drumm paused and double-checked the letters etched into the bow of the key. He stopped outside a door and inserted it in the bolt, but it wouldn't turn.

He moved them down another fifteen feet and tried another door. The lock turned. He nodded to Cody and Eric, who came up beside him, guns across their bodies.

Eric gave him the signal. He opened the door and Eric moved through. It was dark inside except for the slant of light spilling from the hall. Eric scanned the space with his flashlight: a hot and crowded utility room full of ductwork and condensers.

They fanned out, covering the narrow lanes between the equipment. No one was here.

"Is there anything in here they can use?" Eric asked as they searched among the machinery.

"Not really," Drumm said over the noise of the fans. "Not much to sabotage either—it's mostly HVAC for this building."

They searched the room. After five minutes, Drumm stopped near the back, his light going down as he examined something closer to the floor. The beam was focused on a sheet metal assembly where four ducts came together. The heads of the tap screws holding it in were marred, like someone had used a too-small flathead or the tip of a knife to twist them open.

Drumm reached into his pocket and came out with a multitool. He eased out the screws and pried back a panel on the assembly. Shining his light inside, Drumm dropped to one knee to get a better look. Eric could make out the weave of thick black nylon in the duct. The engineer pulled the bag toward him, then hefted it out: a full black duffel big enough to zip a body into. It was heavy enough to be a body too, though the contours of the bulk had Eric thinking it was gear.

"Easy," Eric said. Drumm unzipped it and spread it open on the floor. The gear was organized in stuff sacks and Eric opened one. Neat coils of detonation cord lay inside. Drumm spread open another—a dozen blasting caps. Underneath the sacks were black wrapped bricks with familiar yellow lettering: CHARGE DEMOLITION M112. They were standard American military blocks of C-4 high explosive, one and a quarter pounds each.

The setup was simple. Put the C-4 down, prime it with a blasting cap and det cord, then run that to a detonator. Eric found those in another bag. They were simple affairs, olive cylinders the size of a thick marker, with a pin at the end that would trigger the blast when you pulled it out. Eric had trained with them to breach doors and walls in close-quarters combat and hostage rescue.

"Would this be enough to blast your way through the old construction tunnel?"

Drumm picked up a brick and smiled. "A dozen times."

Eric examined a separate bundle of small charges and fuses.

"What are those?" Drumm asked.

"You can use them to make small bombs on a time delay," Eric said. "Good for setting and running or even tossing to change the equation in a gunfight." Another nylon sack held a half-dozen remote detonators and a unit the size of a walkie-talkie that could be used to trigger them at a distance.

Cody looked over from the door where she was standing guard.

Eric went back to the open panel, looked inside, and pulled out a second bag. From the shape and rattle he knew: small arms. He opened it up on the floor. Two SIG rifles and four M4 carbines with holographic sights lay inside, along with four shotguns—12-gauge Remington 870 Police models with short barrels.

Drumm stared down at them. "They were ready for war."

Eric nodded. "Now we are."

77

ERIC REACHED FARTHER into the duct and pulled out a third bag. It held shells for the Remingtons, and more ammo, still boxed, in 5.56mm for the rifles.

He lifted two duffels, one on each shoulder, and Drumm grabbed the third.

They walked toward the door and Cody held her hand out for one of the bags. He gave her the duffel that wasn't filled with enough high explosive to collapse the mountain.

"If we can get this gear back to the war room and hole up with the president's people," Eric said, "we can hold the plotters off for as long as we need, no matter what their numbers."

"Which way do you want to go?" Drumm asked.

Eric checked his watch. They'd been inside Building C for twenty-three minutes.

"Something concealed. Don't use the stairs near where we shot the attacker. If they zeroed in on the noise or found him, they'll be looking for us there."

Drumm started walking and waved them on. They exited the room and navigated to a door on the north side of Building C.

"Where does this put out?" Eric asked.

"In the cavern, fifty yards from the rear tunnel."

Eric nodded. Cody looked at the bags. "Stay here with the stuff," she said. "We can't risk losing it. I'll scout. Rear tunnel if we can, right?"

"Right," Eric said as she put down her duffel.

He didn't want to send her out alone, but she'd made a good call. This was enough firepower to win the fight for whichever side had it. Eric couldn't leave it to be defended by a guy like Drumm, who fired a gun once a year at a range.

"I'll go," Eric said.

"I can handle it," Cody replied.

Eric nodded. "Take this." He unslung his SIG rifle and gave it to her with a half smile. "I've got plenty."

"Thanks," she said, and eased open the handle on the door. The dirty tunnel air seeped in from the cavern outside. She leaned out and noticed Eric peering out after her. The concern must have been clear enough on his face.

"I'm good, dude," she said. "You're doing that thing again."

For a moment back at the infirmary, he'd feared that she had been taken or killed with the others. It was a struggle not to try to keep her from harm's way, not because he didn't think she could handle it, but because of his guilt about what happened to her father.

He held his hand up. "Course."

"Men," she said, and smiled. "So emotional, right?" She did a chamber check on the SIG. "I'll be right back."

Eric stepped out and watched her go down the steps into the narrow alley between the springs under Building C and the cavern wall. She moved under the building for cover, disappearing from Eric's view.

He waited at the top of the steps, scanning the alley along the cavern wall, the air hot now as the bunker struggled to keep the ventilation going. Sweat soaked into his fatigues along his back.

A minute passed. Two. He lifted his radio. "Cody. Come back."

No reply.

Someone emerged from the darkness in the alley—it was her, eyes wide and breath short.

He trained his gun past her in case anyone was in pursuit. Once she reached the top of the stairs, she waved him inside.

"What's up?" he asked as she closed the door behind them.

"I saw four shooters moving from the north in the rear tunnel toward the president's people."

"Toward us?"

"They already passed us. They went by the back of this building heading south, I assume to Building B. Hardwick and Walsh were in the lead."

From her look he guessed it was a close call.

"They shouldn't be able to get in, right?" she asked. "It's secure."

"We can't risk it. If they're going after Building B, they'll be held up outside, exposed. If we can keep the element of surprise, we might be able to take them."

Eric looked at the bags on the floor. They couldn't engage with the attackers with a hundred pounds of ammo and C-4 on their backs and he couldn't risk losing it.

He crouched down and grabbed a SIG for himself and two M4s to bring to Agents Brimley and Leigh.

Drumm and Cody took the M4s and slung them across their backs. Eric grabbed extra ammo for his rifle and a sack of time-delay charges.

"This could get heavy," Eric said to Drumm. "Are you—"

"Yes. Fuck these guys," Drumm said, and slipped three magazines into his cargo pocket. "Let's go."

Cody looked at the engineer, taken aback. He'd been preparing for a crisis for twenty-three years. Now it was time.

"We stay out front, all right?" Eric said to him.

"Sure."

"Is there a place we can lock up this gear? Somewhere they won't find it?"

"Follow me," Drumm said.

They picked up the duffels and went through a maze of halls to a small office. Drumm led them through it into a storage room in the back with long cabinets along the walls.

"The archives," Drumm said, and dialed open one of the combination locks on the cabinets. He pulled it out—a drawer six feet wide and two feet deep, half-filled with files running left to right.

They stowed the three bags, shoving aside the dusty folders, and locked up. Eric checked the cabinets for any signs that the attackers could find that would indicate something had been hidden here—like prints or swirls in dust—but they were clean.

He lifted his rifle and led the others out.

78

Sunday. 8:41 a.m.

THEY EXITED FROM Building C into the cavern that housed it and slipped under the building, moving between the springs toward the rear tunnel.

Eric stepped out from under Building C, with Cody and Drumm just behind him. He moved south down the rear tunnel toward the wreckage that had fallen behind Building B. The president and his people were inside that building. He didn't see the attackers, but they could have already picked their way through the debris and been trying to get inside B.

As he moved closer, he saw figures—at least three of them—moving near the collapsed framing, shining their lights on the back of Building B. He made out others in the shadows, a fourth, a fifth, seven of them in total.

There were two rear entrances into Building B. Now that the wreckage had settled, Eric saw that it had mostly piled near the center of the building's rear facade. That left the entrance closer to him relatively clear. The attackers gathered around the steps there, lights focusing on the doors.

He stopped and turned to Drumm and Cody. "There are seven."

"Eight," Cody said. Eric nodded. Her eyes were probably better in the dark—he was getting older.

"At least eight," Cody added.

"The crew you saw probably joined up with another party. We should assume they have sentries too."

"Can we take them?" Drumm asked, leaning forward and gripping the barrel of his rifle.

"I like where your head's at, but slow down," Eric said. "Even with surprise, we don't have the numbers."

As soon as Eric and his team pulled triggers, the attackers would take cover in the wreckage, negating any advantage from shooting first.

Eric touched the explosives he carried in an ammo pouch and looked down the tunnel.

"They're bunching up. That may give us an opportunity. If I can get close to them with these charges, I can take out the main group and then between us and the people inside we may be able to finish off the rest. That would even the odds."

"I'll try to raise the others," Cody said, lifting the radio. Eric nodded and she made the call.

Soft static, then a voice came back: "Cody, it's Leigh, where are you?"

"We're in the rear tunnel just south of C," Cody said. "The attackers are all over the back of Building B. Where are you?"

"Inside B, guarding the rear entrances. Are they coming in?"

Eric held his hand out and Cody gave him the radio.

"Lock it down," Eric said. "There are at least eight attackers gathering outside the entrance that's closest to us. We are coming up behind them and will engage if the numbers are right. We'll give you the word if we need you and Brimley to help us take them. But for now, barricade yourselves in and get ready for a siege."

"Copy," she said. "How many are you?"

"Three," Eric said.

"Three?" She couldn't hide the disappointment.

"We have Drumm with us. Stay inside. Warn the others. Defend that space. We'll call you and Brimley out if we need you. Be ready."

"Copy," Leigh said. "Locking down."

The channel went dead.

79

AGENT LEIGH STRODE down the hall to the door that led to the presidential suite.

She knocked. No answer. She banged again, harder, the sweat soaking into her blouse and her bra.

Brimley opened the door. "What's up?"

"The attackers are outside. They may try to breach. Where's the president?"

The older agent turned, and they marched through reception into the office and conference area on the north side of the suite.

The air was hot and close. Before they said a word, their manner announced trouble to those inside. Givens stood in the conference room. Kline was sitting across from them, beside his wife at the table. He got up and walked out to meet Brimley and Leigh in the office bullpen. "What is it?"

"Eight attackers, at least, coming for us. At the rear entrance there." She pointed.

Sarah Kline, now standing in the doorway of the conference room, looked from them to her husband.

"We're secure?" Kline asked.

"Locked tight."

"How long will it hold out?"

"The outer doors should hold up for hours," Brimley said.

"And if they use more explosives?"

"They held up last time. We should be all right."

"Claire, Sarah, come with me," Kline said, waving them forward.

Brimley stepped close beside him. "You four set up in the living quarters. It's the safest spot we have. Don't come out until you hear from me."

A boom shook the office. It sounded and felt like they were on a ship running hard aground.

"They're trying to get in," Brimley said, turning toward the noise as Leigh followed him.

"I'll get the others locked down and come back to help," Kline said.

Brimley faced him. "Sir, we can't take that risk."

"Hill, Cody, and Drumm are coming up behind them and will try to engage," Leigh said.

"We'll hold down the entrances," Brimley said to the president. "They won't be able to get in. Be with your people. You'll be the last wall if, God forbid . . ."

Another clang rocked the building. Kline looked back as his wife and Givens went through the door that led to the living quarters. He put his hand on Brimley's shoulder and looked at the older agent, still wearing the cuts from the attack in the White House basement.

"Thank you," he said, looking from him to Agent Leigh. "You two are an honor to the Service."

"Lock this behind us," Leigh said as she and Brimley stepped through the northern exit.

They left the presidential suite, double-checked that the door was secure, then turned right down the hallway. It ran inside along the northern edge of the building toward the rear entrance.

Another bang shook the structure. This close it felt like they were inside a kettledrum.

She took up a spot on the left side of the hall, dropped to one knee, and aimed at the door ahead. Brimley stood beside her and slightly to her right.

They waited in silence, the adrenaline surging until Leigh had to squeeze tight on the MP5 to keep her muscles from shaking. No sound came from the door.

She glanced back at Brimley. "Gone?" she mouthed.

A deafening blast shot up the hallway. The sound brought pain deep in her ears and she fixed her aim on the door. The attackers must have moved on from trying to ram it down to using breaching charges. The pressure threw off her balance for a moment, but she stayed focused. The door was intact.

"It held," she said, turning back and smiling up at Brimley. He nodded, a pained expression on his face, and pointed to the door.

She looked ahead, then felt the barrel of a gun press in beside her spine.

"What the—"

"Put your gun down, Leigh. Don't turn," Brimley said.

The shock nearly paralyzed her. She knew in an instant that he was bad, but her mind fought back against the fact. *This must be a joke, a nightmare.*

"Listen, Brimley," she said, keeping her voice calm, then she twisted, rising, knocking his gun barrel away and raising her weapon.

He slammed the stock of his MP5 into the side of her head.

Red lights danced across her vision as she fell to the side, her skull in agony. Her shoulder banged into the beige wall as he ripped the gun from her hands.

"Don't—"

He shoved her back and she lost her balance, tumbling against the wall and landing on her back on the thin carpet.

"Stay down," he said, his face a mask of dread as he looked down at her. "Damn it! We don't want to hurt you!"

She tried to rise, but as she got her foot under her the hallway seemed to turn and spin and she fell again.

Through that vertigo, she watched as Brimley went to the end of the hall, drew back the bolt, and hauled open the thick steel door.

He stepped to the side, his gun pointed down as he let Walsh and Hardwick in.

"No!" she called out. Brimley came back and grabbed her by the arm, lifting her off the floor as he moved with Hardwick and Walsh's crew, rifles raised, streaming in through the open door.

Walsh stared at her. She'd worked with him for five years, spent countless hours bullshitting with him on watch. But the cocky frat boy was gone. His eyes were empty, animal.

80

THE CRASH OF metal on metal boomed up the rear tunnel toward Eric, Cody, and Drumm.

"It'll hold?" Eric whispered to the engineer.

"Yes."

They moved closer, and Eric strained to see the men gathered around the rear entrance to Building B. A blast shook the air, red light flaring from the back of B.

"God," Cody said. "They're using the breaching charges."

"They won't get in," Drumm replied.

"Everything has a limit," Eric said.

"They'd have to use enough C-4 to kill everyone inside," Drumm said.

Eric could see that the attackers were in a tight group, which was a mistake. It made them an easy target for a blast or ambush.

"I'll go into Cavern C," he said, "south through the passageway and come up under them under Building B. I'll put a couple of timed charges down and we can take most of them in one go. Then drive the others into the wreckage. You two come from the north in the rear tunnel and we mop up."

Drumm licked his lips, glancing down the tunnel.

"Eric, are you sure?" Cody asked.

He looked to the rear entrance of B, shifting to get a better view. He caught a glimpse of Hardwick standing close to the bottom of the steps, mostly hidden among the fallen framing, holding a rifle across his chest. A brother. Once.

Eric weighed a time-delay charge in his hand. He would have to place it silently, almost directly underneath the steps, to take them all. They'd only have one chance.

"I am," he said, and turned to go.

"Wait," Cody said. "They're moving."

Eric stepped to the side and saw Hardwick lead his team in through the rear entrance. Eric moved forward and raised his rifle, but the last man had already disappeared inside. Someone cried out hurt within. It sounded like Agent Leigh. The door closed behind them, still intact.

"Did they breach it?" Cody asked, flanking to his left and lifting the radio.

Eric faced her. "No. Someone must have let them in."

81

GIVENS AND SARAH Kline stood near the back of the living area of the president's suite, drawing together as they heard a shout of pain echo down the corridors.

"That was Agent Leigh's voice," Givens said.

Kline walked toward the door to the outside, listening, watching. The first lady came up next to him.

"James," she whispered.

"Take Claire and go in the bedroom," he said. "Please. It's okay."

He took another step toward the door. The tramp of boots down the hall, coming closer. Raising the gun, he stepped to the left in case anyone managed to shoot through the door. It was oak veneer over steel, but he wasn't taking any chances. This position would give him the best angle on the side where it opened if anyone burst through.

He kept his gun up, aimed chest high.

Three knocks sounded.

"It's me, Brimley!" the agent shouted through the door. "Are you all right?"

"Fine," Kline said. "What the hell is happening out there?"

"They tried to breach, but we're good. They may come for the other entrances."

Kline didn't answer, just waited, his heart pounding hard enough to rock his whole chest.

"We should double-check them," Brimley said.

"Where's Leigh? Is she all right?"

"She's good. Covering the northern entrance. She was close to the blast, a good scare, but she's all right."

"Bring her to the door."

"We need her at that post, and I need to make sure you're okay."

"We've got it under control."

A long pause from Brimley. "I'm sure you do, sir, but I'll need to check the security posture myself."

Kline looked back to see his wife in the doorway to the bedroom, shaking her head. Something was off about the story. He'd never known Leigh to scare or lose control.

He nodded and backed away. The scream. This bullshit excuse to get inside. He didn't know if Brimley was bad or coerced, but he wasn't getting through that door.

82

AGENT WALSH STOOD a few feet behind Brimley as the older agent called out a third time for the president. Walsh listened for an answer, for any sound, but none came from within the suite.

Reaching into his kit, Walsh pulled out a brick of C-4 and looked to Hardwick.

"Do it," his commander said.

Walsh set to work on the hinge side of the door, the weakest point, laying down two sausages of C-4 at knee and shoulder height and priming them. The outer doors to the secure area holding the presidential suite and the war room were almost impossible to breach, but now that they were inside, the rest would fall easily.

He waved the others back, then retreated from the door, unspooling det cord as he moved. He took cover around the corner with the others, then crimped the cord into the detonator.

A last look to Hardwick. A go-ahead nod. Walsh put his index and middle fingers into the pins and ripped them out. The crack and overpressure smacked him in the face, and he sprinted around the corner toward the blast. The door tilted in toward the president's suite behind rising coils of black smoke.

Walsh strode toward it, raised his foot, and drop-kicked it in, the bolt and lock squealing free as the door opened on the hinge side. He led the others through, turning to cover the living area. Kline was gone.

He and Hardwick stacked beside the door to the bedroom. Walsh spun around and drove a mule kick into it, just beside the knob. Wood splintered. Again. The door frame ripped apart, and Hardwick shoved it open.

There was no one inside.

Walsh crossed to the closets and swept them while Hardwick dropped to check under the bed.

His radio earpiece came to life. It was Foster. "We have the war room secured."

"Kline? The others?"

"No trace."

Walsh ran his hand over the sheets and took a deep breath in through his nose. He could still smell rose and jasmine: Sarah Kline's perfume.

"They were just here," Walsh said. "They must have an escape route, another passage."

He stepped up to the wall, smashed the wood panel with the stock of his rifle, then tore it off.

"Find them," Hardwick called out. "We need Kline alive."

83

KLINE RAISED HIMSELF through an open hatch onto the roof of Building B, careful to avoid the gleaming edges of the metal wreckage that had collapsed here during the fire.

Turning, he reached his hand down and saw his wife's face looking up at him, white among the shadows. They had come up through an emergency escape: a vertical shaft that led from his living quarters to the building's roof, a route known only to him and his wife and possibly Drumm.

Sarah's fingers closed on his and she clambered out. A deep breath and she hugged him, her touch filling him with warmth. They had barely made it to the escape passage before the attackers breached the door to his apartment.

The dread eased only slightly from his neck and shoulders. They were out, but that was only the beginning. He and Sarah crouched to help Givens onto the roof.

Kline picked his way across the broken shielding tiles. The surfaces were greasy with soot from the fires. Building B, like the others, had a round roof that sloped down on the sides, fitting just inside the shape of the cavern that housed it. It was like walking on the roof of a Quonset hut stuffed inside a massive road tunnel.

He measured each step carefully. One slip and he could fall on the shattered panels and drop thirty-something feet to the stone below.

The top of the building was clear of any attackers, and as he turned, he could see a catwalk mounted on the roof about twenty feet to his north. He would have to move down the curved slope to reach it.

The catwalk, a level grated steel walkway, ran east and west along the entire length of the building's roof just where the roof began to curve sharply down to join the side walls of the building.

Looking to the west down the confines of Cavern B, away from the rear tunnel where the attackers had been, he could see that the catwalk was mostly clear of debris—a few shreds of burnt lining and some fallen framing. It offered the easiest escape along the roof, a way around the wreckage that had piled up elsewhere. They could take it west all the way to the main tunnel and find a way down.

He stepped toward it, keeping his eye on the rear tunnel. He was only about five feet from the back of the building. Before he sent his wife and Givens onto that catwalk, he wanted to make sure that no plotters were below with shooting angles on their escape route.

He went on the catwalk, moved to where it reached the back of the building, and dropped to one knee. Raising the gun, he peered over the edge, a thirty-foot drop, scanning through the wreckage behind the building in the rear tunnel below.

Something clanged on the roof behind him, and he turned to see Sarah supporting Givens by her upper arm. The chief of staff's face was frozen in a grimace—she must have stumbled—and she raised her hands as if in apology for the noise.

Kline watched the rear tunnel for any sign of a reaction. The framing and ceiling liners had collapsed there during the fire, leaving a jumble of long steel pipes and scorched material stacked and leaning against the back of Building B like a jungle gym from hell. It was piled more than halfway up the building, filling the tunnel almost completely and crossing over the canal that ran down the center of the rear tunnel.

There was no sign of any shooters, though they could have been hidden among the wreckage.

Kline waved Sarah and Givens toward the catwalk as he kept watch for any attackers.

Movement behind Building B snagged his attention. He scanned over the broken framing and tented liners, looking through the iron sights of the MP5.

He caught a dull sheen among the debris, a rifle aiming his way. He pressed his gun's stock tight against his shoulder and pulled the trigger. Three shots. The man fell, collapsed across a metal bar, and hit the ground.

It was one of the attackers, Captain Foster, the comms officer who had killed Eubanks.

Kline glanced toward Sarah. She had dropped low on the catwalk at the sound of gunfire, potentially vulnerable to shots from below.

He scanned through the debris behind Building B, looking for more shooters, anyone who might have a line of fire on her.

Shots rang out to the north in the rear tunnel. He heard the sound of a body falling somewhere out of sight in the wreckage behind B. His breath pumped in and out. Movement below and to his right, another attacker hiding in the pile behind B. He gestured for Sarah and Givens—thirty feet from him on the catwalk—to keep going back, closer to the center of the roof, before that man could get a shot at them.

Kline peered down into the shadows among the debris, searching over the sights of his weapon.

The man was gone.

Crack crack crack. Three red blasts from the dark below. Three rounds ripped into Kline's chest.

He staggered to the side near the end of the catwalk. The last thing he saw before he dropped over the edge was his wife running toward him, reaching out her hand.

84

WALSH CLIMBED UP the vertical escape route Kline and his people had taken as three shots rang out through the cavern.

He tracked to the right with his SIG rifle and took aim at President Kline standing at the end of a catwalk, but he was already falling, hand to his chest. Kline plunged over the edge at the back of the building, dropping into the rubble in the rear tunnel below.

Walsh turned, aiming at Givens, who was standing on the broken tiles near the center of the roof, then Sarah Kline. The first lady was perched on the narrow catwalk that ran east–west along the length of the roof. Her mouth was open, in shock after watching her husband fall. He aimed at her chest.

"Get back here!" he shouted.

She didn't seem to hear him at first, then looked his way, blinking slowly, seemingly unafraid of the gun.

"Now!"

She stepped away from him. He sent two shots high into the greenstone over her head. Her knees buckled, and she put her hand down to keep from falling.

"Come. Here." He moved north, down the curved slope of the roof, to cut her off on the catwalk so she couldn't escape to the west, toward the main tunnel.

Sarah started walking toward him, step by step, trembling from the near miss.

Walsh heard the metal hatch creaking behind him near the center of the roof and looked back as Hardwick and two others climbed out. They moved toward Givens.

Sarah Kline approached Walsh on the catwalk and he moved in. "Get down!" he said, gesturing with the barrel of the rifle.

She stood up straighter and bore into him with a stare.

He angled to the side, keeping the gun out to his right while he reached for her upper arm with his left. She knocked his hand away, surprising him with the speed, the boldness, and shoved him back.

"You traitor."

Walsh inched closer, appraising her, then backhand-slapped her hard enough for her to stagger to her right. He grabbed her arm, catching her and keeping her upright.

"Easy!" Hardwick warned him.

Walsh aimed the barrel of the gun at her face, inches away, and forced her down.

85

ONE MINUTE BEFORE Kline fell from the roof of Building B, Eric was racing south toward the wreckage behind it in the rear tunnel, with Cody just beside him. Drumm was to their north in the rear tunnel, covering them from that direction. There was no sign of the crowd of attackers. They appeared to all have gone inside Building B.

Then Eric saw a man standing on a catwalk on top of Building B, at the very back. He took aim, looking over his iron sights at the figure.

It was President Kline.

Eric opened both eyes and saw the president fire three shots. A cry of pain sounded from ahead, somewhere in the wreckage.

Satisfaction flared in Eric's chest. The president's gun tracked to the right, and Eric stepped out, searching for the target hidden somewhere deep in the fallen framing and torn liners.

A man leaned out, aiming toward Kline. Eric lit him up, watched him drop, and moved forward, sidestepping right, looking for more threats.

A red blast flared from deep in the debris, a shooter hidden from Eric's view. He glanced up in time to see Kline reeling to the side as more shots rang out. The second and third bullets caught him in the chest. He dropped off the back of Building B and fell forward into the wreckage behind it.

The plunge seemed to take forever. Witnessing it, Eric felt like his lungs were collapsing. He couldn't see where Kline had come down in the tangle of metal framing and liners.

Cody's hand reached out and touched his shoulder, like she was bracing herself. She stared ahead, her throat working. The president was down. There was nothing worse for an agent. They put that man's life above their own.

"Come on," Eric said, steeling himself. He moved south, scanning through the pile behind B.

Voices above: Agent Walsh shouting. Two shots ricocheted high off the cavern wall surrounding Building B. Eric swept toward the sound with his rifle and pointed to Cody to cover the rear tunnel to the south.

Sarah Kline yelled out in pain from the roof of B, out of sight. He heard Hardwick's voice and stepped to the side, aiming up the northern side of Cavern B. His body hungered for the shot, his finger tight against the trigger, desperate to put down these motherfuckers, but the voices grew quieter as they retreated out of sight toward the center of Building B's roof. He had no angle.

He pressed south with Cody. They had to get Kline and take out whoever had shot him. Eric weaved through the debris, creeping along the edge of the narrow canal that ran down the center of the rear tunnel. Ash floated on top of the water. He headed for a teepee of fabric and broken framing. It would offer him concealment, but no protection from gunfire. He edged around it, looking to where he had heard the shots that took down Kline.

His eyes moved over the wreckage, the fallen liners, the metal rods scorched black. He paused. A man leaned out from cover ahead. Eric had him in profile—a person in fatigues he had never seen before—as the attacker inched left for a clearer shot.

Three rounds spat from the end of Eric's rifle. A head shot. A cloud of red. The man dropped.

Eric crept forward, looking for a sign of the president as the water streamed beside him.

The rear entrance to Building B creaked open farther to the south. Another stranger stepped out at the top of the metal steps that led to the rear tunnel. Eric took aim.

The man's head turned toward him.

Crack crack. Eric put him down and heard the tramp of boots running toward that exit. Three figures, then five, then seven emerged—all of them firing toward Eric as he lunged for cover.

Cody shot back, suppressing them, and Drumm fired from farther to the north. That bought Eric time to race to the spot where Cody had taken cover behind a fallen steel panel. He dropped back beside her as gunshots thundered from the debris to their south.

Cody fired three shots, smooth and even on the trigger, and Eric heard a grunt of pain.

She pulled back. "Got one in the plates," she said, her chest pumping like a steam engine, eyes wild with adrenaline. "They're still coming."

Eric edged out and a hail of bullets came their way. One punched through the steel over Cody's head.

"We'll be overrun soon," Eric said.

Cody looked to the north, then back down the tunnel. "What about Kline? He could still be alive down there."

Three shots to the chest and a thirty-foot fall. The odds were he was gone. Still, Eric's training, as strong as instinct, drew him toward Kline.

He looked at Agent Cody, inching forward, pushed by that same drive. In an instant he was back in that ambush fifteen years ago, throwing his body over the president, watching as a bullet tore through Joe Cody's neck. No one else was going to die today. Going head-to-head against these shooters was suicide.

"We fall back," he said, and pulled out one of the timed fuses and a charge. "Blow and go. I cover, you run." He primed the explosive.

She nodded. Eric put his thumb through the pin on the detonator, pulled it, then tossed it over the top of the steel panel they'd ducked behind.

He held his finger up to tell her to wait and readied his rifle.

The blast shook the tunnel. Eric heard the framing collapse to the south as he wheeled out and laid down burst after burst, covering their escape.

86

WALSH KEPT FIVE feet between himself and his hostages as he marched them through the narrow space. He had forced Sarah Kline and Claire Givens back down the hatch in the roof and into the passage they had used to escape from the president's living quarters.

He shined his light on the first lady in the lead, her face spectral white under its beam, eyes wide and pupils dilated with fear.

"Move," Walsh said, and she exited the passage through a hinged panel ahead. They emerged inside a walk-in closet in the president's living quarters and he directed them into the bedroom.

One of Walsh's fellow soldiers was rifling through her bag, her papers and toiletries. Walsh could see the first lady's eyes burning with anger, and he let his satisfaction show in his face as he gestured with the barrel of his SIG. "Outside," he said.

He marched them out of the living quarters and into the office and conference area next to the war room.

Standing by the door, he covered them with his rifle. Givens looked at him disdainfully and shook her head.

"We got word to the top," she said. "This is over."

"It doesn't look over to me," Walsh said, in his chilling whisper of a voice.

"What is your plan here?" Sarah Kline asked.

He didn't answer, just raised the gun slightly higher. The plan had worked beautifully: the initial attack at the White House to get the president to Raven Rock, then cutting him off and cornering him in this bunker. Now Drumm's people were trapped behind the collapse in the northern tunnel, the president's team were outnumbered with no chance of support, and Hardwick and Walsh had the ultimate bargaining chip. He stared at the first lady.

"What do you want?" Dr. Kline insisted.

"The truth," he said. "This is the moment when men of strength, of conviction, stand up and save this country from traitors like you."

She went to speak, and he put the barrel in her face. That kept her quiet. "Now get in the conference room and sit down."

She and Givens obeyed.

Hardwick came in through the side door, along with four other shooters. He carried his rifle in his right hand and a black valise in his left. A steel cable was still locked to it from when they had taken it off of Eubanks's body. Rust-colored patches stained the leather and the clasps had been forced open. They had stowed the military aide's body in an unused break room in Building D.

Givens and Dr. Kline rose and stared at it through the glass of the conference room. Hardwick, who was leading this operation, put fresh guards on the two hostages and brought Walsh into the hall.

Walsh looked down the corridor to see two bodies laid along the hallway—Captain Foster and another comms officer. Rebecca Vaughn, one of the comms staffers who were working with him and Hardwick, looked his way and shook her head. Her hands were stained with blood from trying to save them.

Walsh felt the rage build up, tight in his chest like a heart attack. He stepped closer, looking over the torn flesh, the blood. He embraced the anger, wanted to remind himself what these tyrants were capable of.

"The others, Hill, Cody, and Drumm, where are they?" he asked, his fingers tightening on the grip of his gun.

"Escaped to the north," Hardwick said. "They used an explosive for cover."

"They must have gotten into our cache."

"Yes. The officer we sent to retrieve it is now dead under Building C. He could have led them to it."

Walsh's teeth ground together.

"We'll get them," Hardwick said.

"How?"

"We have leverage," Hardwick replied. "Come on."

He walked him down the hall and through a door on the right. They stepped into the war room, where Hardwick's team had spread out among the workstations. Display after display came to life. Hardwick's tech specialist, a bear of a man, was seated behind one set of triple monitors, chewing on the cap of a Bic pen. On his desk lay a Toughbook laptop that he had connected to the war room workstation. He was a member of Drumm's staff and had been working on the inside for months. Yesterday morning he had used that laptop to hijack and gain control of the bunker's critical systems.

"Are we online?" Hardwick called to him.

The tech held his finger up and worked the keys. "Confirming." After a minute he pumped his fist. "We're in," he said. "The patch worked. You want me to start with the codes?"

Hardwick took in a long breath. "Not yet. Get it all ready." He walked forward, looking to the corner of the war room, where one of the team stepped through a door into an area the size of a small office. A blue drape backdrop stood along one wall, with a presidential seal hanging from it. The wall opposite was all black, with a camera and video-mixing bench set up. It was a broadcast studio established for the country's leadership to address the nation in times of crisis. Tonight it would be a stage for a trial and a confession.

A last display came on, high on the central wall of the war room. It showed a world map in Mercator projection, the borders ghostly green, American military bases, ships, submarines, and launch silos marked out with icon after icon. A stream of white text ran down the right side of the screen.

Walsh's eyes went to the valise in Hardwick's hand.

"What about Kline?" he asked.

Hardwick looked across the war room, taking in the broadcast studio and the screens on the walls. Then he turned his head in the direction of the conference room that held the first lady. His face was grim but determined. "We have everything we need."

87

ERIC TOOK CODY and Drumm north in the rear tunnel to Cavern D. They tried to raise Kline on the radio as they went, but there was no answer. Once they were certain they were clear of pursuers, they circled back to Building C using a passageway. Drumm brought them inside and back to the storeroom where they had stowed the explosives.

Eric went straight to the cabinets and hauled out two duffels.

"Hill," Cody said as he started going through the bags. "Hill!"

"What?" he asked.

"What are we doing?"

He looked at her. "We hit them back. Kline's out there in the rear tunnel, vulnerable, and Hardwick has Givens and the first lady. We need to move."

She looked to Drumm, then back. "Straight at them? You're talking about, what, storming Building B, retaking the war room and the presidential suite?"

Eric felt his pulse pumping in every fingertip, his neck, his chest. The hate flooded him, driving him to move, to answer. "We need to regain the initiative."

"Eric. You're amped right now. Breathe for a minute. Think. There are only three of us," Cody said. "There are at least eight of them that we saw go into Building B. There could be a lot more inside or guarding the approaches by now. They're in a hardened location with hostages. There has to be another way."

"We can't let them control that war room."

"How would we get it back?"

Eric looked over the explosives. "Distract. Breach. Infiltrate. We can find something."

"And if that's what they're hoping for? For you to come at them so they can kill the only resistance they have left?"

"They have the codes. You know what they could do? The kind of hell they could unleash?"

"But not Kline's, not the gold codes. He destroyed them."

"They have the football. They know the system. It's never been tested like this. Kline already authenticated that war room, and they could go straight into the local missile batteries without having to deal with the Joint Chiefs."

He looked to Drumm.

The engineer nodded. "It's possible."

"The Patriot batteries alone would give them the leverage they need to have their demands met. And if they managed to get control of anything nuclear, they win."

"They wouldn't."

"They just executed the president of the United States," Eric said. "Or tried. There's no way to know how far they'll go. We have to stop them, now," Eric said.

Cody took a deep breath. "Kline's dead, isn't he?"

Eric saw the president's body shudder again, saw him fall. An unbearable pressure built up inside him. He slammed his palm into the wall. Pain flared up his arm as the drywall cracked and the metal stud inside bent.

Eric had sworn to protect the president. To protect his family. Today he failed. He broke that faith.

Cody was still looking at him, waiting for an answer.

Kline was most likely dead, he knew, but he wasn't going to say that. "There's a chance he survived. We don't give up on him."

"Then the attackers have him. They swarmed that hall."

Eric faced them, shaking his head. It would almost be better if Kline was dead. "If he is alive and they have him or his wife—and we know they have her—they will get his code out of him."

"You think he remembers it?" Cody asked.

"I do. He's Agency. He's trained."

"And then?"

"They'll try to force him to confess to their bullshit conspiracy that Kline is a tyrant in the making."

"He wouldn't," Cody said.

"Not easily. Not soon. But everyone breaks. They'll get it on camera and air it to prove that they are saving the republic. It would help them finish the coup in Washington."

"We need to be measured," Cody said. "Take our time. The system will hold up. The Pentagon won't go along with any orders. The public will see through some forced confession. These lies aren't going to work."

Eric set his teeth together and stared at her. She still had that Frank Capra fantasy of the good fight, of the people doing the right thing despite the grifters in power. He'd been around long enough to know that the bullshit wins. The crooks come out on top. He'd seen it happen with Joe Cody's death.

"What is it?" she asked.

"We can't trust that the system will hold up."

Her eyes narrowed, wary. "What aren't you telling me, Eric?"

He stayed silent.

"You've been hiding something." She stepped closer, studying his face. "Is it about my father?"

Eric tightened his jaw.

"If you're so tired of the bullshit, stop bullshitting me. What really happened that day?"

"Where are you getting this?"

"When Hardwick came for me after Kline and I ran from the power plant, he told me not to trust you, said you let my dad die and took the glory for yourself. I didn't believe him. Then."

"That's a fucking lie." Hearing Hardwick's name and that accusation snapped something in him.

"Then tell me!" She stared at him. She was daring him to show whether he was the man she'd once looked up to or if he was the son of a bitch who shot people in the back with an off-books gun hidden in his waistband, the man who betrayed her father.

"Your dad shouldn't have been on that street. None of us should have."

Eric thought back to that afternoon in Malaysia fifteen years ago, the day of the ambush, the monsoon heat prickling his skin like a rash.

"Your father flagged the speech as too risky," Eric said, "and all of us agreed, but President Reinhart insisted we do it. He wanted to keep his public schedule to show he wasn't worried about the insurgents who'd been striking in the region. Canceling would seem like weakness. So we went ahead."

Shut up and color, Joe Cody had said, but that seemed too cruel a thing to tell Agent Cody now.

"I could have pushed back more, maybe I could have stopped it, but I went along with the fucking politicians. Did what I was told. I failed him. That's true. When the shots started, I was next to Reinhart. I covered the president. Do you know how many times I played it back and asked if I could have gotten to your dad, could have gotten an angle on that shooter? For years, every time I closed my eyes, I was back on that street. I saved the wrong guy."

"Then you went around as a hero?"

"That was all the work of the brass, the politicians. They needed to hold someone up, to make a silver lining. I wanted no part of it. Reinhart was desperate to avoid any blame for what happened."

A beat. "They put it on my dad," Cody said, gravel in her voice.

Eric nodded. "Quietly, just whispers. They let it fall on the one man who couldn't defend himself."

"And you didn't say anything?"

"I did everything I could to get the truth out, but the bullshit won. The politicians had their story and that's what mattered in the end."

"Why didn't you tell me?"

"Because you believed in this job, the same way your dad did. He gave his life for it. I didn't want to take that away from you."

"I'm not a fucking kid."

"It was wrong," he said. "I'm sorry. And I'm sorry for what I did, and didn't do that day."

She closed her left hand into a fist and opened it, again and again, barely able to restrain the anger.

"I put my faith in this place, in you, and now . . ." Each word was cold, measured. She let out a long breath. "That's why I had to fight so hard to get back to the White House? Them pinning the blame on my dad?"

"No one ever put it into words, but I'm sure it was there, no matter what I said."

Another stare. He'd told himself he was trying to protect her from the truth. He didn't want to disillusion her, or drop a bomb on her in the middle of all this. But now he was starting to wonder if he'd just been trying to protect himself—too chickenshit to tell her everything, to face her and his own failings.

"What they did to him broke my faith in the job," Eric said. "When I see these politicians get away with garbage like that, I get so fucking angry I don't know if I can control it. That's what happened the night I went after Braun. I could have killed him."

"So what *do* you believe in?"

A breath. He looked to Drumm, then back to her. "The men and women who stand beside me when the shots go off. That's it. I failed them that day and I swore it would never happen again. For the people we're up against— the people behind all these lies—ideals and duty are just weaknesses to be exploited, weapons they can use. You have to fight as hard and as dirty as they do."

Sometimes that meant a hidden weapon, a shot in the back. Whatever it took to survive.

She watched him, a hard look on her face. She didn't trust him anymore. Maybe she didn't trust anyone. He hadn't wanted this for her. It was necessary, but dangerous. She was taking a step closer to the cynicism that had plagued Eric, the cynicism that had taken down Hardwick.

He almost didn't recognize her. The only good thing was that she was now prepared, free from illusions. The fact that Hardwick had forced him to drag up all this shit about her father, to bring her into the darkness, only added to Eric's rage. He was ready to kill them all.

A speaker crackled somewhere in the hallways outside. Hardwick's voice boomed through the building, amplified over the public address.

"Cody, Hill. You're outnumbered. You're on the wrong side of this fight. Kline betrayed his oath to the Constitution, and we are keeping ours. He killed your brothers. Join us. We'll show you the truth."

A woman shouted in the background. A commotion. A cry of pain.

"You fought a good fight, but it's over," Hardwick said. "Put down your guns and come to us and no one will be hurt. Don't make me come find you."

The sound cut off.

88

ERIC'S HAND TIGHTENED on the grip of his gun till it shook. That was Sarah Kline's voice. A desperate need to destroy seized him. He walked over and zipped up the bag of explosives, then opened the one holding the shotguns.

Cody had a driven look in her eyes as she came beside him and checked out the guns.

"We're rolling," Eric said, and lifted the duffel of explosives over his shoulder. He reached for one of the shotguns and Cody put her hand on his arm.

"Wait."

He stared at her. "There's no time. Move."

She looked straight back. "No."

He took three long breaths in through his nose. Cody didn't move. "They want us to react. They're using the anger."

"So am I."

"And if it's another trap?"

Eric considered it. The drive to act crowded every other thought out of his mind, but he fought against it. This same anger had brought Hardwick to the conspirators' side, by exploiting his loyalty to two fallen agents—Rivas and Stiles.

She was right. He couldn't let emotion put blinders on him. Though a part of him wondered if she was pushing back because she didn't want to face the possibility of going head-to-head with and killing another Secret Service agent. She had joined to protect her brothers and sisters. It would be anathema to her.

"There's another way," she said.

"I——"

"Listen to me, Hill," she snapped. "The codes. The forced confessions. They all rely on a means to communicate outside the bunker. They must have a way."

Eric looked to Drumm.

"She's right," he said.

"If we find out how they're doing it, we can cut them off and neutralize all of those threats," Cody said. "Tie their hands *before* we attack."

"Or we could use it ourselves to get word to the top," Drumm said.

By long training and new faith, Eric hungered to go straight in, to get Kline and his people safe. But Cody, even after everything she'd just learned, was seeing it clearly. If there was an easy way to take the most extreme risks off the table—Hardwick and Walsh ordering a strike or using the missiles—they needed to do it before they went after the traitors in Building B, to take away their leverage and safeguard against mass casualties.

"What could they be using?" Eric asked.

"We checked every comms line. They're all dead," Drumm said. "Cut."

"They must have something," Cody said.

"There is wiring for power that runs to the surface. Major Moro . . ." Drumm's voice rasped with emotion, and he cleared his throat. "She was trying to patch us out over it. Anything that goes to the top could have been hijacked as a way for them to communicate. It's all copper. It can carry 120 volts AC or a phone call or a full ISDN data stream."

"Where?"

"There are miles and miles of it. Needle in a haystack."

Cody looked to him. "Did the conspirators do anything to tip their hands? Vaughn, Foster? Can you see if they accessed any plans or secure areas?"

Drumm looked down and thought for a moment. "I saw Captain Foster near the S5 junction a couple of weeks ago. It was a little out of place at the time, but I didn't think much of it. Now that I know he was one of the plotters . . ."

"Does that tell you how they might be going to the top?"

"If he was scouting or preparing in that location, that narrows it down to a few circuits."

"Where?"

"They're set in the stone floors of the caverns and passageways and run north–south under the buildings."

"Under us?"

"Yes."

"And you would be able to tell if they were running comms over the wires?"

"If I can find the active line, sure."

Eric looked from Drumm to Cody. He still wasn't going to leave the hostages alone with the killers, but it made sense to cut them off before he attacked, to stop them from taking desperate measures if they were cornered.

"All right," Eric said. "We cut them off, then we take them down."

89

FIVE MINUTES LATER, Eric and Cody were standing one hundred feet apart, hidden among the springs under Building C. He kept his gun aimed toward the rear tunnel, while she guarded the approaches from the west and through the passageways.

Cody had been watching him warily as they headed here from inside C. Eric wasn't sure if it was suspicion or anger for having kept the truth from her.

Metal scraped against metal behind Eric. He glanced toward it, and could barely make out the figure moving deep under C between the silver coils supporting the building. It was Drumm, checking the wires. Another scrape. Every sound drew the muscles in Eric's neck tighter.

He knew what he would do if he were Hardwick—use the numerical advantage and hunt down the enemy.

Footsteps came toward him. Drumm approached, a red multimeter in his hand, then pointed to the north. "There's one more spot we can check for comms links, this way."

Eric and Cody covered him and he crossed through the dark. Metal clanked as Drumm pulled off an access port—a rectangular plate like a small manhole cover—that let him test the old wire running underground.

Eric caught faint light in the rear tunnel and aimed his weapon. The beam turned away and disappeared. The attackers were searching.

He turned and saw Drumm waving him over. The engineer crouched over the access port. Eric and Cody moved in.

"This is it," Drumm said, looking down at the faint glow of his meter, its leads clipped into a set of terminals in the port. "That's a digital RF signal."

"Sending or receiving?"

"Could be both. I'd have to look at it on a computer."

"Can you cut it off?"

"I could, but there are dozens of wires they can use to patch around it if I cut here. We'd be playing Whac-A-Mole unless we cut it off at the terminal."

"Where's that?"

"If he's using this circuit, that means their connection to the top goes out in the rear tunnel behind Building E. The wires connect in a trunk line there. If we cut that off, then we would sever their route to the top. That should put them out of business for at least an hour or two, or maybe for good. They may have a backup."

"Could *we* use it to communicate?"

"Possibly." He glanced at the wires. "I can patch it to the security office in C and look at it on the computer there. Take two minutes."

"You could see what they are saying?"

"That depends on the encryption."

"Do it. We'll check it out and then cut them off at the trunk line behind E."

Drumm reached into the access port. Eric stepped away, turning slowly, searching for threats.

He heard labored breaths as Drumm reached deep into the port, working on the wires. Ninety seconds later, the grate slid closed.

"Let's go," Drumm said.

90

DRUMM LED THEM back inside Building C and navigated through the hallways to bring them into a small office. Yellowing papers were tacked up on the wall beside it—security protocols and checklists. A beige desk with a computer and telephone sitting on it faced eight displays mounted on the wall—thick-bezeled LCD screens that looked like they were at least ten years old.

"This would be a security post if we were fully staffed up," Drumm said. "And the cameras were working."

He opened an equipment cabinet under the displays. Dust swirled out and he reached in among the cables and glowing green LEDs. The monitors blinked to life and Drumm came around to the desk and pulled the keyboard and mouse toward him.

"Do you have the signal?" Eric asked.

After a moment, Drumm said yes without looking up, his fingers flying over the keys. "It's something. Could be phone, radio, data."

Eric cocked his head, listening, then went to the door to stand beside Cody, who was on guard.

"Did you hear something?"

"A creak. The buildings do it sometimes."

Eric focused. He heard the endless rushing of the ventilation systems and the computer's fan.

Drumm pounded his index finger onto the enter key.

"Damn," he said.

"What is it?" Eric asked.

"This signal. It's not the normal comms output from any of the command center systems."

"So—"

A resonant voice jumped out from the computer speakers. ". . . no statement so far from the Chinese premier. Now to New York, where markets are still reacting to unrest . . ."

It sounded like a British broadcaster. "What is that?" Eric asked.

"BBC."

Drumm typed in commands as images appeared on the monitors: a Japanese minister speaking at a conference, a squadron of attack helicopters flying low over the Potomac, a panel of talking heads arguing behind a long cable news desk.

"This is part of the comms package we usually run to monitor the news," Drumm said.

Eric stared at the screens as the engineer switched channels. He'd been down here in the dark for so long it felt like the world above no longer existed. Of course the plotters were watching the media. They were waging a propaganda war and victory would come if their cause was seen as legitimate.

On one screen, a reporter walked in a scrum alongside a senator in the Capitol Rotunda. A cordon of Capitol Police surrounded them. Drumm switched the audio over to that channel as the politician spoke.

". . . President Kline and I have our differences, of course, but there is no place for violence in the political process. We need to get to the bottom of what is happening. That's all I have for now."

The broadcast returned to the studio anchor, who spoke over footage of jets ripping across the sky above a blocked-off road in the Maryland mountains.

"As you can see," the newscaster said, "they have cordoned off the area around Camp David and we have reports of a large military presence moving in."

Eric stepped closer to Drumm. "See if they have a way of communicating with the top, if we can get a message out."

"Working on it," Drumm said.

Cody was watching the screens, her face ashen. "The attorney general made some kind of statement about a confession," she said, pointing to the closed-captioned image on another news network.

"God," Eric said. "Did they get to Kline?" He pointed to a screen on the upper right. "There. NBC. They're playing it again. Put the audio on."

The image showed the Great Hall at DOJ with its blue curtains and statue of blind justice. The attorney general was already at the podium, his left hand on the dark-stained wood, his eyes looking straight at the camera.

". . . we are facing a coup, the most dangerous attempt to overthrow the government in the history of our democracy. But the men and women of the FBI and the Department of Justice have answered that threat. We were able to infiltrate this plot and I am here to announce that we have taken into custody one of the ringleaders of this attack.

"Thomas W. Searle is responsible for coordinating this crime. Using the alias 'Citizen,' he orchestrated it through a series of messages, incitements, and misinformation to the plotters. Though he presented himself to them as a top-ranking government official, Searle is only a congressional aide who has also worked at several think tanks.

"Searle has already admitted to his role in the crimes. This is an active situation and I'm going to go outside of our normal protocols here and play footage from his interview. Anyone associated with him or sympathetic to his aims can see for themselves that this plot will fail. It was driven by lies from the beginning."

The attorney general stepped to his right. On the large television beside him, a video began to play. It was Searle, the aide Eric had talked to early yesterday morning at the White House, the sycophant who pretended to be a friendly emissary from the political opposition. With his fleshy face and round glasses, he was looking down, seemingly in shock. His tie was gone and there were dark circles under his eyes. Seeing his face brought a surge of anger and disgust in Eric.

"I didn't know it would go this far," Searle said. "I never wanted violence. I never touched a gun. I never gave an order."

"The allegations you made about President Kline, were they true?"

"It was more about how I saw the world than their strict facticity. They spoke to a deeper truth. They were intended to have an effect, to move things in the right direction. That's how politics works."

"Were they true?" came the voice from off-screen, patient but firm.

Searle's lips pressed together, trembling slightly. He looked at the camera. "No."

"And this movement of yours, now that you see what's happened, would you support it any longer?"

Searle's eyes went to the interviewer's, then down.

"No," he said, barely a whisper.

After the video finished, the attorney general gripped both sides of the podium. "Searle has verified he is the figure Citizen who has been spreading the disinformation that brought this coup. Anyone who may be involved and in doubt about his identity can check for a new encrypted message from Citizen and confirm for themselves.

"I speak now to anyone who is party to this. There is no basis to this man's claims. You were lied to. It's over. There is no political process that will save you or achieve your goals. The government is secure. We are in communication with the president and his staff. They led us to Searle. The situation is under control. Give yourselves up. We hope to bring this to an end peacefully, but we will bring it to an end."

He closed a portfolio, lifted it, and stepped to the side as a reporter shouted a question about whether Searle was working alone.

Cody raised both hands in the air, her eyes wide as she looked from Eric to Drumm.

"Maddox's evidence," she said. "They got it."

Eric clapped his hand on Drumm's shoulder. "The VLF. The president's transmission went through."

Drumm closed his eyes and sat back in the chair.

"God," Cody said. "Searle was in the White House yesterday."

"I talked to him," Eric said. "Fucking toad."

"He was behind all of this?" Cody asked.

"My assumption is he handled playing the role of Citizen," Eric said, "but he was serving more powerful political forces."

"But Kline's critics disavowed the coup. It's over on the Hill."

"They did in general," Eric said. "We still need to be careful. If Hardwick were to force a confession out of Kline, they could tack back the other way. This isn't over until we return the president safely to the Oval Office."

"All of these news streams have been going to the war room," Cody said. "Hardwick and Walsh must have seen it."

"We'll make sure of that," Eric said, scanning the displays. "Do these screens work like a security system? Can you play back the footage?" he asked Drumm.

He nodded.

"And the public address?"

Drumm pointed to the telephone handset on the desk. "I can patch you in right now."

"Do it."

Drumm lifted the handset and pressed a button on the telephone. A pop and quiet static came from outside the door as the PA went live.

Eric took the handset. "Hardwick," he said, and heard his voice reverberate through the building and the tunnels outside. "You have been lied to. This is the man you call Citizen."

He gestured to Drumm, who started playing back the attorney general's statement and Searle's confession. Eric held the phone near the computer speaker and listened as the broadcast filled Raven Rock. When it finished, with Searle's weak "no" hanging in the air, Eric brought the handset back to his mouth. "It's done. Don't make it any worse for yourself."

He ran his hand across his throat. Drumm cut the PA broadcast.

Eric stood for a moment, the hope feeling like a trap.

Drumm pointed to the screen. "Check this out."

A software window showed a series of horizontal spectra, like oscilloscope patterns, running across the screen in green waves.

"This is the news and information data stream, from the outside," he said, pointing to the top waves, "but these three are encrypted. I can't see inside."

Eric looked at the waves along the bottom.

"Communications. They're talking to someone?"

"Or simply keeping an open line."

"They can still broadcast a confession or issue orders. We have to shut them down," Eric said.

"The trunk line is in the rear tunnel," Drumm said. "On the east wall across from the back of Building E."

"You just cut the wires?" Cody asked.

"They're shielded. If you want to stop them from launching anything, we should take out the whole line and the chase it goes through."

"Explosives?" Eric asked.

Drumm nodded.

"How far are we from the archive where we stashed the duffels?" Eric asked.

"It's right around the corner, down the hall."

"We'll gear up on the way," Eric said.

91

FIFTEEN MINUTES LATER, they were traveling through the springs under Building E, nearing the back of the building.

Once they cut off Hardwick's communications, they could go for the hostages and the war room.

"That's it," Drumm said as they reached the end of the spring foundations. He pointed across the rear tunnel to a steel door. It came up to chest height and was set in the stone on the tunnel's east side.

"What are we looking at?" Eric asked.

"It opens into a small access tunnel, a crawlspace really, carved into the stone. That runs about a hundred meters due east to let people work on the trunk line."

Eric lifted the radio. "Will we be able to keep up communication if Cody stands watch here under the building?"

"We should. It's a straight shot."

"Room to turn around?"

"Only at the end."

"And we're crawling out?"

"You could probably manage a crouch, but it will be slow. Think about that when you're setting the delay on the explosive."

Eric looked up and down the rear tunnel and behind them under Building E. There had been no sign of the person he had seen earlier, searching with the light, but Hardwick's people were out there.

He turned to Cody and pointed to her radio. "Let us know if you see anything or if anyone approaches. If you can't risk a noise, just key the handset twice."

"Got it," she said, then brought her gun across her body and stepped between the springs to the edge of the shadows under Building E.

Eric moved out, did a last scan, then ran across the rear tunnel with Drumm, jumping over the channel of water that ran down its center. Eric covered the approaches while Drumm unlocked the door set in the eastern wall of the tunnel and slipped inside. Crouching down, Eric entered the dark passage and pulled the steel door shut behind him.

Enclosed in the crawlspace, with bundles of cables running along either side, Eric risked a light. The air was warm and close, and Eric was acutely aware of the brick of C-4 and detonators in a small bag on his back. He was careful not to scrape them on the rough stone ceiling of the passage, just inches away.

His clothes were damp with sweat by the time they reached the end and Drumm pulled himself into the corner.

Eric came alongside him, studying where the cables continued through holes bored in the stone face at the end of the passage. He pulled one of the sticks of C-4 and flicked open his knife.

"Twelve ounces?" Eric said. "Should be enough to collapse the passage without bringing down the tunnel wall."

Drumm looked over the stone.

"Make it ten," he said.

Eric slid his knife through the off-white putty. He handed it to Drumm, who pressed it in over the cables where they entered the wall.

"Good?" he asked.

Eric nodded and slid forward, pulling a coil of det cord and a blasting cap from his bag. He primed the explosive, wiped a bead of sweat from his temple, then crimped in the cord.

Tsss tsss. The sound came from his radio. Someone keying an open line. *Tsss tsss.*

Waiting in the dark under Building E, Cody heard a faint scraping coming from the south in the rear tunnel. She gripped the barrel of her SIG rifle and stepped forward, leaning out to get a look down the tunnel.

There was no one, no sound but the whisper of her own breath as she studied the shadows.

A figure emerged from Cavern D. She keyed her radio twice, and then twice again. Then she moved to give herself a better angle of fire as the man approached.

"Who's there!" the figure called out. It was Brimley's voice. The footsteps came closer. "Agent Cody, is that you?"

He had seen her. She inched out from the back of Cavern E into the rear tunnel, gun up, taking aim at him as he strode toward her. The emergency lights lit his face, a look of pure relief. His MP5 was by his side as he approached her in the rear tunnel.

She wasn't taking any chances with him. She had seen the attackers slip inside Building B. It was possible they had somehow forced the door after hitting it with breaching charges, but she and Eric and Drumm had all considered the alternative—that someone inside opened the door for them. They hadn't been able to raise Brimley or Leigh after the breach.

"Wait there," she called out.

"What?" he said, halting. "Who's with you? Are Hill and Drumm all right? The others?"

"How did you get out of the president's suite?" she asked.

"I barely made it," he said.

He looked at her weapon, and his face twisted with suspicion. "How did you get away?"

"We had to fight our way north."

"Put that down, Amber," he said, his voice soft, like a patient teacher's.

He had made it out unscathed after the presidential suite and war room had come under siege, and he was now walking armed in the open. It didn't make sense.

"How did you get free?" she asked.

"I hid," he said. "I made it behind them. I can help you get in, but first, where are the others?"

He took a step forward.

"Stop there," she said.

"Amber, I know there's a lot going on, but you can't go pointing your weapon at another agent like that."

She didn't move.

"Put down the gun. That's an order from your superior."

She steadied her aim, the sights fixed on his chest as he stepped closer, holding up his palm.

"Stop," she said, surprising him with the command in her voice.

He looked back, as if checking if there was a threat behind him. Or perhaps he was waiting for someone, expecting more to come.

Brimley continued toward her. She took aim, her finger drawing against the trigger.

"Drop it, Cody! You're going to get someone hurt."

She looked at his face over the sights and remembered every kindness Brimley had ever shown her. Her focus fixed on his lapel pin, like the pitted one of her father's she still carried in her pocket. She couldn't pull the trigger, couldn't kill one of her brothers or sisters in the Service.

His eyes darted to the left. Cody turned her head that way and saw a figure coming toward her from deeper under Building E, a man raising a gun. She pivoted and fired. The red flash from her rifle filled her vision and the man's left hand went to his chest. He turned to the side like someone had shoved his shoulder.

She spun back to Brimley to see the barrel of his MP5 pointed straight at her head, his face pained, the gun's muzzle a perfect black circle. He had the shot. Her body tensed, waiting for the sting, the end, as her gun spun toward him in what felt like slow motion.

A whip cracked over her shoulder. Brimley fell back. Eric had fired the shot. He and Drumm were on the east side of the tunnel, moving toward her, Drumm already aiming his weapon toward the man under Building E.

Drumm fired three three-round bursts. Some bullets sparked off the springs under the building, ricocheting, but some found their mark. The man under E dropped even before Cody could take aim again.

Drumm and Eric jumped across the water toward her. Blood dripped down Hill's neck. Drumm covered the north and west while she moved with Hill toward Brimley, lying on the stone floor of the rear tunnel.

One look confirmed the veteran agent was gone, the face she had known since childhood now a lifeless mask. She dragged his MP5 away with her boot, then kept her aim up as she picked it off the floor and slung it over her left shoulder.

Eric covered the southern approaches. "Move back under E," he said as he crouched down, took Brimley's radio, and searched his pockets. "More will be coming."

She moved north and joined Drumm among the springs under Building E. Eric finished with Brimley, then crossed to the east side of the rear tunnel. He ducked into the small passage where he and Drumm had set the charges to take out the communications trunk line.

He came out running a second later and jumped over the water toward her. They all headed west between the springs and were thirty feet under Building E when the blast hit, a wall of noise and heat that slammed into her back like a truck.

She kept going, running through the dark as the blast pressured her inner ears, disorienting her.

She was shocked that she was still alive somehow. A sick feeling rose in her—she had the shot on Brimley and didn't take it.

92

THE GUNFIRE AND the blast would telegraph their location to the attackers, so they ran hard, moving deeper under Building E until they reached the narrow passageway in the cavern wall that led south to Cavern D. They took it to Building D and Drumm brought them up a side entrance and inside.

Cody's chest burned from the sprint as Drumm led them down a hall. They slowed the pace, each step sounding like a drumbeat on the floors with their spring foundations.

Walking to Eric's right, she could see blood drying on his neck and the collar of his shirt.

He could have been killed, because she was too cowed by Brimley to fire her damn weapon.

"Jesus, Hill. I'm sorry," she said.

"What for?"

"I didn't take him when I had a chance. I . . . I couldn't."

Eric faced her, but before he could speak, the sound of muffled voices came from the outside: shouts.

They froze, covering both ends of the passage. All she could hear was her own breath and her pulse deep in her ears. She didn't know how long they waited; it felt like minutes. All was silent. Finally, Hill waved them forward, picking each step carefully, not making a sound.

Eric carried Brimley's radio, but nothing came over it. The attackers must have started using another channel or key for their operations.

They were moving east inside Building D now, toward the rear. Drumm took them into a small break area with lockers along one side. An orange and yellow stripe decorated the opposite wall, running horizontally. It reminded Cody of the graphics she'd seen on old custom vans rolling around LA.

"Where are we?" she asked.

"The original gym. Rarely gets used since we put in the fitness center."

The place looked like it hadn't been touched since the 1980s.

Drumm crouched next to a set of cabinets under a countertop. He rifled through boxes and came back with some gauze and tape.

"Sit," he said to Eric.

Eric dabbed at his neck, looked at the smear of blood, and sat on one of the benches. Cody watched Drumm pick at a section of athletic tape, trying and failing to get it started. She stepped toward him and held out her hands.

He seemed relieved as he gave the first aid gear to her. She walked over to Hill and looked at the cut high on his neck near his jaw—two parallel scratches about an eighth of an inch deep.

"It's not bad," she said.

Hill tilted his head to the left and winced. "Frag, I think."

Cody remembered the chaos of the shooting. Neither Brimley nor the other attacker fired. Only Hill and Drumm. The ricochet from Drumm's shots must have caught him.

"Was that me?" Drumm said, looking to the injury. "God. I'm sorry."

"Don't be," Hill said. "You dropped him. All that matters."

"Right," Drumm said, his voice distant. Cody assumed he had never killed anyone before. His hands were in his pockets, maybe to hide any shaking. He looked like he might be ill.

She ran gauze over Hill's cuts, then taped it down. He gave her a faint smile and said, "Thank you."

He still didn't seem to know where he stood with her after everything he'd revealed about her father and the anger it elicited in her. She wasn't sure herself, hadn't had a second to think it through.

"Welcome."

Eric got up, walked to the door on the right, and peered through its window. Cody could see it was a small weight room filled with Nautilus machines and a tanning bed along the wall.

She turned back to see Drumm with a jar of Folgers crystals.

"We have time?" he asked Eric.

"It'll do us good, thanks," Hill replied. "We need to plan."

Drumm filled three Dixie cups from the hot water tap and stirred in the crystals. He handed one to Cody. The water was only warm and the coffee gritty, but as she took her first bitter sip, her whole body seemed to lighten in anticipation of the caffeine.

She checked her watch. "God," she said, and looked at Hill. "It's Sunday."

"Did you think we'd been down here for a couple hours or a couple weeks?"

"Both."

Twenty-eight hours in this bunker, and she'd been awake for forty-five.

She sat on a bench, leaning forward, elbows on her thighs. She needed to move, to act. "They're cut off. Now we hit the suite?"

"That's right," Eric said. Taking out their comms first was the right strategy, but she could tell that he'd been dying to fight back every second since he watched Kline fall from that building. "Let's see those building plans," he called out to Drumm.

He nodded, reached into his pocket, and pulled out a sheaf of papers—blueprints for Building B that they had grabbed along with the explosives before they hit the trunk line. He laid them out on the counter, and they gathered around them.

Cody's attention fixed on the walls that secured the war room and the president's suite—six inches of steel.

"Ways in?" Eric asked Drumm.

"The two secret passages into the president's suite are out. The one to the roof is known and the hatch through the floor we took earlier is impassable after the fire, probably both be guarded anyway."

"The doors?"

"Assume they'll be locked from the inside."

"Breach them?" Cody asked.

"We probably have enough explosive," Drumm said. "But anything strong enough to rip through those outer walls or doors would be fatal or damn close inside. Then we would have to clear it room to room."

"I got this off Brimley," Eric said, and pulled a flash-bang from his pocket, a nonlethal grenade that can temporarily stun with a powerful blast of pressure and light. "But one won't be enough."

"Flush them out?" she asked. "Cut off the air?"

He looked to Drumm.

"They're good on air for a day at least even if we shut down every HVAC line, and there are dozens of them."

"If we run in smoke or exhaust?" she asked, pacing across the tile floors.

"It's not tear gas," Drumm said. "The diesel plant puts out carbon monoxide. The first lady and Claire Givens are inside and possibly the president. Decent chance you'd kill them all."

"Agent Leigh could be a hostage too. I heard her shout when they took the suite. It sounded like she was being attacked." Eric studied the building plans. "What if we shape the charges?" he asked. "Don't blow the doors in, cut off the hinges."

"We don't have the gear. Linear shaped charges are built around a copper core. We might be able to blow them anyway, especially if we can find some weakness from the previous attacks. But even if you get in . . ."

"They can guard every entrance," Eric said. "We don't have intel on their numbers and disposition. And there's more of them, dug in, with hostages, human shields."

"There has to be a way," Cody said. "They could be in there working over Kline and the others right now."

Eric ran his hand along his jaw, his eyes tracing the corridors on the map. She caught him glancing toward her, looking at the gun hanging from her shoulder. She crossed her arms.

She could see the rage burning in him. He wanted to attack as badly as she did. He was right before—you have to fight as hard and as dirty as they do.

"No," Eric said. "It'll be a bloodbath."

"What?"

"We won't make it. Or the hostages won't."

"So we just leave them?" she said, almost an accusation. "Why don't we get these fuckers?"

He stared at her, his eyes going back to her gun, then he turned and waved her with him as he walked toward the far side of the room.

She followed him until he stopped by the door to the weight room and looked at her.

"You've never killed anyone," he said.

She glanced down. "No. Listen. I had the shot."

"You didn't know he was bad. Not a hundred percent."

"I knew. I just didn't pull. I should have taken him down. I'm sorry. Next time I won't hesitate." She felt a flush of shame working through her cheeks.

"That's not it, Cody. I'm glad you didn't."

"But he could have killed you. He nearly killed me."

"I don't know. He hesitated on you. You talked me down before, when I needed it. So listen to me now. You're angry at yourself. You want to prove something out there, but you didn't do anything wrong. It's hard to kill a man. It's hard to watch an old friend die." The muscles in his jaw tightened, and he breathed out through his nose. She wondered if he was thinking about her father. "Here you'd be doing both. If we go after that suite, you're going to have to take out your fellow agents all while shooting within a couple inches of hostages. This is beyond what we train for."

"I can do it," she seethed, her fists closing tight.

People had been telling her she wasn't good enough her whole life. The most fucked-up thing was, part of her believed them. That fear stalked her, the idea that she would fight her way back to the White House only to find out that the people who doubted her were right. She couldn't hack it and it would end with another agent dead on the ground like her father.

"I know you can, Cody. There's no doubt in my mind. That's not the issue." He clasped his hands together. "You were right before, about me. I was on tilt. The same way I was that night I went after Braun. You think there's no way to push back against the evil in the world. You get so fed up all you want to do is tear it down, blow it all away. I know. That's the danger, seeing all the bullshit and letting the anger get the best of you. It's what happened to Hardwick.

"I was either going to walk away—just give up and let them win—or end up like him," Eric went on. "Shit, I could have killed Braun. I fed that cynicism. I let the anger blind me. I could have ended up in that fucking war room by Hardwick's side myself.

"You were right to call me out. And you were right to tell me to have some faith. And I'm returning the favor now. I'm glad you didn't put a bullet in Brimley's brain. Maybe you believed there was some good in him. You still think that the people will do the right thing? The institutions will hold? The truth always comes out in the end?"

She thought for a moment. "I do. Always been partial to lost causes. A little self-delusion is the only way to make it out of Mesa Springs."

"You saved me with it, Cody. Thank you. You're a good agent, as good as any I've ever met. And I think you were the one to figure out how we can get our people safe."

"You want to fill me in? Because I'm not seeing it."

Eric pulled out the radio he'd taken from Brimley. "The truth," he said. "I need to talk to Hardwick."

93

CODY LOOKED AT the radio like it was an armed grenade.

"What's the plan?" she asked.

"We already won. I can turn Hardwick, or try."

"They've gone this far."

"He's cut off. He knows that the coup failed up top. He may not fully believe it yet, but he has seen that everything driving him was a lie."

"But he won't back down until he admits that. He could think that broadcast was a trick."

"Searle sent a message out as Citizen. That's the first thing the FBI would have him do once he confessed, to call off the other plotters. Now Hardwick and his people are on their own, isolated down here."

"You're going to make a deal with him?"

"No. But I'll put the truth in front of him. I know why he's doing this. Loyalty to Rivas and Stiles, duty. That same drive can bring him around if he's faced with the truth. I have to try. I've spent too long believing that nothing can beat back the bullshit except sinking to their level or shooting them dead."

Cody's eyebrows rose. "He might just try to kill you."

"No doubt," Eric said. "I think it'll work, but it's not all kumbaya. If I can get him to come out in person, it will give us a sense of what their security posture is, their numbers, everything we're up against."

Eric thought about the layout of Raven Rock. He was in Building D, and Hardwick and the hostages were in the presidential suite that made up the back of Building B, next to the rear tunnel. "You and Drumm can spot while I talk to him, look for weaknesses, access routes. It's the only way we'll get intel inside that building."

Eric looked across the room to Drumm. The engineer joined the conversation.

"We'll see whether the hostages are all right," Eric went on. "And get a sense of where they are. More than that, I need Hardwick to see what they've turned him into, a terrorist. If forced to acknowledge that, he'll back down."

"You're sure?" Cody asked.

"Sure enough."

"How?"

"Because I could have been him."

"And if he decides to shoot you on sight?"

"Shoot back. But I saw it before when we squared off. He could have killed me. He didn't. He's not all gone. They were lied to, and now they have to face the truth."

"You'll bet your life on that?"

Eric weighed the radio in his hand. "Yes."

He watched her for a second. Things had been strained between them ever since he told her the truth about her father's death. "Listen, before we head out . . ." He was so bad at this kind of thing. "Are we all right? I'm sorry, for keeping all that from you, for what happened that day with your dad, for not doing more to stop it."

She regarded him for a moment. "We're cool. Just be straight with me. I can handle it."

"I know. And if I was . . . trying to keep you safe, it wasn't because I doubted you, at all. It was only because after what happened to him, I couldn't stand the thought of anything happening to you, of failing again . . ."

A half smile. "Scared? Eric Hill?"

"I guess I was."

She put her hand on his shoulder. "I've watched the tape of the ambush. I know. There's nothing more you could have done."

"I—"

"You did your job. And my dad made his own decisions that day. Everyone blames themselves after something like that. 'If only I had . . .'" She shook her head. "Just let it go, man."

"Have you?"

"I'm getting there."

A silent moment passed between them. "Thank you," Eric said.

"You're welcome." She gave a look around the room, then ran her hand along her cheek. "All right, fuck it," she said. "Let's do this."

They walked toward Drumm. "Everyone set?" Eric asked.

Cody's and Drumm's eyes met, and they nodded.

Eric brought his shoulders back, lifted Brimley's radio, and keyed the mic. "Hardwick, this is Eric Hill. Come back."

He waited, staring at the black grille of the speaker. He went to try another frequency, but the line was already alive: "Go ahead." It was Hardwick's voice, brusque and cold.

"We need to talk," Eric said. "Face-to-face."

94

EIGHT MINUTES LATER, Eric was walking down the rear tunnel south toward the back of Building B, his rifle hanging at the end of its sling. The terms Hardwick gave for the meeting were simple. Hands off your weapon. Stay on the east side of the tunnel, away from the building.

Hardwick had agreed to meet in ten minutes, no later. That didn't give Eric much time to set up—which was almost certainly the point—but Eric had sent Drumm and Cody ahead to watch over and case the building for possible weaknesses.

His boots ground through the grit on the stone as he approached the wreckage behind Building B, moving into the glow of the emergency light.

He had to force himself to keep his hands at his side. They kept drawing naturally toward his weapon, the muscles in his wrists and forearms tense and ready.

Agent Cody was planning to cover him from the south by traveling through the passageways and setting up just south of Building B in the rear tunnel. He examined the shadows ahead among the debris behind B. She would only just have time to get into position.

Drumm had taken the passageways to hide along the northern edge of Cavern B, in the narrow alley between the springs under Building B and the cavern wall, where he could protect Eric from the west.

They were watching, but Eric had to assume Hardwick's men were too.

Fifty feet, Hardwick had said, come no closer. Eric stepped over a few pieces of rubble, then stopped at that distance. The rear doors to B were closed. The air burned in his lungs with every breath.

A long creak. Eric fought the impulse to raise his weapon as the rear entrance closest to him opened and a sliver of light poured out. A shadow passed over the gap—Hardwick standing inside, his gun hanging from a sling over his shoulder. Eric peered around him into the hallway and saw Walsh, rifle held at a high ready, the muscles tensed in his jaw.

Hardwick said something to his accomplice, and Walsh stepped back, out of sight. Then Hardwick walked through the door onto the steel landing at the top of the entrance steps.

"Is everyone all right in there?" Eric called out.

"What do you want?"

"To end this. I know you saw what's happening in Washington."

Hardwick took long, even breaths.

"You've done what you wanted to do, Mike. The entire world has its eye on you and on Kline. The truth *will* come out. You can make your case to the country, but holding innocent women at gunpoint isn't going to help your side. Let's start by getting Sarah Kline and Claire Givens out of there. Handle this between the professionals."

Everything Eric said came out of Hostage Negotiation 101. Hardwick knew it. Eric wanted him to feel it, to understand what he had become, a terrorist standing over a couple of terrified victims. It would tear at his instincts, everything he had once been, and probably still thought of himself as—a protector.

"They're not innocent," Hardwick said, shaking his head. "They murdered Rivas and Stiles, for a start."

"There's no cavalry coming to save you. There's no coup. I understand that you're doing this out of a sense of honor, of getting justice for them. But this isn't the way. There's a lot of military massing out there. It's only a matter of time before they find a way in. It will be ugly. Get out now, and tell your story while you can, on your own terms, before this ends in bloodshed. That's not who you are."

"He threatened everything we swore to protect. It had to be done."

"It will only hurt your cause if you get more of them killed." It pained Eric to even come close to sympathizing with Hardwick's crusade after he and his men had killed so many, but building a rapport was the key early step in hostage negotiations. "Just let Dr. Kline go. She's innocent."

Hardwick crossed his arms, looked through the door, then back. He wasn't biting.

"I heard Laura Leigh cry out before, when you took this building. She sounded like she was hurt. Is she all right?"

"It couldn't be helped."

"What happened?"

He didn't answer.

"Hardwick, I need to know that they're still alive and that you haven't hurt anyone."

"They're all fine . . . except Agent Leigh."

Eric felt the blood burning in his face. "Damn it, Mike. What happened?"

"Leigh. She's gone. It was a fair fight."

"You shot her?"

"She engaged," Hardwick said, then swallowed. "We finished it. There was nothing else we could do."

The anger coursed through Eric like a jolt of electricity, but he stayed in control.

"Was anyone else hurt? Do you have Kline?"

Hardwick looked down for a moment.

"Is he alive?"

Eric's old friend's eyes bored into him. "He fell into the water. It pulled him toward the intake for the diesel plant."

"He might have made it," Eric said, stepping closer.

Hardwick shook his head. "He took three shots. We saw the blood."

Eric had suspected as much, but hearing it out loud left him with a feeling of free fall. After a moment of disbelief, the rage gripped him. This was the ultimate betrayal for an agent: killing one of those he had sworn to protect and taking out a fellow officer. He tightened his fists and didn't give voice to it. He didn't need to. It had to be working on Hardwick in the same way. After almost two decades in the Service, that mission was a part of them.

"I can try to resolve this," Eric said. "So it doesn't end in a massacre. But I need to know that the others are okay."

"You're not giving orders here."

"Just walk Dr. Kline and Givens out to the door." Hardwick and his people probably considered them as guilty as the president. They might have tried to force a statement out of them, a confession, anything to try to turn the public to their side, to make their lies into the truth.

"If they're dead, it's a very different story."

"They're okay."

"I need proof." He glared at Hardwick, accusing him, questioning his honor, working him.

Hardwick held up his hand, stepped inside, and looked like he was talking to someone. Eric assumed he would give proof of life, if only to demonstrate the leverage he still had to prevent Eric or anyone else from trying to take that building by force. Any information Eric could get on the situation inside would help him plan his attack.

Hardwick returned and stood on the landing just outside the door. Two figures came down the hall, lit from behind. Givens walked in front, her shoulders back in that same dignified posture she always had, though her steps—fearful, tentative—gave away her true feelings. Dr. Kline walked behind her, her eyes darting from her captors to the exit.

"Far enough," Walsh barked from behind them, deeper inside the building. They froze. Eric couldn't see him, but he must have had a gun on the hostages.

Eric shifted to the side to get a better view. Hardwick might be keeping them back from the door so they couldn't escape, or because he was hiding something. Sarah Kline looked slightly to the side, and Eric noticed a red mark on her cheek. His eyes went to her hands, hanging by her legs against the front of her dress. She moved them, one at a time, subtly, starting with the thumb on her right hand. It looked like she was counting—one through five on her right, six through ten on her left, eleven and twelve on her right.

Eric assumed it meant she had seen a dozen attackers inside. He met her gaze but did nothing to acknowledge or give away the signal.

"That's it!" Hardwick shouted. Another bark from Walsh. A plea in the first lady's eyes as Walsh stepped closer to her, only his shadow visible, clearly holding a weapon to her back. He ordered her away.

Eric looked to Hardwick. He let the contempt show. "Someone hit Dr. Kline. Was it you?" he asked.

A clenched jaw. "No," Hardwick said. "I have it under control." He stood a little taller, searching for the sense of command, of pride, that Eric knew was eroding inside him.

"Did Citizen tell you to stand down?"

He saw a spark of defensiveness in Hardwick's eyes.

"Searle? He was an errand boy. Citizen . . ." Hardwick looked down for an instant, then stabbed his finger into his chest.

"I'm Citizen. Walsh is Citizen. Every one of my people is Citizen, and there are millions more. It's a movement for the truth. You can't stop it by taking out one functionary."

Eric stared back at him. Hardwick was trying to convince himself. "Did he call it off?"

A long pause before Hardwick answered. "We knew the risks we were facing going into this. We were all willing to make that sacrifice for what we believed in."

"I understand."

Eric thought he might go on, defending himself, even trying to bring Eric to his side, but he simply went quiet. He had spoken in the past tense. That was good.

"You're the one they call Brutus, then?" Eric figured him for the leader.

"Just Marcus," he said.

"And Walsh is Cassius?"

He nodded.

"Those are the only two hostages?"

"The only two detainees. Correct."

"Kline's gone," Eric said. "You can make your case without him pulling the strings now. There's no need for any more of this."

"Say my piece and drink my hemlock," Hardwick said.

"It doesn't have to go that far. But if you hide, or try to use those women as a shield, history will judge you."

"I was never afraid of the consequences, the law. I'll face it. You saw the corruption yourself, Eric. I know you felt the same anger I did."

"This isn't the way."

Hardwick didn't answer. Eric was surprised he didn't try harder to sway him to the plotters' side. He must have known it wouldn't work. That was probably why he never approached Eric to join the conspiracy in the first place. He was more certain of Eric's loyalty to the job than Eric had been himself.

"Let them go, Mike. You made your stand."

Hardwick looked down at his hands, then back to Eric. "Wait here," he said, and stepped inside. The door closed.

Eric waited, tracing the darkness, looking for snipers above. He caught movement—Cody crouched down on the far side of the debris, taking cover just at the edge of the light. He thought he heard raised voices inside, and his hand went to his gun. Then there was nothing but the hum of the fans and the rush of the water under the fallen metal.

95

THE DOOR SQUEALED open. Eric moved his hand a few inches farther from the gun. Hardwick stepped onto the landing and this time shut the door behind him. No backup. No audience.

He took the steps slowly, and Eric moved closer, facing him across the water and the wreckage.

"We took the risk to save this country. You need to understand that. This was all done to keep Kline from subverting a legitimate political process."

Justification, practically an excuse. Eric let himself hope that this was the beginning of Hardwick's climbdown. It had a valedictory feel to it.

"We can follow this wherever it goes, find out what happened to Rivas and Stiles, but no one else needs to get hurt."

"What are you proposing?" Hardwick asked.

"You let the women go. Out of the bunker. I'll stay."

"If I do that, if we bring this to a close, we will need safe passage, and the chance to make a televised statement on the networks. I'm not alone in this. There are powerful men and women, patriots, behind me."

"Who?"

"Senators. Congressmen. This isn't a coup. It's a necessity, safeguarding the exercise of a constitutional process."

Hardwick was right about one thing: Searle was surely a go-between, and Citizen wasn't simply one man—it was a mask hiding the real power, the true authors of this attack. He wondered how much Hardwick really knew about who was ultimately behind the conspiracy.

"Names," Eric said.

"Not yet. There has to be a full airing of the truth," Hardwick said.

"Open hearings in the Senate, equal time, subpoenas. I need to talk to my people on the surface."

"Get me Givens and an open line and I'm sure we can make that happen."

"That will take some time. Our lines are down."

Eric nodded, grateful for the confirmation. Hardwick was cut off.

"This was always about the truth, Eric."

"I know." They all had their faiths. Hardwick had chosen a false god.

"Ellie didn't know anything about this. Not one thing."

Hardwick's girlfriend. Maybe that was why Hardwick hadn't married her. He didn't want to tie her to his fate, the prospect of going down as a traitor.

"I believe you," Eric said. "I'll do everything I can for her."

Hardwick's eyes narrowed as he looked down in thought. He ran his knuckles along his cheek and faced Eric. "We connect up top, and work out the terms, then I'll let them go."

Eric had to fight to still any reaction. It felt like he had taken his first full breath in twenty-eight hours. He had him. He played it steady, didn't want to do anything that would knock Hardwick off this path.

Hardwick looked at him, relief showing in his face. He stood there for a moment, maybe processing it, then gestured to Eric's neck.

"You all right?" he asked, looking like himself again.

"Fine," Eric said. "Thanks."

"All right," Hardwick said, drawing his shoulders back. "First, we—"

The bullet entered Hardwick's right temple and blew out in a cloud on the other side of his head. The crack followed an instant later, booming down the tunnel. Hardwick dropped like a marionette with its strings cut.

Eric had his gun up before the body came to rest, aiming where he had seen the flash of the shot—a catwalk that ran along the roof of Building B and ended at the top of the building's rear facade above him. He saw Liam Walsh lowering his rifle and caught a glimpse of his face, his hollow stare. Eric let nine rounds fly in a long burst, but Walsh had already pulled back and disappeared into the dark above Building B.

96

MORE GUNSHOTS SOUNDED to the south, where he had seen Cody. She was pouring fire onto the roof as well.

Eric vaulted over a fallen piece of framing. There was no time to absorb Hardwick's death or the prospect of peace being ripped away.

He called Cody and Drumm on the radio. "Walsh is on the roof. Look for a way up so we can take him."

As Eric raced from the rear tunnel into Cavern B along its north side, he could see Cody already entering the cavern on its southern edge. The fallen framing should let them find a way to climb up and cut him off. He stepped into the narrow alley along the northern edge of B.

"Going deeper on the south side," Cody said over the radio. "No access yet."

"Same on the north," Drumm said. Eric could see him moving ahead in the alley, deeper in on the north side, about a third of the way down Cavern B. All of them were moving away from the rear tunnel, though Cody and Drumm were well ahead of Eric.

He slipped through the narrow space between the springs under Building B and the rough stone wall, holding his gun high, looking for any sign of Walsh on the catwalks overhead.

Twenty-five feet in, he reached a section of the building's exterior where the shielding tiles had fallen away, revealing the framing that had supported them. He dropped his gun to the end of its sling, reached up, closed his fist on a bent piece of framing, and climbed. Eight feet up he looked for a way to continue, his eyes fixing on a thin horizontal bar about five feet above him.

The tramp of boots sounded through the cavern. Eric guessed it was a half-dozen men. It sounded like they were under the building, deeper in the cavern, separating him from Drumm and Cody.

The footsteps came closer. The drive to close in and kill Walsh after he'd murdered Hardwick was all-consuming, but Eric would be an easy mark hanging off the side of the building.

A last look up, then he lowered himself and dropped, absorbing the fall with his knees to soften the sound of his landing.

Lights flooded through the springs under B, coming from where he'd heard the attackers. There were at least six of them, spread wide enough that one of the timed charges he carried wouldn't be able to take them all down at once. He wanted the fight, but it was suicide. If he engaged with them, Walsh could send backup out of the rear entrances of Building B, cutting off his escape to the rear tunnel.

He held for an instant, then slipped toward the rear tunnel as the lights swung toward him. At least Eric would draw the shooters away from his two allies, who were farther down in B, moving west toward the main tunnel.

He tracked through the springs under B, slipping fast between the dusty coils to avoid their lights and angling toward the southern side of the cavern. A close crack of gunfire lit the darkness red. He heard the bullet hiss past him, within a foot or two, and ran ahead before the shooter could fix his aim.

The other lights closed on him. More shots rang out. He reached the end of Cavern B and cut right around the corner into the rear tunnel as the stone wall exploded near his head. His hands and neck pulsed with his racing heart as he pressed against the western wall of the rear tunnel, staying close to the corner, ready to take anyone who came for him.

Staying low, he edged out, looking for targets following him among the springs under Building B. A figure emerged in the lead. Eric aimed and fired. A groan.

Three shots cracked toward him. As he dodged, his gun jumped in his hands. Sparks. Something stung his face. He squeezed the trigger to return fire. Nothing.

Dropping back around the corner into the rear tunnel, he looked at his weapon and saw the mangled ejection port. A bullet had hit it. He hauled back on the charging handle, but it would only move back an inch. The shooters would round the corner toward him any minute. He grabbed the handle with both hands, put his boot on the back of the grip, and pulled. Metal ground against metal.

Crack.

Pressure bloomed in his back. It felt like somebody had shoved a tent stake through his ribs. The shot had come from behind him, to the south in the rear tunnel, and caught him in the Kevlar vest. He pulled on the handle again. Nothing. He slung the gun over his shoulder and turned.

The shooter, a man with olive skin and a furrowed brow, approached him, his gun up and aimed straight at Eric's face. He was twenty feet away now—too close to take out with an explosive. He must have come from farther down in the rear tunnel, near Building A. His hand tightened on the grip, his knuckles going white.

Eric wasn't going down easy. He pulled his knife and charged.

Crack.

Eric braced, but the man hadn't fired. His arms fell slowly, his strength draining out. He'd been shot in the neck from behind.

He sat straight down, clumsy as a toddler, straining to lift the gun, refusing to give in. Then he slumped to the side, a question in his eyes as the life left him.

President Kline stood behind him, rifle raised, a line of smoke curling from the barrel as he moved toward Eric.

97

KLINE RAN TO the fallen attacker, grabbed his rifle, and tossed it to Eric. He caught it by the barrel, scanned the tunnel to the south, then faced the corner where the shooters were approaching from under Building B.

The president came to Eric's side, his uniform stained with blood near his shoulder. There were three holes in his cammies. He'd changed into them last night in the infirmary, after they escaped the fire by diving into the canal. His clothes were damp again. He must have fled the attackers by using the canal after they shot him, or fallen into it. Through the rips, Eric could make out the thin Kevlar vest the president wore for low-profile protection.

"You're hurt?" Eric asked.

"It's all right. You?"

A shadow lengthened around the corner, coming from Cavern B.

"Fine. I'll cover this, sir. Drop back, head south in the rear tunnel, and get out under Building A."

"There's too many for you to take alone."

"They can't know you're alive. If they take you, it's the ultimate leverage. They may be able to swing this whole thing back their way."

Kline shook his head. "If I run, they'll kill you, then me. Sarah's in there. How do we take them?"

A gun barrel appeared around the corner. Eric fired three more times, bullets skipping off the stone, and the shooter pulled back. "Go," he growled.

"Damn it, let me help you," Kline said.

"You can run?"

"Yes."

"Hold them off. Keep them from coming around that corner into this tunnel. Suppressive fire. I need five seconds."

Kline nodded and dropped to one knee, taking aim. He propped the elbow of his left hand against his raised knee, steadying the barrel.

Eric reached down and pulled out one of the charges. He needed a second to put a time-delay fuse on it. Lights poured out from Cavern B and fixed on him and Kline.

Kline laid down shots, holding the attackers back as Eric set the blasting cap. They probably had recognized the president by now. They would know he was alive.

Eric pulled the pin on the timed charge and tossed it in front of the attackers, just inside the back opening of Cavern B.

"Go!" he called out.

Kline raced south, and Eric followed him, moving sideways, keeping his gun trained on the attackers, squeezing off three-round peals of fire as he and the president went down the rear tunnel toward Building A.

Gunshots slit through the air to his left. Eric's charge blew, the blast running down the tunnel like a bullet train. A pressure wave slammed into Eric's ribs, compressing his organs and ringing his ears. He heard the fallen framing behind Building B collapsing as a cloud of black smoke and dust filled the rear tunnel between them and the attackers. Eric turned to the south. The path ahead was clear.

98

Sunday. 1:50 p.m.

AGENT LIAM WALSH marched down the hall inside Building B, blood staining his right hand from aiding the wounded. Two more of his people murdered, dying in front of him. He felt the veins in his neck standing out. Kline needed to answer for this.

"Eric Hill comes to us to negotiate," he said to the four shooters walking alongside him. "Hardwick goes out there in good faith, and what does Hill do? Shoots him in the fucking back!"

He looked at the others, shaking his head in disgust. It was a lie in the service of a larger truth. "It was on Kline's orders. He would put us all down like dogs. This is the treachery we've been fighting from the beginning."

Walsh pushed through the doors into the presidential suite's office and conference area, leaving streaks of red on the oak.

Major Rebecca Vaughn and another guard stood inside the conference room, both armed with rifles. They watched the hostages, Sarah Kline and Claire Givens, both sitting on armless office chairs against the far wall. Walsh strode closer and opened the glass door.

"You two," he said, pointing at the captives, and raised his hand. "Up."

Vaughn, standing over the two women with a rifle, looked his way.

"Command center," he said, staring at Sarah Kline.

"What is—"

"Move!" Walsh shouted, grabbing her by the upper arm and pulling her toward the door.

They led the two hostages out of the room and down a narrow hallway into the command center.

"There." Walsh pointed, and she and the other guards brought Givens and Sarah Kline to the far corner of the war room.

He turned right and looked to the tech, who was sitting in an office chair, grinding a ballpoint between his teeth as he worked the keyboard at the main workstation. The nuclear football, pried open, sat by his side. The binders it once carried were arrayed on his desk.

"Where are we?" Walsh asked, looking at the triple monitors.

"Reconnecting to the top. I'm close."

"How long?"

"I'll know in three minutes."

Walsh looked at the red digits of the clocks set high on the wall.

"Get it done," he said. "The missile batteries? We have local control?"

"That's set."

Walsh clapped him twice on the shoulder. "Good. Armed?"

"Not yet, but I can work backwards on the authorizations from these," he said, nodding to the binders. "I'll get it."

Walsh walked toward the hostages. "Against the wall," he called out to Vaughn.

She and the other guards directed Sarah Kline and Claire Givens with the barrels of their guns. The hostages looked to each other nervously, then saw Walsh coming toward them, his hand tight on his weapon.

They backed up toward the wall. Sarah Kline hit it first and touched her palm to the wood paneling.

Walsh paced toward them and stopped in front of the first lady. He inched forward, looking down at her, picking up that faint trace of flowers from the perfume she wore.

"Your husband left you here. He ran and hid." Walsh shook his head, disgusted.

Hesitation on her face, like she didn't dare believe it. She brought her hands together. "He's alive?"

Walsh nodded slowly. "His people offered to talk to us under a truce. Hardwick believed them. Then they shot him in the back of the head."

"No," she said.

He looked at Givens. "That's how you operate, isn't it? Round up and kill anyone who stands in your way. You're a poison to this nation.

"Your husband is a coward," he said to Sarah Kline. "Afraid to face us and afraid of the truth. But there's nowhere he can run. You know what's in that room?" He tilted his head toward the small broadcast studio off the corner of the war room.

"Yes."

"You're going to answer for your crimes."

"You're delusional," she said.

A low laugh escaped him. He took hold of her shoulder. "The people are going to hear the truth from your lips, and his."

"With a gun to our heads?"

"If necessary."

Walsh let his hand fall along her upper arm and pointed to the left, the studio.

"Get inside," he said.

She didn't move. He raised the gun toward her face.

The chief of staff stepped forward. "Don't touch her," Givens said.

"Get back," he said. "It's the last time I'll warn you."

"I could give a fuck what—"

He punched her in the stomach, a short, vicious blow that cut her words off and dropped her onto one knee.

Sarah Kline reached for her, and Walsh brought the barrel of his gun under the first lady's jaw.

"The studio. Now."

Her chin trembled. She swallowed as she looked at him, then moved toward it.

Two guards ushered the hostages in. Walsh remained just outside, looking over the camera, the teleprompter, and the presidential seal as the door closed.

Vaughn put down her radio and walked toward him. "No trace of Hill and Kline," she whispered.

"It doesn't matter how far he runs," Walsh said quietly, looking over the hostages. "We have him." They could broadcast the audio from the studio throughout the bunker over the public address and put the video out on the security camera monitor feeds. Kline would give in once he heard his wife's pleas.

"You're sure about this?" Vaughn asked.

"He murdered our people in cold blood under a flag of truce. He left us no choice. This ends now," he said. "Go turn the camera on."

99

THE ACHE IN Eric's ribs had spread to cover half his back on his right side. His vest had stopped the bullet, but its energy had gone straight into his body. He and Kline had used the passageways to return to Building C.

The injury pulsed with pain as he hauled a door open inside C and stepped through, pivoting right and covering the corridor with his rifle.

Kline followed him, scanning the left side. A quiet creak sounded from around the corner ahead—someone moving toward them.

"Hill?" It was Agent Cody's voice.

"It's me," he said.

"We're clear."

Eric rounded the corner. Cody was waiting, holding her gun across her body, with Drumm behind her, watching the other direction. They had arranged to meet back here before Eric went out to talk with Hardwick. She came forward and put her hand on his shoulder. "Thank God."

"You're both good?" he asked.

She didn't answer, only stared straight ahead as Kline walked toward them.

"You're okay," she said to the president, seeming to forget herself at the sight of him alive. She'd always called him "sir."

"A little scratched and dented, but I'll live," he said, smiling at her and Drumm. "You two are holding up?"

"Better now, sir," she said, emotion creeping into her voice.

"Thank you, Agent Cody." He turned to Eric. "Is there someplace safe we can talk?"

"This way," Eric said, and led them down the hall.

He brought them to the archive where they had stored the duffel bags full of gear, while Drumm went to get Kline a fresh pair of fatigues. Eric examined the storage room—it looked undisturbed—while Cody went to the back and opened the cabinets.

Three black bags lay inside. It was all still there.

"What is that?" Kline asked.

"Guns and explosives," Eric said. "We found one of the attackers' caches."

Kline opened one of the duffels, reached in, and pulled out a Glock 26. He checked that it was loaded, slipped it into a pocket, then peered into the bag.

Cody was looking over the holes in Kline's fatigues. "You were wearing a vest?"

"It seemed wise," Kline said.

"Why didn't you tell us?" she asked.

"Trust no one," he said, with a nod to Eric for the advice. "I didn't know who might shoot me in the back, so I didn't let on that I was wearing it. If they knew, I figured they would shoot me in the head."

Drumm announced himself quietly, then came in, with a fresh set of cammies and a small first aid kit. He went to Kline and started cleaning up the wound on his shoulder, a nasty quarter-inch-wide gouge through the skin.

"We thought you were dead," Cody said, as if still trying to process it.

"I almost was," Kline replied. "The liners broke my fall, but I still hit hard. I pulled myself into the water to get away from them. I was in bad shape."

He stared into space for a moment, remembering the ordeal. Then he looked to Eric. "We were in a better position when everyone thought I was gone."

"They saw him," Eric said. "They know he's alive."

Cody pressed her lips together. "Damn it."

"We'd both be dead if he hadn't stepped out," Eric said.

"They'll try to use Sarah and the others to bring me in?" Kline asked.

Eric nodded. "We need to be prepared for it. Walsh is running the show now. He's far gone. He killed Hardwick to stop him from backing down."

Kline closed his left hand around his right fist. "The gear is right here. We arm up, go in, and get them."

Eric wanted nothing more than to put a bullet through Walsh's skull.

The anger gripped him again, as he flashed on images of Hardwick's murder and the fear in Sarah Kline's eyes.

Eric looked to Cody. "We all want to take them down," she said. "The odds aren't good."

"We've gone through the scenarios, sir," Eric said, watching as Drumm finished putting a bandage on the president's wound. "A straight assault is extremely risky. We are in a good position now. I recommend we play for time."

"Play for time? How the hell are we in a good position?"

"We cut off all their communications to the top, for a while at least, so we don't have to worry about them trying something with the nuclear codes or missile batteries. And the attackers' plan to force a confession out of you or the others won't work."

"Because they can't air it."

"Yes."

"Not this moment," Kline said. "But they still will try to get it out of them. Record it. Play it when they can."

"The coup failed," Eric said. "They know it, know they're losing, and they're desperate."

"Which makes them more dangerous." Kline looked at Eric. "You made contact with Washington?"

"No, we were able to see what was happening in DC and up top from a live communications line that the attackers had set up. We tapped into it."

"The confession I heard over the PA. Searle. That was real?"

"One hundred percent."

"I was so out of it when I heard it. I thought maybe it was a psy op, some way you were trying to demoralize the attackers."

"We were, but it's true. Hardwick and Walsh had political support. The plan was for them to hold you down here while politicians maneuvered to get you out of office. For now, the institutions have held. They got the evidence from Will Maddox's work, from your transmission over the VLF radio."

Kline touched his fingers to his temple. "Thank God."

"The military is massing around Raven Rock. They'll be able to get in eventually. That's why we play for time."

"Or help them out," Drumm said. "We have the explosives now. I can try to blast through the old construction tunnel, give us an escape route."

"Would the military know about it?"

Drumm thought for an instant, then shook his head. "Not likely. It's not on any current plans. I only know about it from the old guard who were around when it was built."

"We get out through it and then use it to bring in backup?" Cody asked. "Enough to take back the war room and presidential suite?"

"If we get through. Decent chance it collapses on me when I blow it, but . . ." He shrugged. "Fuck it. Life's not a dress rehearsal."

Eric looked at the engineer. He seemed so different now, grim and confident.

"That's priority one," Eric said. "Get the president out and get the cavalry in."

Kline shook his head. "I'm not running. I'm not leaving her or Givens."

"They want you down here. If they get control of you, they can take everything. Walsh's political backers are still up there. They're watching which way the wind blows. If Walsh can coerce a false confession out of you, it could still turn the tide. We could lose the government."

"It's not just me they want," Kline said, staring at Eric. "What are they going to do to her? What have they done?"

"She was okay. Though they put some pressure on her already . . . I saw a red mark on her cheekbone. It looked like she'd been slapped."

Kline's fingers wrapped around the barrel of his gun and squeezed, a hard look on his face.

"Can we get into the war room?" he asked.

"Sir, you need to be clear-eyed about this. The country—"

"Enough with being a politician. I need to be a human being for fucking once. A husband. A father. I never put her or Jill first," he said, his mouth drawing tight at the thought of his daughter. "How do we get her out of there?"

Eric studied the president's face. He'd almost lost everything. That changes a man.

"We've run through the scenarios," Eric said. "They're not good. We believe Dr. Kline signaled the number of attackers inside Building B to us when I negotiated with Hardwick—twelve. And there could have easily been more that she didn't see."

"But we just took out two," Kline said. "And Hardwick is gone."

"And Brimley."

"That leaves eight," Kline said. "We use the explosives and take them by surprise."

"We have to assume there are more," Eric said. "I saw at least six coming after us, and they wouldn't have sent everyone out and left the hostages and war room protected by only a couple of people."

"They were able to sneak in gear and personnel. There could be sixteen, twenty-four . . . We really have no idea," Cody said.

Eric kneaded his right palm with his left hand. Of the thirteen people who had come from the White House, seven were now dead. Of the six remaining, one was a traitor: Walsh. Two had been taken captive: Givens and Dr. Kline. The last three, two agents and the president, were in this room.

"They may use the hostages as shields or kill them if we try to breach. Is there another way into your suite we don't know about?"

"No. Just the route we took during the fire, and the one that goes out to the catwalks."

"They'll have both of them covered by now."

"I want to see the plans," Kline said.

"Let's get Drumm started on the escape route first," Eric said. "Then we can see if there's a way into B."

Kline nodded.

"What do you need?" Eric said to Drumm, and they went to the cabinets. The engineer opened the duffel of explosives and started taking out gear.

Kline walked over, looked at the C-4, and paced back, shaking his head.

"She's in there with that psychopath. I'm not going to sit here and do nothing. Give me the plans for Building B."

Eric glanced to Drumm, who was pulling det cord and crimpers from the duffel and loading them into a smaller bag. Drumm reached into his pocket and handed him a sheaf of papers.

Kline took a few steps away and laid them on top of the cabinet, his hands shaking with anger.

He wasn't thinking straight. Eric could see it in his face, the tunnel vision of protecting what he loved. Eric understood it, respected it, but the priority was to get Kline out of here, to save his life and deprive the attackers of what they most wanted. Once Drumm had a route to the top, they could bring in backup in overwhelming numbers, and do a full-force siege against Walsh and his crew.

Kline traced his finger over the blueprints. "What about—"

A voice sounded throughout the building, the murmur barely audible through the thick door to the storage room. Eric held up one finger, then moved toward the door. Gun raised, he opened it.

". . . stop hiding like a coward and face up to what you've done." It was Walsh's voice over the public address system, the acid tone of a demagogue. "Are you going to let them die to serve your ambitions? Look at the security monitors, pick up your radio. It's time to answer for your crimes."

A low whimper of pain sounded over the PA, a woman's voice.

100

"THE MONITORS, WHERE are they?" Kline asked Drumm. The engineer pointed down the hall.

"Grab the gear," Eric said.

They picked up the duffels and headed out, moving down the hall and into the security office they had used earlier to view the news footage. Drumm set to work at the computer and a moment later a video feed appeared in the top left monitor.

It showed Claire Givens standing in front of a wall of blue drapery, the presidential seal hanging behind her. She was in the broadcast studio attached to the command center. Her eyes were fixed on something behind the camera. Givens's right hand gripped her left, both trembling.

Sarah Kline stepped into frame, as if pushed.

The president moved closer to the screen, his hands balling into fists.

"Turn on the radio, Kline," Walsh's voice blared over the public address. "The one you people stole from Brimley after you murdered him. The channel is live. We need to talk."

"Where the fuck is it?" the president asked Eric, looking for the handset.

"You can't deal with him."

"Give it to me." Kline drew out the words, his voice cold and low.

Eric pulled out the radio, powered it on, and handed it to him.

Kline keyed the mic. "This is the president."

"You have twelve minutes, Kline. That's enough time to get you from wherever you're hiding to the back door of Building B, off the rear tunnel. Come alone, unarmed. Lie on your face on the stone at the foot of the steps with your hands behind your head. If you vary from these instructions in any way, there will be blood."

The women pressed together on the security monitor's screen, Givens reaching for Sarah Kline's hand. There was no audio on the feed, only what Walsh broadcast over the radio or the PA.

"Walsh, listen. There's no need for any more violence," the president said into the handset. "You want me. We can work this out."

"You're not in charge, Kline. I am. Battery three four seven."

Kline lowered the radio. "What does that mean?" he asked Drumm.

Drumm worked the keyboard, staring at the monitor as Cody stepped in from the hallway.

"The Patriot missile batteries are armed," Walsh said over the radio. "Any attempt to take this bunker by force will bring grave consequences. I am in control here, James. Understand that. I will not negotiate. I will not hesitate. You people have dishonored the republic and the Constitution you swore to defend. We have targets in Washington, institutions complicit in your crimes. Anyone tries to get in here and we launch. I will wash that city clean, I swear. Now give yourself up or they die."

Kline lowered the radio, his eyes fixed on the screen.

"They're armed," Drumm said. "Under local control. He doesn't need Strategic Command in the loop. It's hardwired to the war room."

Kline took a step back and put his hand over his mouth. "He wouldn't launch a strike on DC."

"He shot his commander in the back," Eric said. "You know more about The Order than I do, but don't underestimate how far he'll go."

"Some of the writing is borderline messianic," Kline said. "Bringing down the capital, washing it clean with blood. The dawn of a new era. We thought it was rhetoric, but now . . ."

Walsh stared at the camera. "Ten minutes," he said over the radio.

The president stared at his wife's face on the screen, shut his eyes, and took a long breath in.

Eric, Drumm, and Cody exchanged looks. Eric felt a knot in his stomach like the worst hunger he'd ever known.

"Don't engage, sir," he said. Kline stared back at him, rubbed his hand along his cheek, then keyed the radio.

"I can work with you on this, Walsh, make a trade, me for them, but I need good faith."

He released the key on the microphone. No answer, just a static hum. Walsh stepped off-screen.

The two hostages pressed back against the wall, responding to some command that Eric and the president now couldn't hear. Their eyes narrowed and their heads turned away as if bracing for a blow.

"You're not listening," Walsh said over the radio in a disappointed tone.

He walked back into view on the security monitor, holding a pistol in his right hand. The two women backed away, but he grabbed Givens by the wrist.

"Wait!" Kline shouted. "Stop!"

Sarah stepped in front of Walsh, and he shoved her to the side, out of view.

"Don't do this!" Kline yelled.

Only silence over the radio as Walsh pulled Givens forward. "Please," she mouthed to the camera.

"I'll come in!" Kline said.

Walsh leveled the pistol at her from the right. She looked at him defiantly and said something. The screen flashed white. Givens collapsed, falling back, out of frame.

"No!" Kline shouted.

Cody's hand rose to cover her mouth.

Eric stepped toward the monitor, his fists rising, a clammy feeling passing along his skin as he watched her fall.

Walsh stepped into the frame and raised the radio to his lips.

"I warned you," he said, the words just slightly out of sync between the image and the canned voice coming through the radio.

He gestured off-screen with the gun, and a man in fatigues pulled Sarah Kline into the shot.

She was yelling. No sound came through, but the words were clear enough from reading her lips: "Don't do it! Don't!"

"The blood is on your hands," Walsh said. The first lady shouted in the back and seemed to gesture subtly with her fingers. He gripped her arm and raised the gun toward her. "Eight minutes."

The video cut out.

. . .

Liam Walsh checked his watch, then looked down at Givens's body. "Get her out of here," he said.

As he turned, Sarah Kline broke away from the guards and lunged at him. "Monster!"

Vaughn and another officer grabbed her by the arms, and she strained against them.

Walsh stepped closer, his face inches from hers, looking over her snarling expression with the calm of a museum patron.

"For her crimes," he said. "Justice is coming for you all."

He gestured with his head and the two guards pushed her back against the wall.

He exited the studio into the command center and called across the room.

"Where are we?" he asked the tech.

"Ready," he said.

Walsh walked up to him and looked over his shoulder at the screen.

"Bring up the targeting."

The officer looked up at him, a mangled pen in his hand. "Are you sure? I thought—"

"Half measures prolong wars," Walsh said. "Decisive action is a mercy. Do it now."

The tech reached for the computer and brought up a map of the capital.

101

THE PRESIDENT'S EYES were closed. A low growl escaped from deep in his throat, his body coiling with rage until it shook. Eric felt it too, anger like steam rising, burning under his skin, his face.

He slung his rifle and gave the president an extra foot of space, waiting for the explosion. The only way to vent the feeling, Eric knew, was movement— driving a fist into the steel side of a cabinet, screaming at the top of his lungs. He was ready to catch him, to restrain him if necessary. They couldn't give away their position.

Kline forced out a long breath through pursed lips, shivering as he rolled his shoulders back, then opened his eyes.

"We get them now," he said.

Eric looked at the bag full of explosives. "Head-on won't work. Did you hear what Sarah was saying at the end of the radio transmission, from behind Walsh?"

"'You know the way,'" Kline said.

"What does that mean?" Eric asked.

The president thought for an instant. "'You know what to do.' You saw what she was saying before: 'Don't do it. Don't give in.' She wants us to hold out."

"Maybe she meant the actual way," Eric said. "Did you see her hands?"

He made a T with his hands, then raised two fingers, the same gesture Sarah Kline had made before Walsh killed the transmission.

"Did anyone else see it?"

"I did," Cody said. "A time-out? Two minutes?"

"That's a door on the north side of Building B, designated T-2, that leads toward the command center," Drumm said, laying the plans out on the desk.

"Have you ever seen her do anything like that before?"

"No," Kline said. "It was a sign. I missed it. You're sure?"

"She was trying not to make it too obvious, but it was there."

"You think she overheard Walsh talking about a weakness? Or saw it herself?"

Drumm tapped the northern wall of Building B on the map, showing the T-2 entrance. It would let someone enter from the exterior of the building, in Cavern B, into the secure area that held the presidential suite and the war room. "It could have been damaged during the incendiary attack, or when Hardwick and Walsh were trying to blast their way in themselves," Drumm said. "Or she was just wringing her hands."

"No," Eric replied, in awe of that woman's courage. "It was deliberate."

"If Walsh knows it's a weakness," Cody said, "he'll be guarding it."

"With what we have." Kline cocked his head toward the bags. "What happens if we get through and they're prepared, guarding that door? Could we still overwhelm them?"

Eric considered the thick steel of the doors on the building plans, the warren of hallways and suites they would have to take back room by room, outnumbered.

The attackers had been preparing for this for months or years. The hostage would certainly be killed, and Walsh would have time to launch a strike.

"No," Eric said.

Drumm stared at the computer. "My God," he said.

"What?"

"The Patriots are armed and locked on."

"You have targeting?"

"No. But DC is in range."

"What kind of damage would those do on the ground?" Cody asked.

"With one, a smoking crater about the size of the West Wing. And they have sixteen."

"Jesus Christ," Kline said.

"Can we cut the lines?" Eric asked. "Take away control?"

"They're buried deep," Drumm said.

"Grab your gear," Eric said to the engineer. "Find that escape tunnel. Blow your way through and get us some backup."

Drumm nodded and picked up his bag.

Eric put his arm around his shoulders. "You're a hell of a soldier, Drumm. It's an honor working with you. Keep your radio on. We'll see you in a few."

"Will do," he said, and eyed the exit.

"Good luck," Kline said.

Drumm dipped his head and walked toward the door. Cody put her hand on his shoulder as he walked past her to the exit. After he left, she looked up at the clock.

"Sir, you need to go now if we're going to make the deadline," she said. "Do you want to try to take them or . . ."

"Give in?" Kline looked down, like he was praying. "I never put them first."

He was thinking about his family. Claire Givens would never see her daughters again.

"You walk in there, he could kill you both," Eric said. "Or force a false confession out of you, turn all those lies into the truth."

"There's no more time," Cody said.

Kline looked at them both, a new clarity in his eyes. He'd made his decision.

102

WALSH WALKED ACROSS the war room and looked at the red digits of the clock, the seconds ticking off one by one. Kline had one minute left.

He glanced to the man at the desk behind him, looking over the feeds from the security cameras they'd activated over the main entrances.

"Nothing," he said.

Walsh drew his pistol and pointed to Sarah Kline.

"Bring her in," he said, and started walking toward the studio.

Rebecca Vaughn raised her gun and grabbed Sarah Kline by the arm.

"Hold up," the man watching the cameras said. "I've got something."

Walsh walked over and looked down at the video feeds.

A figure emerged from the wreckage behind Building B: President Kline, walking slowly, his hands out to the sides in surrender.

"No," the first lady whispered.

"You should be honored," Walsh said. "He's giving up his country for you."

Kline walked over the stone floor in the rear tunnel behind Building B, his footsteps muffled by the soot the fires left behind.

He had heard a blast of thunder through the tunnels two minutes ago—Drumm trying for the escape tunnel, he assumed. He had attempted to raise him on the radio, but only silence came back.

He ducked under a fallen piece of framing and stopped ten feet from the base of the steps that led up to the rear entrance of Building B. He got down on one knee, then two, and lowered himself in a push-up position until his face rested against the floor among the debris. His arms went out to the side, and he laced his fingers behind his head.

"Do not move," Walsh's voice boomed over the PA, echoing back for seconds along the tunnel.

A door creaked above, then slammed shut. He heard boots pounding down the metal steps from the entrance as one of the attackers circled him. A heavy palm ran along his waist and his legs, then his ribs, searching him for weapons.

"Up," the man said. "Eyes forward."

Kline climbed to his feet and looked at the conspirator—six four, maybe two hundred and twenty pounds, pale with short blond hair and eyebrows and a smug look on his face. He had never seen him before.

"Hands behind your head."

Kline complied. The guard circled around and shoved him forward. "Go."

The president climbed the steps, then stopped outside the door and looked up at the camera mounted over it.

The door opened to a rifle aimed at his face. He recognized the woman holding it from Drumm's staff, brown hair and high cheekbones. She still wore her fatigues with her name on a patch: Major Vaughn.

"In," said the guard behind Kline. Six steps brought him over the threshold. Vaughn walked backward, her aim steady, a cold efficiency to her look and movements. The door clanged shut and locked behind him.

"Forward," Vaughn said.

Kline walked down a long corridor that ran inside Building B along its northern wall. After ten feet, the woman took her hand off the barrel of her rifle and rapped on the door that led south to the military command center: knock knock, pause, knock knock.

It opened, and Liam Walsh stepped out, a carbine hanging from his hand and a pistol on his hip. Two guards flanked him with M4s drawn.

"Now you see where things stand," he said, his lip curling with satisfaction. "James Harrington Kline, I am taking you into custody until such time as the Congress may try you for the high crimes you have committed."

A gesture with his finger, and the guards seized Kline and brought him forward into the war room. His wife was sitting on a chair against the far wall, guarded by another unknown in an army uniform.

She stood, heartbroken, when she saw Kline. Her hands reached out toward him.

"Down," the guard said, aiming his gun toward her.

"You have me," Kline said. "Now let her go."

Walsh shook his head. "Still think you're giving orders. You don't understand."

"I'll do what you ask, but please—"

Walsh drove the stock of his rifle into Kline's stomach, forcing the breath out of him. The president leaned forward as pain filled his body.

"Don't beg. It's pathetic," Walsh said. "Where are the others?"

Kline raised his head. The blow left his diaphragm in spasm. He saw the guard shove Sarah back again. Her eyes met his with a mix of love and anguish as he managed a breath.

"I only connected with Eric Hill. He wouldn't come."

"Where is he now?"

"I don't know. He tried to talk me out of it. I broke away."

"Stop fucking lying."

"It's true, I—"

"Bring her here," Walsh said, without looking back. The guard dragged Sarah closer by her upper arm.

Walsh turned toward her with the weapon and aimed the barrel at her chest.

A blast rocked the building, slamming Kline's body like he was inside a drum. The floor shifted under their feet and rocked on the springs.

Two of Walsh's people grabbed Kline's arms.

"Piece of shit," Walsh said, and drove the rifle butt into the same spot, just below his solar plexus. A sickening wave of pain passed through him.

Crack. Another blast shook the room. Walsh's eyes went around the command center, tracking the source of the noise. "They're coming from the south side of the building," he said. "Check the entrances there. What do you see at doors T-9 and T-10?"

"No breach," the man at the surveillance cameras called back.

"You two," Walsh called out to a pair of soldiers. "Join the other men on guard in the hallways and cover those doors," he said. "Vaughn, get on the radio. I want shooters on the roof, on the catwalks firing down on the entrances."

He walked back to Kline.

"It's not going to work," Walsh said, with a manic laugh. "The doors are fine. But you're fucking done, traitor." He looked to Sarah and raised his rifle. "Bring her here!"

103

ERIC FELT THE springs under Building B sway against him as it shook from the second blast. He and Cody were in the dark, taking cover under the building, thirty feet from the steps that led up to the T-2 door on the northern side of B.

"Hold," he whispered. "Hold." It took all his strength to stay still, to not rush in, but he had planted the distraction charges on the south side of B and needed time for the first two blasts to draw Walsh's people away from this door.

T-2 led from the alley along the northern side of Cavern B into the building, offering a way into the same hallway where President Kline had entered. It would bring Hill and Cody in at a spot deeper in the building, to the west of where he had gone in. Eric hoped that if Kline was still in that hall, this entrance would let Eric and Cody get the jump on his guards.

Eric had already prepared the attack. The T-2 door had seemed as secure as the others, until Eric noticed the fatigue marks in the steel around the frame and hinges, strain from the incendiaries and blasting. They looked like the whorls of a fingerprint. Dr. Kline had been right to bring them here.

He'd placed a line of C-4 along the door's bottom edge, working from under the building. If it wasn't enough, if the steel was too strong, this whole plan might fail, and Eric would have simply handed the president over to his enemies. Eric put that out of his mind as he drew in a long breath. Kline had insisted on going in first, to distract Walsh and buy Eric and Cody time to set up.

"Ready?" he said to Cody.

She nodded slowly.

"Firing," he said. They turned their heads away, and he tugged the pins from the detonators.

The charges on T-2 blew in a single pop. Eric waited for the frag to stop falling, then ran out from under the springs into the alley, the narrow space between the foundations of B and the cavern wall. The door leaned out, the bottom hinge torn from the frame, the top barely holding on.

He sprinted up the steps, braced himself against the railing, and drove his boot into the edge of the twisted metal, breaking it free. The door toppled out and Cody shoved it, sending it over the other rail. It crashed onto the stone floor of the cavern below.

Eric sprinted through the entrance with Cody just beside him, guns ready, high and low, left and right, searching for the killers inside.

Back in that security office, they had watched Sarah Kline stand up to Walsh and tell them not to give in. She knew it could cost her her life. The decision to take the attackers by force was torture for the president, but in the end, he and Cody and Eric were all of the same mind: the truth was worth dying for.

The hallway was clear. Looking down it toward the rear of the building, to the east, he could see the door to the war room and hear voices from within. That was where they would have taken Kline, where they would hole up to keep control of the military command center.

"This way," he said, leading her in the other direction. They needed to circle around the war room, to take another way in to keep the element of surprise.

But as they moved, four figures stepped out from the door to the war room and looked their way. Cody put two rounds into the lead man's chest, and he stumbled back as Eric pulled a time-delay charge, ripped the pin, and threw it down the hall. It landed between them and the shooters.

"Come on," he said, laying down suppressive fire and waving Cody back with him. They reached an intersection with a north–south hallway and ducked around the corner to the south.

The blast blew down the corridor they had just left, the pressure over-whelming in these confined spaces. A high droning noise sounded in Eric's ears, but behind it he could hear debris falling, blocking that hall.

It would buy him the time he needed. He lined up his iron sights on an overhead camera and blew it apart, then tracked to a second and took it out, blinding the watchers within.

"Let's go," he said, unslinging the shotgun from across his body as he raced south down the hall.

104

ERIC STOPPED TEN feet down the hall and put a small charge on a steel door that led straight into the war room, then wired it with a remote detonator.

Cody covered him, and when he rose, she stacked against the door, the northwest entrance to the war room, ready for him to blast it so they could rush in.

"No," he said, picking up the shotgun. "They'll be expecting us here. This way."

He took them down the hall.

"There's access to the war room through the president's office," he said. "That charge I laid on the other door will draw them away from it so we can rush in there."

It was the only way to take out superior numbers—outthink them, hit them fast, and move.

He stopped at the outer door to the president's office. The attackers had forced its lock when they broke into the suite earlier. He threw it open and moved in, shotgun up, looking over the striped silk sofas and the oak desk.

He walked to the far left corner, where a doorway concealed in the paneling opened into the war room near its southwest corner. That lock was still intact.

He heard shouts inside, a woman's cry. "This is it." He handed her the remote detonator and a flash-bang.

Blowing the charge he'd laid on the other door would distract them from this entrance. He needed the diversion. They only had one stun grenade to take the war room.

Cody rested her thumb on the detonator trigger. "Ready."

Eric shouldered the Remington and aimed it at the lock on the war room door.

While two of his men restrained Kline's arms, Walsh grabbed the president's fatigues near the neck and threw him to the ground. He stood over him, rifle in his hand, squeezing hard to steady his muscles against the adrenaline flooding through his system.

"Of course," Walsh said. "Of fucking course."

His finger tightened on the trigger. A long breath.

"Cover him," he said to one of his men. "Kill him if he gets up." The officer took aim.

Walsh strode toward Sarah Kline and pulled her to him by her wrist, wrenching her arm behind her back and drawing her in, pressing against her, both looking in the same direction now, his face just beside hers. He dropped the rifle to the end of its sling, drew his pistol, and pressed it in hard under her jaw. "Now you'll see what happens—"

Another blast, closer, rocked the northwest door into the war room, the metal creaking with strain. Walsh shoved her away and took aim. One officer kept his rifle trained on the president while the others arrayed themselves around that door. Walsh had just sent four of his guards into the northern corridor to go after the intruder, and now he wished he'd kept them here.

The metal around the lock was bent, but it had held.

"They're coming," Major Vaughn said.

Walsh holstered his pistol and drew the rifle, warm sweat on his palms. He took a step to the side and turned slowly, eyeing the other entrances.

"Cover them all," he said.

They spread out. Vaughn aimed her rifle at the door in the southwest corner that led to the president's office.

105

THE SHOTGUN KICKED against Eric's shoulder and the slug punched out the lock with a squeal. He drove his boot into the war room door, flinging it open as Cody threw the flash-bang through.

Major Vaughn was waiting with a rifle aimed straight at him. Three shots exploded from it, drilling into Eric's vest, knocking him to the rear. He caught himself with a long backward step.

They were ready, Eric thought as the white blast of the flash-bang rocked the air around them.

Even as the pain of the impacts spread through his chest, there was no other choice than to move, to exploit the instant of advantage from the stun grenade she'd tossed.

"Go!" he said, driving sideways through the door, rifle up. Vaughn was blinking, looking around the room, coming out of the daze from the flash-bang. Her weapon tracked toward Eric's face, and Eric dropped her with two shots.

Scanning to the left, he saw President Kline, his legs unsteady, going for another guard's gun. That man—strong, with pale skin and fair hair—pulled away, recovering from the blast, and aimed at the president.

Crack crack. The man reeled back, hand to his chest, as Cody fired twice. Eric put a bullet into his head as he fell.

"Stop him! The controls!" Kline called out to them, pointing to a soldier running across the room toward a workstation. The black valise that had been stolen from Eubanks's body stood next to it, and the binders from within it lay beside the monitor. He was trying to launch an attack. Eric recognized the running figure as one of the comms officers, a computer specialist. The man drew a pistol and reached for the desk.

Eric put him down with a single shot before he could touch a key.

Moving into the room and scanning right, Eric saw his primary target: Liam Walsh. He appeared to be the only attacker left alive in the war room. He'd drawn his pistol and was holding Dr. Kline in front of him, the gun pressed into the skin under her jaw. He hauled her backward through an open door into an office in the southeast corner of the command center.

"Try anything and she's dead," he hissed as he disappeared from Eric's view.

Kline lifted a rifle from the dead guard as Eric moved farther into the command center, angling to the left to get a better view inside the office.

Eric didn't have a direct line of sight into the room, but he could see Walsh and Sarah within it by their reflection in the dark displays on the wall. From the way the traitor's eyes tracked him, he knew Walsh could see him too. Eric stepped closer.

"Don't move!" Walsh called out, backing deeper into the office. They only had a moment to take him before the rest of his team, drawn away by the distractions, returned. Eric looked at the door frame—steel like all the other walls of the war room. He couldn't shoot Walsh through it.

Sarah squirmed as Walsh forced the .45 in harder. Kline inched closer to the door, his weapon rising.

The sound of footsteps came from behind Eric, echoing through the president's office where he had entered. Walsh must have sent some of his people out to investigate the blasts and guard the hallways, and now, drawn by the gunfire, they were coming back to the war room. Cody was already on it—she returned to the door where she and Eric had entered and aimed her weapon through.

"Use the charges to hold them off," Eric called to her.

She let out a three-round burst, nodded, then slipped through. She carried two explosives. That would stop them, but not for long.

Eric used the distraction to move toward the office door, trying to get a shot at Walsh.

A murmur of pain came from inside. Eric could still see them reflected in the displays. Sarah Kline shut her eyes and pressed her lips together as Walsh drove the pistol up under her jaw.

"Another inch and I shoot!" Walsh yelled, a rabid look on his face. Eric didn't doubt he would pull and exchanged a glance with the president. Kline held up his hand: wait.

"It's over," Walsh said. "You're outnumbered and surrounded. Guns down or she dies."

Another burst of gunfire boomed from the president's office, where Cody was.

"Put them down!" Walsh shouted. A quiet groan from Dr. Kline as he dug the gun into her skin.

The president looked to Eric, stricken by the choice. If he gave in, the attackers could force a confession out of him and have their allies in Washington use it to spin that all of this was somehow legitimate. They would rob him of his honor, and use those lies to rally support for their side as they continued their attempts to seize power. Eric would take nothing for granted anymore. He now understood how insidious those lies could be, and how fragile were the institutions he'd spent his life protecting.

And Walsh could simply kill them all.

"Time's up," Walsh called out, his hand tightening on the handle of the pistol.

"Wait!" Kline shouted, raising his weapon and his free hand.

Walsh nodded and licked his lips. "Put it down and kick it away."

Kline's mouth clamped tight. He lowered his gun to the ground and kicked it across the linoleum. There was a blood trail across the floor leading from the studio where Givens had been killed, a reminder of Walsh's savagery. Kline would do whatever he needed to save his wife, though Eric prayed this move was simply a feint, not a real surrender.

"Now you, Hill!" Walsh shouted. Kline turned to him with the face of a grieving man and nodded. More shots sounded from the president's office. It was over.

Reflected in the display, Eric saw Sarah Kline snap her head back into Walsh's face. He grunted and she broke away, running for the door as Eric sprinted to the left to get an angle on him.

She'd gone two feet through it when the first shot caught her—Walsh firing his pistol from inside the office, still out of Eric's direct view. She stumbled with three long steps and fell to the ground, her hand clasping her side, blood welling out through her fingers and the fabric of her blouse.

Kline ran to her and dropped to one knee.

Eric saw the traitor's face in reflection, twisted with rage, taking aim at the couple on the ground. He ran straight into the line of fire, rifle up, readying the shot though he knew the odds—Walsh had cover, he didn't.

His mind cleared. All that remained was the drive to protect and a simple faith in the job that he'd missed for so long.

A hail of bullets met him before he had a line on Walsh. He pulled the trigger, but the first two rounds from Walsh drove into his vest and sent his aim high. The third ripped through his skin near his neck along his collarbone. An awful numbness spread through his chest. His right arm dropped, useless, and the rifle fell from it. He crouched, reaching for the gun with his left hand as the strength went out of his legs and the room tilted to the side.

His focus wavered as he fell, his vision a long black tunnel. The last thing he saw before the darkness came was Kline and the first lady, still alive, staring at him with a kind of awe. The bullets had stopped with him.

106

AGENT CODY PRESSED against the wall in the president's office, her body tightening with every gunshot. She held a timed charge in her hand and watched the shadows move beyond the open door at the far end of the room.

Wait, she told herself. *Wait. Let them come.*

She counted two attackers, then three, four. She pulled the pin on the timed charge, counted off two seconds, and tossed it. It hit the carpet and rolled through the far door.

She lunged through the door into the war room as the blast filled the office behind her.

As she entered the command center, she saw the blood trails. Eric and Dr. Kline were down, and Walsh was pulling the president in front of him by twisting his arm up behind his back. He held him close, with a pistol to President Kline's head, shielding himself behind the taller man's body.

Cody took aim. All she needed was a stray movement, a few inches of target, to get her shot, but Walsh kept Kline in front of him. A welt was growing on the president's temple, and something about his eyes made her think he'd taken a hard blow to the head.

Glancing to the side, she saw Dr. Kline slumped against the wall, her hand against her ribs, eyes narrowed in agony. Eric Hill lay on his back to her right, blood pooling on the floor beneath him. His face looked strangely at peace.

A chill ran through her body, and for an instant her mind refused to believe what she was seeing. Anger and fear followed in a flood soon after. She looked back to Kline and Walsh, taking short breaths as she leveled the rifle at Kline's head, waiting for the moment when Walsh's face would slip out from behind it and give her a target.

"Put it down," Walsh said. "It's over. My people will be here any second."

She kept her aim, hunting for a chance through the sights.

"You don't have it. And you're not stupid enough to risk shooting *him*."

She fixed her vision on a quarter inch of Walsh's face, the edge of his right eyebrow, wavering just beside the president's temple. Her finger tightened on the trigger, but the shot was too close, then it was gone.

"You won't kill him," Cody said. "You need him."

"You're right. I'll kill her, to start." She saw him shift behind the president, keeping the pistol close to his body, aiming it to the side. He had an easy angle to finish Sarah Kline.

The president drove his free elbow back into Walsh's ribs and twisted. Cody readied the shot. But Walsh only let out a sigh of pain as he wrenched Kline's arm up, keeping him in front.

"Put down the fucking gun or Sarah dies," Walsh said. "Tell her, Kline. She's so good about following orders."

The president seethed but said nothing.

"I will paint the walls with her," Walsh said. "Three . . . two . . ."

Cody glanced at the first lady, her eyes fixed on Walsh's pistol, resolute. "One."

"Put it down, Cody!" Kline said. He looked to his wife and his face fell.

"Don't, James," the first lady said.

"I know what matters here."

He was choosing his family. Cody let her breath fill in, paused, steadied. All she wanted was to kill that traitor.

"Agent Cody," the president said. "That's an order."

"Drop it, Cody," Walsh said. "It's over."

Kline nodded. Cody had to believe he was only playing along, buying time, not giving up.

She took her finger off the trigger and brought the rifle to her side.

"On the floor," Walsh said.

She laid it down, forcing her fingers to let go despite the voice screaming in her head to hang on to her weapon.

"Kick it away."

She toed it across the linoleum.

Walsh pulled the president closer, revealing his own face for the first time.

He moved toward her and dragged the rifle away with his foot. She could smell the sweat on him, mixing with the old-penny scent of blood in the room.

"That's a good girl. You were right not to try," he said in that strange, hollow voice of his. The corner of his mouth curled into a leering half smile. "I took your measure the moment I saw you. You don't have it, *Amber*. Stick to paper targets."

He gestured for her to move back, and she took a few steps until she hit a desk.

"Knees," he said.

She glared at him.

"On your fucking knees!" he screamed, a blue vein in his forehead standing out against his pale skin.

She lowered herself down. The president's lips tightened as Walsh pulled him back, still aiming the .45 at Dr. Kline.

"You will understand that there are consequences to your actions," Walsh said to the president, sounding like a father doing his best to control his anger. "You'll confess to what you've done, or she dies, and then I turn Washington to ash. Don't fuck with me here. Now you know this isn't a game."

Kline closed his eyes for a moment and forced air out of his nose. He was shaking with rage.

"Are you ready to answer for what you've done?" Walsh asked.

No response.

Walsh extended the gun toward the first lady. His finger tightened on the trigger.

"Don't," Kline said.

"Answer me."

"Yes," the president said, his voice firm and clear.

Cody looked at Hill, the life pouring out of him onto the thin carpet. He'd given everything for the truth, and now the lies would win.

"In the studio, come on," Walsh said, and pulled the president to the side.

Cody watched him, waiting for this one chance. She rose. Her hand flashed behind her back and pulled the Glock from her belt. *Always carry a backup piece.*

Walsh swung his gun toward her and pulled the president closer. She had a four-inch target, then three, as his head slipped behind Kline's. She squeezed the trigger. The gun jumped, then came back level, steady in her hands as the bullet slipped past the president's face and tore through Walsh's cheek, twisting him to the side. She pulled the trigger a second time and caught him over his left eye.

He fell to the ground and found the strength to raise the pistol toward her.

She fired twice more, her aim perfect. "It's Agent Cody, and that's enough of your bullshit."

Kline crouched and took Walsh's pistol, then looked to Cody as she closed in, smoke rising from the barrel of the Glock.

Walsh was done.

The president ran to his wife. "Bandage," Dr. Kline said, her voice strained.

Kline tore off his sleeve, balled it, and held it to her wound as she sucked air through her teeth.

"Watch that door," Cody barked at Kline as she went to Hill. ". . . sir."

"Fuck *sir,*" Kline said, aiming Walsh's .45 toward the entrance with his free hand. He looked at Hill. "Is he going to make it?"

Cody took his pulse while she watched the other door, waiting for the rest of Walsh's men to arrive.

"Anything?" the first lady called out.

Cody could barely tell; her heart was pounding so hard. She took two long, deep breaths, then felt it, faint but there in his carotid.

"He's alive."

"Direct pressure on it," Dr. Kline said. "We'll get him through this."

Cody started undoing the Velcro on Hill's plate carrier so she could get a compress on the wound.

Footsteps sounded behind her, in the president's office. She turned and took aim. A shooter appeared, the barrel of his gun coming toward her. She dropped him and heard a gunshot over her shoulder.

Kline was holding the pistol in front of him, facing the other direction as another attacker fell dead in the other door. Dr. Kline held his torn sleeve tight over her injury.

"How many more are there?" the president asked.

"I don't know," Cody said. "But they're trying to surround us."

107

LOUD CLANGS CAME from the north, then the west. Cody spun, covering the other entrances.

"They're everywhere," Kline said.

"You cover these doors, and I—"

A rattle of gunfire. A pause. Another burst.

She looked to Kline. Someone was fighting out there.

"Could it be Drumm?" she asked.

"I heard a blast. It could be him with the backup."

"Or the attackers turned on each other."

Boots marched up the hallway on the northern side of the building, coming closer, enough of them to shake the floor.

Cody moved to cover that approach, standing side by side with Kline watching the half-open door to the hall. Two long shadows stretched past it.

"Who's there?" Kline shouted.

"Friendly! It's Drumm!"

"Is the building clear?" Cody yelled.

"This hallway is."

"Come in," she said.

Drumm stepped through the door, holding an M4 across his body. He had black dust in his hair and on his face.

"They're with me," he said, pointing behind him. "I made it through. Barely."

"Thank God." Cody moved forward and put her hand on his shoulder.

A hard-looking soldier with a beard stepped inside, followed by five more, spreading through the room in some unspoken choreography. They wore army uniforms with no insignia. Joint Special Operations Command boys, Cody assumed, probably Delta.

"You're good, sir?" the leader asked Kline.

"Fine," he said. "We have wounded." He led them to Eric and his wife.

Two of the men dropped beside them while the others secured the fallen weapons and covered the far doors. Radio chatter filled the room.

Kline turned to the leader. "My daughter, Jill—"

"She's fine, sir. Joint team of U.S. Marshals and JSOC standing post."

The president took a long breath in, and his eyes met Sarah Kline's.

"How many reinforcements are there?" Cody asked Drumm.

"Two dozen," he said. "And more coming." He looked at Liam Walsh's corpse and the desk with the dead tech's body and the black valise lying beside it.

"What's the escape tunnel like?" Kline asked Drumm. The engineer looked at the first lady and Hill as one of the soldiers cut away Hill's shirt near the wound. "It'll be hard to get him through. Dr. Kline, can you walk?"

"I'm not sure," she said as the medic worked on her.

Kline's gaze came to rest on Hill. "Those shots were meant for us."

"It's what he wanted," Cody said.

The president looked to her.

"To believe in it again," she said. "Something worth dying for."

Kline nodded solemnly and his attention went to the desk where the nuclear football sat. One of the special operators secured it and Drumm had already pulled up a chair to the workstation.

"Stop whatever they were doing with the Patriot batteries," Kline told him.

"On it."

The soldiers unfolded a collapsible litter next to Hill, and Cody took a spot by his side as the medic poured grains of Celox, a clotting agent, from a pouch into the wound. Hill sighed in pain, barely conscious as they worked on him.

She could hear Sarah Kline quietly talking to the other soldier, helping to guide him as he treated her.

"Fuckers," Drumm said.

Cody looked up to see him leaning over the laptop, its screen casting a white glow on his face.

"What is it?" Kline asked.

"They had a secondary lock on the blast door bolts. That's how they kept them sealed."

"Can you release it?"

"We'll see," Drumm said.

He leaned over the computer and set to work. Two minutes later, he took a deep breath, cast his eyes upward like he was praying, then pressed a key. "Roll away the stone."

108

THEY LEFT THE war room a few minutes later, with the Delta boys carrying Hill and Sarah Kline on litters. The medic held an IV bag up, running into Eric's arm. Stepping into the northern hallway, Cody saw two special operators posted where she and Hill had entered Building B, and two more at the rear entrance behind them where Kline had been brought in.

The JSOC soldiers from the war room formed a tight box around them, with Cody stepping in at the seven o'clock position as they moved through the corridor. Drumm led them to the front entrance of Building B and they exited into the main tunnel.

Two special operators approached from the north, eyeing Drumm. With the streaks on his face, he looked like he'd just fought his way through hell.

"What unit are you with?" one asked.

"114th Signal Battalion," Drumm said, gripping his rifle and scanning to the right. Amazement on the faces of the JSOC shooters that he was a comms engineer, but Drumm went on. "I'm the commander. My people are trapped in the far north of the main tunnel," Drumm said, "by the blast doors. There was a collapse."

"We have two teams working our way to them. They'll be all right."

A black haze hung in the air, which was now as close and hot as a DC August. Cody saw flashlights moving in the main tunnel to the north, half a dozen of them, and raised her rifle to her shoulder.

"They're ours," the soldier ahead of her said. "We're good."

They loaded onto two pickups parked along the side of the tunnel and drove south, headed for the blast doors where they had first entered the building, almost thirty-one hours ago.

Cody sat on the side of the bed, and the medic passed her Hill's IV bag to hold as he worked on the fallen agent by headlamp.

After five minutes, the vehicles came to a stop by the southern blast doors, and the soldier injected something with a syringe into a port on the IV.

Hill stirred, his muscles tightening.

"Is he okay?" she asked.

"Yes. That'll keep him going till we get to trauma."

The others jumped out, some posting security and others following Drumm to a control room the size of a phone booth built into the stone wall beside the inner blast door.

"Crafty."

She looked down, shocked to see Hill's eyes half-open.

"Eric!" She took his hand.

"Got him in the back? I didn't see it all."

"Eye to eye."

He coughed weakly. "Well done, Agent Cody."

"Always have a backup piece," she said, and squeezed his hand.

She laughed, a lightness spreading through her on seeing him alive. "I thought taking a shot for a politician was a sucker's game."

"Here's your proof."

A loud buzzing noise filled the tunnel, Drumm and the others powering up some hydraulics deep in the stone wall beside the blast door.

"You were right all along, Cody," he said, and did his best attempt at a smile. "Kline knew you had the second gun? He was playing for time?"

"I don't know. I tried to turn so he could see it. In the end I just made the call and took the shot."

He put his other hand on top of hers. "That's—"

He bore down and clenched his teeth as a wave of pain swept through him. A low groan escaped his throat, and he closed his eyes.

The medic reached for the side of his neck, checked his pulse, then pushed another syringe into the IV. Hill took three long breaths, and then a peaceful look came over his face.

Cody didn't like the medic's expression, mouth tight, concentrating on every beat of his pulse.

"Is he going to make it?"

"We need to move," he said.

A heavy grating sound filled the tunnel, metal pulling against metal. She looked up at the expanse of white that made up the first blast door. It looked as big as a drive-in theater screen. She couldn't imagine it moving.

"More!" Drumm yelled.

An engine roared.

"More!"

The door pulled back, inch by inch, darkness showing beyond it. The gap widened and the operators shined their flashlights through, lighting up the outer blast door. The motors ground on so loudly that she couldn't hear the voices anymore. Through the widening gap she could see the metal shaking on the outer door.

The engine revved higher. Drumm shouted something she couldn't make out. The far door jumped six inches on its track, shuddered, and pulled back again, moving smoothly now.

Sunlight poured through the gap. It lit up the haze and spread across the tunnel, covering the soldiers ahead and Eric lying on the truck bed, then warming Cody's face. A breeze pushed in, twisting the smoke into spirals, passing over her with the scent of freshly cut grass.

109

THE TRUCKS ROLLED through the inner blast door as soon as it was wide enough for them to pass. Kline sat on the side of the bed of the first Ford, watching over his wife. Hill and Cody were in the second pickup, and Drumm had stayed behind to see to his people and his post.

The operators moved ahead of them in a chevron formation, guns raised. The light felt like it was washing him clean as they passed the massive bolts of the outer door. Kline narrowed his eyes, squinting against the afternoon sun burning between the oaks.

A company of soldiers stood outside with their rifles ready, guarding the approaches and the hillside above along with a dozen snipers on mobile observation posts. As the president and the others cleared the Raven Rock entrance, he saw earthmovers and long drilling rigs stationed throughout the lot. Helicopters circled overhead, and tents and mobile command centers filled the property.

It looked like an army division had set up in the Pennsylvania hills. The soldiers guarding the perimeter kept their attention focused outward while the others faced him, snapped their rifles to their shoulders, and brought their hands to their brows, hundreds of them in unison.

Kline returned the salute, then brought his hand sharply down to his side.

A medevac Black Hawk came in low and landed beside the trucks. Kline's clothes snapped in the downdraft as the medics ran toward him.

He reached down and took Sarah's hand.

"You hanging in there?"

A smile with some tears waiting behind it. "I'll be all right."

He looked at her for a long moment.

"Next time you want to show me you care, hon," she said, "just give me a quiet weekend far, far from DC. No need for all that." She waved her free hand toward the bunker.

He laughed, leaned down, and touched her cheek. "Deal."

"Did you know that Cody had another gun?"

"I had faith."

She was the one person who could read him, and she gave him a skeptical look. "You see everything. You saw it. You played him."

"Never trust an old spy," he said, and squeezed her hand. "You and Jill are everything. I've always known it, but I've never seen it so clearly."

The crew from the medevac climbed onto the bed of the truck and he helped them carry her down.

"They're with us," Kline said, pointing to the second truck. "There's a Secret Service agent down. He goes in the first helo. Straight to Walter Reed."

"Yes, sir."

They brought Sarah into the Black Hawk, and Kline reached down to help Cody as she and the other corpsmen brought Hill on board.

The door closed. The helicopter lifted and turned. They flew fast and low over the treetops as the hills of Raven Rock disappeared behind them.

110

Four months later

THE BEAST ROLLED down Pennsylvania Avenue with the Capitol towering ahead. Eric sat in the passenger compartment of the limousine across from the president and first lady, with Cody to his right. Normally agents traveled in the follow-up vehicle, but the Klines had invited them to ride in the limo.

The president looked over his remarks—an address to a joint session of Congress. The pundits had been trading takes all week about how the president would play it. Some argued he would clamp down on resistance and go to war against anyone who had opposed him, while others said he would try to bring peace to a divided country.

"Advance, this is Stagecoach," Eric said into his wrist mic. "How we looking on the eastern entrance?"

"All clear, chief."

"We're Bravo," Eric said. Five minutes out.

"Eyes on," came the reply.

Eric brought his hand down. He was working out of Chilton's office now, heading the White House detail, one of four posts that had been left empty by the Raven Rock attack. Those who had fallen still haunted the West Wing. A memorial stood just outside the Oval. Whenever Cody walked past Maddox's old office, not much bigger than a broom closet, she would glance inside as if expecting him to still be there.

Kline still hadn't selected a replacement for Givens—couldn't bear to,

Eric assumed. Her office remained vacant. A single photo of her stood on the desk in remembrance.

It was only after they had escaped Raven Rock that Sarah Kline shared Givens's last words as she stared down Walsh and his pistol: "You don't deserve my fear."

Cody had been promoted and was the shift whip on Dr. Kline's detail. Raven Rock had changed her. She was as optimistic as ever, but not willing to take any shit, even from Eric. Command suited her.

Drumm had become the commander of Raven Rock—the Grand High Mole—and Major Ashley Moro would take over his old job once she returned from medical leave and time with her family. The communications staffers had pulled her from the rubble—she had nearly outrun the collapse—and stabilized her until the Army Corps of Engineers broke through the northern blast door. Eric had met with Drumm twice since the escape, and Drumm had proudly shown him the checklist—sixty pages long—he was working through to restore his underground home.

The FBI, using the leads from Maddox's undercover work, had traced the conspiracy from Citizen to a tight network of politicians and power brokers working behind the scenes to stop Kline's anticorruption campaign, along with the security personnel they had co-opted.

Two congressmen had already resigned. Searle had been cooperating to bring down the rest until he was found dead by apparent suicide in his cell in the special housing unit of the Alexandria jail.

The conspiracy to take down Kline had been driven by his enemies in the opposition, but not exclusively. Alexander Braun, Kline's primary opponent, was his closest rival for power within the party and, as one of the wealthiest men in Washington, a defender of the behind-the-scenes players who were threatened by Kline's antigraft work. Braun had quietly fanned the rumors that Kline was staging a slow-motion power grab and needed to be stopped.

One beautiful October morning, Braun opened the door of his Alexandria mansion at 5 a.m. to find two dozen windbreaker boys from the FBI's Washington Field Office, there to serve a search warrant looking for any links between him and the conspiracy.

His political career was over, though politicians are never really done in DC; they just fade into the money rackets, trading on influence and old connections, working out of sight. Eric hoped the law would put him away for good, and if it didn't, he would work to keep Braun in check himself.

In the back of the limo, Cody raised her mic to her lips.

"No," she said. "Three agents. North, east, and south. Good. Tell me when they're in place."

Kline looked over at her, and pointed to the weapon on her right hip, a worn SIG P229.

"Looks well loved," he said.

"My father's."

Kline nodded. "And a backup?"

"Of course."

He smiled. "You look like him when you stand guard," he said. "Something about the way you hold your hands, the posture. It might be time we told his story a little better, his work, the sacrifice he made."

"Thank you, sir."

"He'd be proud of you, Cody."

She met his gaze and an easy silence passed.

His phone buzzed in his pocket. He read something on it, brought his fist to his lips, then looked out the window for a moment. Eric caught his eye, and Kline passed the phone to him.

It was an intercept the FBI had picked up, a message that had gone out that morning over encrypted chat.

"The tyrant speaks . . ." the text began. It was a screed warning that Kline would use the speech as the beginning of a massive consolidation of power. It ended by calling for resistance by any means necessary.

At the bottom, it was signed, "Citizen."

Eric leaned forward and handed the phone back to him. The president passed it to Sarah Kline.

"Citizen is dead," she said.

"Long live," Kline said. "You cut off one head."

He looked out the window as the limo pulled into the plaza in front of the Capitol.

"This is a call to arms," Eric said. "We can go in through the underground entrance."

The first lady passed the phone to Cody, then exchanged a look with the president.

"No," Kline said. "No hiding in tunnels."

"I want counterassault posted around the steps," Eric said.

Kline shook his head. "We're not going in heavy. That's what they want—fear, overreaction. These people are going to keep up the provocations until I turn into the monster they make me out to be. Not today."

He peered at the flag over the Capitol, and Eric knew he was thinking about how to walk that line, how far he would have to go to keep this country whole.

"We proceed on foot in the open. Keep the CAT team out of sight, but ready."

Eric watched him, saw the determination in his face.

"Yes, sir," he said. He radioed the command. Once the teams were in place, he opened the door; it only opened from the inside. Standing guard just outside the limo, Eric scanned the plaza. The president stepped out and waved back to the people gathered along the barricades. Hill kept his body between him and the open lanes of fire, studying the crowd, watching their hands.

Eric had three surgeries at Walter Reed National Military Medical Center after he made it out of Raven Rock. He spent twenty-one days in that hospital and started physical therapy with the stitches still in, building up to four hours a day, six days a week. A deep ache pained his chest with every breath, but he never let it show on the job.

Cody rolled out with Dr. Kline on the other side of the limo as the president's top staffers emerged from a follow SUV with Ellen O'Hara, the communications secretary, in the lead.

"Hill," she said, smiling as she came up beside him.

"You want to give me a heads-up on tonight's message?" he asked her. "It'd be good to know up front if it's a declaration of war."

"Wouldn't that ruin all the fun?"

Eric shook his head.

"I heard you're getting serious with a French ambassador," she said.

"Second secretary."

She whistled. "How's that going?"

"Merveilleux."

"Nice. You look good . . . clear."

His eyebrows rose. "Clear?"

She laughed as the ready call came in over his radio.

Eric led the president's people up the steps. The sergeant at arms met them at the eastern portico and escorted them through the Rotunda into the Speaker's Lobby, an ornate chamber leading to the House Floor.

"Are you ready, sir?" the sergeant at arms asked.

"Yes," Kline said.

The doors opened, and Eric looked out over the faces of the representatives, standing and clapping, a sea of practiced smiles.

Eric led them in, his eyes constantly moving, his hands ready by his waist.

"Keep your guard up," Kline whispered.

"Always."

ACKNOWLEDGMENTS

A huge thank you to my wife, Heather, for her love, unwavering support, and for cracking me up all the time. She encouraged me to take a leap of faith on this writing thing way back when and I'm forever grateful. We recently welcomed our first child and the whole experience has left me completely in awe of her.

And thank you to my family for their invaluable first reads, especially my mother, Ellen, who has a terrific eye and gave feedback at every stage. And I am so grateful to my wife's mother, Eileen Burke, for all her help over the past year. She's a lifesaver and a joy to be around.

Tisha Martz and Chris Holm were kind enough to read early versions of the book and offered great notes. And thanks to my agent, Dan Conaway, for his excellent advice as always, and to Chaim Lipskar, Peggy Boulos Smith, and everyone at Writers House. And a very big thank you to Will Watkins, my television and film agent, for all that he's achieved and the faith he's had in these books.

I had the great fortune to work with Emily Krump as my editor on this novel. She dramatically improved the story and characters and saved me from many of my literary bad habits. The team at William Morrow and HarperCollins continues to amaze me with their excellent editorial and publishing insights—thank you to Liate Stehlik, Jennifer Hart, Kaitlin Harri, Beatrice Jason, Brittani Hilles, Tessa James, Andy LeCount, Carla Parker, Mary Beth Thomas, and the entire sales team.

I'd also like to thank David Highfill, recently retired from Morrow and a stellar editor and human being, for taking a chance on me and *The Night Agent*. I'm so grateful to have had the opportunity to work with him.

I had a blast talking with Chris Albanese, a former Secret Service agent and thriller writer to watch, as I researched the story. He was incredibly helpful and generous with his time and expertise.

Raven Rock is very much a real place. I have my friend Garrett Graff to thank for his painstakingly researched nonfiction book *Raven Rock*, which delves into the many secrets of the government's doomsday plans. I can't recommend it highly enough.

I did take a few liberties to simplify the bunker complex's layout and (hopefully) make it easier for readers to keep their bearings. In real life, the blast doors swing, rather than retract, and the springs under the buildings aren't actually tall enough to walk through. I made them a little higher so I could have a few good fight scenes under there. Thanks to Kushan Kalpa for his help with the map.

And finally, I would like to thank my new writing partner, Emily, born February 2022. She very kindly slept for hours in a carrier while I polished this manuscript at a standup desk. She's a hilarious, determined, beautiful child, a daily wonder, and the best thing that's ever happened to me. Love you, Bear.